Outlaw's Vow:
Grizzlies MC Romance

Nicole Snow

Content copyright © Nicole Snow. All rights reserved.
Published in the United States of America.
First published in December, 2015.

Disclaimer: The following ebook is a work of fiction. Any resemblance characters in this story may have to real people is only coincidental.

Please respect this author's hard work! No section of this book may be reproduced or copied without permission. Exception for brief quotations used in reviews or promotions. This book is licensed for your personal enjoyment only. Thanks!

Cover Design – L.J. Anderson – Mayhem Cover Creations. Photo by Allan Spiers Photography.

Description

I'M MARRYING AN OUTLAW AND I CAN'T FAKE IT...

ELLE JO

Forget the flowers and tender kisses. I'm marrying a man who took a bullet for me tomorrow, and I don't have a choice.

Did I say he's an outlaw? Asphalt has slayed more men on the road and taken more women between the sheets than I can ever count.

He's arrogant. Savage. So handsome and wild I should slap him for being this beautiful while he does every sin in the book. When he tells me I'm going to say I do, and mean it, I want to believe him.

Especially when he's the boy I left behind. All the insanity I tried to escape when I stopped being the sheltered club princess.

So, why the *hell* can't I keep my lips off his when he gives me that smirk and whispers filthy things in my ear?

ASPHALT

She thinks it's pretend, and club business is the only reason I'm slapping my brand on her skin. What a damned joke.

Elle got away from me years ago. Never again.

I'm putting her where she belongs the second I hear "kiss the bride." Yeah, I told my brothers I'd go along with this sham marriage to save the Grizzlies MC. They don't know how bad I need her.

This isn't pretend anymore. The good girl act won't save her this time. I'm keeping my bride.

I can't forget the kiss that turned me into an obsessed lunatic. I'll own her on my bike, in my bed, wreck her for any other man, or I'll be dead.

Elle's always been mine. Don't care how much I suffer 'til she learns that's law...

The Outlaw Love books are stand alone romance novels featuring unique lovers and happy endings. No cliffhangers! This is Asphalt and Elle Jo's story in the Grizzlies MC series.

I: Love Interrupted (Elle Jo)

Four Years Earlier

The bastard had a heart of gold.

I called him "bastard" because he'd earned it. Austin Graham left Steen High when I was just a freshmen, but his legends lived on. He still lived down the street from me too, a big, mean-eyed, heavily tattooed young man who'd just hit twenty-one, always on his shiny new motorcycle, pulling into his beat up driveway with a keg or a bimbo on the back.

If I hadn't been born into the life, I would've hated him. Austin's teasing didn't help, whenever he actually noticed me.

Instead of getting mad, I got butterflies.

All over. They beat their wings through my bloodstream and flapped into my heart, sending that strange energy every girl discovers at this age straight between my legs.

Besides, I had another advantage for handling the boy next door. I didn't fear the bastard or swoon for him like everyone else because I'd already grown up with the roughest biker in Washington.

Nobody on a motorcycle put hell's terror into me like daddy.

Every single bastard in Tacoma paid Gil the respect he'd earned as President of this Grizzlies MC charter, including the kid down the street.

But he didn't grovel to my father like the other boys wearing the bear patch, even though he was only a prospect. Talk about interesting, as if I didn't spend enough time thinking about him with this stupid crush.

Some days, his teasing and lewd gestures exploded into the open. He sat across the street, smoking on his mom's porch, and then he'd look up at me, pierce my soul with those bright green lips, and make a motion like he was shoving a banana into his cheek.

Blowjob, Ell-Bell, he'd mouth to me, before he got up and walked inside like it was the most natural thing in the world. He usually did it when daddy was in the garage too, just a few feet away from seeing the crude jokes that would've brought out his knife.

I should've learned to expect anything from the badass next door. I knew he was crazy, and he'd had a rough life with both his parents as screwed up as they were. Maybe something about that made a young man fearless, or else he'd just run out of fucks to give.

But then prom night came, and Austin showed some *serious* balls that left my jaw hanging open for the next four years of my life.

"Here we are, Elle Jo." My date hadn't said anything since we'd left the dance. "Thanks for the awesome night."

We'd just pulled into the driveway with Mike Wilkie, half an hour earlier than the curfew my dad set with his dead eyes and booming voice.

Mike was a good kid and a nice dancer. A handsome lacrosse player, his looks promised to set a few panties on fire in a once he went off to university and grew up a little more. Someday, he'd wind up with a good job, beautiful babies, and a lovely wife to take to dinner every Friday night.

Everything I should've wanted.

Everything daddy hinted he wanted for me since I'd gotten older. He'd stroke my cheek with a beer in his hand and a tear in his eye, mumbling something about how I "wasn't cut out for half this fucking shit. Gotta get what your ma would've wanted."

In other words, he wanted me to settle for everything that bored me to death.

I flashed Mike a soft smile and tucked my blonde locks behind my ear. "I had a great time. I'll see you in Calc next week. Can't *wait* to get the final over and never see Miss Faith again!"

He chuckled. "Aw, come on, Elle Jo. She's not so bad. I hear the principle wants to have her talking at graduation so none of us go off to college thinking we've got it easy."

Another smile. A shallow nod. I pressed the button on my seatbelt and slid toward the door.

No sooner than I popped it open, Mike reached over and grabbed my wrist. I looked back, staring into his watery, nervous eyes.

"I didn't get a chance to tell you...god damn, you look so beautiful tonight, Elle. Good enough to kiss. All the kids say you've never done anything before. That can't be true, can it?"

His voice sounded strange. Anxious. Disbelieving. Desperate.

Like a little boy, rather than a man who'd just turned eighteen. A wet blanket instantly smothered what little attraction I'd had for him on the dance floor.

Great way to end the night, Mike, I thought. *I wouldn't have wasted my first kiss on you anyway, but you've just lost your chance after graduation by bringing up crappy gossip.*

Ugh, this was only my third real date, and I already hated this part. I softened my face and shook my head, trying to give him those puppy dog eyes so he'd let me off thinking *maybe* there's a chance. My stomach twisted in knots.

"Have a great night. I really need to go."

If only it were that easy. The idiot wouldn't let go. I turned, losing the friendly pity I'd worn on my face earlier.

"Let me show you what it's like to be a woman, baby. Please. Seriously. I can make you feel so good...we don't have to fight this. I saw the way you were looking at me on the dance floor. Your dad's not even home, is he?"

Mike nodded to my house with the porch light on. No, daddy was probably out at the clubhouse handing very important biker badass business, but he always came back by curfew, or else sent a prospect around to check that I was home safe.

We wouldn't be alone out here long, thank god.

"He'll be home anytime, if he isn't already. Early morning and all. Thanks again for the wonderful night." The door popped and I flung it open, ready for my escape.

His face twisted. Releasing my hand with a snarl, he gripped the steering wheel, looking more than ready to rev the engine and tear down the street.

"Whatever, you uptight fucking bitch. You know I was the only one man enough to even ask you to prom. Figures that I wouldn't get a boob out of it."

For a second, I sat there with one foot out the door, frozen in shock at the Jekyll and Hyde transformation unfolding before my eyes.

Asshole! I wanted to slap him across the face.

Before I could do anything, a rock hit the glass on Mike's side. We both jumped, watching a long, jagged fracture spreading across the window.

"What the —"

Mike never got the last word out before somebody ripped his door open. Muscular arms striped with lightning reached inside, pulled him out, and slammed him against the hood.

He had his back turned to me, but I knew it was the bastard next door before I saw the back of his cut with the roaring bear on the back. *Holy shit.*

Mike screamed like a girl as Austin held him down, one tight fist hovering over his face, ready to wreck his good looks forever.

"Austin, don't! Are you *crazy?!*"

I should've already known the answer.

He looked up with his freshly shaven head, his jaw tight, causing the lightning bolts he'd had inked on his temples earlier this year to twitch. Our eyes met, and I heard thunder. Or maybe it was just the blood hissing in my ears.

"No fucking way, princess. What's crazy is overhearing this shithead talking to you like a piece of meat when his balls haven't even dropped yet. Maybe I oughta put my boot up his ass and help 'em pop."

Mike made another noise, a garbled plea to let him up. Austin growled, and slammed him into the metal again, hard enough to rattle bones.

"Shut the fuck up. Give your date an apology, and maybe I'll think about it if you talk real nice and really mean it."

I wasn't sure whether I'd die first from embarrassment

or laughter. Seeing Mike in his place had a crazy kind of satisfaction. And there was *another* satisfaction I didn't want to acknowledge when I saw the boy down the street at his baddest, his muscles flexed, that killer glint his eye I'd seen on daddy's face several times in my life.

"Austin, please, he didn't mean any harm. Did you, Mike?" I walked over, pursing my lips, staring at the little jackass who'd just ruined my prom night forever.

Tears messed up Mike's hot, red face. He looked at me for a split second and then shook his head violently.

"No ma'am. No way, no fucking way! I'm sorry. I really am. I got a little hot under the collar, a little disappointed, that's all. Please believe me! I don't want any trouble with these biker guys, just tell him to –"

My jaw dropped as Austin picked him up again, spun him around, and slammed him face first into the car like he was nothing. "You think I take orders from her just because her old man's fucking god on the open road around here? Fuck, kid, you're stupider than you look."

Crap. He was really going to hurt if I didn't get Austin away from him soon.

"Let him go," I sighed, trying to focus on my anger, and not the heat building between my thighs.

It was strange to be looking at the bastard all dressed up. He stopped, holding Mike down, slowly running his eyes up and down my body.

"All right. Say the words, little boy, and you can run home to mommy." The biker eased up just enough for

Mike's beet red face to twist. Austin grabbed his short hair and jerked his face toward me. "To *her*. I don't do apologies. You take a big, deep breath and let the lady know how fucking sorry you are for shitting up her special night."

Mike's bleary eyes opened and looked at me. My heart beat faster. All for the bastard, and nothing for him, except a slim hum of sympathy churning in my veins.

"I'm really sorry, Elle Jo. He's right. I shouldn't have acted like such a prick. You were just so beautiful. I expected too much. I –"

Austin's elbow slammed into Mike's spine so hard he went speechless. "I didn't say shit about making excuses. Ell-bell, are we done here, or do you want me to bust his nose?"

I shook my head furiously. "No, no, we're good. Just...let him go."

Austin snorted. At last, he stepped back. Mike popped up in disbelief, walking as quickly as he could back to the driver's seat. The bastard joined me on the sidewalk as we watched him struggle with his seat belt, then do a crooked lap up the street.

Crickets. Literally. The night was suddenly deadly silent, but tense as all hell with his green eyes washing over me, teasing every inch of my skin.

A couple lightning bolts were stamped into his temples, making him look even more fearsome than before with his shaved head and wild stare. Muscles I didn't know I had went taut.

"Shame you had to waste such a hot dress on a little pissant like him. Fuck, baby, you look good." He stepped up, wrapping one arm around me, smoothing his palm over my lower back.

Before I knew what was happening, the bastard pulled me in. He towered over me by several inches, six-feet-something of testosterone and violence. Raw masculinity at its worst, which also meant its finest.

He was everything that was supposed to be off limits for a girl who'd grown up with the MC in her life, but who was never supposed to be a part of it.

"Was he telling the truth?" Austin demanded, leaning down. I could practically feel him smiling inwardly when he felt me tense, pulling me a little closer, just enough to feel my nipples turning to rocks against his chest. "That shit the kid said about you being a prude? I heard everything with the window cracked."

"Austin, please!" I couldn't believe it.

As if I really wanted to talk about how sexually starved and inexperienced I was with this killer who oozed sex?

"I should go inside. The boys'll be by any second, and they probably won't take kindly to seeing us out here like this."

He snorted. "Answer the damned question, princess. I'm already on Gil's bad side. Thank fuck I'm heading down to join the crew in California soon. They know how to party. The brothers down there aren't such hard asses they keep their hot daughters under lock and key neither."

My lungs turned to cement. I couldn't tell if this was more teasing, or if he really meant every word about how hot I looked.

He wasn't looking at me like I was a bratty sister anymore. Gone was the bastard who'd whistle or jeer at me from across the street, the man who'd pulled up on his bike last year when I was learning to drive and give me crap about it, while daddy swore at him from the passenger side.

The man looking at me now was too serious. Too hungry. Ripping through my clothes with just his eyes.

And I loved it. God help me.

"Austin..."

"Stop calling me that," he growled, tightening his hold around my waist. "It's Asphalt tonight and every night for every day I'm still breathing."

He reached up and tapped the new patch on his chest. So, he'd chosen a road name, just like they always did. I wondered how he'd gotten it, but didn't have the courage to ask just then.

I wrinkled my nose. "Whatever, Asphalt. Maybe if you stop calling me princess, I'll think about addressing you properly."

"Come on, your highness," he said with a smile. "Let me walk you to your doorstep like the little bitch in the car wouldn't."

It was only a few stairs up to the porch, but we took the long way, and it became the longest walk of my life. My hand practically burned in his as he led me on, up our hilly driveway, and then across the wooden ramp we'd made for mom's wheelchair when she was in her last days.

We stopped just outside the door. Or, more accurately, *I* stopped, not wanting the night to end just yet.

Before tonight went to hell, I'd imagined my first kiss with Mike. If only he'd been man enough, with a little more edge, and few less tantrums...

I looked at Austin's – Asphalt's? – lips. God, they looked good. My pussy tingled, more soaked than I think I'd ever been in my life, my entire core a tight, wanting mess.

"Go." His hand slid down my ass and squeezed when he said the word. "Before I throw you on the back of my bike and ride off to NorCal with you, babe. Don't need an even bigger death warrant from your old man, and you're pretty damned tempting since you're finally legal for some lucky bastard to fuck."

"Austin..."

His eyes narrowed, and he pinched my ass until I whimpered. "Last time I'm telling ya, it's Asphalt now. Asphalt forever. Tomorrow, I'm leaving this town behind with no regrets. You're the only thing I'll be missing when I think about this shithole."

His voice rang solid. No sarcasm, no lie – just plain truth.

I couldn't take it. His hand pushed against my ass as I stood up on my tiptoes, pursing my lips. His mouth covered mine with a growl, and the heat in my blood turned into fireworks.

We kissed, hotter and longer than anything I'd ever imagined. He gave me passion, so much it threatened to consume me. I lost myself in his strong, sexy lips, relishing his arms around me, and offered him my heat like the world was about to end.

I think it did when his tongue slipped past my lips. He conquered me, opened me like no man ever had. My lips were all over the bastard, Asphalt and Austin, a kiss equal parts beginning and end, hello and goodbye.

My heart banged like a car crash by the time he finally let go.

For a second, we stood there, staring. Both shocked from the sudden explosion of lust, disbelief over what just happened mingling with the howling need for more.

I flipped my hair back and wrapped my hands around his neck. I hadn't planned to lose my virginity tonight, but suddenly, I was totally ready.

If his mouth felt like heaven, then his body promised ecstasy I couldn't imagine. I didn't want fantasy anymore, I wanted this for real, embracing the wet, greedy urge to feel him between my legs.

"Come inside," I whispered, my voice turning into a

moan. "The prospects don't normally come in as long as they see the TV going in the living room. And daddy's out late all the time, he usually doesn't get in until two or three, sometimes later..."

"Fuck, babe, do you even know what the hell you're saying?" He grinned, his powerful jaw tensing with the same dark energy in his beautiful emerald eyes.

"Yeah, Asphalt. I do." I slipped my hand back into his and reached for the door, twisting my key into it, ready to lead him straight to my bed.

But we never got that far.

The door burst open before I could finish unlocking it. A huge, angry hand reached for my wrist, flinging me against the wall.

I saw a blur of the murder on daddy's face before he marched out to kill the only man I'd ever kissed.

"What in the ever living fuckity fuck were doing with my little girl?" For an older man, daddy had the strength of ten raging bulls when he got mad.

I watched him fling the big badass I'd just had on my lips against the wall like he was a ragdoll, one hand around his throat, his handlebar mustache twitching with pure venom.

"Jesus Christ, Prez, ease up!"

"Don't think so, motherfucker." I had to lean close, one ear out the door, as daddy's voice lowered to a deadly boom. "You've been going behind my goddamned back too many times, treating this patch like it's the only reason you've got for growing a dick. No more. These colors aren't a fuckin' joke, kid. They've got blood behind them."

I poked the rest of my head out just in time to see daddy land a savage blow to Asphalt's gut. My crush doubled over, dropped to his knees, and hit the ground. Then my father looked up and saw me, his eyes blazing full bloodlust.

I think I died on the spot.

My head shook slowly, tears welling in my eyes. So much for salvaging this prom, the beauty of a first kiss, much less pretending I wasn't waist deep in this violent, secretive life.

"Elle Jo, get the hell inside. Now! I'm not gonna ask you again, sweetheart."

The tears came, hot and poisonous, as I slinked away. Just before the screen door slammed shut, I heard daddy let out a heavy sigh, his face dangerously close to Asphalt's.

"You're a lucky fuckin' punk tonight. You deserve to be gutted for putting your filthy hands on my daughter, but even I don't have the heart to do it right in front of her. Let's go, cockmongler. You can lick some of your fuckin' namesake off my driveway while we go out back for a chat."

My hand shook, holding the screen door open, just enough to hear Austin groan. Then there was nothing but the sound of a body being dragged behind the fence, into our backyard. My heart beat wild, on the verge of giving out.

Couldn't believe it. Just couldn't.

The full horror of what was happening made me wretch.

It wasn't going to get better, was it? I hadn't seen my father this pissed for months – not since he was screaming at that other club President from California on the phone.

Daddy sent me to the safe house that night, surrounded by three burly prospects. Something about a reckoning coming one day with the national MC because someone called Fang had fucked up everything, and the Mexican cartels would be sawing everyone's heads off to pay for his mistakes.

Who knows what he'll do when he's like this? I can't just sit on my hands. I have to save Austin!

My feet didn't match my brain's courage. I couldn't just rush out and meet them head on, especially if I stumbled into daddy with a gun against my neighbor's head.

So, I compromised. I crept toward the back door, undid the latch, and held my breath as I tried to push the screen open as carefully as possible.

"You're taking this shit way too seriously, Prez. Elle Jo's becoming a young woman. She's grown up. A few more months, and she'll be out on her own. Good fucking luck telling her who she should kiss then."

The lump building in my throat was like solid stone. Asphalt had balls, talking back to my father like that, especially when he faced an execution on our patio. It made me love him even more.

Wait, love? No, maybe not, but at least a stupid little crush that had finally come into full bloom tonight.

It wouldn't have worked out, of course. I wasn't stupid. He didn't call me *princess* for nothing.

In a year's time I'd be sitting in a Seattle sorority with new friends and some handsome jocks who'd never held guns in their lives. My life here would be a distant memory, I hoped, and if I didn't see another switchblade shining in the light or a grizzly bear patch for years, then I'd consider myself very lucky.

No, Austin and me, we didn't have a prayer. Even if I wasn't heading off to college, Asphalt – god it felt strange to think of him as that – was leaving the state. Assuming daddy let him off the hook still breathing tonight.

Right now, that was all I cared about.

"She's my daughter, damn it. My own flesh and blood, asshole! If I want to hear your horseshit excuses, trust me, I'll ask." A heavy thud landed in someone's chest, cutting through the night.

Asphalt swore, barely able to vocalize. Daddy's voice boomed loud, dangerous as ever.

"Shut your yap. You breathe another fuckin' word

about what she wants or how I oughta treat her, and I *will* put hot lead through your skull. I don't give a single fuck who she winds up with, as long as she's happy, respected, and safe. My girl deserves better than some boozin' and whorin' shit-for-brains prospect sticking his clap filled dick in her, and she's gonna get it."

"Yeah, she does, Gil," Asphalt growled, staggering up, blood running between his teeth and out his mouth. "A girl as smart as her deserves to make her own damned decisions. She was smart enough to lay off the kid she took to prom tonight who acted like he owned her. She picked me, Prez, just like it was meant to be. All these years of flirting and teasing, don't tell me you're fucking blind?"

My heart nosedived and swooned back up in my chest. Ballsy and arrogant as ever, yeah, but he told the truth. It wasn't just the fact that he'd given grabby Mike a harsh send off.

"Thing is, she wants me. I know I can't have her. I'm leaving your fucked up club. I know when to let you go. You've gotta learn to let her go, too, let her live on her own," Asphalt continued. "I won't be anything you've gotta worry about in a few more weeks. The boys in California are more my style. This fucking transfer can't come soon enough."

I'd fought my little crush on the bastard forever. Ever since the day he'd stopped in town to help me change a flat on my bike, I'd known there was a deeper side to him than the pretend killer with the take-no-prisoners attitude.

This crush didn't mean I wanted to marry him. He'd never be husband material or anyone I'd hitch myself to forever, but god, his lips were just perfect tonight.

Too good to lose forever.

I clenched my teeth and threw the screen door open, stepping outside. I was just in time to see the death stare between the two men end with daddy pulling his gun.

My jaw dropped. Before I could say anything, he pushed a boot into Asphalt's guts, knocking him to the ground. His pistol flew up and barked two deafening gunshots.

Asphalt, Austin, the first man I'd ever tasted, screamed on the ground. Daddy spun around, and we locked eyes, sharing the same look of mutual horror.

"No! Jesus, daddy, you...you...didn't..." I stumbled a couple steps backward.

I couldn't bring myself to finish it, to ask if he'd killed him. My eyes danced to the body on the ground. Some tiny relief flickered through me when I saw Asphalt moving, rolling on the ground in agony, clenching his shoulder.

Then I saw the long, thick crimson stream making its way across the cracked patio. So much for barbecues. I'd never see it the same way with a man's blood trickling across the tile.

"God damn it, Elle Jo, I told you to stay inside! What

the fuck's the matter with you, girl? You gone deaf today?" Snarling, he shoved his gun back in its holster, and caught up to me before I could run.

I screamed as he grabbed my arms and pushed me inside, firmly but gently, slamming the screen shut between us.

"You're too good to care about what happens to this piece of shit. I raised you better than to fall for bastards like him, and you know it. Your ma knows it, bless her soul."

I winced, pinched my eyes shut, and shook my head.

"Daddy, don't." I looked up, letting him see my anger, even if it threatened to get someone killed. "Don't *ever* use her name like that again."

"It's the God's truth, sweetheart. We both know it. I'm taking out the trash before he leaves his fuckin' stink all over you. I get it, you think he's just a cute boy with a chip on his shoulder." Growling, daddy pulled out his gun, and motioned again to my crush, bleeding on the ground. "I'm saving you from making one helluva mistake. You won't understand tonight, sweetheart, but you will someday."

"No, daddy, you're the one making a mistake. Austin's right. I deserve to make my own choices. I'm eighteen now, and I'll be out on my own this fall. You can't treat me like a little girl forever."

The rage on his face cracked. The soft smile that appeared was totally out of place. But that's the kind of man my father was, a storm in a bottle who gave all his love to me while went away to kill, abuse, and do who knows what else.

"You can choose whatever the fuck you want, baby doll, just as long as it isn't him or any other sorry bastard wearing a one-percenter patch." Daddy turned, his hawk eyes focusing on the unfinished business a few feet away. "Wish you'd understand. This maggot's dirty, and I don't just mean bitches and smokes kinda filthy. He's already been hanging with the NorCal boys, and that's where he belongs. Those fuckers aren't like us. Not anymore. They lost their damned honor years ago and made this club a fucking laughing stock. Your boy here will fit right in."

"Wait!" I rammed the screen as hard as I could until it flew open, forcing him to pause. "You can't kill him. I know you don't like him and you're punishing him for what he's done. But I brought it on. I let him kiss me. I *wanted* him to."

I locked eyes with the man laying on the ground. There was a glimmer of the heat we'd shared when our mouths locked behind his pain. I had to look away, before it totally consumed me.

"Do this for me, daddy. Everyone deserves a second chance, and you know it. He's too young to die, he's still finding his way. He...he treated me good."

Several dozen teases flashed through my mind at once, all the mysterious little moments I'd shared with the bastard. I'd relived them a few hundred more times with girlfriends over the years, listening to them chattering about me, the only girl he'd ever been sweet on.

"Back inside. *Now.* I'm not asking again, Elle, and you'll do it if you want me to consider anything you've said tonight."

He wasn't playing around anymore. Slowly, I pivoted and headed back into the house, flattening myself against the wall in the kitchen, where I could still hear what was going on while staying out of sight.

"Fuck's sake, Prez. You really gonna kill a brother out here in your own backyard? I – ah, fuck!" The soft strain in Asphalt's voice fragmented with new pain.

"No. Let me tell you, boy, you're a lucky sonofabitch. I'm letting you off with a few warning slugs in that fucked up shoulder. When I pull my fuckin' boot off your chest, I'm gonna walk to the gate and open it up. You'll crawl through it, straight down the street, get on your bike, and never, ever come anywhere within fifty miles of Seattle-Tacoma."

"Shit."

"Yeah, you got yourself a whole pile," daddy growled. "I'll talk to Blackjack. He's always been good at keeping the boys down there in line and putting 'em where they need to go. One of the only good men left south of Klamath."

"Okay. Okay. Whatever you say."

"Now you're starting to learn, *Ass*-fault. Maybe there's hope for you yet, but I'm not holding my goddamned breath. Fuck's sake, I'd suffocate."

I shuddered. My father's voice took on a wicked satisfaction, the way a lion would talk if it was able to while playing with its prey.

"It's go time. Just one more thing." He paused, and somewhere in that blank space his voice became daggers. "Stay away from my little girl. Forever. Don't ever come near her again, you bald headed fuck, or I swear to Christ I'll put you in the ground."

Another long pause. Then the sound of a boot kicking, straight into Asphalt's chest, hard enough to splinter several ribs.

My stomach churned. I covered my mouth, fighting the sick need to throw up, wiping at the tears rolling down my cheeks with the other hand.

The gate creaked open, and several new boots clattered on the old patio outside. Daddy spoke to several of his men in hushed whispers before he pulled out his lighter. I listened to him flick the flame on. In my mind, I could see him holding it to light another one of the cigarettes he rolled by hand as part of his morning ritual.

"Carry this sack of shit out, brothers. Make sure that Tacoma bottom rocker's off his cut before he leaves town. Don't ever want this dumbass kid embarrassing our charter again."

"You got it, Prez." I heard Uncle Line whistle, leading the prospects out, imagining his one-eyed face staring over the grisly scene.

Asphalt groaned as they dragged him out. My signal to make my feet work again. I fought the urge to throw up as I tottered up the stairs. I barely shut my door and crashed out on my bed before daddy came inside, slamming the screen shut behind him.

By some miracle, he never heard me cry myself to sleep that night.

The only man worthy of putting his lips on mine was gone forever, if he even lived through the night.

II: Blowout (Asphalt)

Present Day

"Shit. It's always some fucking thing, isn't it?" Brass slapped the table so hard I could feel it vibrate beneath my palms.

The other brothers weren't looking at me like the hothead for once. The Veep was pissed, and who the fuck could blame him? Hell, with all the guys hooking up and taking old ladies left and right, they had more reason than ever to hate the bloodshed coming our way.

"Enough, son. What's going on up in Tacoma cuts straight to the heart of this club's future." The Prez slicked his long gray hair back and tightened his grip on the bear claw serving as his gavel.

When Blackjack spoke, everybody listened. I tensed up in my seat and sat a little straighter. He'd led us through some crazy, fucked up shit the last few months, and we were so close to peace everybody could taste it.

I didn't mind the peace and quiet, honestly. Every man needed a break after all the life and death, old lady drama shit we'd been through. But fuck if my fists weren't hungry to break some bones.

"We could've easily ended up with a new civil war on our hands if it hadn't been for you boys." Blackjack looked across to me, Roman, and Stryker. "No charter tolerates having their Prez hog-tied and roughed up. But Gil didn't leave us any choice."

"No, he didn't," I growled. "Him and I go way back. You'd better believe the man was pissed off when we strapped him down and grilled his ass about the Chinese in his own damned office. No small miracle we managed to get him on the phone with you, Prez, and diffuse a fucking shootout with Tacoma."

"So, no evidence of dirty deals?" The Prez's sharp eyes narrowed on Roman, our overgrown Enforcer.

"None. If he's been dealing extra ammo and weapons behind our back, he's doing a damned good job of covering it up."

Blackjack's lips twitched and he pulled out a fresh smoke, making a show of slowly lighting it and taking a long drag before he spoke. "Well, if he's up to the bullshit we think he is, we need to find out before anybody else does."

"Damned straight," I said. "If the Devils see some shit and think we're skimming off their shipments to new suppliers, it'll fuck up the whole alliance we've had since Fang bit the dirt."

"Nobody needs that shit." Brass leaned back in his chair, locking eyes with his blood brother, Rabid. They shared a nod.

I could've rolled my damned eyes.

This wasn't about how glad we all were that the old Prez was dead and we'd put Blackjack in his place, turning this club right-side up. All the boys in this MC were going soft since they'd taken women.

Shit, some of 'em were family guys now, even the giant next to me. I'd only helped his ass move in a few weeks ago with his babe, Sally, and the change was fucking obvious.

Ever since Roman found out his old flame had popped out a kid, he'd gone from hardass goliath to diaper changing daddy. Spent more time with his family than he did at the clubhouse, except when we all had to get dirty.

His transformation freaked me the fuck out most.

"Nobody in this club needs to worry, as long as we get a man inside." Blackjack looked at his Veep.

"I'm guessing you've already got a plan, Prez, yeah?" Brass said hopefully.

"That's right. In all my years, nothing cements loyalty between clubs like mixing blood. Gil has a daughter who's back from college to help with his biz up there. We have a few eligible boys, and that gives us an in to —"

I jerked up so hard in my seat my knees banged the fucking table. Everybody looked at me, and a couple guys laughed.

Fuck them all. He was talking about Elle Jo, the only

chick I'd ever touched and still thought about without dragging her to bed.

That hot, blonde, blue eyed brat still caused my cock to strain some nights. I thought about her when I jerked off alone or dragged some club whore into my room to fill. I came like a wild fucking animal when I imagined what I'd lost with her, getting nothing but that sly little kiss before her old man put lead into my bones.

Then I got pissed, thinking about everything I'd lost, wondering where she'd gone and who she was fucking. It wasn't me, damn it, and the sick truth made me wanna ram my fist through the wall.

The razors in my blood didn't take too kindly to hearing her being talked about like a piece of fucking meat neither. That pussy was meant for me one time, and I'd let it fucking go because the Tacoma boys chased me outta town.

That spoiled, sexy club princess had the only cunt I wanted to fuck, and hadn't. My whole vision went red and the world spun when I thought about her coming back to taunt me, wrapped in some fucked up Grizzlies intrigue she didn't deserve.

All the brothers around this table had been through some serious shit, sure, but had we lost our goddamned minds?

"Wait, what the fuck, Prez," I grunted, pretending like I hadn't heard him right. "You can't be saying what I think you're saying. I thought the arranged marriage shit in this club died out with Fang?"

"Easy, son." Blackjack looked at me and smiled. "I know you have roots up there, but she's not your kid sister. She's our ticket to smoothing hell over and finding out whether or not Gil deserves more than a rope around his hands and a blade in his throat."

"Fuck..." My head was spinning.

Elle Jo.

The bitch. The tease. The princess.

I hadn't seen her since the night I'd grabbed her ass and put my mouth on hers. She was probably the tenth woman I'd kissed, and I'd had at least fifty more since I'd blown town and left her sweet ass forever.

Her old man gave me the greatest regret I'd carried like a ball and chain for four fucking years. That night he put a couple bullets in my shoulder, broke my ribs, warned me away from ever sniffing around her again...

I'd been fucking robbed.

My fists tensed. Roman shifted next to me, sensing my body language, ready to restrain my crazy ass if he needed to. Wouldn't be the first time.

"We've come too close to let it all slip away, boys. We've turned this club around and sent the cartel packing. We did it without losing lives. Is having one of our men take an old lady on the fly extreme?" He paused, pointing at us with the bright orange end of his smoke. "Hell yes, it is. And you'd better believe I'd go crazier to see every one of you and your families safe from more bloodshed. I'm not asking anybody who's already hitched up with a woman and a kid to take on this job."

Fuck, fuck, fuck.

Talk about a narrow damned field for a ludicrous mission. Blackjack's eyes pivoted to me, then to Stryker, the only two eligible bastards left, excluding himself.

But there was no way in hell the Prez would ever volunteer for this shit himself. Besides being old enough to be Elle's father, he hadn't let go of that woman who'd locked his heart in a tomb years ago, some chick I'd only heard vague rumblings about.

Karolyn? Carol? Whoever the fuck she was, she was a big damned secret, one so bad he'd sworn off pussy forever.

Stryker and I looked at each other. Our newest brother had come back into the fold after we'd thought he turned rat and nearly dropped his ass dead a couple months back. Lucky for him, we'd been wrong.

"Prez," he said slowly, "I'll do it to take the load off brother Asphalt's back. Just let me –"

"No, you fucking won't. I can handle all the fucked up weight in the world." I looked him dead in the eye, trying like hell to control the hornets swarming through my veins. "Elle, Gil, and me, we all got history. Let me do this. I'm the only other fucker here who hasn't married himself off to some chick."

Rabid cleared his throat, staring at me with wild

smirk. "Damn, brother, no need to jump the gun. Christa and me, we're not official yet."

I nodded. Roman was the only boy at the table formally hitched, but the weddings for Brass and Rabid would be coming soon, and they were just itching for the right time.

"Fuck me. Never thought I'd see Asphalt beat me to the altar." Rabid did a long take with the Veep, no doubt thinking the same shit, and the other guys laughed.

"No time for bullshit." Blackjack stood up, one eye wincing through the pain he still carried on his battered old bones. "We've found our man. Asphalt's right. I don't enjoy forcing that sonofabitch to give up his spoiled brat so we can play secret agent to protect this club. If they've been on good terms before, it'll soften the blow."

Yeah fucking right.

Nobody in their right mind would've called the shit Ell-Bell and I had 'good.' I'd treated her like a dog 'til the night we kissed. Yeah, I'd taken a break from the teasing one long evening to help her fix her bike when I was sixteen, but she must've thought I was the biggest prick outside her old man's charter, and fuck if she wasn't right.

'Course, I could afford those mistakes when I was young and stupid. Now? Prez was sending me into a viper's nest. There wasn't any crawling away without someone getting bit.

Roman turned to Blackjack, his huge arms folded.

"What happens if he goes up there and finds out Gil's been fucking with the Chinese like we thought?"

"Then we'll fuck Tacoma *hard*. We've seen it all by now, boys. Brothers' blood spilled on the ground. The worst the cartel had to offer. Half of you've pulled the girls you're with straight out of hell. One rogue charter isn't gonna break us – so long as we get them into line before they go completely off the chain."

The Prez locked eyes with me. Slowly, I nodded.

Every man at this table understood. My mind was going crazy thinking about dealing with Elle again, making her my no shit, white dress and bitch heels *bride*.

But I wasn't marrying her because I had butterflies flapping in my heart.

We weren't getting hitched because I still had a hard-on to fuck her 'til she screamed my name, tore my skin, went outta her mind beneath me. No, no, fuck no.

This was all about the club, and I never let the patch down.

Had to tell myself that shit. Had to believe it. Had to get this over with.

"No questions?" Blackjack growled, waiting for a few tense seconds.

Silence.

The petrified bear claw smacked the table hard. "Meeting adjourned. Now, go get this poor bastard drunk while I tell Gil exactly how it's going down tomorrow."

"A married man! Holy fucking shit." Brass slid a fresh bottle of Jack into my hands and slapped me on the back. "Rabid's right. I would've bet my right nut we would've been next after Roman."

"Good fucking thing you didn't. You'd be half a man right now if you'd put that shit on the table." I ripped off the cap and took a long swig.

Pure amber fire washed down my throat. Hellfire blazed in my guts, churning away with their usual mix of anger, piss, lust.

My cock wouldn't stay down every time I thought about Elle Jo. I hadn't even seen the chick for four years. Not since I'd blown Tacoma with my shoulder wrapped in gauze.

The ache her asshole dad left behind still hit me sometimes in the heat of battle, or when the winters were rough. Flesh and bone remembered what the brain wanted to forget with crystal-fucking-clarity.

"That's it, brother. Drink up." Roman's gorilla-sized hand squeezed my arm. "We've all had our differences here, you and me, but this is something for the club to celebrate. Family always is."

"Oh, fuck." I rolled my eyes. "Come on, guys. It's not like this bitch means shit to me. I'm taking one for the club. Probably won't even fuck her."

My dick wanted to bust out and choke me when I lied.

Brass grinned. "That doesn't sound like the Asphalt I

know."

"Don't tell me. You're gonna keep getting your dick wet in sluts while she's wearing your brand?" Roman's eyebrows furrowed, disapproving as all hell.

"Not your fucking business, brother. None of you." Goddamn I needed another swig of liquid courage, and I took a big one. "You're all acting like you've never heard of a marriage of convenience. You know me. I don't settle for that shit, and I'm sure as hell not gonna be a married man. She won't tame me. No woman ever will."

Rabid stood up, polishing off his beer, and almost spat the shit out when he started laughing. "Good one, brother. You oughta know by now it's a bunch of bullshit. Just look how many boys here have fallen head over heels. If this Elle isn't the one for you, somebody else will be."

"I can see it now..." Brass smiled. "Asphalt and Roman's kids making play dates. Swapping recipes with their old ladies. Keep that shit up, and the Prez'll have to patch in some new prospects just so he's got guys ready to ride at all hours."

"Fuck you," Roman growled. "I'm still doing everything an Enforcer should, and you know it. Raising my boy and loving my wife hasn't changed one lick of that shit. Never will."

"Easy, big guy. You know I'm just fucking around. All for our soon-to-be-ex bachelor's sake."

"Whatever, VP," I said, taking another long pull of

whiskey.

Fire surrounded my brain, turning the world to a delicious red. Only thing I loved more than being toasty in booze was being balls deep inside some hot, tight pussy.

My dick pounded, hard as a fucking brick, whenever I thought about Elle's. No, I wouldn't force her to fuck me, bride or not. Shit wouldn't be right.

But damn if I'd put up a fight if she came along naturally. My shoulder remembered taking bullets for her on our last night together, just like my lips remembered that kiss.

Her breath. Her need. The little moan she pushed into my mouth when my tongue twined with hers, held it down, stroked it the same way I wanted to spread her legs apart and drive into her virgin cunt.

Fuck.

"Yeah, Brass, let's not get cocky. The way it's going, we're gonna have ourselves a double wedding, if somebody doesn't knock up their girl first. We can still put our brother here behind us, right where he belongs." Rabid winked at the VP and tilted his bottle at me.

"You boys go do that. As for me, I'm gonna find something to fuck around here while I'm a free man, without taking more shit."

"It's your bachelor party, bro." Rabid said, raising a drink to me. "You know we'll be right behind you, whatever happens."

Grabbing my bottle, I staggered away from the bar. The brothers meant well, but their barbs left my ass sore, seeing how this wasn't a real marriage.

Wished the Prez had told me I'd end up the butt of everybody's bullshit jokes for taking this job on. Not that I would've let Stryker or anybody else do it.

Shit, just imaging another man in this club taking Elle Jo to the altar made me want to smash my bottle to pieces on the nearest wall, stab the nearest asshole I could find.

One of our new prospects, Glassy, was standing out by the gate, smoking. "You need something, Asphalt?"

"I'm too fucked up to drive. You're gonna bring me into town for some tits and ass." Another swig, and I dropped the Jack, spilling the shit all over the pavement. "Not that clean new place Rabid's old lady runs. I'm talking about the dirty tonight."

Glassy grinned, tilting his head. Hated when he looked at me like that because his fake eye pulled apart from the other one, making him look like a goddamned chameleon for a split second.

"You're the boss. Let's take my truck."

I didn't come all the way to the last big whorehouse outside Redding to fuck. I came for therapy.

Sat down at the bar and ordered a beer. I sipped it slowly, just waiting for some chucklefuck to make the first move.

No matter how much my dick hurt tonight, my fists hurt more. They needed serious action.

When you've fucked dozens of whores, sluts, and one-night wonders your whole damned life, fucking takes a backseat. The other F interested me a whole lot more, and nothing but a good, hard fight was calming my nerves tonight.

I stared into my half-empty glass, realizing I shouldn't even be here.

Well, fuck, shoulda, coulda, woulda never sat well with me anyway. That shit, that uncertainty, became an integral part of my life since the day my balls dropped and I got my bottom rocker.

Nothing tonight made sense without blood.

Marrying Elle Jo wasn't supposed to be in the cards. I wasn't supposed to take an old lady and a wife. I wasn't supposed to come up to Tacoma and face down Aaron "Gil" Mathers after he'd barely spared my life that night four years ago.

Fuck what was supposed to happen. Destiny held an Ace in her hands tonight, but I could still control a few things, make them go my way or the motherfucking highway.

They didn't call me Asphalt for nothing. I'd lost count of how many fucks I'd hitched to my bike over the years and shredded on the pavement.

Too bad I couldn't do one more tonight. My fists would have to do the talking instead. And those sons of bitches *sang* when I saw the greasy, redneck piece of shit across the room, fondling some bitch swaying in stockings, refusing to let go when she tried to push him away.

The girls out here were supposed to be off limits. This place looked like a strip joint on the outside by Blackjack's order – all part of the agreement July Kitty paid the club for being allowed to operate an old school fuckhouse in our territory.

So, Kitty put the nice girls, the ones who weren't down to fuck, out to shake their tail near the bars. The real meat was out back, and the asshole ripping at her thong outta known it.

I threw the rest of my brew back and slid the empty glass over to the bartender, who gave me the stink eye. Bastard knew what was coming.

Too bad. No way would any of these assholes call the cops unless the place was riddled with bullets and blood.

Rule number two, by the Prez's order – any attention to this place by the authorities was too much. They depended on our club's protection, and tonight, I was gonna give it to the girl.

My feet felt like cement logs in my boots as I walked up to the handsy fuck. He had a firm hand around her thighs now, trying to pull her off the stage, more than a little dangerous for a woman in heels as tall as hers.

"Whatdafuck, baby?" he slurred. "Come hang out on papa's lap. That little ass was made for this dick, and I ain't paying. You should be fuckin' paying me after all the shit I dropped on booze here. I –"

"Hey, asshole." Two words plus a finger jabbing his shoulder like a spear was all it took to spin him around.

My fist exploded into the motherfucker's jaw before he even looked at me. He was fat, muscular, probably the former bodybuilder type. Bone crunched underneath the meat I'd punched through, and he recovered pretty fast for a drunken, horny hog.

Clasping his hands, he took a step back, and swung. He had a wicked swing that barely missed caving in my skull. The bastard was fast for a fucker who'd seen his share of brawls.

I was faster. My boots smashed into his shins so hard he went crashing down. The girls on the stage screamed, and several drunken jackasses laughed, forming a circle around us.

Goliath got me in the knee as he went down, and I fell with him. Shit.

For a second, I wished I'd taken it easier on the booze before I decided to get into the thick of it. But second guessing wasn't my style. Ever.

The whiskey in my system had its advantages when he got a glancing blow in against my ear. The punch rattled my whole skull, turning everything into a numb, ringing mess, but it didn't make me skip my next punch.

I bellowed like a motherfucker and lunged, kneed him the spine, just the right spot to hold his drunken ass down while I wrapped my hands around his fat neck. He kicked something fierce for more than a minute, just like a tiger going down from a dart.

Asshole nearly threw me off several times. I hung on, pressed my fingers deeper, choking him out, throttled his neck all the way through the last desperate thrashes.

Now, it was time to see my shrink, that killer lightning surging up inside me every time I had some fucker's life in my hands.

I squeezed so hard I swore I could've ripped his head off. Down on the ground, ready to take his life, we talked. I told him shit with my violent, bloody need to kill that nobody else would ever know.

One shaking finger, deep in his throat, for all the times my parents screamed, all the nights the Tacoma PD showed up at the house, all the way up 'til my old man walked out, never to be seen again. Ma died in a hospice her sister brought her to in Olympia a couple years later, and he didn't even come to her fucking funeral.

Another finger for the blood on my soul, a dozen men I'd shot or stabbed or shredded on the road, all devils who deserved it.

One more for Elle Jo, the only girl I'd wanted to kiss twice.

Three more fingernails scratching so hard they drew blood for this fucked up, fake, arranged marriage.

Two more for the satisfaction I'd get watching Gil seethe while I threw back princess' veil and kissed her deep, my hand on her ass, feeling my cock swell for the only pussy who'd ever got away.

Last three fingers for everything I'd never have with her – love, kids, shaking her in bed while she howled out my name like a fucking mad woman.

No, wait. That last one, I wasn't ready to give up on yet. But all that other shit – everything that seemed to come natural to all the brothers who shared my clubhouse?

Fuck no. Not this week, not this year, not ever.

My hands squeezed so hard I could feel the fire in my chest, bringing the crude drunk to death's doorstep.

Didn't let up 'til he was finally limp underneath me. I checked his pulse to make sure I hadn't killed the asshole. Fucker had a heartbeat, however weak.

Maybe somebody would bludgeon him to death another night, or maybe he'd learned a powerful lesson here. That shit wasn't up to me. I staggered to my feet, rubbing my temple and hot, damaged ear.

Fuck. Just my luck that I'd probably have a nasty bruise across my face for the wedding later this week.

I looked up. The girl he'd been groping clung to her pole on stage, staring at me with those *fuck me* eyes I'd seen on wet pussy a hundred times.

I nodded respectfully and turned around, refusing to look at her again. I wasn't here to fuck, like I said before, and I kept my word.

Two burly bouncers stood behind me, right in the

middle of the spectators. I threw my arms out and pushed through them, grinding my teeth as I did.

"Lazy motherfuckers. You're damned lucky I was here to do your dirty work for you. Outta my way."

When I said jump, they did. Nobody fucked with a man wearing Grizzlies colors on his cut, and Kitty herself would personally have the hide of any employee who did.

When I got back to the bar, I threw my arms out, supporting my weight. "What the hell you looking at? Get me some ice and a fresh bottle. Don't worry, I've got a sober cab tonight."

"Shit, brother, I want some of what you've had tonight." Glassy chuckled from the other end of the bar and winked with his good eye.

"Then go off and marry the girl next door for a club op. Shit, maybe you and Stryker can share the next bitch Blackjack wants to use to keep us safe."

Did I really just say that shit? Yeah, I did.

Glassy looked down awkwardly at his drink and turned away. Well, fuck him too.

Fuck the past. Fuck the endless stream of sewage the club had been dealing with ever since I hooked up with the Redding crew. Fuck the poison running in my veins.

And fuck Elle Jo more than anything else for giving me the shakes every time I thought about crushing my mouth to hers, much less sliding into that sweet puss I'd been denied for four hellish years. Fuck her for making my dick so hard I could've pounded railroad spikes, and fuck her for knowing I'd never be driving it into her, ripping at her hair, spilling my come up inside her.

Fuck. Everything.

I didn't know what the hell fate had in store after I saw my name inked on her skin and she started calling me her old man. But I could damned well guarantee it meant watching a few worlds turn to ashes by the time it was all over.

III: Down the Aisle (Elle Jo)

"All right. *All right,* you motherfucking, cocksucking, hard balling sack of shit. You've got your time and place. Which one is it? No, no wait. Don't fuckin' tell me. I'll find out Sunday. I gotta get the fuck off the phone and break the news..."

The coldest chill of my life ran up my spine. I hadn't slept for the last hour, listening to daddy rant and rave, my ear pressed against the door.

The walls in this old house had always been paper thin. Whatever had him upset had shook up him worse than I'd heard since the night he almost murdered Austin.

I pinched my eyes shut, trying to take long, slow breaths, my hot little ear pressed to the door.

Is this what I've returned for? Really?

I was coming home already. But what choice did I have when grad school was a bust, and I didn't want to go all the way to San Francisco for a crappy translation job that wouldn't even let me afford an apartment?

Daddy offered me a roof over my head, and some work. He offered me club money – *a lot* of club money for my help on a business deal. Enough to finally be an adult and do grown up things, to get the latest boots and drink nice cocktails in upscale Seattle lounges.

Not that I really cared for those things. Mostly, I just wanted my own space, a condo to share with friends in the city, maybe some imported wines and good chocolate. All the things that let me pretend I still had a shot at a normal life, even though I was twenty-two, and about to crawl deeper than ever down the club's throat.

Jesus. What was I thinking?

I hadn't taken four years of Mandarin Chinese and done an entire summer studying abroad for *this*.

Too bad life has a funny way of throwing the last thing I ever wanted in my face, dragging me back to Tacoma.

Perfect timing, too. My father was ready to put ink on paper for a black market trade deal with the Shanghai mafia. I'd studied the infamous Black Dragons in an international crime seminar.

They were as dangerous as they were masters in the underworld, and they'd been trying to get a foothold on the West Coast for years. They also had a lot of money and a serious demand for weapons – just what daddy needed to make his chapter the richest one in the entire Grizzlies MC.

Or that's what little he told me, anyway. I doubted the fine print here, whatever it is, even if I couldn't say no because *so much money.*

"Elle Jo! Open up!" I jumped when I heard his fist

pounding on my door. "We gotta talk."

I'd been so deep in thought I hadn't heard him coming. Slowly, I twisted my lock and pulled it open, pretending to rub fake grog from my eyes.

"Sorry, I know it's late...but this is too damned important. Better we get this shit done sooner than later." He stepped in and walked over to my bed, sat down with his face in his hands.

This was going to be bad. His defeated posture said it all.

My heart ratcheted up, doubling in speed. I tried to prepare myself, like I always had growing up in this house when something terrible happened to him or the club. But, hell, he hadn't looked like this since the day he told me mom wouldn't be coming home from the hospital...

"Daddy, what is it?" I walked over and spoke to him softly, cautiously, gingerly laying my fingers on his shoulder. "You're really upset."

"Yeah, isn't that a fuckin' understatement. Shit." He sighed, filling the long pause before he formed words again. "There's no easy way to say this, darling. So let me just lay it out. Elle, You're getting married this Sunday."

"What?!"

The whole world went out from under me. I stepped back, shaking my head, wondering if I'd heard him right.

"Yeah, I know it's a clusterfuck of a surprise. This

wasn't what I wanted for you, or the club, but the fuckers down in NorCal are twisting my nuts so hard they're about to bust off. I told you about this shit with the Chinese, the big deal coming up that I really need your help with. It's for the good of the club, and they're too stupid to realize it. So, me and the boys are going it alone with the Dragons. And Redding'll have my head on a pike if they find out what's going on up here. I gotta stall those fuckers out, keep the peace, just long enough to wheel and deal those mean motherfuckers from Shanghai. You follow?"

"No, daddy, I don't! What's that got to do with me...getting married?" I could barely force out the last part.

My stomach lurched every time I thought about it. Every girl's dream is to meet a handsome man, a best friend, a boy who lights a fire in her belly and an inferno in the bed.

Did I want a husband someday? Sure.

It just wasn't supposed to be happening like this. There should've been a courtship, a proposal, a slow, delicious season of falling in love – not being handed off to a man I'd never even seen like a piece of meat!

"You're out of your mind!" I shouted, throwing my fists in the air. "I can't go along with this. I won't. Nothing could possibly be worth trading me for...for what, exactly?"

"Saving lives and keeping the peace, that's what.

Blackjack down in Redding, the national Prez, he doesn't trust my ass for good fuckin' reason. We're gonna give him one so he'll shut his fuckin' yap. He wants a guy embedded up here to scope things out, and we'll show him exactly what he's allowed to see. We'll make that long haired old fart think we're playing right along, and by the time the deal's done, he'll be none the wiser. We'll send his boy packing after a few weeks and I'll get your names on the divorce papers. Easy, peasy."

"That's asking a lot." I snapped. "I...I don't think I can do it, dad. I'm sorry."

Daddy's hand shot out, seized mine, and pulled it close. He hadn't held my hand to his rough, scarred cheek for years. He did that thing that made me think of a loyal old dog, one who'd jealously guarded me a thousand times.

Except now he had a splinter in his paw, and he was looking at me to pull it out.

"Baby, don't apologize. You just listen. If it were up to me, I'd have you marrying a guy with charm and fortune behind his name. Shit, you remember how I got when boys would come sniffing around you while you lived at home...I chased all the rats away because I wanted the *best* for you. I still do. Unfortunately, shit's not working out that way. I can't get you shit if I'm no longer breathin' because Redding blows my brains out." He opened his big blue eyes and looked at me, the same ones I'd inherited.

"You're a smart girl. You've had more schoolin' than anybody in this family ever did. I saw your transcripts, you took political science and shit for that fancy foreign language degree. Well, this is politics. Real world, outlaw fuckin' politics, and it gets nuts. We're dealing with the lifeblood of Tacoma here. Life and death. An olive branch. A marriage of convenience to Redding while we slay some Dragons – in trade, I mean – nothing more. You walk down the aisle, share a place with this guy for a few months, distract him while I keep things rolling on the home front here in Tacoma, and we'll forget this ever happened."

"But, daddy..."

"No buts. I'm asking you to play pretend. Sure, we'll make it look official for club moral with a ceremony and all, but that's as far as it goes. You don't have to ride with this asshole or sleep with him. Just act like a nice old lady out in public for his dumb ass, help me bide time, and I'll keep the divorce papers warm in my desk drawer. He'll be out of your hair before you can say 'fuckin' go,' and one day you'll find a man who won't give a shit that you had a three month marriage with some random outlaw asshole from California."

I pulled away from my father. I had to turn away, processing the brutally insane offer he'd thrown in my face.

I walked backwards until the wall wouldn't let me go any further. His big blue eyes stayed on me. I couldn't stop seeing the desperate, wounded dog, all the pride and joy he'd shown me over the years, melding with a plea.

Do this for me, Elle Jo. I didn't have to hear him say it. His face did all the talking. Please. Just this once.

"Well, baby? What do you say? It'll be a good excuse to try on your ma's old wedding dress."

Daggers. My intestines twisted so hard I wanted to throw up in his face. I lunged, stepped up, and slapped him.

Hard.

"Fuck you, dad!" The air I sucked in singed my lungs. "I'll do it for you, for the good of this family and your club. But don't you *ever* invoke her name to make me fall in line again. I'm not a damned teenager anymore."

"Fair point." Taking it like a champ, he stood up.

Physical pain never bothered him, and emotional agony didn't seem to do much either. Not when he got exactly what he wanted anyway. And I'd just handed him everything on a silver platter.

Again. So much for being a grown woman, right?

God damn it.

"Who's the man I'm supposed to wed, anyway?" I said, chewing on the words. All so bitter.

Maybe the more I talked about it, the easier it would be. *Ha ha, right.*

"Didn't ask that part when I cut the deal," he said, scratching the scarlet mark I'd left on his face through his salt and pepper stubble. "Does it really matter?

Nobody's asking you to love the dog."

I didn't say anything, just lowered my eyes.

He really didn't grasp the full insanity of what he was asking me to do. It didn't matter if I even liked the bastard I'd be forced to wed. He'd still be my first husband, the first man I lived with, my first tender kiss as a wife.

That last part was a maybe. It scared me, honestly, especially when I hadn't been kissed since that night with Austin more than four years.

"Darling, listen, it's gonna be okay," he said, reaching for me.

I jerked away. "Just go. I need some time to process. Not to mention start getting ready for everything with what little notice you've given me."

"Yeah, I'm real sorry about that. Only finalized the shit last night, when I realized there was no way out of it. That bastard, Blackjack, he's already nipping at my heels, just looking for a chance to eighty-six me and put another puppet in place who'll dance for the Redding club. Greedy, demanding fucks. All of 'em." He softened his anger before he spoke again. "Look, I already promised you work up here, and that part doesn't change. I'm gonna need you around, helping with the Chinese deal when it's all patched up. You can understand those boys like we can't. They'll never see it coming. We're gonna make a lot of money from this, baby. I'll be a dead man before anybody tries to take your fair share."

I turned away. He wasn't making me feel better.

For a second, he lingered, probably feeling a pang of fatherly guilt over this whole thing. That should've counted for something. But it didn't. Not when Gil, the Grizzlies MC President, overruled it.

"Okay, Elle Jo. Try to get some sleep." One more command, and he was gone, gently closing the door behind me. Just like he used to when I was a little girl and he stopped in to check on me while I lay in my bed, pretending to be asleep.

Kind of ironic that money was suddenly the furthest thing from my mind when it was my whole reason for coming home. Finding a man and getting married in Tacoma was last on my list of dreams.

Well, I hadn't exactly found one, but now marriage was in the cards. I had to make myself think he kept his words, that he was serious about sharing the profits from whatever came out of this dirty deal with the foreign mafia.

Just think about the money, I told myself. A few weeks married, a few six figure payments, and you can go anywhere. Do anything. Forget all of this crap forever.

It had its appeal. Now, I just had to repeat it to myself a few thousand times, until I actually believed it.

If I survived the next few weeks – a *very* big if – I swore I'd walk away rich. And once I had my money and dumped my fake husband, no man was *ever* going to order me around again.

"Christ, you're beautiful, Elle Jo." Daddy didn't look half bad in his charcoal jeans and fresh, clean cut.

He hooked his arm over mine as we stood in front of the double doors, ready to be hoisted open any second by the two prospects on the other side.

"I wish it wasn't going down this way. I'm sorry, sweetheart. One of these days, I'm gonna lead you down the aisle in that getup to marry a man you want to be with. Mark my words."

"Let's just get this over with," I whined, fidgeting in my heels.

I'd had about half an hour to practice walking around in them, careful not to trip all over my mom's ivory skirt. I knew at least a few of the tears in daddy's eyes weren't because of what he had to do, or because he was still handing off his daughter for a biker wedding.

He had to be remembering his own, the day she wore this, coming down the aisle toward him with love and hope in her eyes. I tried to hang onto that memory, focus on the greater good.

Hell, I tried to focus on all the compensation I'd get from this sideshow – *if* it worked out.

I just had to grin and bear it, stay out of harm's way, and then do my thing when he went to negotiate with the Chinese. I hadn't begun to plan how I was going to keep my new husband's eyes off what was going on in the club, but daddy said he'd help with all that.

Whatever else, he lived by his word. I had to count on it. I had to —

The doors swung open. Rock and roll blasted in our faces, and several dozen bikers lined up near the pews roared, holding their hands across their chests in a salute.

Two big, burly prospects from Tacoma nodded, their beards waving. We stepped onto the bright red carpet, heading for the trio gathered near the altar. A tall man with long, gray hair who had to be the infamous Blackjack, a brother who doubled as a priest, and...

Fuck. Daddy mouthed it first. I was right behind him.

I practically stopped in my tracks, staring in disbelief.

Even after all these years, I recognized him. Asphalt had gotten at least an inch taller and filled out with pure muscle since the night he kissed me. He'd been handsome at twenty-one, and now he was an absolute panty melter.

I saw green lights facing my way, and the dizziness hit me like a rocket. They hadn't changed a bit. He beamed the same sharp jade eyes that gazed into mine right before daddy blasted him in the shoulder and pulled him away from me forever.

Except forever wasn't so permanent.

Somehow, I started walking again, toward the handsome shock of my life, pulling on daddy's arm. He'd come to a dead stop, his hand near his side, dangerously close to his holster.

The Redding guys on the other side of us tensed up. Several went for their guns. In this kind of standoff, everything has an equal and opposite reaction.

Before I knew what was happening, guns were raised, locked, and loaded over the booming music. Two crews were about to blow each other apart, and we were right in the middle.

"Oh, God."

Blackjack burst between us with a snarl, jerking my hand away from my father's, pushing him into a group of Redding Grizzlies.

Daddy wasn't deterred. Just when I didn't think his face could get redder, it turned completely crimson.

Then he exploded.

"Is this a fuckin' joke, Blackjack? Him? *Him?!* It's bad enough you're asking me to give my daughter up so you can fuck with my club, and now you had to go and rub my goddamned face in it too? Bullshit!"

A man grabbed my shoulders. I spun around, and came face-to-face with those deep green eyes. Each one flickered like a soft, warm ocean, pulling me deep, calming me.

Familiar electricity raced through my veins. My blood turned thick and hot like candle wax, and my sick brain imagined everything else he could do with that grip.

What the hell would it feel like to have those fingers between my legs?

"Come on. Follow me up to the altar. Can't leave you

standing in the way where you could get hurt." Asphalt pulled.

I started to walk, letting him guide me like the numb, awestruck zombie I'd become.

"Gil, listen to me very closely," Blackjack growled. "On my count, you're going to put your popgun down and pop a tranquilizer before you get two charters killed, plus your little girl. We're going to get on with this wedding, exactly like we said. Deal's a deal. It'll be smooth as good whiskey and you'll have some fun, once the shock isn't frying your balls anymore. Don't be a goddamned fool."

"Fuckin' two faced prick," daddy growled, pressing his handgun into the older man's chest. "You knew. So did he. This is a humiliation!"

He pivoted to face us, aiming his gun right at Asphalt. Daddy only let up when I threw my arms around my surprise groom, savoring his heat for the first time in four years.

"Daddy, don't. You're going to get everybody killed."

"God damn it, Elle Jo. You remember what this prick did, right? It's a sick fuckin' joke that my baby, my girl, is being forced to marry this savage little turd. I should've aimed my gun higher that night. Fuck, he wouldn't be standing here today, grinning like he just ate a fuckin' pile. I shoud've –"

A gunshot barked, interrupting his seething anger. Asphalt threw me down. We hit the ground, and he covered me with his huge muscles, protecting me from the imminent shootout.

It never came.

When I looked up, forcing my head up between his big hands, I saw daddy's gun on the floor. He kneeled on the floor, cradling his hand.

Several men looked toward the rafters. I followed their eyes and saw a *massive* man poised on a beam, a long sniper rifle in his hands.

"Great shot, Roman. Knocked the toy clean out of his hands." Blackjack stepped up, leaning over my father, his face lined like an old tree that had seen too many storms. "Let's try this one more time, Gil."

My father snarled as the old man's hand reached for his collar and pulled him up, back on his feet. "Fuck you, Blackjack. Fuck you."

"Don't ruin your girl's special day. This is all about peace between clubs, brotherly love. We still have a chance to make it that way. You can scream all you want, go out back after the ceremony and punch holes in the walls, suck down Jack 'til you black out. None of my concern. But if you point a gun at one of my men again, I *will* have my boy blow your brains all over this holy ground. A deal's a deal, and I never take shit from a man who goes back on his word."

I struggled out of Asphalt's grip and stood. He wrapped his hands around me, cradling me close, and we watched the two biker chiefs face off. I struggled harder when my back leaned against his torso, catching something hard, eager, alive in his pants with my butt.

Oh, shit. I blushed like I was about to burst into flames.

We'd barely been reunited for five minutes, and he already wanted to fuck me, finish what we'd started four years ago on a cold, awkward night.

I wiggled away, shaking my veil to try to cover the wild, shameful red blooming on my cheeks. Asphalt grabbed my wrists and clenched tight, that hold a man has that says you're not going anywhere, babe.

He said more, too. Every single part of him. I heard that rough, eager bulge between his legs talking to me loud and clear when it pressed against me again.

Stay close. Stay horny. I'm not letting you up 'til you feel every fucking inch of this, babe. Everything I should've made you feel years ago.

We took a long delay, and we lost time to kill. I'm gonna fuck your damned brains out.

"You keep your damned distance," daddy spat. "We're brothers by patch, but no man in your club's any kind of blood brother of mine. Stay on your fucking side of the church, and we'll get through this freak show."

Satisfied, Blackjack nodded, turning his attention back to the altar. The older brother who'd flattened himself against the nearby wooden column approached, clearing his throat.

"You two ready to get hitched, or what?"

I looked at Asphalt. Without smiling, he nodded, leading me up the four steps with him.

Our makeshift minister waited a few more minutes while the commotion died down, and men on both sides returned to their seats. When the music cranked up again, the rest of the music poured out, finishing in a booming bass crescendo about how it's better for a man to live on the road than die on his knees.

A couple men behind us coughed. The tall, thin biker with the long mustache marrying us looked through us, his eyes scanning the sizable crowd. I looked at his name patch, ANGUS.

"Everybody gathered here knows this ain't a real wedding, so I'll keep this shit quick." His eyes flicked to the beautiful bastard next to me. "Asphalt, brother, you're claiming this girl and marrying her on the same day. Only God knows how long you'll keep her, but every second you do, your duties are the same. Love her. Honor her. Protect her. Treat her as sacred as your patch. She's one with this club, and one with you. Get it?"

"Yeah, I do. Me and this girl, we go way back. It's been a few years and we've got a lot of catching up to do. We'll be solid, come hell or death. I promise." He thumped the name patch on his chest the same way he did when he put my rude prom date in his place.

Four years ago. Up here, it felt like four minutes.

Asphalt's fingers pushed through mine and squeezed. Such an innocent gesture, surprisingly sweet, but damn if it didn't turn my blood to magma. I melted in the messy, confusing attraction I thought I'd lost years ago, resisting his eyes.

"Elle Jo Mathers," Angus said, fixing his dark eyes on me. "Peace brings love. And so it will with you, when you're on the back of his bike, wearing his brand. You're Tacoma's daughter. He's Redding's son. Both Grizzlies blood forever. Keep him true. Serve him. Love him."

I bristled at the *serve him* part. I caught Asphalt – Austin – wearing the same cocky glint in his eye that I'd seen a dozen times when we were kids, teasing and flirting our way against an uncertain future that was never meant for us.

Well, except now, it was. But I didn't feel it when the biker-priest nodded, and Asphalt grabbed the heavy ring off the altar, sliding it onto my finger.

"Fuck, that thing looks good where it belongs."

"The brother's right," Angus said. "Asphalt, whenever you're ready, you can go ahead and –"

Oh. Sweet. Jesus.

His green eyes swallowed me up before his lips crashed on mine. Asphalt kissed me with a feral, starving passion I hadn't expected.

He kissed me like he wanted to destroy my whole world, and replace it with his. His lips moved like they wanted me, deserved me, owned me. This kiss left me a nervous, shaking wreck, too scared to admit how incredible it felt, but too horny to resist it.

So many years gone, stamped out in his fiery lips. This kiss took me back to our only other kiss, four years ago on daddy's doorstep, before we'd caught hell for it. Our lips moved, divine and right, replacing all that hell with heaven instead.

I hadn't given up the fight yet. Hell, I was still so numb from what was happening it was a miracle I could stand in these stupid heels.

For a single second, though, I surrendered. I moaned into his mouth, just like I did the very first time. His strong arms swept me up, pushed me even deeper into his tongue, into the embrace with every molecule letting me know how bad he wanted to fuck me.

And I wanted it too.

I wanted everything I couldn't have tonight. I wanted it more than the urge to slap him across the face for hiding the fact that he was my groom, for this insane arranged marriage, for never reaching out to me all these years, even if it would've ignited another war with my very pissed off father.

The men in the audience were roaring and laughing by the time it was over. Angus grinned behind the altar, slapped Asphalt on the back, and murmured something about hitting the road before he stripped me down right here.

"I still fucking want you," he growled into my ear. "Never stopped all these years, Elle Jo. We don't have to waste more time. We can pick up right where we left off, with my cock going between your legs, taking everything it should've had years ago."

Holy shit.

As if I'd let him. *No, no, this isn't happening.*

I can't give in. Not like this. Not ever.

I leaned in close, his green eyes shimmering with happy mischief, and whispered in his ear. "If you think you can walk back into my life and sweep me off my feet with one great kiss, think again. I'm your bride, Austin, but I am *not* your woman. I don't love you."

He pulled away and his eyes darkened to an angry jungle green before he answered. He didn't say anything. Just picked me up and threw me over his shoulder, carrying me down the aisle like his latest conquest.

I quietly fumed, hating the fact that his kiss left me soaking wet underneath the wedding dress. My body could mutiny, maybe, but my heart wouldn't.

I just wouldn't let it. This was all business, all for my father, and nothing else.

"Be careful!" I yelped, just as he narrowly avoided tripping over an empty bottle that had fallen and rolled out into our path. He steadied us, put his hand on my ass, and I pursed my lips. "Austin, don't you dare get any screwed up ideas. I told you where we stand, and that isn't changing. Let's just get out –"

"Ell-bell, kindly shut the fuck up. If you don't start calling me by my proper name, I *will* bend you over and slap your ass red like I should've years ago. We're having a honeymoon, one way or another, and you're gonna enjoy it."

Great.

So, he'd really bought into this whole outlaw bride and groom thing. I rolled my eyes, just barely faster than my heart began to beat.

Then his hands clenched my long skirt and ripped it clean off, leaving me with nothing but the thin, short lily white one underneath, all I'd be left with when we climbed on his bike.

IV: Tamer (Asphalt)

"Asphalt, look. What happened at the altar this morning was all for show. So is this honeymoon. I know what's up, my father explained everything. We're not *really* married. It's all club politics." She stopped, smiled nervously, batting her eyes. "And...you know, I really shouldn't have to say this, but...we can't have sex."

Bullshit. She hadn't held me like she was playing games when we rode into town, straight to the place where I'd get her branded as mine.

I wanted to throw her over the leather chair in the tattoo parlor and fuck the ever living hell out of her on the spot. But only after I'd spanked her raw first.

Her hands moved across my abs like she wanted it on my bike. So did her lips at the altar. What the fuck were we doing, pretending otherwise?

My cock hammered in my pants the whole way through that damned ceremony, and it hadn't eased up a beat since we rode into town, my bike decked out in its colors, her losing that long ass wedding skirt before we hit the pavement.

'Course, the girl was completely right. This shit was

all a political stunt, and Gil must've done a pretty good job of convincing her. Didn't change the fact that my body knew what it wanted.

Hers did, too. Fuck, she touched me like she was starving, and I wanted to make every inch of her a feast.

I looked her up and down, not even trying to hide the lust in my eyes. Couldn't stop picturing those high, white bitch heels she had on digging into my ass, her long legs wrapped around me, spurring me on like a bull 'til I broke the fucking bed and left her sore for days.

Shit. My gaze crawled up her body, only stopping when I caught her bright blue eyes, watching as she tucked a stray blonde lock behind her ear.

"We'll see what happens, babe. Keep your panties on. It won't be tonight unless you want it to be."

"It won't be any night, Asphalt." She sniffed, shook her head, taking on a tone like she needed to convince herself. "I just needed to get that out there, given our history. You wanted me. There was a time when I wanted you. And I'm only wearing this because we've both been roped into it with a shotgun to our backs."

"Shotgun wedding? I thought they only did that shit if I knocked you up. This isn't half as much fun." I grinned.

Elle stopped and scowled.

She'd been fidgeting with the new gold ring since we sat down. It already looked like it belonged on her, from the moment I'd slipped it on her hand. Something about that slow up-down-up-down fidgeting motion as she pushed it along her finger made my balls taste fire, tempted me to grab her damned hand right here and shove it on my cock.

Then she'd understand. She'd get that we were gonna share a bed one way or another, no more avoidable than giving her my vows earlier today.

I watched her while we waited, wondering how many bastards had gotten to that body before me. I wanted to handcuff her to the nearest bed and find out, then start over with my face between her legs. The caveman urge to fuck away every last trace of everyone she'd ever had grabbed me by the throat and whispered in my ear, *what the hell are you waiting for, boy?*

"Missus Graham?" She looked up and twisted her head around, then did a double take. Took her a couple seconds to remember she'd taken my name, plus the missus part.

A tall man covered in ink and piercings appeared from around the corner, and he did a double take when he saw us sitting together. "Oh, shit! I'm sorry for keeping you guys on hold. Didn't know another one of Blackjack's boys was getting married."

"Whatever, man, you know the drill." I stood, taking the opportunity to grab her hand and pull her up with me. "Just do your best work. Whatever she wants, wherever she wants it, as long as it says Property of Asphalt, Grizzlies MC. You make it damned near perfect, and we won't have a problem."

He swallowed nervously. The ink jockey in front of me had tatted up plenty of brothers and their girls since we took over this town, and I knew he knew his shit.

For some reason, he never got over shitting his fucking pants whenever he saw any man with a bear patch walk in. Even worse when he needed his old lady inked, too.

I walked her over to him 'til she gave me a sour look and snatched her hand away.

"I can do this alone with the artist, Asphalt. I don't need you looking over my shoulder..."

"Don't bullshit me, babe. I'm coming back there with you," I growled, ripping open the curtain around the little workstation where he had his bench and his inks. "You're mine now. I protect you day and night, make sure you *always* get what you deserve. This marriage thing might have gone differently than I wanted, but as long as you're wearing my brand, you'd better believe I'm treating it like a man should. Deadly fucking serious."

She didn't say anything, just laid down and worked her small fingers down her zipper, exposing her back. When Ink Man stepped in to take it down, I beat him to the punch, giving him the dirtiest damned look in the world as my big hand peeled her dress open, exposing her tender back.

Virgin flesh for my mark. My cock jerked, enjoying the fact that I'd get to claim her one way, even if it wasn't the one I wanted most.

I'd missed my chance to take her cherry before she ran off to college, yeah, but I'd take over every single inch of her. It wasn't close to too late for that.

Fuck, what the hell's happening to me? I watched my reflection in Ink Man's big mirror, listening to the hum of his tools while he worked.

My brand slowly came into view. It had the same theme as lots of other brothers' old ladies. A halo of thorns and barbed wire around the letters, my name writ large on her flesh.

Elle Jo laid completely limp for the next hour, barely murmuring or shrugging her shoulders when the artist asked her for input. I clenched my jaw, trying to keep myself from blowing the fuck up here.

What's wrong with me? What the fuck's gotten into her? Doesn't she realize this is the most important day of her goddamned life, sham marriage or not?

"Easy, girl. Just gonna do the finishing touches."

"Not yet." I stepped up, putting my hand on her free shoulder, giving it a possessive squeeze. "I want something more unique with this one. Put some lightning bolts around it. The same glorious shit I've got stamped here."

I tapped one temple with my free hand, making absolutely sure Ink Man understood. I wanted her to match what I had on my skull. He cleared his throat and looked at Elle.

"That all right with you, ma'am?"

Finally, she sat up, her face tortured. "No. I think we're done here. I've got his name on my skin, all the club legalese an old lady should wear. That's enough, right?"

"Fuck no, baby. The brand's all up to your old man, and asking you for input is just a fucking courtesy. I told you exactly what I wanted. You wanna wear my name, be my property for real? You'll sport my symbol too. Nothing says Asphalt like these lightning bolts. I want my girl wearing 'em too."

We locked eyes, two wills warring. She pursed her lips before they parted slightly and she answered in a haughty, sharp tone.

"You know that isn't what I am. Not really. Come on, Austin, can't we just –"

I snapped. Seized both wrists and flipped her around, pinning her down on the bench, making her feel my weight on top of her. Ink Man jumped back like he'd just come face to face with a mad dog.

Obviously, he had. And now I was laying down the law, telling her *exactly* what was happening here, leading the way an old man should.

"No, goddamn it. We can't." I shook her arms gently, but firmly, lowering my face 'til my hot breath caressed her throat. "I don't give a shit if your old man and my Prez put us both up to this. Don't give a microscopic fuck if you've got a boyfriend back home, holding his dick and getting the worst fucking case of blue balls in the last ten thousand years. Babe, I don't even care if you hate me now, if that sweet, lost little brat I remember in Tacoma's nothing more than ancient history."

Her breath rose, matching mine, her big blue eyes sparkling. Same beautiful eyes I wanted to be looking at when I rocked her ass and spilled my load deep inside her.

She looked at me with that mix of disbelief and desire a woman gets when her body's begging for my dick, but her mind's screaming no.

I rammed my hips into hers, one quick, long stroke, just enough force to make the crappy leather beneath us rock with our combined weight.

"You're mine as long as we're married, woman. That means you follow my lead, and you stop talking back. You start calling me by my proper road name, and you forget all about that troubled kid you grew up with named Austin. He's dead as a fucking doornail. Doing the shit I do makes a man grow up, turns him into a beast." She squirmed as I pushed my face lower, not stopping 'til our foreheads touched. "Baby, you gotta forget the past. So do I. We need to make this work for peace between our charters and our own damned sanity. Forget all about Austin. You're Asphalt's now. And don't you *ever* think you can get away with fucking me over or running your mouth with disrespect just because I went soft on you years ago. Got it?"

Her eyes narrowed into a message I heard without the words.

Fuck. You.

Whatever, at least she wasn't giving me shit from those sweet, plump lips anymore. I resisted the urge to crush my mouth on 'em again and devour her, pushed myself up, and staggered back against the mirror. Didn't bother hiding the raging warhead in my pants, about ten minutes of hard fucking away from exploding deep inside her as soon as I ripped her clothes off.

But not here. Not today. As long as she got the fucking message, we could get by – all we needed to make this sham marriage work.

"You heard what I said. Put the lightning on her and do it right."

Ink Man got back to work. I folded my arms and watched, loving the way he put them around her brand, perfect carbon copies of what I'd worn on my face for years.

Now, she was truly, uniquely mine. Maybe not forever, it was true.

Rings could be taken off. Divorce papers could be signed. Tattoos could be scrubbed away with tears and salt.

But today, I owned her completely. Only a matter of time 'til I took over the rest of that sweet body too.

"Come on, babe. Don't hate me forever. I had to show

you who's boss back there for good reason, and now that it's through, we can have some fun. Let's make the most of this fucked up honeymoon."

She wasn't holding me as tight as we rode toward the lodge, just a short jump outside Redding proper. The girl hadn't made a peep since I'd walked her outta the tattoo parlor and back to my bike.

I wasn't worried. I could deal with her shit, especially the silent treatment, just as long as she'd internalized what I'd told her.

Something about little Ell-Bell was different. Couldn't quite pin it down, but she wasn't the same woman anymore.

She'd grown up. Blossomed like girls do when they add brains and experience to their beauty. She didn't flirt, didn't give me those sappy doe eyes, not even when I tipped her back and gave her the kiss I'd been waiting years to plant at the church.

She'd changed, ripened like a rare delicacy I wanted every fucking piece of. The girl was gone. When she wasn't bathing me in pure hate rays, she looked at me like a woman who wanted to fuck. Not a nervous virgin living in daddy's shadow who didn't know what the fuck she wanted.

If I played my cards right, I'd use my dick to slam the hate right outta her system. I'd show her exactly what she wanted. I'd fill every hole 'til she couldn't do anything but scream my name, and I had an Ace up my sleeve because I was Asphalt, the bastard she'd loved before she changed from baby doll into beautiful broad.

Half an hour later, we pulled up at the big lodge. Place was a little too fancy for my tastes, but it had an awesome view. Maybe seeing Mount Shasta would get her extra wet.

"Come on. Helmet off. Let's check our asses in."

I helped her take off her headgear and then threw it in the back, not missing an opportunity to slap her ass beneath that pretty white fabric.

She glowered. "Don't. I'm not afraid to hit you back if you start treating me like a piece of –"

"Aw, come the fuck on, babe. If you were a piece of ass, I'd have fucked you half a dozen times by now. I'd slap those sweet cheeks three times harder. I'll do whatever the hell I want, and you can try and stop me."

I grinned, putting on my King Asshole face. Fuck, if I didn't know any better, the look she gave me said she had a dagger hiding between her tits, ready to come out and shank me in the guts.

Good. I wanted to test her limits. I wanted to fuck with her, make her come at me, anything to make her lose control and give me all her hate so I could turn it into sopping wet sex.

Hell, I was already giving her more patience than I'd ever doled out to any girl. They might as well call me King Fucking Midas for turning everything to gold, and if she finally gave me a chance, I'd make her sparkle on my arm for good.

I checked in quick, eyeballing her the entire time as she stood at least five feet away from me. The sorry fuck at the counter learned awhile ago not to look at the brothers like they were animals. The other boys had shown him what this patch meant the last few seasons when they came here with their girls, and the media did the rest.

The Grizzlies were the biggest swinging dicks in NorCal again ever since we'd chased off the cartel. The Prez meant to keep it that way by keeping our Tacoma charter locked down tight, reminding me I was just a cog in a greater machine.

Just like her.

I got our keys from the nervous asshole behind the counter, then grabbed her tense little hand and led her to the elevator. A man could've cut the tension in the small space between us with a goddamned knife. I couldn't wait to get her clothes off and diffuse all that manic energy the best way I knew how.

When we stepped into the room, she walked straight to the window and paused, looking over the darkening mountains. Elle turned, hitting me with those ocean blue eyes for the first time since I reminded her what wearing my name meant.

"Don't get any ideas. I meant everything I said. I swear to God, Asphalt, if you try to force anything, I will tell my father. The truce won't hold if he knows you're treating me like shit. You'd better believe you're not just holding the ball, but the whole court." She took a tentative step closer, her lips trembling, trying to lay down the law like I did – and failing miserably.

Sure looked cute when she tried to twist my balls, though. I fought the instinct to tear her lily white clothes to shreds and take what was mine.

But I wasn't a complete sonofabitch. I used my ears and shut off my cock, striding across the room, closing the distance between us.

"So, you're telling me if I toss you on that bed and throw those panties across the room, a whole bunch of people are gonna die? It'll all be my fault, yeah?" I gestured to the huge king sized bed, so plush the damned thing was begging to be defiled. "Because that's what's gonna happen if this fuckery between us falls through."

"Yep," she said coldly. "Go ahead and try it. I won't be able to stop you. But I can scream from the rooftops after the fact, and that won't be on me. It'll be you, asshole, and nobody else."

It must've taken every little molecule of courage she had to reach out and jab her finger into my chest. I waited all of five seconds before I lunged, grabbed her wrist, spun her around, and had her against the wall so fast her head spun like a damned rocket misfiring.

"I'm not the evil motherfucker you think I am. I'm your husband, babe, and you're my old lady. My wife. You'd better believe I own you, but you're a fucking fool if you think I'd ever hurt you." I tore myself away from her, listening as relief poured out her lungs.

She stopped back on the bed. We stared at each other for several hellish seconds, her eyes softening as she met the anger, the want, the shame in mine.

I still couldn't believe she thought I'd fuck her without any of it. I'd never sunk so low, and I sure as shit wasn't gonna start with Elle.

I'd have her sooner or later, oh yeah. But I'd make her beg for my cock. Wouldn't give her a single inch 'til she was dripping, moaning, coming apart at the seams if I didn't fuck her that very second.

"Asphalt...Austin...I didn't mean it like that. I don't know what to think. This whole thing is just so much to take in, and then after you talked to me like a Neanderthal at the tattoo shop..."

"Save your words," I said with a nod. "Seriously, babe. Get cleaned up and get some sleep. We've got a weekend together before we decide what the fuck to do. I'll be a complete gentleman when I'm around, if that's what you're worried about."

She tilted her head, making her gold locks catch the dying evening light. Damn if I didn't imagine that soft hair clenched in my fist, pulling on it while I bent her over and pounded her like keeping my patch depended on it.

"When you're around?" she repeated.

"Yeah. Look, I'm not sharing a bed with a chick who

thinks I'll tear her up while she's fighting it the whole way. I had a dinner planned for tonight since the guys couldn't agree to a reception with so much bad blood between the crews. Fuck it, we can do that tomorrow. Tonight, I'm giving you the greatest wedding gift of all – I'm getting the fuck out and leaving you alone."

"Austin!"

She yelled my name – the *wrong* goddamned name – and I cut it off by slamming the door before the whole thing was even outta her mouth.

It'd be a long ride back to Redding. Harder when I made the return trip to the lodge with poison in my veins and my balls much lighter.

If she thought I was gonna stick around and argue all evening on my own fucking wedding night, she was dead wrong. I'd take out my frustrations some other way. I was heading into town for some fun, and I wouldn't be back to deal with her shit 'til sunrise.

"What the hell you doing back here, bro? Guess this means the honeymoon's off." Rabid came up to me at the bar, his old lady at his side.

Home, sweet home. The clubhouse always had that vibe, and I headed straight for it after blowing outta the lodge.

I hadn't seen much of his scarred beauty lately. Tutoring and managing the new bar attached to our strip joint was a full time gig for Christa.

"I'm having some fun here that I can't with her," I said, knocking back another shot of whiskey. "The babe's cold as ice, brother. What the fuck do you expect for an arranged marriage?"

Rabid grinned. "Shit, you say it like it's a bad thing. Give it some time. Wouldn't be the first time some chick's thawed out after getting off to a rocky start."

He grabbed his old lady's hand. Christa smiled as I watched my brother lift it to his lips.

"I feel sorry for both of you," she said softly. "It must be a tough thing, growing up in this club from day one."

"Yeah, tough fucking titties in the old days, for sure," I growled. "Thing is, Tacoma was always one of the cleaner ones. They lost some guys back when we were fighting the Devils, but Gil took care of his shit like Fang didn't when that sonofabitch was still in charge of national. I'm halfway surprised her old man didn't wind up with lead in his head years ago for defying California."

"That's what makes him dangerous. We gotta keep his ass in line, and if we have to do it through his daughter, so be it."

Christa cocked her head. "Rabid, baby, you talk like she's just there to be used."

I looked at them both and gave a shallow nod. "That's because she is. I'm not proud of it, but a club's gotta do what a club's gotta do. Beats having brothers under the same patch shooting and stabbing each other's guts out again. We all had enough of that shit when Fang went down."

Rabid understood like every brother sharing this patch. We'd been through so much shit in the last few years, cleaning house and restoring this MC to its old glory. Time for it to stop.

Kicking the cartel's dick off had been a small miracle. Fuck if we needed more trouble now that things were finally settling down, drifting toward quieter, more peaceful times.

All the boys here with women and kids needed it. Wild bastards like Brass, Rabid, and Roman would do whatever the fuck they needed to get it, too.

"I'm gonna get the girl back in her natural habitat tomorrow. Calm her ass down, and get to work scoping out our 'brothers' up north." My voice oozed contempt when I talked about brotherly love with Tacoma.

"What are you saying, bro?" Rabid said, reaching up and scratching the dark stubble on his chin. "The Prez said we're supposed to coordinate this shit. You can't just ride up there on your own and –"

"Nobody tells me what to do with my old lady – especially when I've got the club's good interest swinging from my heart." I pounded my chest. "Go ahead and tell Blackjack what I'm doing. It's not like they're gonna beat my ass up or skin me alive for going alone. We've got Gil's girl as collateral, yeah, but she doesn't need to be miserable the entire fucking time."

"Bro, I know you're solid. But I think you're letting this wedding crap go to your head." Rabid pressed a friendly hand to my shoulder. It pissed me right off. "You're not really married, and she isn't really your old lady. You'd be smart to take a step back, talk to the MC, and let us all handle it the way we're supposed to."

I jumped up from the bar and flung his hand off me. "Outta my way. Tomorrow I'll have a bunch of assholes up in Washington treating me like I don't know my ass from my own head. Don't need one of my own brothers doing it too."

"Fuck...Asphalt!" Rabid called after me, but it was already too late.

I looked over my shoulder just long enough to catch a glimpse of Christa pulling him back, keeping his ass in line. An old lady was good for something besides fucking, at least when putting your brand on her really meant something.

I stopped by the drinking fountain and sucked down cold water 'til I thought my guts would blow. I'd come to fuck and drink my woes away, but all my instincts wouldn't let me do anything except flush out my damned system and ride back to her as soon as I could.

Didn't stop my boots from moving toward the empty rooms we had since more brothers moved out. Whores and prospects used them a lot now, crashing there with booze and condoms.

First door I hit, I stopped and inched it open. A burnt

out lava lamp pumped violet light through the room. A dark haired girl sat on the bed, turned away from me, her bare back shaking.

Hadn't ever seen her before. The chick looked fuckable as all sin, but the way she quivered screamed junkie.

Blackjack didn't allow the hard shit since we'd cleaned this club up, and everybody agreed with the Prez. I balled my fists, ready to burst into the room and run her the fuck outta the clubhouse.

But the loud, sexy moan bursting out her lips stopped me in my tracks. She arched her back suddenly, panting and moaning, purring like a fucking jet engine as she came.

Somebody else moved under the covers.

Stryker's hands pushed her off his face, grinning from ear to ear, his mouth slick with the juice her pussy left behind. I turned away with a growl, suppressing the hard-on banging in my jeans.

"Asphalt? What the fuck you doing back here?"

I didn't answer. Just turned and slammed the door shut behind me, walking out to the garages, not even bothering to check for free chicks in the other rooms.

Seeing him making that bitch squirm reminded me of everything I'd lost in this goddamned sham marriage. I hadn't gotten any appreciation so far, and I sure as shit hadn't gotten laid.

My brother looked *happy* when he reared up after

having his tongue inside her. He'd be happier in a few more minutes when he went balls deep, railing that slut to the headboard 'til she screamed and milked his dick for all her whore ass was worth.

I couldn't do it. Sure, I could fuck 'em, but what the hell good would it do?

My cock pulsed lightning, hard as solid granite, begging for a tight, warm hole to fill for the night. It'd been at least a solid week since I'd pounded my last slut deep into the mattress.

I thought about her and snorted, amazed how freely I could fuck and drink just a week ago. I had her all to myself, this little country bumpkin who'd come into Redding just for Grizzlies cock. I pulled her short blonde hair and pinched her tits rough, half the size of Elle's, shoving her lipstick smeared lips down on my cock when I blew my second load down her throat.

First one, I'd fucked straight into her, emptying my balls in the condom. Had to check it after to make sure I hadn't split the rubber from slamming her loose cunt.

I'd been a mean, angry fuck during the best of times. Now?

I wouldn't even smile. I wouldn't take any joy winding faceless sluts up and making 'em come themselves blind. Not when the only woman I could fuck without blowing a gasket was still at the lodge, sleeping off her nightmare, this arranged marriage to me.

I had to go. I had to blow the clubhouse without a

second glance 'til the Tacoma charter was under our control.

Stopping by the storeroom, I grabbed a few extra beers for the road and walked to my bike. I pulled out a smoke – a luxury I'd gone light on the past few years to help my lungs – lit it up and stared at the sky 'til the buzz of Jack wore off.

The stars yawned high and wild. I'd seen a similar sky that first night I'd crushed my lips to hers, back when we were two dumb kids with dreams as different as yin and yang.

She wanted to take the world by the balls, prove being a club princess wasn't all she could do. I just wanted to ride and fuck my way to the top of this MC, line my cut with a few more patches earned in blood, sweat, and playing hero.

I snorted and stubbed out my cigarette when it wore down, thinking about the bitter irony we shared. We'd both tried to escape the black holes trying so hard to swallow us, chew us up, and shit us back out.

She'd run away from the club. I'd gotten as far as I could from Tacoma, Gil and the rest of those bastards. They'd have never given me my bottom rocker if I hadn't met Blackjack.

I'd fought side-by-side with the old man when he was California's chief Enforcer, back when he had pull with Fang, enough to bust Gil's balls 'til they made me a brother with full voting rights.

As for Elle, she'd fought her own battles, shit I didn't even know about. Had we both lost, being sucked right back into the worlds we'd clawed our way out of?

No. No fucking way.

I wouldn't allow it. I climbed on my bike and let the engine roar, riding hard toward the gate. Those bars peeling open exposed the road to a whole new world, hard and promising as anything I'd ever seen.

This job wasn't gonna be easy. Shit, marriage wasn't by definition, especially when I'd shacked up with an old almost-flame who still hated my ass.

Let her fucking hate. Let her moan. Let her do everything in her power to push me away and curse the ground she walked on for this miserable fate.

I couldn't scrape the black, hateful tar outta her heart, but I could damn sure set us both free. And by the time I got through with those sorry sonsofbitches in Tacoma, I'd hear my Ell-Bell ring like brass clanging up in a church steeple.

"Holy shit. What're you doing here? Get off me, Asphalt. Get. Off!"

She elbowed me hard in the gut. I groaned awake, rubbed my eyes, and flopped over on the bed. I'd gotten in late, after I'd sucked down another beer in the lodge parking lot. Found her sleeping like the dead.

The girl dropped off without a blanket. I'd tucked her in like a little girl, threw my arm around her, covering her with my heat.

So much for a thanks. I shot her the dirtiest look as I put my hands back where they belonged, wrapped around her waist, and pulled her tight. She stiffened up like a goddamned cat about to be thrown in water.

"I'm keeping you warm like a good husband should," I growled. "What time is it?"

"Huh?" She reached for her phone on the nightstand. "Ugh. Seven o'clock. Too early to wake up like this."

"Then shut it and go back to sleep, Elle Jo. You're gonna need your beauty rest. We've got a long ride ahead."

"Ride?" She turned toward me, the anger lining her face smoothing to that sweet innocence my cock ached to corrupt like nobody's business. "We're supposed to stay here for two more days. I don't know what you're –"

I reached up and pushed my hand across her mouth. She struggled, only relaxing when I held her down and whispered in her ear.

"Things change. You're pissed off and unhappy with the whole situation, I get it. I'm not fucking stupid. Only thing you'll hate more than having me by your side is all the other brothers here in Redding, keeping you under lock and key. So, I'm taking your ass back home, where we can calm the hell down and play house."

Her eyes widened. I stared into those baby blues and twisted away from her, all I could do to stop my dick from pressing into her thigh.

"I know you're a smart girl, Ell-Bell. We're both perfectly able to stuff the rage for a few shitty weeks and play pretend. That's what I'm offering. I'm about to give you the whole damned world, babe, and I just need you to close your pretty lips, roll the fuck over, and get some shut eye." I pressed my face to hers, so close she could feel the stubble on my cheek against it.

"That's all this is. Theater. Pretend. I'm gonna act like the best old man a lady ever hoped for. I'll help you on my bike, pull out chairs for you, and share a bed without ripping off everything clinging to your body and claiming that hot little puss like I should. Hell, I'll even pretend I like your old man instead of wanting to drive smoking lead in his brain. It's not hard. It's pretty fucking simple. And we can get right to it as soon as we're rested for the road and ready to make this shit work. Okay?"

There wasn't much response for ten long seconds. She just stared at me, her eyes two vast oceans, studying mine to figure out what kinda game I'd decided to play now.

Finally, she nodded. Perfect.

Loosening my grip, I let her breathe freely again and rolled away, giving her an inch of sorely needed space. I never took my arm off her waist, just held in place without moving between her legs or across her ass, fighting the wild urge.

Elle turned away from me, without making any effort

to throw me off. For now, she'd been tamed. Pacified. And maybe, just fucking maybe, she'd started to trust me.

We slept like two kids who'd fallen down after screaming and chasing each other all day.

V: Baby Steps (Elle Jo)

Drifting in and out of sleep shouldn't have been so easy. I shouldn't have let him take over, shouldn't have let him keep my hips against his, shouldn't have surrendered to the powerful arms with the black, murderous ink wrapped so possessively around me.

But I did, and I slept better than I had all week, ever since I'd found out I needed to play bride to keep daddy's schemes from falling apart and putting us all in danger.

The danger wasn't even close to gone. I'd found a second of peace with my fake husband, sure, but soon we'd both be caught between two Grizzlies charters at each other's throats. Plus I'd be carted off to play interpreter whenever daddy decided to meet the Chinese, a negotiation promising tension.

I reached for my phone and checked it, careful not to disturb the biker holding me. Eleven o'clock now. Four hours slipped by in a haze, dreams and manly heat that temporarily carried me away from the hellish joke called my life.

Holding my breath, I rolled to face him. I watched Asphalt as he slept, feeling his big chest rising and falling against me.

I wondered why I'd lost the desire to pull his switchblade out of his belt and cut his throat in his sleep. No, of course I'd never do it – I wasn't a violent girl. My father's obsession with shielding me from MC blood had paid off over the years, except I'd grown up scared of having to fight for my life.

But in this case, I should've wanted to. I thought I'd be ready to do anything to have him off me and be free from this mess, this outlaw freak who'd had his name tattooed into my flesh.

That wasn't how I felt just now. God, no.

My heart beat a little faster as my eyes traced his strong jaw, stopping at his lips. I remembered their heat against mine, the fire in his kiss. The way he kissed me during the wedding brought me to my knees, awed that he'd lost none of the shock and awe from that first night four years ago, before either of us dreamed about being prisoners to each other.

We'd wanted passion then. If my father hadn't nearly killed him that night, I probably would've led him into our house, up to my room, and straight between my legs.

Gnawing my bottom lip, I reached out, gingerly running my fingers across the lightning bolt on his temple. I shared the same dark ink on my shoulders, symbols that were quintessentially Asphalt.

Jesus. Why the hell did I feel so connected to a man I was supposed to hate?

All this outlaw crap had gone to my head, obviously. That didn't stop my hands from brushing up above the lightning as he slept, across a small knife scar just above his temple, and then circling his smooth scalp.

He'd kept his head shaved all these years. I vaguely remembered the thick, sandy hair of the boy I'd grown up with down the street, back when both his parents still lived there, and he hadn't so much as wrapped his hands around a motorcycle's bars.

The hair went when he joined the MC as a prospect. All the older girls at school told stories about how incredibly smooth his face felt between their thighs, all the wicked, marvelous things he could do with his tongue...

I chewed my lip harder. My hand other hand slipped down between the soft sheets, down below my belly, tentatively dipping into my panties to check for what I feared most.

Yep. It was there, a molten wetness gliding across my fingertips like somebody had cast a spell and given form to desire.

I shuddered, resisting the urge to play with my clit. I wanted to believe the urge to fuck him was as dead as the sheltered, naïve girl who'd left Tacoma years ago.

I'd tried to leave her behind with the town. But I was going back for the third time, wasn't I? Back to the life I'd tried to ditch, chained to a man I'd told myself would never fit into the stable fabric of my life I'd tried too damned hard to hold together, before the club's stupid politics ripped it to tatters.

Everything came apart.

Elle Jo the budding businesswoman.

Elle the independent woman, who told herself she'd never be up close and personal with a man wearing the bear patch ever again.

Elle, the idiot, who thought she could walk away from this life, when I'd seen what it did to my parents and every brother who was ever a guest in our home.

My world cracked apart a little more with every second ticking by. And for some ludicrous reason, it didn't kill me.

I closed my eyes and pressed my face into the pillow, enjoying his heat, his rock hard body so close to mine.

If he wanted to play pretend, fine. We could do it here in this bed just the same.

I could pretend to be his, if only in my own mind, so I didn't actually show him and die from the embarrassment. I let my fingers wander, closer to my aching pussy, the pussy I'd once quietly promised him in a kiss on prom night.

My lips parted in a soft, instinctive moan I couldn't control when my thumb grazed my clit. Eyes shuddering, I let myself rub deeper, drawing little circles that were nothing against what his big, strong hands could do.

I opened my eyes to look on his masculine glory while

I touched myself.

My heart stopped. His eyes were open. Bright, green, and predatory, watching me so close to fucking myself.

"Oh!" I made a little sound and ripped my hand away.

"What the fuck, babe?" He grinned, his handsome lips curling up in a smile that ended my world. "Are you seriously jilling off after giving me all that shit about how you'd never want this?"

His hips moved. I tensed when I felt his hard cock roll against my thigh.

Raging, pulsing, ready to fuck me in two, promising an explosive release from this suffocating tension...

"Ew, no!" I jumped out of bed, splaying my hands over my lap.

I ran to the bathroom as he laughed, hoping he wouldn't notice the burning suns my cheeks had become. I'd never been so red in my life.

So much for playing pretend.

It took forever to come out and face him again. I had the longest shower of my life. Cold because I needed so badly to ice down the lava in my veins left by shame and lust.

"Let's get some breakfast before we check out and hit the road. Fuck, black coffee and bagels never sounded so good." He was standing by the door when I walked out, a fresh change of clothes on, the same powerful arms that held me the night before now folded across his barrel chest.

"Asphalt, I don't know what you thought you saw this morning, but..."

"Already forgotten, babe." The bastard silenced me with a swift hand through the air. "I told you, everything we've got going on between us is a fucking illusion. You go ahead and act like you weren't strumming your sweet pussy because I turned you on so bad. I'll pretend I never saw it. Mostly, I'm just really fucking hungry right now, and if you don't wanna move, then I'm heading down for breakfast without you."

He grabbed the door.

"Okay, okay!" I chirped, throwing back my half-dried hair and following him.

His words were strangely comforting. I didn't completely believe that we'd forgotten anything as we headed down to the lodge's small rustic eatery, but food was a good distraction.

We ate in silence, or close enough, making small talk about the forecast and the surprise trip to Tacoma.

"I hope we make it before nightfall. We're getting such a late start, and I still have to pack all our things."

"You worry too much, Ell-Bell." He shook his head, swallowing his last bite of bagel and cream cheese. He'd inhaled it after demolishing a plate of eggs and bacon stacked high. "I see some shit never changes. Don't worry about bringing anything besides your clothes and toothbrush. I'll leave all the wedding shit with the staff and a prospect'll be by later to pick it up."

"So, that means your brothers are okay with us heading up to Washington alone?"

He'd just raised his coffee to his lips and stopped in mid-sip. Slowly, he put the mug down, narrowing those brilliant green eyes on me like search lights.

"The club knows I can handle their shit, the same way I know how to handle my woman. They won't care. This sham marriage is just a damned olive branch. Long as we're together, safe and plastering on our best fake smiles, nothing else matters."

"Uh, okay." I rolled my eyes.

The pretend theme started to wear on me. He leaned back, stretched, and cocked his head.

"What?" I said finally, waiting for him to deliver whatever smartass remark he had written on his face, waiting to come out.

"Just remembering how cute you can be when you let that feisty attitude go to your head, princess. It's like I said – some things never change."

I glared. Much as I didn't want to admit it, the bastard was right. Some things never did.

We rode so hard and long everything below my waist went numb. I'd had some long trips with daddy growing up, back before the MC had to fear for its life, but I hadn't been on a motorcycle for more than four hours in just as many years, probably more.

Five hours put us deep into Oregon, close to Eugene and our halfway mark. We stopped for gas.

I walked away from the bike, desperate to stretch my legs, watching him do the same as he pulled out a cigarette and stuffed it into his mouth. I wrinkled my nose.

Being around men who puffed like chimneys hadn't made it seem like any less of a bad habit in all these years. I kept my distance, staring off at the mountains and trying to enjoy the fresh cedar air sweeping in from the state's pristine forests.

The perfectly crisp air curdled all the more easily when he came close, blowing a long jet of smoke over his shoulder.

"Do you really have to ruin this with your smoke signals? You could talk to me like a normal human being, Asphalt."

He waited until he was right next to me. For a second, I feared he'd blow smoke right in my face like a total jackass. Then I'd kick him square in the balls.

Instead, he let the cigarette hit the pavement, before he brought his boot down on it. "You're lucky I wanna make this easy on you."

"Whatever. I'm doing your health a favor. That crap is bad for you."

He snorted. "You gotta be fucking kidding me, right? I haven't touched this shit for years 'til just recently. I gave it up shortly after I came to NorCal because I saw what it did to the older guys' lungs. Last thing I want is some motherfucker getting the jump on me just because I can't breathe right."

"Sure, hubby. Whatever you say." I gave him my biggest, fakest smile, and even batted my eyes.

That did it.

His face darkened. He grabbed me by the shoulders, jerked me close to him so fast I didn't know what happened until I was drowning in his angry green eyes.

"Listen, babe, there are times when that spitfire shit drives me wild. This isn't one of them. You can either turn the sass off, or there *will* be consequences. You're my old lady, my woman, and my wife. You owe me some respect. I don't give a shit how fake this thing is."

My cheeks overheated for the second time that day. Maybe challenging him was just my way of venting, or maybe I'd lost my mind.

"Respect is earned, Austin. You're old enough to know that."

He smiled, sharp as a knife. "You're right. And I'm gonna earn it by pulling your jeans to the ground and spanking the fuck outta you right here if you call me the wrong name again. No bullshit."

My jaw dropped. My eyes fell with it, a crazy, submissive gesture I'd later regret when we were back on the bike, following the long road to SeaTac.

Regardless, my body language told him I'd gotten the message. He released his iron grip and I followed him to his bike, angrily fixing my helmet without saying a word. He stopped inside to pay for our fuel and picked up a few bottles of water for the road.

"Hands around my waist, babe," he reminded me, just as he started the engine. "Now."

"You know, all these years, I thanked my lucky stars daddy didn't actually kill you that night we kissed," I whispered in his ear, tucking my hands across his tight abs. "I wish I'd remembered what a huge bastard you can be."

"Only when I gotta remind somebody how hard these balls can swing, babe. You put on your sweet old lady act, and they won't have to slap you again. I'll give you the same respect I did years ago, when I didn't mind taking a few bullets for you. Still don't, princess, in case you give a damn. This is all just peacekeeping shit, and we both know it. So let's forget the insults and act real peaceful-like."

I pressed my tongue to the roof of my mouth, all I could do to avoid more trouble. His words surprised me, softening the fire in my blood more than I expected.

I shouldn't have mocked him about the shooting when we were kids, something that truly had twisted my stomach in knots in all the years I'd left him, wondering if he'd been permanently disfigured by a bad shoulder.

The bike kicked hard as we headed onto the highway. Soon, it wasn't a struggle to hold onto him, though I wished it were.

Clinging to this crude devil while we pierced the wind shouldn't have felt so horribly natural. Especially when it was just 'peacekeeping shit' like he said, without a prayer of ever becoming anything real.

It was late by the time we finally got into town. We headed straight for daddy's place, after I insisted it was as good an option as any.

The club wouldn't be any happier if they learned we'd snuck into town under their noses. I wanted to give my father a head's up so he could tell the rest of his guys. Hopefully preventing any bloody noses or broken bones if they ran into Asphalt around town.

"Whatever, babe," he grunted at a stoplight on the edge of town. "You'd better get your shit fast. I'm not staying a second longer in your old man's place than I really need to."

"Oh?" I suppressed a smile. "Thought you were my old man now?"

Something possessed me to throw my arms around his neck. I breathed his scent deep, letting it flow into me, warm and strong and curiously soothing.

Maybe riding so close with him all damned day had done something to my brain chemistry. I didn't want to admit how badly I craved him, his body at least, but mine wasn't giving me much choice.

He pushed my hands away just as the light turned green. The bike jerked forward, and I heard him clear his throat.

"You know what I mean," he growled. "I'm trying to do you a favor, bringing you back to your home turf where you can feel like you're solid in your own skin. Let's get this over with."

I studied his face in the mirror. He'd turned so stone cold, and it caused my heart to sink like an anchor.

I'd played too many games. He didn't want me. He was on a run for his club, and it'd finally sunken into his head that I was just his cargo, nothing more.

The new distance between us was what I'd wanted badly before. But now, it rattled me to my very core.

We pulled up to my old house with a steady Seattle rain falling. Asphalt shook off the drops like they were nothing. I folded my arms tight like a cocoon, trying to stop my teeth from chattering.

He stood quietly while I ripped off my helmet and pushed it into his hands, then watched as he shoved it in storage. He'd been staring at the house, the place where he'd first put those scoundrel lips on mine.

The same place where he'd nearly lost his life. More than four years ago, but for some damnable reason, it seemed like yesterday.

He held a fresh cigarette, filling his lungs with a long pull of smoke. He let it drop when he saw me looking, stomping it out on the cracked sidewalk with his boot.

"What's the deal?" I asked, trying to figure him out.

"Nothing. We've got bigger business ahead. Hope you've still got a key to this place, babe, 'cause I'm not kicking down the door and letting some jumpy prospect blast a hole in my head."

Smiling, I fished out my keys and followed him up. I undid the lock and pushed my way inside, wondering if daddy had lightened up on the constant guard around his house since I'd moved out.

I stopped for a moment, breathing in the familiar scent of smoke, beer, and long lost memories. The door clicked gently shut behind me, and Asphalt rubbed my shoulder. Time to move.

We headed down the hall, aiming for the staircase leading to my room. Asphalt stayed close behind me.

When I heard a snarl like a cougar getting caught in a trap, I thought I'd gone deaf.

"Holy shit!" The words exploded from my mouth just as three of my father's guys appeared from nowhere, grabbed him, and smashed against the wall so hard I thought he'd leave a human imprint.

"What the fuck you doing here, asshole? One of Blackjack's boys, coming in our Prez's house without warning? Smells like shit!" The prospect with the beefy arms and a huge gut shook Asphalt again.

"Don't hurt him!" I screamed, but they all ignored me, too focused on roughing up their target.

Three big, savage looking bastards. The kind of men I'd seen before, except they normally weren't posted here on guard duty.

Were they expecting us? Didn't make sense.

Regardless, there wasn't time to figure it out. Asphalt's eyes beamed hot, red murder straight through the fat prospect's face as they sized each other up. Then my man's smooth forehead darted out like a wrecking ball, cracking straight into the other man's face.

"Fuck!" The prospect's nose made a sickening pop, and he lost his grip on Asphalt. He stumbled backward, both hands covering his face, blood pouring out between his fingers in the darkness.

The other two Tacoma boys went to town. Asphalt grunted as the punches started, going straight into his stomach, knocking the air out of him so he couldn't do anything else.

I stood there with my mouth hanging open, not sure if I should try to jump them, or else grab a knife from the kitchen. Normally, my presence alone should've done it.

Didn't they know who the fuck I was? I'd have to show them if this kept up. *Nobody* had the balls to lay a finger on the President's daughter!

"Sear, Jack-O, Peak, lay the fuck off. Let him speak." I heard a familiar voice behind me.

I turned to see Line, my adopted Uncle and Tacoma's VP, his face as unreadable as ever behind one eye patch and shaggy salt and pepper hair.

"Shit, Veep, you gotta be kidding me," the one called Jack-O snorted, barely holding back on his superior's orders, his fists trembling at his sides. "Fucker walked in here without a peep to the club. He should've called the clubhouse, and we would've been expecting him. Last I knew, that was against whatever fucked up terms California set with us."

"Our Prez'll be the judge of that. Elle?" Uncle Line cocked his head, finally acknowledging me. "What're you doing back here with your old man?"

He practically spat the last words like he'd bitten into something rotten. I stepped up, pushed my way between the two men, tugging on Asphalt's shoulders.

He tried to throw me off, but he was still too busy sucking air back into his lungs. I looked at Line.

"I'm here to see daddy, but I'm guessing he isn't here." Line said nothing, telling me everything I needed to know. "We're going upstairs to pack so we can find some different lodging. Tell daddy we're home. And for God's sake, make sure he knows his guys should point their guns away a man who shares your patch. I thought we had a peace deal?"

I gestured to Asphalt. He finally stood up straight, shot me a look that said, *I don't need your damned help.*

Line snorted. "Trust me, baby doll, your dad's got bigger dragons breathing down his neck. He's gonna want to see you tomorrow. I'll tell the boys to lay off – for now."

Dragons was right. I wondered how long we had before the ticking time that was his deal with the

Shanghai mob exploded in all our faces.

Smiling, the VP looked Asphalt up and down, just as he began to move. He didn't look back as he raced upstairs, and I could only follow.

"Make sure you keep him on a short leash, Elle Jo. I remember the shit he used to get into years ago, back when we gave him his prospect patch. Doubt this boy's changed one bit from all the drinkin' and whorin'. I know a rat when I see one. He's bad for you, girl."

"Funny, I only see feral fucking animal with his lips moving, one-eye," Asphalt snarled from the top floor.

That was my cue to run up. I stopped on the top step, slid my hands against his chest, and pushed as hard as I could. "Come on. Just ignore him. It isn't worth it when we're this outnumbered."

At last, he relented. I pointed to my room behind him. Asphalt turned, walked, and shoved my door open so hard it banged against the wall.

He was in like a tornado. I stood with my legs totally stuck for the third time that night, watching him fling my closet open and rip the drawers out of my dresser.

"Start fucking packing. We gotta get the hell outta here, babe. Clock's ticking."

I couldn't deal with the way he was manhandling my things, tearing through them like a bad cop without a warrant. I just walked into the closet and pulled out my old suitcase from college, unzipped it, and began gingerly folding the clothes he'd thrown out on a heap inside it.

I tried to focus on my work, ignoring everything else that was happening until I saw him rip my bottom drawer open. *Oh, Jesus.*

Shit!

"Hey, hold up a second, there's fragile stuff in there!" My warning didn't stop him. He paused for a single second, eyeballing me, and then dug in harder. He shoved aside my diplomas, old homework, a couple precious birthday cards from mom.

Then he hit gold.

I should've known the bastard's hands would find it, no different than a dog digging up a bone. I still died a little when his hand came up triumphantly, his fingers around the silver bullet, the purple cord dangling from his fingers.

"Fucking shit, is this what you do for fun?" His hand swept through the bottom drawer again. "There's gotta be more than this little dick on a wire."

When he didn't find anything else, he chuckled. Loud, thick, and seriously amused. That pit in my stomach became a fucking chasm.

"Asphalt!"

"Christ, no dong in here to go with this clit grinder? I'm surprised, babe. How do you fuck yourself when there's no man around?" His green eyes pierced mine, curious mischief shining. "Fuck, I'm starting to think you really live that good girl shit night and day. Just how far does the act go? Don't tell me you've never had nothing bigger than this! I know you can take it *deep*, woman."

"Damn it, get out!" I swung, snatching to take my vibrator back. He was way too fast, moving it high over my head to the other hand, where I couldn't reach. "Of course, it's all I've ever had! And it's none of your damned business!"

The shitty grin on his face evaporated. I turned around, all my blood suddenly lava, shame so intense at spilling my stupid secret that two fiery tears instantly ran down my cheeks.

"Holy fucking Moses," he said softly. "You're just giving me shit, yeah? Jerking my balls around? There's no way – *no fucking way* – you're still a virgin, Elle. You've been to college, for fuck's sake!"

No more. I spun, dragging my half-zipped duffel bag behind me, and jumped at his hand. He didn't resist this time as I jerked my toy away from him, throwing it into the empty pocket. I pulled my suitcase hard, listening as it rolled over the toe of his boot.

"Babe, hold up, I didn't know you were so goddamned sensitive about –"

I slammed the door behind me before he could finish. I had to get out of there. Preferably before I suffocated from embarrassment, choking on my own lost secret.

The suitcase banged hard on the stairs behind me.

Line and the other Tacoma men were sprawled out in the living room, watching an old Western on the big, dusty TV daddy hadn't used since mom's last days. Thank God for small distractions.

They didn't have to see the hot mess I'd become. Nobody came to check on me when I flung the door open and wandered out into the night. Unfortunately, I hadn't closed the suitcase on my way out. It banged down the steps leading down the sidewalk.

I lost my grip and watched it tumble. A couple shirts and a black bra spilled out. I kicked the pavement so hard I stubbed my toe, resisting the urge to scream into the night and wake up the whole neighborhood.

Nobody here was a stranger to noise after living next to bikers and hardened vets-turned-mechanics over the years, but the last thing in the world I wanted was more attention.

Not when I just wanted to disappear, the only thing I wanted.

I pulled my coat tight, shoved my hands into my pockets, and headed for the old park.

The rain had softened into a cool, soft mist. It helped draw out my tears, taking them like orphans into the great fog settling over the city, away from the crude joke I'd been forced to live.

When the tears became too hot and too many for the mist to claim, I put my palms over my eyes, and let my sadness stab deep into the night.

He found me sometime later, soaked and sitting on a

swing. His feet crunched the sand as he approached. I was too tired to move, so I could only flinch when his hands landed on my shoulders.

"Babe, come on. Let's find somewhere to crash inside before you get fucking pneumonia."

I jerked up, desperate to get away from him, speed walking through the wet, sticky sand.

"What the fuck!?"

I heard him call after me. It didn't stop me. No words would. I just kept going, though I knew walking through the muck wouldn't save me. He'd catch me sooner or later, and then I'd have to scream.

I was on the wet, thick grass before he caught up, heading toward the paved trail into the hills. Didn't have a clue where I was going or how I'd survive the night, but every second away from him was precious. It prolonged my escape from this hell just a little bit longer.

"Ell-Bell, baby, stop running." I didn't listen, ignoring the rough edge in his voice. He caught up to me and tried to grab me.

I swung around so hard I crashed into his chest, hit the ground, and he went down with me. We fought hard.

Screaming, thrashing, I swiped my nails across his face, tearing over the stubble I'd dreamed about gently caressing a thousand times before. The same rough patch that caused a firestorm in my blood a dozen times before, always so close to my skin, but never as close as

I needed. And now, it repulsed me, so much I wanted to destroy it.

"Ah, fuck! Stop moving, woman. You hear me?" Growling, he got on top of me, rolled me over. Grabbing both shoulders, he slammed down hard, pinning me underneath him. "I said *fucking stop!*"

"No, Austin! You don't control me. You don't –"

His hand swept behind my head. Seizing my hair, he folded my wet locks into a ponytail, and gave it a rough jerk so hard I went speechless.

"Told you I'm not having you calling me that shit! What don't you understand, baby girl? Why the fuck can't you get it through your damned pretty head? Are you fucking blind? Deaf? Dumb?"

Every word barked out a little louder, sharper, hitting me in the face like fists.

"Jesus Christ, Elle Jo! You're the whole reason we're back here. You're why I didn't break all those fuckers' noses back at the house, why I tried to play fucking nice. You're everything that's keeping me sane while we both deal with this clusterfuck of a marriage thrown on us by a buncha bastards who really don't give a shit. Can't you see it yet? No? Work with me, goddammit!"

My legs kicked against his. He had too much leverage for me to do any damage.

It just enraged him more. His grip on me tightened, pushing me into the soft soil. His hand tore at my hair, tilted my face, forcing me to look into those bright green eyes I loved and hated all at once.

"Go to hell! I don't owe you anything, and you don't need to know all my secrets. You're not really my husband. You're nothing, Asphalt." I paused, taking a deep breath, too afraid to tempt him again by using the wrong name. "*This,* everything between us, it's nothing too. It's pretend, just like you called it. You don't get to treat me like shit, humiliate me in my family's house. You keep treating me like the bratty little sister you never had, and that's *not fucking me!* I'm not the girl who watched you get shot years ago, or the one you could catcall across the street. I'm a grown woman now, and all I'm going to do the first chance I get is leave this evil biker bullshit behind – including you. You can't stop me. You can't!"

"Babe," he said quietly, as if he'd been carefully listening to everything.

"What?" I spat, waiting for the next load of crap to drop on my head from his dirty mouth.

"Shut up."

The asshole kissed me. He kissed me harder than he'd ever smashed his lips on mine any time in my life. We were numb from the cold rain, messy and dirty, rolling on the ground, but he just kept coming like I'd told him I loved him, rather than screaming a stream of abuse.

The emotional dam building up inside me completely shattered.

I cried. I punched him, I thought about biting off his

tongue when he pushed it into my mouth. But I never once took my lips off his.

Asphalt kissed me deeper. Before I knew what was happening, he eased his weight off my arms, and I threw them around his neck, pulling him as close as two people could possibly get.

Damn it, damn it, god damn it, the bastard could kiss. Deep down, I adored him, even when he overpowered me.

Hell, *especially* when he overpowered me.

He put out the fire in my mouth and ignited a new one in my body. My nipples tingled, my pussy ached, the insane desire to give it up to him here in the park, the dirt, took over my brain.

His head twisted, pulling his mouth off me, leaving me stunned and breathless. My senses only went crazier when his teeth grazed my throat. He planted new, rough kisses there, so possessive they were bound to leave a few marks.

And I loved it. I loved him, or if that was a little too premature, then I was falling so fast I'd be flattened in another week. But that didn't mean I'd stopped hating him, too, as fucked up as it sounds.

"Fuck, Asphalt!" I moaned, feeling the hard bulge in his jeans against my pussy.

Our hips began grinding together. Ruthless, wanton, crazed with desire.

One more sucking, biting kiss and he reared up,

burying me in his jade green gaze like he'd never done it a hundred other times. It felt new, and it lit every inch of me ablaze.

I tried to twist away, but his thick hand caught my chin, tipped it toward him. "You keep looking at me like that, babe. I'm gonna settle you the fuck down by making that little pussy come wild for me."

Holy shit.

"Here?!" I gasped. He couldn't be serious.

He nodded, dry humping me harder, grabbing my hips and pulling me into him. He rubbed his swollen cock through the fabric, his strokes lengthening, scraping my clit.

Already on the edge, it didn't take much. All the worries about sorting out my feelings came apart as he humped me, thrusting like a madman, growling each time I jerked against him and moaned.

My hands went out, flattened against his chest. I tore at his shirt, struggled to lift it off, and succeeded in getting a glimpse of the wild lightning and grizzly bear in full roar stamped across his torso.

My fingers ran down his rock hard abs, just as my resistance completely ran out.

"Fuck!"

My whole body tensed. His hips slammed into mine, pushing me into the dirty, wet soil, fucking me through my clothes so bad I wanted him in me like nothing else.

No joke. No lie.

I wanted the bastard. I wanted the brute. I wanted Asphalt, Austin, the biker badass and the tender next door neighbor all in one. I wanted everything we'd given up for years, wanted him just as much as I wanted to make up for lost time with flesh, sweat, screams.

Just before I came, he twisted me around, hoisting me up on his lap. He grabbed my ass and crushed my mouth against his, stifling the shrill pleasure that came pouring out of me a second later when my pussy overheated and exploded.

I came so hard through my panties and my jeans that the toy he'd teased me about was nothing but a distant memory. Everything below the waist became as soaked as the rest of me, a throbbing, clutching mess.

Lightning zipped through my legs. I could feel the bolts on my shoulder tingling, the fresh tattoo reminding me I belonged to him.

And this was why.

His raw, masculine power couldn't be denied. It claimed me like magic, took me over, set off the time bomb I'd had building up inside me for four long years.

His fingers tore at my belt, slipped down to my bare pussy, and he stroked my clit while I slowly came down from the peak.

Virgin fire raged hotter, higher, longer. I tried to scream out into the night, if only to remind myself I was still alive, but his relentless kisses stopped me every time.

I came until I couldn't anymore. My legs shaking up to my hips, my ass, now digging into his fingers.

He slowly peeled me off. For a second, I thought he'd take down his belt and undress me. Instead, he got up and walked back toward the swing, leaving me all alone.

What the hell? I got up, shaking off the last few shocks in my legs, and ran after him.

He couldn't be that much of a pig – right? Surely, he wouldn't just leave me all alone after he'd taken me further than any man before.

I couldn't possibly be that wrong about him...I hoped.

"Asphalt, what're you –"

He turned around holding a towel before I could finish the question. My suitcase was at his feet. He'd found it outside the house and brought it with him. He walked toward me, spreading the smooth white cloth, and wrapped it around me like a protective shroud.

"I know I fucked up back at your place. Here's my way of saying sorry, babe. I'm keeping you healthy and beautiful. It's fucking cold out here. Hold still."

He dried me from head to toe. I held my face up, cooling my hot little mouth in the rainy night, amazed that those rough hands running the towel over me could be so gentle and so absolutely brutal.

The walking paradox in front of me finally stopped when my hair wasn't dripping. He let the towel drop, smoothed my hair with his hands, and pulled me into his embrace.

"Asphalt...you're a real dick sometimes. But I guess I can forgive you this once."

"That's what I wanna hear. I take care of what's mine – damned good care. Whether you've figured that out yet or not, I don't give a shit. You will."

"Was what just happened taking care of me too?" I pulled away and met his eyes, studying the untamed fires he hadn't satisfied with me on the ground.

"We're just getting started. Fuck if I'm gonna take you on the dirty goddamned ground your very first time. Can't believe you're a virgin, babe. Shit, Ell-Bell, all those years and you've never..."

He closed his eyes, unable to finish. He leaned into me, and the raging hard-on he hadn't lost dug into my thigh, so hard and promising.

I trembled. "There were a few guys I dated at college, yeah. We kissed, we messed around, but I never gave it up to them. I couldn't. They were like that stupid little boy I went to prom with – not worth my time. They just couldn't measure up to what I really wanted."

You. I wouldn't say it, but he heard me loud and clear.

Asphalt looked at me for a long second before he leaned in for another kiss. We let our lips, tongues, and teeth wander for the next few minutes.

His taste, his scent...God, it was just like a drug. Just as addictive too. I knew I'd never be able to get enough.

This utter bastard did something to me I couldn't understand. He'd always had a magic spark no other man in the world could match.

Tonight, when he'd been a total dick, I'd thought that might be change for the worse, just like I had hundreds of times over the years. But he always pulled me back, always proved me wrong.

He always reminded me there was a man with a heart and a brain behind the ruthless muscle.

"Fuck, baby, I gotta have you," he growled, pulling me deeper into his arms. "Tonight. Let's get on the damned bike and go."

"Where?" I whispered, just as he seized my hand and started pulling me up the path to the road, my suitcase bobbing in his other hand.

"We'll find a spot for some R and R. Just you and me. The shit with the club can wait. The fuckers at the house'll fill everybody else in Tacoma in. They'll know we're in town." He packed up my suitcase and passed my helmet to me. "We're picking up right where we left off, Elle Joy. I'm giving you a real honeymoon, and you're giving me every fucking inch of you. Everything I've been jerking off to for four fucking years, what I thought I'd missed forever."

Oh, crap. Did he really just say that?

I could barely climb onto the bike from the tremor in my nerves. And I visibly shook when he leaned in close, pouring his hot breath against my neck, and then straight into my ear.

"I'm breaking you in tonight, babe. I'm gonna fuck

you 'til neither one of us can even walk straight. You belonged to me the second my fucking ink went on you, woman, and now it's time to make it official by mixing like a man and woman should." He stopped, just long enough to wrap his hands around me, searching for my ass. He squeezed me so hard I moaned. "Fuck, you're so tight. Goddamned beautiful. All mine."

I smiled. He wanted it so bad he couldn't form complete sentences anymore, but at least he could speak. I couldn't even do that.

He started his bike while I wrapped my hands around him. I hugged him tighter than I'd ever held anyone in my life while we rode.

My blood crackling with carnal expectation kept me more alive than I'd been for four painful years away from my destiny.

I didn't even look at where we were until I stepped off his bike. He had a sixth sense for finding these incredible off-the-map places like most bikers did. This one was no exception.

It was a nice little lodge just outside town. If the rain ever cleared up, we'd probably have an awesome view of Mount Rainier, something I'd realized how badly I missed since going away to college.

The look in his eye was the only signal he gave me as he took my hand and led me inside. We got checked in and headed for our room. I slicked my hair, taking out the latest moisture, feeling the wetness running down my shoulders.

Cool and weirdly refreshing, in a way. It masked the blazing, wet heat between my thighs – everything that wouldn't be calmed until he found his way there.

As soon as we were in our room, he dropped my bag, plus the small one he'd brought with fresh clothes from Redding.

I wasn't sure who lunged for who first. Hot, heavy, muscular man gripped me, threw me against the big bed in the center of the room, and smothered me in fresh kisses. His hands roamed my body, taking what he'd teased before.

My breasts, my ass, the soft, ticklish spaces along my sides...he explored them in slow, eager strokes, far more controlled than anything I could muster. I threw one arm over his strong neck and tugged at his leather cut with the other.

"Take that off and fuck me," I whispered, when he finally broke the kiss for air.

"No."

My jaw dropped when he growled it, and I moaned a little Oh!, feeling his cock pressing hard into my thigh again. The wrong place for it. That was when I realized he'd tease me until my heart exploded.

"You don't get this dick 'til I say you do, babe. If you want me to fuck your brains out, you'd better come for me a few more times, and hard."

His hands went to my waist and found my jeans. Asphalt had them down in a single jerk, exposing my bare legs. He ripped my shoes off and pulled my pants down, flinging them against the wall. He kissed up my right thigh while his hand went for my panties, grabbing them in the middle and tugging the way a man throws a grenade.

Gone, in half a heartbeat.

Oh, shit. He's really going to –

My mind blanked when his mouth began to climb up. Hot, searching kisses stamped my legs, then my inner thighs. He found the soft skin humming expectantly next to my pussy and sank his teeth into it.

I jumped, moaned, covered the back of his head with my hands. His hot breath blew over my pussy, making every inch of me feel the lightning need pooling there.

Asphalt, please.

Please.

Fucking please!

I couldn't say it. Words escaped me. The best I could do was dig my fingers into his smooth head, pressing hard while his tongue darted out in one quick, teasing flick across my molten center.

Fuck! My fingers gripped the sheets, tangling them for support.

And I had to hold on for dear life once he really started in. The same tongue that teased me, cursed me, and conquered my mouth owned the space between my legs.

His rough hands held me down, spreading me open, wider for his face to work its wicked, dirty magic. I couldn't think what else to call the sensations he summoned in my blood, the way every nerve crackled to life at once, burning like taut guitar strings beneath a rockstar's skilled fingertips.

Asphalt's mouth licked, nipped, and fucked my pussy for the longest minutes of my life. When he found my clit and sucked it, I rolled my hips forward, surrendering to the urge to throw myself into him.

This was giving everything up, and holy shit did it feel right.

He introduced me to a dozen feelings I didn't know a woman could have. My clit throbbed against his broad tongue strokes, circles quickening in around it. He honed my pleasure, slipping two stiff fingers in below the spot where his mouth made me delirious.

His fingers fucked my pussy while his tongue took me higher, higher, straight up into a wide yawning sky until I couldn't climb an inch more.

"Asphalt! Oh, God, if you keep doing that, you're going to make me –"

He doubled his speed. The last word lodged in my throat, as my eyes filled with stars.

Come, woman. Come like you fucking mean it.

I could hear him say it without him actually saying a word. And I did.

Sweet merciful God, *I came.*

All the shame and doubt died in a second of blinding white tension building in my hips, feeding the fireball he'd fanned in my womb.

Now, it exploded outward. The lightning that bound us together zipped through me in a huge wave, exploding out the center and mastering everything to my fingertips and the ends of my toes.

I came so hard I thought I died.

He growled the whole way through it, pistoning his fingers in my virgin pussy like he owned me, and I suppose he finally did. His mouth sucked harder, his tongue went so fast it made me dizzy, strumming my clit in mad, devilish whirls.

I crashed over the edge again and again, trying to scream his name. Each time, nothing but breathless pleasure rasped out my lips. The sheets pulled in my hands so hard I thought they'd rip.

He did it hard, soft, and everything in between, more than any man ought to be able to do with nothing except his fingers and hands. This pleasure softened me, soothed my body and soul, opening me to the inevitable bliss he promised next.

"My. Fuck. Just...fuck." I didn't notice I was mumbling incoherently until he sat up, wiped his mouth, and stroked my cheek with his hand.

"You're off to a good start, babe. I'll have you swearing like a fucking sailor by the time we're through.

You think you're finally ready for this?"

He shifted between my legs, running the thick bulge in his jeans against my bare slit.

Impossible pleasure hummed through me, reigniting my desire. I thought it'd be impossible so soon after what he'd just done to me. But I looked up, stared into his green eyes, now alive and sharp as a wolf's with raw lust.

"You know I am, baby," I whispered, running my hand over his cheek. He drew his fingers closer to my lips, and I smelled my scent on him.

"Make me believe it, girl. You lick this shit I did to you clean. Show me you understand how wet that sweet cunt gets for me, how wet I fucking make it."

The two fingers he'd used to fuck me numb pushed into my mouth. For a second, I hesitated, but then I took them like a whore, blushing as I sucked them as deep as I could, running my tongue up and down his fingers, tasting my explosion.

Good practice for working on a much more sensitive part of him later. Sexy as hell too, and it made me far hornier than I had any business being just for taking a man's fingers into my mouth.

But he wasn't just any man, was he?

Husband. Old man. Lover. Inquisitor. Bastard.

I ran my tongue across his skin like I loved every part of him. In truth, I was starting to, and I finally began to understand why he had so many wild contrasts wrapped up in the same rock hard man with the ruthless tattoos.

My fingers ripped at his shirt. With a smug grin, he pulled his fingers from my mouth and rolled his shoulders, then took off his cut. The soft black Grizzlies MC shirt underneath it rolled up over his head, exposing the crazy broad canvass of pure muscle and pitch black ink he called a chest.

My hands roamed his flesh, and for a few glorious seconds, he let me. I touched everything. The lightning, the thorns, the bear stamped forever in his chest, its mouth open in a roar threatening to tear the hell out of anyone who crossed him and his club.

These men were dangerous. I'd known it from the first day I was old enough to realize my father was leading an outlaw pack. I'd been warned away from it, nudged away from the men my screwed up brain craved, and it had all come crashing down like it inevitably needed to.

Tonight, I'd gone to bed with a bastard. My pussy tingled, soaked itself on the evil taboo I'd tried to run away from. It pulsed harder as I embraced my destiny, the only one that seemed right since the night I'd put my lips on his so many years ago.

"Fuck me, Asphalt. Take what you've wanted for so long." My voice shook as I said the words, spreading my legs. I wasn't sure if I could take one more second without having him inside me.

My hand ran down his tightly packed, perfect abs, resting on his bulge. He grabbed my wrist in a fierce snatch, and then leaned in to take the other one, dragging me upright.

"Told you before, babe, you're gonna work for this cock in your pussy. You sucked yourself off my hands real nice. Show me what that hot little mouth can do where it belongs."

I didn't need any more encouragement. I gripped his jeans and slowly pulled down his zipper, reached inside with his hand covering mine, fishing out the massive root inside.

His cock popped out in my hand, pulsing and filled with lava. I'd never seen a live one before, much less held it. I couldn't get over the heat, burning even hotter than the ache between my legs.

I could feel the insane, feral need underneath his skin. God, I wanted to feel it inside me, every single inch of his desire mingling with mine.

Taking me, owning me, fucking me senseless.

Soon. You have to drive him just as crazy, I told myself, kneeling next to him and moving my hand in a slow fist across his length.

"Fuck, Elle Jo..."

Must've done something right. His head rolled back and he cursed, soft and encouraging, pressing his hand over mine a little harder.

I gripped him tighter and quickened my next couple strokes. The tip of his cock jerked, pulsed a long, clear trail of sticky wetness down my hand.

Okay, I had to taste him. Now.

My mouth parted and I sank down on his cock.

"Fuck!" he roared, grunted, and pulled at my hair as I went down, exploring him with my lips, my tongue, inch-by-trembling-inch.

Salt and manly musk became my whole world. I sucked him hard, pressed my tongue up under his length and rolled it around his swollen head, learning the parts that caused his breath to hitch.

This ownership thing was a two way street. If he wanted to possess every part of me, then it was only fair that I did the same, treating him with the reverence and focus an outlaw bride was supposed to give to her man.

"Fucking shit," he growled, pushing his hand into the back of my head, forcing me to take him deeper. "You're a goddamned natural, Elle. Can't believe you've wasted that tongue all these years. Hell, can't believe I wasted years without having your lips wrapped around my dick."

His eyes widened. He studied me with my mouth full of him as I sucked, eyes bright and admiring, like he'd just stumbled on a work of art.

Whatever he saw, he liked it, and my need to please him nearly suffocated me.

The hand in my hair pulled tighter the more I sucked him. His cock went from iron to solid granite, so impossibly hard I swore he had a steel pipe embedded in his flesh.

I moaned on his length, feeling my own wetness pooling in my thighs, twitching together in their plea for sweet relief. The vibration must've been the last thing he could take.

Asphalt fisted my hair and jerked my head back in one rough pull. We stared at each other, his huge chest rising and falling, his pupils wide with frenzied want.

"What? Did I do something wrong?" I asked softly.

"Yeah." He reached behind me and tore the clasp from my bra. "You weren't fucking me ten seconds ago."

I laughed and toppled backward as he pulled the rest of my clothes off. He finished peeling his away even faster, kicking off his jeans and boxers behind him, fully exposing the magnificent bottom half I'd only gotten a small taste of.

Asphalt's hands gripped my wrists, pinned them to the mattress. The bed sank beneath our combined weight.

I felt his hot, strong heat against my slit, pressed against me in one final tease.

"Once I'm balls deep in you, Ell-Bell, I've never going anywhere else. You fucking realize that?" He spoke into my ear, leaning in close so I could feel his prickly stubble against my cheek."Four years, I've waited for this. So have you. Four goddamn, fucked up years when I should've had your pussy wrapped around me that first night – fuck!"

I wasn't sure what throbbed harder – my heart or the muscles unraveling below my waist. I rolled my head and kissed him on the forehead, officially dying from the heat, the desire, the need.

"It's okay. We don't have to think about the past, baby. Be here with me," I whispered. "Look at us."

His arms jerked and he raised himself up. His cock shifted, moving until he angled it against my slit, ready to pierce deep.

The whole world seemed to stop.

"You're right, babe, the now's all that matters here. I'm taking everything tonight. Everything that's mine since I put my brand on your skin – everything that's always belonged to me since we were kids. You, Elle Jo, you and that hot little cunt that's been made for this dick since the day you were born!"

His hips rolled, pushing him into me.

My back arched and my legs folded around him. I ran on raw, feminine instinct when I felt him opening me, stretching me apart, changing my flesh to accommodate his thick, hard length.

There was a slight tearing sensation, and then a terrible itch. He moved his cock deep and then stopped, swearing underneath his breath, taking a moment to soak in the fact that we were finally, *finally* one.

"Love this fucking pussy, Elle Jo," he growled, lowering his mouth to mine, cutting off a moan. "Fucking love you."

I couldn't even answer. He started fucking me. Long, tense, gradual strokes that came a little harder and faster each time his hips met mine.

The fiery itch in my pussy became a raging inferno. My head rolled from side to side. A pleasure I'd never known before, not even with his hands or mouth, opened up below us and swallowed me whole.

Oh, God. Oh, Shit. Oh, Asphalt!

I pushed my hips into his, learning how to fuck him back. Loving every single second of it, everything our bodies could do when they were bound together like this. Of course, we'd barely scratched the surface, but something told me we weren't going to stop until he'd scratched me so deep I'd be lucky to walk.

"Hold the fuck on, baby," he ordered, pulling at my ass with his thick hands.

He hoisted me onto his cock, lifting my hips up in the air, all the better to deepen his strokes. He pounded into me, really hit me *deep*. His expression transformed from soft, eager lover to outlaw killer.

Nothing was stopping him now. Not even death could've prevented him from fucking me straight to the headboard, and I practically climbed it when his pubic bone ground against my clit, shoving me deeper, deeper, deeper into ecstasy.

Muscles I didn't know I had around my spine tensed up. This tension with him was awful before. This time, it was totally stupefying, and it would've destroyed me if he hadn't power fucked me like a maniac.

His hips crashed into mine. The sharp creak of the bed

and the slap our skin disappeared in the roar of my own blood, my heartbeat, pounding like a clock ticking down the last seconds to the greatest release of my life.

Asphalt.

Austin.

Husband. Lover. Alpha. Omega.

I wasn't sure if I screamed them all or just thought every word. It didn't matter a second later when the pleasure swept me away in a storm, tossing and turning, howling up at the ceiling that had turned into a hot, white sky.

His cock shook me without mercy while my pussy convulsed. Asphalt sounded like a wild animal, dragged my body into his, pinching my ass so hard it would've hurt something fierce if I wasn't so drunk on pleasure.

My climax shook me apart, tore apart time, making me lose track of everything except the bombs exploding all over my body. My senses came back while he fucked me with wild abandon.

No reserve. Nothing except the bestial need that had fully taken him over, driven him to own me the most primal way a man could.

"Fuck, fuck, I'm gonna bust inside you, babe. Spill every damned drop 'til you're leaking me for days!" His eyes narrowed, like it took all his energy to hold onto the great weight inside him. "Tell me you're on the pill, the patch – fuck, I don't care! I'm not wasting shit."

"Yes! Come, please come." I went stark raving mad.

My legs pinched tight to his legs, holding on like vices so he couldn't even think about pulling away. I'd been on the pill for about a year, hoping I'd finally find the right man, though the last few days had been screwed up.

If I'd missed a few, it didn't matter. Just then, I didn't fucking care about anything except the blinding pleasure tearing me in two. Nothing else mattered except being wed to him at a fluid level, filled and mated with his seed, the only thing in the world that could put out this fire.

"Fuck, fuck, fuck!" He threw his head back and drove into me, jerking my ass with all his might.

Our hips wedged together and his cock swelled inside me, a new, wild heat hotter than anything else.

We came together. My pussy massaged his length just as his first hot jet hurled inside me, streaking right to my womb. He spilled his fiery load as deep as it would possibly go, making me feel his weight the whole time as he held me down, fucking his come into me.

He owned my body like nobody ever had, like no man ever would. I loved it – freaking *loved it* – couldn't imagine sex any other way now that I'd had it at its finest.

Asphalt wasn't lying about filling me. His seed pulsed again and again, completely flooded me, then spilled out onto the sheets, even as he held his cock in me for several minutes. Slow, shallow strokes worked it deeper still, rubbed it into me until our very DNA tangled like our bodies.

The rough, slow fade of his growl brought me back to life. I opened my eyes and the room and tried to stop the room from spinning.

His kiss helped. Our lips pressed together, desperately seeking a more tender satisfaction. Everything we needed to take the savage edge off the coupling that left my thighs shaking, and probably bruised my butt cheeks where his fingers had almost pinched the life out of me.

"We're going to pay for this tomorrow. This has to be the longest day of my life," I said softly, loving how his forehead rested against mine.

"Fuck tomorrow, baby girl. The next twenty-four hours are just you, me, and this bed. You'd better hope I pass the fuck out next to you, or I'll keep owning this sweet pussy in your sleep." He kissed me again, pulling my bottom lip into his mouth biting it until I whimpered. "I've had my taste, and it's not enough. Not even fuckin' close! I'm addicted to you, Ell-Bell, if you want the cold truth. You thought we'd fuck some of this shit outta our system? I thought so too. I hoped it'd go down that way. Fuck, babe, I was wrong. I've gotta fuck you at least ten more times before I even think about stopping."

His hand cupped my mound and squeezed. More of his seed spilled out into his palm. He caught it, held it, pushed it back into me with thunder in his throat.

"Jesus, Asphalt...what's happened tonight?"

He sounded insane. But damn if it didn't turn me on,

until I started questioning my own sanity too.

"I've finally found a pussy attached to a chick worth filling, fucking, claiming for the rest of my life. You're all I ever wanted, Elle, and that shit hasn't changed a single bit since I finally got you in my bed." He sucked my lip again, biting it harder, drawing a tiny drop of blood.

I moaned, kissed him back, pulled at his strong lips with my own teeth. Seriously, what the *hell* was going on?

"Mark my words, babe. You're my property, and it's goddamned beautiful. I'm *never, ever* letting this go unfucked for more than a day. Shit, I'm never letting you go anywhere without me again. You belong to me, Elle Jo. Tonight's the start of forever."

VI: Fissure (Asphalt)

Don't know how the hell we managed to get a single wink in overnight. The exhaustion must've just knocked our asses down at some point.

Didn't matter that I fucked and filled her perfect cunt more times than I could count before we crashed. I woke up with my balls aching like they hadn't spat fire for days, my cock hammering so hard it tented the damned sheets.

I'd spilled pre-come all over her sweet, round ass in my sleep. My hips rolled. One push between her cheeks, and her eyes fluttered open. I shoved my length down, holding it against her pussy, moving my hand across her 'til she rolled the fuck over.

"Wow, so it wasn't just a dream," she mused, then made a face and winced. "I'm hungry."

I laughed. "Babe, I'll get us a feast after you work up an appetite. Spread your legs."

She didn't resist as I pulled her smooth thighs apart. My tongue went to work, taking her tits in my hands and mouth. I hadn't even begun to tease her pink, perky nipples with my tongue.

How many times had I felt those fucking things poking me in the chest? How many times did I imagine those perfectly palm-sized tits in my hands, squeezing 'em like pillows as I fucked her raw?

Now, they melted in my mouth. She moaned as I sucked her buds deep, flicking my tongue against each one, hungrily devouring her inch by inch.

I couldn't take it a second longer. Flipped her over 'til she had her ass up, then spread her legs again and shoved my cock against her slit.

Hot, wet heat enveloped my dick. I bared my teeth, clenched my damned jaw 'til I thought I'd shatter all my teeth. The rough, primal urge to fuck this woman to ashes clashed with the mad desire to keep her safe.

My fucked up brain wanted to take her, own her, destroy her all at once.

She infuriated me. She twisted me the fuck up and did a thousand other sorts of sappy shit no other woman had ever pumped into my guts. Really, my Ell-Bell turned me on like nothing else ever would, and my dick ached when I wasn't in her.

I remedied that here in bed.

Long, vicious, bed shaking strokes slid down into her pussy. She started to cry out when I got ten thrusts in, pressing her little hands against the pillows, tearing at them for support. I covered her with my body, grabbed her wrists, and held her the fuck down.

Only caused her ass to slam against me harder.

Perfect.

We fucked hard, relentless. Fucked her like I thought I'd never have this pussy again, because I'd been craving it like a motherfucking junkie for the past four years. And now that I had it, I was *never* going back to anything else.

I'd taken a few cherries in my life, but Elle's was the last, only virgin pussy that ever mattered. I'd broken her in and I still stretched her sweet flesh every time my cock sank balls deep.

I'd make her *mine* every fucking way a man could. My wife, my old lady, my whore, no holes barred.

I fucked to tame her too. Reaching between her legs, I found her clit and stroked it furious while my cock slammed into her. She arched her back and screamed, legs shaking, proof she was about to come.

When I saw that shit, I *really* laid into her. Grabbed her hair with my free hand, held her down by the weight of my thrusts, just fucking her 'til she smashed her face into the pillows.

It was all she could do to stifle the earsplitting scream. I ripped her up by her golden hair halfway through so I could listen to what I'd done.

"Don't stop coming for me, babe. Don't hide it. Not today, not ever," I growled, giving her ass a firm swat when she calmed down.

She came hard. Music to my ears.

Her pussy clenched, sucked, milked every inch of me.

I almost busted then and there, but I wasn't done with this pussy yet. Not by half.

Pulling out, I yanked her against me and we rolled together. I flopped back and tugged her onto my cock, manhandling her tits while she slowly sank down on every inch, learning to ride me.

"Faster, baby girl," I ordered, my balls starting to burn.

Fuck, she looked hot. Her blue eyes shone so bright, her blonde hair bobbed wild when she started picking up speed, those soft lips I could bite all day slowly opening as new pleasure took her over.

Didn't start fucking her back 'til she'd found her groove. Then I laid into her, grabbed her ass, pulled her up, down, sideways on my cock, angling my thrusts to find new spots in her pussy to own.

"Asphalt!"

She looked at me as her eyes rolled, breaking my name to draw in a few desperate breaths. I slapped her ass harder and grinned. Tried to be reassuring, but fuck if I didn't want her thinking I ever did this shit gentle or tender.

I'd never hurt her, of course. But I wanted the girl to get used to rough, hard, wild animal fucking. I also knew enough to know tension did something special to a girl, caused her pussy to burn and gush like nothing else when she didn't know what the hell I had up my sleeve.

This morning, I had pure, rabid dick. And I slammed it

up into her 'til my balls slapped her ass, snarling like a beast, driving her over the edge 'til she collided headfirst with ecstasy.

Her tits flopped in my hands. I brought my face to her throat and bit – hard – marking her in that fucked up way I couldn't resist.

I wanted my imprint all over her. My ink, my teeth, soft bruises left by my hands on the rump of her sweet ass. The whole damned world deserved to see the war I'd fought to win this woman, and now that I had her, I'd keep reminding her who she belonged to 'til kingdom fucking come.

And come, we did.

She threw her head back, blonde hair tangled in my hands, this time not doing anything to stifle the scream. Her pussy jerked me off, coiled like a vice around my length 'til I couldn't hold back.

"Fuck!" One staccato burst raged from my throat, barely ahead of the fire shooting up from my balls.

I filled her the fuck up all over again.

Hot come poured inside her, into the empty void I was always meant to fill. I locked my arms around her and held her down on my cock, hurling every spurt, every molten burst as deep as it would go.

Elle squirmed, whimpered, begged with those incoherent little yelps that drove me mad. Her pussy clenched harder, told me she loved every damned second, even though she'd been fucked too hard to say so.

I held my dick in and emptied my balls in her 'til I went soft. Regret seeped outta my throat in a snarl when I finally pulled out a couple minutes later, watching my seed slip out and run down her thighs.

We locked lips for a minute more, and I finally let her roll off me, amazed that I'd be sated for the next thirty seconds.

Then I'd be aching to fill her all over again.

She flopped back on the bed, her eyes half-closed, a little smile plastered on her lips. I'd seen that *holy mother of god* look on girls a hundred times before. I knew how to own their bodies, but I'd never given more than a passing shit 'til I saw Elle's sweet, satisfied face in the morning light.

Something came alive, pulsing deep inside me. Wasn't just my cock begging me to fuck her once again neither.

Shit. I had that warm, rosy glow rolling down my chest and into my guts. The kinda warmth I'd always heard the family guys in the club talk about together when the bachelors weren't around, squawking about how much they loved their old ladies.

They talked about how fucking 'em was different than any other slut they'd pounded. Hell if I believed it 'til now.

Now, Elle's pussy pried my eyes wide open. I'd been converted, brought to a new faith that involved me getting in deep and feeling her pulse on my cock for the rest of my life.

I walked into the bathroom to wash up. Splashed my face and scalp in cold water, smoothing it into my skin. When I looked in the mirror, I saw the same homey glint in my eyes I'd seen on Brass, Rabid, Roman.

That's when I realized I was really, truly fucked. I hadn't just claimed the beautiful woman stretched out on the bed a few feet away. She'd got her claws in deep.

Damn if I didn't love it.

We got our grub and I picked up a case of beer from a liquor shop around the corner. Looked at my phone a couple times expecting calls from the brothers, maybe even Gil's assholes, but it was weirdly quiet.

Switched off my phone for good measure by the time I got back to our room. She'd cleaned up nicely and sat at the table, scribbling something like a mad woman on a stack of cheap hotel paper.

"Hey!" Elle called out as I grabbed a couple sheets and held them up to see.

"What the fuck is this?" I couldn't make heads or tails of it.

Whatever the fuck she was writing, it wasn't English. Everything was in some alien looking Asian script I'd only seen in bad kung fu movies, or sometimes the authentic Chinese places in the cities.

"None of your business." She snatched the remaining papers closer to her chest, giving me a dirty look. "Don't worry. It's nothing that's going to ruffle your feathers, Asphalt. It won't interfere with your precious club business either."

I rolled my eyes. Why the hell did every old lady have to make a mockery of that damned phrase? She'd beaten me to saying it, for fuck's sake!

For a second, I almost ripped them up, crushed them into a ball, and hurled them into the waste basket. Too bad I remembered what was at stake home in Redding.

We weren't here to play fucking patty cake, no matter how real this marriage was getting. I marched up and looked her in the eyes, holding her gaze 'til she cracked.

"What?!" she whispered, annoyed, looking away. "I told you already, I —"

"Babe, don't talk. I know you went to school for this shit and maybe you're just practicing." I licked my lips, closing the distance between us, 'til our faces were only an inch apart. "But I also know there's some real stone cold fuckery going on here in Tacoma. Your old man, trading with outsiders, probably the Chinese mafia. I married you to keep the peace, and I don't wanna play you if I don't have to. Best way for me to do that is if you start talking honest, telling me exactly what the fuck's going on here, if there's something I oughta know."

"God damn it, Asphalt!" She jerked up, managed to slip away from me before I could grab her. "Is that what you think this is? Me, seducing you and pretending to be the good wife, just so I can screw with your stupid club?"

"Don't know what your old man would put you up to, Elle Jo. He's a real sneaky sonofabitch when he wants to be." I stepped closer, working to soften my face, turn back into her loving husband instead of the biker asshole interrogating her. "Look..."

I grabbed her shoulder. She tensed, but didn't fight me off, giving me an opening to pull her to my chest.

"Things don't need to be this fucked, Elle. Not between you and me. Things were going good a couple hours ago, just like it oughta be between a man and his old lady. Fuck, club politics is the only reason I'm not ripping down those pants right now, bending you over the bathroom counter, and making you watch in the mirror while I make those big blue eyes roll backwards."

I grabbed her chin, held her face, even as she tried to pull away. Looked straight into those pearly blues 'til I saw green reflecting back. Her pupils widened. Red splotches appeared on her cheeks.

I'd taken her cherry, yeah, but I hadn't fucked out every last trace of the shy, virgin Tacoma princess.

"God, you're so crude."

"Yeah, baby, you know I am. Doesn't take a damned psychologist to figure out you fucking love it too." I pressed her against the wall, shoved my hips between her legs, and rubbed my cock into her. She pinched her eyes shut and hissed desire when she felt my bulge. "Did you really think we were done this morning? Put that translation shit on hold for the rest of the night. Doesn't matter what the fuck you're doing. Only thing you need to be thinking about is how amazing my balls feel when they're slapping your clit raw."

Her mouth dropped open in that *holy shit* look that turned me on more. Like a deer in headlights, and now it was time for the shock and awe.

I grabbed her blonde locks and pulled 'til she followed me into the bathroom. Once I was behind her, I grabbed her wrists, pinned them in front of her, and tore at her jeans with my free hand.

"You keep your eyes glued to your pretty reflection there, and don't you move them off. Not once. I want you to see how beautiful you look when you're coming on my cock, Elle Jo."

My free hand went for her clit. Then the defiant little minx leaned over and bit my hand, sinking her teeth in so hard I fought the instinct to draw my knife.

She pulled her teeth away with a grin, just as her panties fell. My cock pushed inside her in one mean thrust, taking away her little flash of power.

Bullshit. She needed a stern reminder who the fuck owned her.

"What the hell was that, babe?" My words died in a in a guttural growl when she pushed back, warming me to the hilt with her tight, wet cunt.

"Just a reminder. You want to keep this, then you're

going to work for it, old man." She clenched her pussy muscles so damned tight I almost went full psycho.

Fuck. I hadn't tamed her tongue yet – and amen to that.

With my hand on her head, I jerked her face close to mine and kissed her from the side, quickening my strokes inside her.

We fucked in front of our own reflections. Kissing, biting, scratching, growling, screaming.

Every dirty, nasty thing I'd always wanted to do with the love of my life was possible with her. And that shit caused my balls to meltdown. I couldn't hold back nearly as fast.

My thrusts wedged her to the counter, and I twisted her face up, just as I started to power fuck her to the grand finale. Elle moaned, staring at us in the glass like a good girl.

Good, bad, whatever the hell she was, she'd always be mine. Mine, mine, and nothing else.

Club politics and mafia assholes be damned.

My cock went wild, stroking deep inside her. Held her face up the whole damned time, making her watch what I was doing. I had to show her there was something behind the rough fucking – something crazy, wicked, and special – I fucking *had to*.

She took it all in, but I wasn't sure how much she understood when her lips popped open and she let out that feral moan.

Her pussy gushed, clutched my cock, shook me down to my balls like a greedy little thief. I came fire, watching her tits swing, and she joined me as soon as I lost the first couple hot jets inside her.

"Fucking love you, Ell-Bell," I whispered, when I could finally speak, running my fingers through her soft gold hair. "That's not gonna change, however tangled and nasty shit gets."

The next day wasn't so peaceful. We spent the night with pizza and beer. I told her we'd save the fancier shit for another time, when we didn't have to worry about all this other criminal bullshit getting between us.

I stepped outside early in the morning, sliding out of bed, careful not to wake her. Had an urge to enjoy my last good smoke in peace with the sunrise, maybe the last one I'd ever need now that I had a better drug purring in my system every time that woman made me come.

I wanted to enjoy the cool morning air and think about our next fuck. Then the one after that, and the one after that, all the ways I'd shake her, slam her, make her fucking scream.

My cock jerked, an image of her arms and legs tied to the bed in my brain. Knew damned well this vision wouldn't come unlodged 'til I made it happen, too.

She still had a lot to learn, and I was gonna teach her, show her all the ways a man like me could work her body over 'til the end of fucking time.

No sooner than I lit my cig and stuffed it in my mouth, the phone rang.

Looked at the screen on my burner phone and saw the Veep's number lit up. Shit.

"Yeah?" I snapped, trying not to sound like an asshole who'd just been pulled outta heaven.

"Fuck you," he growled on the other end of the line. "Word is you've been in Tacoma for days, and I'm guessing you haven't brought back shit? Roman says he's high and dry on intel, and so's the Prez."

"Christ, I'm working on it, brother. Settle your ass down. It's not easy gaining her trust. I gotta get her mind locked down before she'll open up and let me the fuck in."

Fuck me. Talking like that gutted me, especially when I had to make these assholes think this was just an info pump, without any real feelings involved.

"I don't care how hard it is," the Veep said, murder in his voice. "You do what you were fucking sent up there to do. Take what you need from that bitch and keep her outta the way if we've got to gut her old man."

"I'm her old man now," I growled. "But I know what you mean. Her dad's a sneaky sonofabitch, and I'm sure he's hiding something."

"Yeah, so's the rest of the club. Fucking Blaze is starting to ride our asses about the rumors slipping back to Montana. He's got a bug up his ass about Grizzlies selling their shit and cutting the Devils out, breaking the only damned agreement that keeps us from stabbing each other."

"Shit," I grunted. Serious business.

The President of the Prairie Devils Montana wouldn't stay fooled long, no matter how sweet Brass' sis, Saffron, was on him. They'd gotten married shortly before Blackjack took the wheel, and we'd been on good terms ever since. But that alliance was fragile as fuck, and it could all go to hell, leading Grizzlies and Devils right back to each other's throats.

"You remember the last time we all sat together in church, Asphalt? The club agreed to do this thing the nice way, as long as you deliver. You'd better do it soon. We already stood like penguins through that fucked up wedding while the Prez shook Tacoma asshole's hand."

"Let me do my work. You'll have answers within the week, Veep, I promise."

Brass sighed on the other end of the line. "What the fuck's happened to you, brother? You were always solid. Not so wrapped up in emotional cesspool like the rest of us. Don't tell me she's getting to your head through your cock?"

"No."

Total fucking lie. Brass knew it too.

"Bullshit. I know a man who's falling when I hear him, and you're crashing like a goddamned redwood." He paused, mumbling a few more curses under his breath. "You're lucky my breakfast just showed up, and Missy's the best fucking cook in the world."

Another pause. I heard lips smacking over the other end of the line before he came back. "I'm not gonna jerk your balls all day, Asphalt. Get your answers and then you can sort the rest of this shit out. This is your last chance before we ride up there ourselves. We've gotta move, before we all wind up with the Chinese and Tacoma kneecapping the whole club."

"Yeah, you know I will, Brass. Take your fucking doubt and choke on it."

The line went dead. *Motherfucker.*

I took a long pull from my smoke. Couldn't even enjoy it, the fucking thing tasted like ash. I ripped it outta my mouth and stomped it flat with my bare foot, not caring about the burn.

Turning back and looking into our room was almost as bad as some asshole shoving a gun in my face. I'd have to risk the miracle we'd found over the last week for the damned club, or else I'd be putting a lot of brothers' lives on the line.

I needed answers. I had to drill deep, break her wide open, or else I'd be giving up my patch for a chick who couldn't even tell me the damned truth.

Rock, meet fucking hard place. All I could do was try not to get smashed between boulders.

We sat in a cool Tacoma park, overlooking the

coastline. Several ships were rolling in, big steel bastards hauling wares from distant shores. Some illegal cargo too, no doubt.

Funny thing about the underworld, once you're in it, you realize it's everywhere, like a foundation to everyday life.

She gripped my hand on the bench, going on about her big career plans, everything she'd wanted before her asshole father interrupted 'em with this arranged marriage.

"I know, it probably seems like a useless degree sometimes, but I swear it isn't. China's going to be a powerhouse in a few more years. I can do anything, Asphalt, go anywhere."

"You can own the fucking moon, babe, as long as you're still riding behind me and looking cute. You'd damned well better keep riding me like a nun in heat, too."

She elbowed me in the side playfully and laughed. "Oh, God. That's really all you think about, isn't it?"

"Fuck, girl, you tell me." I smiled.

Elle didn't know I'd softened her up as much as I could before I lobbed the grenade I'd been hanging onto all evening. And if I didn't throw that fucker at her soon, get it out in the goddamned open, it'd blow us both to pieces, everything we'd built.

"It's okay, I know it's really me you're after," she said, nuzzling into my shoulder, breathing my scent. "I can't believe I actually want this to work out. I told myself it wouldn't all those years at college, and then when I came back, and saw how big an asshole you could be..."

"That's when you fell for me, babe. You didn't have a prayer, and you fucking know it." I stroked her soft blonde locks and looked into her eyes. Those baby blues beamed like lighthouses.

"There's something I gotta ask you again," I said, shuffling my feet together like a nervous fucking kid.

She gave me a sharp look when she sensed the pause. *Spit it the fuck out,* I told myself, and my lips started moving.

"What's really going on that I don't know about? If your old man's been fucking with the Chinese behind my club's back, then we've got a bigger problem than just you and me, babe. Give me the truth. We're solid now. You can trust me, open up, give it to me straight."

For a second, her face rippled. I thought she might actually spill it.

Then the girl's hand crashed across my cheek like I'd just pinched her ass without her loving it. The sting shot up to my temple and down through my jaw.

"Shit!" I snarled, jumping up and moving my fingers across the hot, numb patch on my cheek. "Did you just fucking hit me, Elle Jo?"

"You're damned right I did," she said, getting up and moving several steps back. "You should know better than to bring that crap up. We were having a nice time. I was starting to think I was wrong about you, Asphalt, but I can see the club still comes first."

Fuck, no. My fists balled into stones at my sides. I ran after her as she began quick-stepping away, weaving between some old couple walking a big, spindly mutt on a pink leash.

"Goddamn it, Elle, you're wrong." I grabbed her, twisted her 'til she looked at me. "You're wrong about everything. Don't you get it? We're all fucked if this deal goes off and your daddy's doing wrong. Yeah, I got my club duties, but I'm doing this for you, babe. I'm saving all our asses. I'm trying to get this shit dead and over with for us. Long as you're keeping secrets, I'm gonna keep drilling you, and that's poison for all the sweet fucking moments we could be having, without all this bullshit piling up in the way."

Elle's phone started going off. Horrific fucking timing.

I blinked in surprise as she snapped it up, let out a long sigh, and tore herself away from me.

The dog started barking behind us. The raging shitstorm coming outta my mouth must've caught the old farts off guard.

I looked behind me, saw they were staring at us. The old geezer had one hand in his pocket, probably thinking about calling up the cops and reporting me for disturbing the peace or some shit.

Fuck. I couldn't go after her with all these damned civilians hanging around. Not the way I wanted to.

Heard her talking to somebody as she put more distance between us. I crept up slowly, staying just outta her view, behind a thick tree. I had to find out if that important call had anything to do with this whole sick situation.

"Daddy, please. It's really a bad time. I –"

Her voice sounded soft, angry, unsure of everything. She stopped, took a long pause while a garbled, older voice that made me see red bitched her out over something. Couldn't quite make out Gil's words, but fuck if his tone didn't curl my fists tighter.

"I mean, I can be there if you really need it. You're sure about now?" She sniffed while he mumbled a few words. "Yeah, he's close behind. He won't follow if you send a prospect. We're...going through some troubles. No, no, nothing I'd need any help from your guys with. It's just a little argument. I'm a big girl, daddy, I can take care of myself."

A little argument? Was she fucking joking?

Shit, was she yanking my dick off, standing there and jabbering away with her asshole, traitor father while I stood just a few feet away?

It hit me like a nuclear bomb in my guts. This entire sham marriage is the fucking joke.

I grit my teeth, straining to make out what the asshole who'd blasted my shoulder a small eternity ago was saying.

"Okay. I understand, daddy – if it can't wait, I'll be

there," she said at last, a little sadness entering her voice. "Just give me a little time. I'll get over there as soon as I can."

Gil exploded on the other end of the line. Something about *leaving that fuckwit out of it,* and how bad he'd wished he'd *sent that dirty bald bitch to the reaper years ago.*

I dug my boots into the ground, seething. Wished I could've reached right through her fucking phone and snapped his worthless neck. Then I heard her murmur a few more words under her breath and end the call.

My cue to move. I marched up, grabbed her, whipped her around. The dog barked like a damned fiend behind us, and those shitheads eavesdropping were probably dialing up the Tacoma PD right now.

Fuck if I cared. She'd defied me for the last time, and I had to set things straight, before she got us and the Grizzlies MC balls deep in something that would get our brains blown out our ears.

"Let me go!" Elle snapped, kicking at my shin. "Asphalt, you don't understand. I need to get out of here and –"

"Shut your fucking mouth, babe. Now. You've been lying to me the whole cocksucking time, haven't you?"

I spun her around and pinned her to the nearest tree. The hot rage burning in my eyes shut her up. I tried to keep my eyes off her chest, those tits I'd ravaged the last couple nights pressed tight against me, rolling with her ragged breaths.

Fuck me. Was I really thinking about sex right now when she'd just shoved a knife in my back?

"Last warning," she snarled, giving me her best war face. "Let. Me. Go."

"You're not going anywhere 'til you tell me what the hell's going on, woman. I know your old man wants you for something dirty, and I've got a feeling it involves crushing all my brothers' balls. Did you think I'd never find out? That I'd let you ride off on your merry little way and bullshit me through a river of blood?" Anger surged in my heart, so hot it almost popped the thing like a fucking balloon. "I'm your old man, Elle Jo, but I'm not your fucking chump!"

She flinched when I spat the last word like I'd hit her in the face. I had a pang of guilt, yeah, but it did fuck all to slow the white, blinding rage crackling through my system.

"Take your hands off me," she said coldly. "Right fucking now, Austin. I'm not playing around. That couple behind us, they're going to –"

"Fuck!" I spun so hard I lost my damned grip and shot the old folks a death glare. Also had to get my hands off her so I wouldn't do some shit I'd regret. "What did I tell you about using that name? You know what to call me, and you won't fucking do it!"

"I'm not playing games when you're acting like a complete ass." She stood up straighter, stiffening in place, trying to stare me down.

She didn't have a chance. I bathed her in my angry green gaze 'til she broke eye contact and withered.

"This shit's not a game, babe. None of it. I don't know what that fucking asshole said to you, but –"

"Don't call him that." Death ruled her eyes as they focused on me again. "Look, I know you two have a history, but he's my father. He raised me proper. He always tried to do the right thing, and I've got to help him, just like you're going to do everything you can for your club."

"History?" I snorted. "That's fucking cute. Last I checked, we're still clashing right here in the present because he's shitting up the chain of command, Elle. You were raised in this MC, so I know you're not stupid. What Redding says goes – right across the fucking board. It's mother charter. If he's gonna do something stupid, then you'd be smart to stay the hell outta the way. Let us deal with this."

"You don't understand, Asphalt. You really don't." She looked past me, over my shoulder. "I have to go. We can sort this out later, if there is one, I mean."

I lost it. The hellfire boiling my brain spilled over, and I wanted to curse her to the fucking moon, throw her over my lap and spank her defiant little ass, if I didn't just chain her to the nearest post first.

God help me, I loved her. I really had.

It shocked my whole system to start hating the bitch

too.

"Don't do it, Elle. I'm telling you. You take one more step outta line, and this thing between us, it's over. You want to put the club first, your scheming fuck of father? So will I. Trust me, I can make this shit we've got as dead and business-like as any ordinary run. Your choice. Not mine."

It ripped my guts out to say it, but I did. I had to make her understand, had to make sure she knew I was goddamned serious.

She didn't even waver. At least, her feet didn't, but the way she snatched her face away from me said some serious tears were about to fall.

The girl moved quick. Zipped right past me before I could catch her, wondering why the fuck she thought she could walk right out.

"Babe?"

Holy shit. I couldn't believe what I'd seen. She'd really, truly just thrown in the fucking towel, choosing that fucknut Gil over me?

What. The. Fuck?!

"Elle! Jesus Christ, where the hell do you think you're –" I started running, one reach away from grabbing her and cuffing her to my fucking wrist.

Suddenly, I saw the asshole standing on the hill, waiting.

It was that fat piece of shit from the night we blew into town. He wore tape over his nose, trying to soothe

the damage my knuckles had done to his ugly face.

He looked at me and grinned, one hand by his belt. He was sending a message, and I knew the bastard wouldn't hesitate to draw if I stepped up, even if this place was crawling with civilians.

Elle Jo looked back over her shoulder once. Saw her wipe one hot tear away as it rolled down her cheek before she turned back to the Tacoma brother and redoubled her steps.

I didn't move a muscle. That pitch black stone in my chest I called a heart splintered apart and turned into gravel by the time I heard fat boy's truck starting up, squealing outta the parking lot like they were in a real fucking hurry.

Then another sound. Sirens.

I couldn't take a chance just waiting with my thumb up my ass. If that old couple had truly called a buncha badges, I'd be gone like a phantom before they caught up here.

My bike started and I rode without direction. I swerved through the rush hour traffic heading toward SeaTac proper, not giving a shit if I wrecked.

I had my mission for Blackjack, for the club, but that was all I had now. I'd just lost the best thing that ever happened to me, plus my own damned mind.

Blinking back the angry red veil clouding my vision, I swore I'd *never, ever* let myself be this stupid again as long as I breathed.

VII: Lost in Translation (Elle Jo)

"Shit, still no answer. Fuck." Sear swore, slamming his phone down on the dashboard. "Aw, come on little Elle, that fucking asshole won't follow us a single step unless he wants a bullet in his skull."

"Just shut up. I need a moment."

And I did. The man I'd left behind had been a bastard all my life, but I'd also fallen for him.

What started as a sham was starting to feel real – before he started making these cruel demands. What's worse, Asphalt had been *right*.

Of course I was hiding my father's deal with the Chinese from him. It couldn't get back to his club, or Tacoma would find itself at the mercy of swarms of angry Grizzlies several charters over.

Of course I'd disrespected him, thrown him off, and walked away. Blood ran thick – always had since daddy sat me on his knee as a little girl and told me it was everything. It ran like mud in my veins, cementing my loyalties, even when I wanted to break and tell the man with the beautiful green eyes everything weighing down my shoulders.

Of course I loved the bastard too, and I'd meant it when I told him. Now, whenever this crap was finally done, I just hoped I could hold it all together until he shoved the divorce papers in my face and broke me a second time.

I couldn't let him see how bad he'd hurt me. Not today, and not ever.

"Your dad's gonna make it all right, Elle Jo. He knows what he's doing. If those fucks down in California had a little more brains, we wouldn't be having this shitty problem right now," Sear growled, pounding his truck's steering wheel. "You wouldn't be wearing that bald fuck's brand neither. We've done a damned good job throwing them off the trail, but if that won't work no more, then we'll throw fists instead."

I grimaced. Civil war was brewing in the club, and nothing would slow it down.

I looked at him, eyeing the bandage on his nose. Asphalt had smashed it just a few nights ago at daddy's house, and I'd fought him too.

He'd won me over, and lost me in the same agonizing week. I couldn't believe how fast the world raised me up and smashed me on my face again.

"Sear, I didn't ask for any commentary. Just drive."

He listened. The big prospect chomped a cheap cigar and drove on, toward daddy's house.

When we got out, everything seemed eerily quiet. As far as he knew, my father was supposed to meet us here, and we'd all ride down with the club to deal with the Chinese.

There hadn't been much notice. I fought more tears, remembering how I'd listened to daddy with one ear, more worried about losing what I had with Asphalt, rather than this stupid gun trade going right.

"Fuck." Sear came upstairs, slamming the basement door shut behind him. "No sign of 'em anywhere. The other brothers aren't answering their phones, but I got a message from Line – we gotta go to the warehouse downtown, Elle. They're probably all waiting for us."

"The warehouse?" I cocked my head and squinted. "Daddy always said that was off limits for me. Too dangerous."

That was the word he'd used for the club storage site since I was a little girl. He probably had good reason for scaring my teenage self straight, but he'd talked about it just before the wedding, reminding me that was where club business began and my involvement ended.

"That's what the VP says," Sear growled. "Come on. Let's get our asses down there."

Back into the truck we went. I couldn't take my mind off the stink beginning to rise from this situation the entire ride there.

It was almost dark by the time we rolled through the huge, high gate with a rusted sign marking club territory.

PROPERTY OF THE GRIZZLIES MC. KEEP THE FUCK OUT.

I clenched my jaw. Sear seemed a little more tense than usual too, his knuckles turning white as he gripped the steering wheel.

His eyes lit up when he saw two familiar club trucks and a sleek row of bikes parked near the side. "Oh, thank fuck. Everybody's here. Guess they're all inside. I'll get this thing parked, and then we can head in. Let me go a ways ahead, just to make sure nothing fucking crazy happens. I'll –"

One second, Sear's lips were moving like he'd been rattling off this week's groceries for pickup. Then something whizzed by my face, tore through the windshield, and went right through him.

Quick. Hot. Blinding.

I opened my eyes and took in the gruesome scene. Something had totally taken out the driver's window, shattered it to little bits. Sear's head went with it.

The bloody crater where his face had been slumped forward, leaking red gore all over the seat. Only the seat belt stopped his body from totally falling on the steering wheel and blasting the horn.

My eyes snapped down, trying to comprehend what I'd seen without losing my sanity. My hands, my arms, my shirt was completely sprayed with blood, and more red droplets rained down on me. I opened my mouth and screamed.

The world spun, went silent. I barely noticed my door ripping open, and two sets of angry hands pulling me out of the truck before I blacked out.

When the world stopped spinning, it blurred. I woke up with a terrible headache, woozy like I'd taken a long road trip on an upset stomach.

The blood all over me, now dried to a rusty brown color, caused me to heave. My hands were tied to the back of the chair I found myself in. There was nowhere to go but to the side.

I tipped my head and vomited, then barfed some more when I thought about how incredibly fucked we all were if these assholes could kill Sear in cold blood.

Cold, rapid fire words in Chinese echoed a few feet away. I struggled to make them out.

Girl's awake. Go say hi. Maybe she'll talk more than these dead fucking Grizzlies, if she knows anything.

Three cold faced Chinese men leaned over me. The one in the middle looked older, wearing a salt and pepper goatee. He reached into his gray suit pocket and pulled out a small LED flashlight.

"Oh!" The asshole shined it right in my eyes. I jerked, feeling the light stabbing into my brain.

"Very responsive, just like your father," a voice said, switching to English. "Miss Mathers, please call me Zee. You, sweet thing, are going to tell us everything we need to know about this ambush."

Ambush? What the hell was he talking about?

"I don't know what you're getting at. I came here to

help my father with a business deal. You were supposed to be doing a contract together. Weapons, I think? He never really told me the specifics." I paused, considering my words. "He never really told me anything. Club business."

I managed a shaky smile, repeating the phrase that had always worked before as a substitute for *fuck off.* I had to play dumb. If I could convince them I was just a stupid little girl helping with the family business, I might walk out of this alive, or at least delay them until Tacoma could get some backup.

But the entire club was here, wasn't it? I'd seen the bikes outside. Jesus, how many of them were still alive?

"You know, I might believe you." Zee smiled, slowly pacing around me, circling like a menacing gray shark. "Why would dear old dad tell you anything about what's really going on when he was willing to put you between two dragons?"

Zee whirled, faced one of his men, and started talking Chinese.

What a piece of shit! Bring him in here. We'll just see how much she knows.

If she's telling the truth, we'll finish off his men, just like we planned. Sell her into slavery, perhaps.

If she's lying...we do them all. I'll garrote this bitch myself.

A cold, crazy chill ran up my spine. I saw him pull on something half-hidden in his pocket. A sharp cord, which he pulled up to his chest in the corner of my eye. Zee fiddled with it a few times, undoubtedly thinking about slicing into my throat with it, and then stuffed it back into place.

"We wait," he said, staring at me with his dark brown eyes. "Dear old dad really must think he's hot shit. I flew here all the way from Shanghai, you know. My own fucking time and money, only to find out he meant to have me in that chair, ransoming me off after he killed my men!" Zee's hand slammed the wooden backside over my shoulder, rattling the chair so hard I could feel it in my bones. "Fucking idiot. Biker trash! I'll rip his balls off myself and he can watch them laying on the ground. You too, Miss Mathers, if you're telling the truth. He's wasted your time just as much as ours."

His eyes bulged. He leaned in, looking like a total maniac.

Great, so I had Jekyll and Hyde to contend with. That terrified me, even if it gave me a few narrow options for survival.

No emotion. I couldn't let it come.

I didn't flinch, didn't protest, didn't show any reaction to the psychopath whispering in my ear.

When he stepped away, his face looked relaxed again, back to his somber, business-like expression.

Zee rolled up his sleeve and tapped his watch, an expensive platinum-plated luxury fit for a mafia don. A minute later, I heard several pairs of feet scraping on the concrete.

When I looked up, two of Zee's men were dragging my father into the vast room. His hands were tied together tight, and he looked like he was barely conscious. His movements were jerky, erratic, the protests on his lips so incredibly soft for being pulled along like an animal to slaughter.

"No, no, no," he whispered, over and over, as if he could've believe it.

Neither could I. Hell, I could hardly handle what was happening in front of me. In all the years I'd grown up with daddy disappearing, going away and coming back cut, bruised, or bloody, he'd never looked as terrible as this.

So defeated. Dead, like they'd already done him in.

They'd bludgeoned him in the head. Blood dried in his hair and spread across his face, a rust red spiderweb coming out of the huge scar on his head.

Oh, God. Imagining the pain, my heart sank like a stone. It took everything inside me to hold back tears.

The Chinese released him and he toppled to the ground, laying like he'd just died. Zee walked over slowly, calmly, and then slammed his polished shoe into my father's ribs. His bones cracked so hard I winced.

"You have a visitor, old man. Do you still recognize your own daughter, or did that blow to the head fuck something up?" Zee grabbed my father's hair and pulled, yanked his head up like a doll's until we looked at each other.

Daddy's eyes went big and dark as soon as he saw me. I could've counted – five, four, three, two, one – before he flew into a biting, kicking rage.

"Let her fucking go! I made a mistake. I fucked up bad, asshole, but she doesn't need to be here like me and my guys. Just let her –"

Zee nodded. Half a second later, his boys shoved my father back on the ground. One held him down while the other bastard punched him in the stomach until he stopped making any sounds at all.

I pinched my eyes shut. Zee grabbed my face, pressing his hands tight to both sides, and twisted my head around hard, forcing my eyes where he wanted them.

"Look, you stupid little bitch. I want you to understand – he's going to die. It's just a question of whether or not you go with him. Now, tell me truthfully, girl...were you involved in this ambush?"

"No!"

I could barely hear my own voice. It came out sharp, cold and distant, like I'd tried to shout down a long, vacant tunnel to someone on the other side.

"Hm. I almost believe you, Elle Mathers. Let's see if your daddy's got a little life left in him..."

Zee spun, and began walking over to my father, corralled by the two dead-eyed killers at his side. I hung my head, refusing to watch, even though it risked the mafia don doing something much worse.

God damn it, daddy, you screwed up BAD, I thought, hiding my tears. *I can't watch you die like this.*

I can't.

Zee had other ideas. He pulled my father's face up and lifted something from his pocket. I flinched, thinking it was going to be the garrote.

Oh God, I was going to watch the mobster slash his throat in front of me. No, wait. It was *just* a handgun.

Sighing relief at the sight was so sick and twisted I wanted to laugh.

Then the Dragon don slammed it hard across daddy's jaw. His blue eyes opened, going gray with anger.

"What the fuck?!" Daddy screamed through the blood filling his mouth.

"Shut up, Gil!" Another vicious blow landed on his jaw, this time the opposite side. "So nice of you to join the living again – for just a little while longer, anyway. I'm giving you one chance to save your daughter. Only one. And just to show you I'm serious..."

Zee turned to his men and shouted in Chinese.

Bring the others in, the ones we haven't killed.

Daddy groaned in Zee's grip, his head turning, like he wanted so badly to shake off the dizzy, hellish pain clouding his mind. For a second, our eyes met.

I had to look away. One more moment, and I'd have lost it, seeing nothing but *I'm sorry, I'm sorry, I'm sorry* mirrored in his eyes, over and over again.

Apologies wouldn't help us now. We needed a miracle.

"Ahhh, there they are." Zee smiled and let my father fall to the dusty concrete floor, clapping his hands together.

He switched to Chinese, barking his orders with bloodlust. *Line them up. That's right, one by one, and keep your eyes on these fucking bastards. They'll try anything when they figure out how fucked they are.*

Six guys were still alive. It was a small relief, but my heart thudded hopefully, amazed to see anyone in the club alive.

Uncle Line looked up, his single good eye going wide when he saw me. His mouth opened in a silent, round curse.

Oh, shit.

Zee's two underlings were joined by two more, all of them cold, quiet men in business suits. They went down the line one-by-one, checking the handcuffs on each man, then stepping behind them on opposite ends of the row when they were finished.

Their bastard leader turned his attention back to my poor father, grabbing his hair. "Nice, clear view, yes? How strange it must be to see your men lined up, defeated, completely at my mercy, Gil."

"Fuck you," daddy growled. "Don't know how yet, but I'm gonna fuckin' kill you, motherfucker. I'll rip your balls off with my bare fuckin' hands."

Zee laughed. Not just a throaty chuckle, but a full,

high pitched, scary-as-shit hyena cackle. I wished I could've covered my ears, if only to pretend we weren't all at the mercy of this ruthless psychopath.

"Aww, so feisty. I wonder what it will take to break a man like you, Gil. Yes, I could take the easy route and execute your daughter in front of you." Zee looked at me, and I froze, my blood running glacial. "No, too easy. She only dies if she's guilty. We don't kill the innocent here. Fortunately, I have my pick of you and your troops, all of them guilty as sin. You'll die, Gil, but not too quickly, I hope."

"Fuck..." Daddy tried to twist in the mafia devil's grip, but he was too dazed, too screwed up to fight the death grip the man had on his throat.

"I'm going to break you first. We'll start with that one-eyed jackal at the end, and see how far we get today. Sound good?"

"Line..."

Oh, God. No. No, no, no.
Not Uncle Line!

The Vice President shared a look with daddy, and he nodded, accepting whatever fate these animals had planned. Daddy's eyes bulged in horror, and he shook his head, refusing to accept it.

I just cowered, trying not to remember all the times my Uncle Line bounced me on his knee, or let me stay up late when daddy was gone, watching crappy reruns and eating pizza.

The mafia men all seemed to have garrote wires like Zee. I watched one of them step up, put his arm around Line's throat, then pull a sharp string around it.

His life would be over in less than a minute, dying in a bloody, gushing heap. I imagined it before it even happened, and that sent me over the edge.

No more strong, brave MC princess. Just a scared one, a frightened young woman who'd never been cut out for any of this shit.

I cracked. I cried. I fucking *bawled* until my sobs echoed off the high rafters, wishing I could be anywhere but here.

Hell, wishing I could be back in my husband's embrace, the one who'd just disowned me because I'd been stupid enough to come here.

Fuck everything. Fuck my life.

I saw the mafia grunt's arm twitch, ready to do the deed on Zee's command. But he held up his hand instead, and barked orders in Chinese, a little more softly than before.

No, wait. Wait.

This little girl hasn't given us good reason to make her throw a tantrum just yet. Besides, this man doesn't even flinch. He's a fighter. Respectable.

Lay off, Yu. Back the fuck up.

We kill a coward first.

I couldn't believe my ears. Was I really hearing everything he said right, or had I just lost my mind with wishful thinking?

No, he'd actually changed his mind. I saw it a second later when the killer backed up, bitter disappointment on his face, fidgeting with his outstretched garrote wire.

Zee motioned, waving his hand to the right. *We'll go down the line. Choose the next man. Make this one bleed like the biker trash hogs they all are.*

Mercy wouldn't be so kind two times in a row.

"Wormwood? Worm! Fuck, fuck, fuck!" Daddy went berserk, screaming as the killer lifted the skinny man's head up.

Wormwood opened his mouth to beg, or else curse the man about to kill him, but he never got that far. The Black Dragon hovering over him pushed his wire deep into the biker's throat.

I turned away as the brother died. He choked, sputtered, bled all over the place. The men down the line next to him screamed or cursed or shook like bombs about to go off while the demon killed him, just inches away, and they were all powerless to do anything.

When the commotion finally died, I realized Zee had gotten exactly what he wanted.

My father faced the ground, several teardrops underneath him on the dirty floor. He'd made a terrible mistake, but he'd been so sure about double-crossing these assholes, and now they were going to kill all of us, slow and torturous.

Zee wasn't kidding around. I'd only seen daddy cry a

couple times over the years when he was losing mom.

Now, he did it again, except there wasn't any relief coming. No end to this nightmare, except for death.

The Chinese mobster had ruined him. And that scared me more than anything. It would've sent me into another hysterical, crying fit, if only I wasn't so achingly numb.

Zee's fingers trembled as he lowered his hand – probably drunk on triumph, the kind of glee a serial killer has when he's claimed a new victim.

Take them all away and clean up this fucking mess, he said in Chinese, nodding at Wormwood's limp body, face down in his own blood. *We're off to a good start. We can afford a few more days here.*

I came all the way from fucking Shanghai to have this foreign devil waste my time, try to kill me like a fool. This isn't just about making them all pay, and making sure their stupid biker club never does this again.

I want to have some fun.

It didn't sound any less insane in Mandarin Chinese. I closed my eyes and tried not to panic, slowly counting as I heard them moving around us, probably taking the five living club members back to their cage.

When I finally looked up, Zee crouched next to my father, his arm around him like an old friend ready to pass the bottle.

"This is how it works, Mister Hard Cock President. When we ask, you answer. Simple, Gil. Easy."

"Fuck. You." My father's blue eyes still reflected red,

murder, revenge.

"Now, now. I'm going to kill more of your men and I'm going to kill you. But every time you tell us the truth, you prevent us from putting little Miss Mathers under the wire instead. You're a sensible man," Zee said softly. "Surely, you'd rather watch the men you call brothers die rather than your own flesh and blood, yes? I know how it is. I have a daughter too. She would've been very sad if your little plot here had gone your way and you'd kept me from ever coming home again. Lucky for us, you fucked up bad, and I'm going to make sure it's your little girl crying instead of mine."

"Elle, darling, fuck...I'm sorry."

I'm sorry, I'm sorry, I'm sorry.

I wouldn't even listen to daddy's apology, even though he kept moaning it over and over until they dragged him away.

If I heard him say it one more time with Wormwood's blood still tarnishing the ground, I swear I'd lose my mind.

They threw me in an old shipping container with a bottle of water and a bucket to pee in.

A few boxes were left to sit on, empty wooden crates just sturdy enough to support my weight. When I couldn't stand anymore, I finally gave in, and sat on them.

What kind of illegal cargo had they held one time?

Guns? Ammo? Drugs?

The club had been involved in selling and smuggling all sorts of stuff over the years. Now, the chickens had come home to roost, and they wouldn't stop until they'd pecked out the eyeballs of everyone I ever loved.

I couldn't believe how dumb and stubborn I'd been. Jesus, how absolutely fucked in the head daddy had been to think this was a good idea, drawing the Chinese here to stab them in the back and gain – *what, exactly?*

I didn't even know. I regretted walking away from Asphalt in the park.

Not just because I missed his love, his touch, the way he faced down the world to keep me safe...I regretted it because Wormwood might be alive right now if I'd only told him the truth.

He wouldn't have let this fly. He'd have called up his brothers in California the second he found out, brought them up here, and they'd crash right through the walls of this dirty warehouse.

They could've wiped out the Chinese before they killed another Tacoma man wearing the Grizzlies patch. They could've –

Fuck it. What was the use?

All of this would've-could've thinking wouldn't save me.

I let my train of thought derail because it wasn't happening, however bad I hoped it might. If Asphalt didn't just decide to throw up his strong hands and walk away from all this, he'd have hit the nearest bar after everything that went down between us.

And I couldn't blame him one bit.

It started as a sham marriage, but I'd wanted to open up so badly. I should've told him everything, like I'd started to before he interrogated me, beginning with how badly I'd wanted us to be real.

But I'd lied to him instead. I'd taken on this stupid obligation to my father's club, all on a dirty secret daddy had kept from even me, and now I just might pay for it with my life.

No clue how I slept, but I did.

A day or two passed in that dirty, dark container. Pulling down my pants and carefully pissing in the bucket was humiliating enough. So was having to thank the bastards who came to feed me stale crackers a couple times a day.

They wouldn't turn them over, or the fresh bottles of water that came with them, until I said thank you.

And I did, pretending I didn't understand the vicious comments they made in Chinese between their laughter.

Bitch thinks so much of herself, doesn't she?

Let's bring her down. Zee won't notice. There's nobody back here – bet she sucks like a starving village whore.

Hell, maybe the boss'll let us fuck her in front of daddy if the shithead keeps us waiting. Still no secrets.

How many we got to kill to loosen up his lips? Maybe if we hold her down, fuck her instead, let him hear her screams...

Bitch is too polite. We'll play a game. First time she spits in our face and doesn't thank us for keeping her alive, we'll teach her a fucking lesson.

I learned to smile real big and say thank you each and every time. Thank God, there weren't very many of them.

They only came twice a day. Somehow, I walked on just enough eggshells to stop them from pushing me back inside the storage unit and closing the door behind them, leaving me alone with their dirty mafia cocks and savage threats.

I ate and drank to stay alive. Same reason I covered my ears every evening – or what I thought was evening – when I heard distant voices, screams, howls drowning in the unmistakable gurgle of human blood.

They were still torturing daddy and the brothers. Killing them.

I wondered who was left.

Jack-O? Line? Herc?

These men understood the risks of playing the outlaw game better than anyone. But *nobody* deserved to die with their hands bound while a bastard behind them slashed their throat.

So weak, so cowardly, and so fucking brutal.

I cried for them all. I prayed for my own miserable

life, and daddy's too, not caring about the fact that he'd put us here.

I swore that if, by some crazy miracle, I ever got out of here alive, I'd find Asphalt. Any way I could. Next time I grabbed him, and I wouldn't let go.

I'd be the best old lady I could be to the only man who'd ever been completely straight with me, the man I knew I'd been born to meet.

God, please, just one more chance. Don't take my love, my life, before I can confess it.

Mom had always been more faithful than me. It hadn't saved her from dying once the cancer ate her up, no, but it had eased her pain.

I was about to learn that sometimes when you pray hard enough, when nothing gets lost in translation, and luck is on your side, heave and hell both answer at once.

VIII: Uncaged (Asphalt)

Forty Hours Earlier

I needed a stiff goddamned drink after that shit in the park.

I was still in shock, squeezing the bars of my bike as it rattled down the road so hard I let the force shake me numb.

Didn't understand how the fuck she'd done it, but she had.

My baby girl fucked away everything. Showed me she didn't really give a shit, that she wasn't my babe after all, that she put her old man's dangerous games ahead of common sense.

Fuck, fuck, a thousand times, FUCK.

I'd have to tell the club now. Bring all the boys in to rain down hell on Tacoma, put a stop to whatever shit they were getting into with the Chinese. Had to move fast, too, before the motherfuckers ruined everything we'd fought for over the past year.

Then I could deal with the mad bloodlust burning in my fists, the need to shatter the whole fucking world over Elle Jo ripping out my heart.

I found a little watering hole just outside town. Recognized it from other runs, and I knew the owner had a loose affiliation with the club for years.

No sooner than I burst in and the boy behind the bar saw my patch, he motioned me over to a corner stool and slammed a shot of good whiskey down in front of me. I took it down my gullet without a word, closing my eyes as that hot, honey burn exploded in my guts.

Thank fuck for booze. Jack, Jim, and Johnny had never betrayed me. Not like pussy had.

I punched my empty glass down on the counter, making the only sound I needed for more, then ripped out my phone while I waited.

"Yeah?" Roman the Enforcer answered in his booming voice.

"Gonna need support from the guys up here after all, man. She wouldn't cooperate. Shit's coming down fast with the Chinese. Motherfucking imminent."

"What the fuck happened?"

I explained everything. Left out the part where I'd started to feel real fucking attached to Elle Jo, when I'd stupidly believed she might really be my old lady, instead of just being the woman I'd fucked before she fucked me over.

"She just took off with one of their prospects and you didn't stop them?"

I shrugged. "You really want me going martyr alone in

Tacoma?"

Roman growled his consideration on the other end of the line, and a sharp noise interrupted us. I heard his kid crying in the background.

His girl Sally made some soft, cooing noises to calm the boy down.

"Sorry. Yeah, brother, guess you're right. I'll get the boys together quick. Should get our asses up there by tomorrow evening. You keep your shit straight and try to get more intel. Find out if that bitch of a princess you married is just running, or if she's trying to lure us into a trap."

I knocked back my second shot while Roman put the phone down, his killer voice softening as he talked to his kid, his old lady. Something about that shit made me smile.

Too bad it also made me rage, reminded me of all the shit I'd lost.

No, the shit I'd never even had. Everything Elle started to make me hope for before she flung it around, broke it, smashed it to smithereens.

"It's not like that, brother. She's a crafty little girl, being who she is, yeah, but she doesn't want any bloodshed. We both agreed on that before she stepped out. There's no fucking way she'd help her daddy draw us into a meatgrinder."

Wasn't sure why the fuck I bothered to defend her, but I did.

"Well, she's made her choice, and so has her old man. She's eaten up her goodwill," Roman thundered. "Get moving. Find out what you can. The Prez won't wanna put a hole through her chest if we can avoid it. Doesn't sound like we're gonna be as lucky with the rest of those Tacoma fucks."

I nodded, feeling my chest tighten. One more day in the life where the bloodshed didn't end. It never bothered me before, but for some shitty reason, it did now.

"Take care of yourself and your family, brother. A man never knows how or when he's going to come back from the trenches every time we get ourselves into this shit." I meant it.

Roman just chuckled, hungry as ever for raw violence. Becoming a family man had barely lessened his appetite for ripping fuckers' arms outta their sockets, though he was more careful to reign in those urges since we'd all nearly died in our shootout with the cartel a few months back.

"Worry about your own ass, hothead. Shit, you're usually itching to settle the score more than me. What's gotten into you?"

I held up my empty shot glass and studied the light streaming across it. I knew *damned well* what – or who – had gotten underneath my skin.

That was for me. He didn't need to know it.

I'd just given him all he needed for a club briefing. The giant who'd held me down and knocked me out cold on a couple occasions when I got out of line was the last brother I'd confess anything to.

"Nothing. Just being up here by myself in their fucking den, I guess. Don't worry about it. I'll get as much as I can outta the locals for you and the Prez by the time you show up. I'll be ready."

"We'll be there in thirty hours. Thirty hours or so to get our shit together and ride."

The line went dead. I pushed the phone back into my pocket and ordered one more shot to clear my fucking head.

Once the poison wore off, I'd be back on the road. This time, I'd be demanding answers, and I wasn't letting *anybody* blind me again.

Gil's place was first on the itinerary. She'd always run back there before when shit went raw.

Daddy would probably be there to console her, tell her what a good girl she'd been to walk out on the bald headed fuck who'd always been too bad for her.

My body tightened, ready to tear open throats like a tiger. Didn't get any better as I rolled into our old neighborhood.

Hit the breaks when I circled by my parents place, now property of some young couple who'd probably make their kids a hundred times happier than I'd been. I let myself have one long glance at my the home I'd left years ago, feeling the grim past staring out the windows, looking right at me.

The fucks who'd bought my parents' place changed the color and the landscaping, but they couldn't do anything to banish the ghosts inside.

I could still hear my folks bitching at each other, before my old man walked out. Then the shitty soap operas and dog shows my ma used to watch, smoking and drinking herself to death. The woman put away more poison than half the guys I'd ever met in the club.

She hadn't lasted more than a year or two after I'd gotten patched in and blew town. Spent her last half year on this earth in a shitty fucking hospice, all she could afford on her meager bennies.

I remembered how shell-shocked Elle Jo used to look when she walked outside, not long after her ma died. Saw the girl cry while she was alone at the bus stop several times, while I played hooky at home and smoked in my room.

How many times had I wanted to march out there, pull her into my arms, and squeeze her 'til all her tears stopped coming, if only for a day? Shit, how many times had I stared at her ass while she disappeared inside her house? How many fucking times had I thought about her later while I fucked the nameless sluts I started pulling as a prospect, the only good thing that came outta my time with the Tacoma charter?

Too many brutal memories in this old neighborhood. I sped the rest of the way to her doorstep, letting my engine roar loud and lonely.

Maybe it was the Jack in my system, or else the hole in my chest that bitch left behind when she walked away. It hit me hard to stop and stare up at her old man's porch, remembering the first kiss that hooked me forever.

Even now, I'd kill a man to taste those lips. Preferably her old man, but fuck, anybody would do if it got me back in bed with that woman. I'd spill blood to feel her nipples go soft on my tongue, sink my teeth into her shoulder while her pussy clenched around me.

I had to shake off the lust. Remember why the fuck I was standing here, stepping off my bike and pulling out my binoculars about a block up to take a good look at the house.

The whole neighborhood was dead silent. I stood my ground and watched for a solid half hour, waiting for somebody to stagger out for some fresh air or a piss.

Her old man always had a prospect or two hanging around, but I didn't see so much as the dot of a lit cigarette shining into the night.

My girl had either avoided daddy's place entirely, or else there was nobody home.

Fuck it. I ran down the street and snuck near the back, climbing over the locked gate. There wasn't a bike in sight, the biggest sign yet the place was deserted.

If Gil's boys were here, they'd be guarding the back door, the flimsy weak spot most homes had. With one hand on my gun, I slammed my boot across the knob.

Fucking thing splintered with barely any effort.

Nobody greeted me with a bullet or a blow to the head as I stepped inside. The interior was just as pitch black as the porch outside. I latched onto the adrenaline in my blood and didn't let my guard down, but I took a quick scan through the entire house.

The basement was a little more interesting. A couple shotguns were laid out on a work bench, too clean and new to be antiques hanging out in Gil's place.

Papers were strewn across the chipped table, next to a couple hammers and a case of beer. I grabbed them and flicked on my lighter for some light.

"Holy shit." Couldn't stop the words when I saw what the fuck I had.

It was some shit scrawled in black ink over a ledger with the Ivankov logo at the top. The Russian mobsters based around Chicago did business with us sometimes out West, usually smuggled their shit through Seattle with our blessing and a hefty protection tax.

Chinese dealings ramping up in SeaTac, and they mean business. They'll hit your club hard if you don't hit the fuckers harder first.

Fool them. Play nice. Then break their skulls open. We'd rather do business with your boys than the Black Dragon assholes any day.

-Lev

Shit was dated about a month ago. Snarling, I tore the corner, stuffing it into my pocket. The other shit was a mishmash of notes back and forth between Gil and some asshole in the Black Dragon mob.

The lying Tacoma Prez acted real friendly, pretending he wanted to sit down for drinks and deals with the fuckers.

I wanted to believe he did all this shit by paper like a hundred fucking years ago because the cock hanging outta his mouth was too big to talk.

I flipped through more, taking it all in, quick little notes between Elle's old man and some mafia fucker – Zee.

It all made sense. Finally.

Gil hadn't turned rat. He wasn't the greedy asshole I'd thought, trying to make a special deal behind California's back with the goddamned Chinese.

It was worse than that. The stupid, stupid, *stupid* motherfucker was trying to gut the Chinese all alone, and he'd dragged Elle into it too.

Had to get this shit to the Prez. There'd be time to ball the Russians out later for going to Gil first instead of Blackjack.

Fuck, I had to save my girl!

I tucked the rest of the papers underneath my arm and ran outta the house. Still didn't have a clue where those fuckers were, but I'd find them. Just hoped to hell I'd get there before I turned on the radio tomorrow and heard about a massacre with one dead blonde caught in it on the local news.

Tacoma's clubhouse was almost as empty. When I rolled up, a couple scared looking prospects pointed guns my way, hiding behind the gates.

I marched up to the iron bars and put my hands on 'em, shoving my face through the middle. They nearly shit their pants.

"You're wearing the wrong bottom rocker," a kid named Carbon said, trying to sound tough. "We're not letting you in. Don't give a shit if you're the asshole who married the Prez's daughter."

"Open the fuck up. The whole Redding crew's on its way, and there's only two of you. Otherwise, you'd be calling for more guys when I'm standing on your doorstep like a fucking wolf."

The two prospects looked at each other. The other one had smaller balls. His gun went down so fast his buddy swore, reluctantly walked over, and pounded the switch for the gate.

I waited while it slid open.

Soon as I was inside, I put my arms around them both, and shoved them to the fucking ground in one swift push.

"Ow! What the fuck?!" Carbon roared, squealing louder when I stomped on his leg. Hard enough to scare him, press his ass into line, rather than do any real damage.

"Listen up, boys, *both* of you. Club rules say you're both with me now. You've been drafted. I'm guessing your officers are all MIA. That puts you under Redding's control since I'm the only full patch brother here."

"Brother? You? Fuck me!" The other guy rolled, trying not to choke on the irony.

"Yeah, asshole," I growled. "We'd better start acting like it, too. I'm guessing you wanna earn your bottom rockers and save your boys. Can't say I give a fuck about your futures in this club, but my old lady's with your boys, wherever the fuck they scampered off to. Here's how it's gonna go down..."

They didn't protest when I finally let 'em up. They took me inside the clubhouse and went to the bar.

They spilled everything there – all they knew, anyway.

I listened to 'em talk about the big raid, the dirty deal going down with the Chinese that wasn't really a deal. It was a goddamned ambush, just like I already knew.

None of these boys could've been any older than twenty-one. About the same age I was when I took on the patch for life and drew my first blood for these colors. They'd both made the right choice, saved themselves from a blade in the guts.

If Lady Luck decided to give us all a nice, big kiss today, then they'd both have a long life of drinking and whoring ahead.

I'd settle for undoing everything that happened yesterday at the park. As soon as backup came, we'd all be heading down to that warehouse where something had obviously gotten fucked up. They said their guys left hours ago, and hadn't checked in since.

I wasn't waiting to save my girl. Forget the divorce, forget disowning her, I hadn't meant any of that shit when she forced my hand.

I'd win her back, and make sure she knew her place forever this time. I'd tape her sweet lips shut if it saved her from ever risking her life again. And I'd also kill every last brain dead sack of shit who'd dared to put her in danger – even her old man. Shit, *especially* her old man.

Didn't care if the fuck was dead and I had to drag his ass up outta hell to do it. I'd make him pay for putting my woman's life on the line, so help me God.

I hadn't been fully sober this long in years by the time I heard the roar of my brothers' bikes. It felt like a fucking eternity waiting for them to show, and now that they were here, it was like a lightning bolt struck down my throat and got me moving.

Fists at my sides, I marched out before they climbed off their bikes and started busting open the gate. Soon as they saw me coming, everybody relaxed, Roman especially. I motioned to Carbon, and he smashed his hand on the gate's button with a sour look on his face.

"It's clean. No need to do a sweep," I said, nodding at Blackjack. "Just a couple prospects inside, and they're with us now. Come on, we can't waste another minute."

"Easy, son. Chances are the Chinese have already

ambushed Gil and his men. We've got to make sure we aren't wandering into the same trap." Blackjack got off his bike and stormed past me, moving as fast as his old war wound in the leg would carry him.

No way was he fucking serious, right? I wasn't gonna sit down and rehash all the intel I'd already fed Roman.

We'd wasted too much precious fucking time already. Elle Jo could be rotting away in some goddamned pit for all I knew!

"I can't let her die with them, for fuck's sake!" I started heading for my bike, pulled off just to the side. "We've gotta go now. The Chinese think they got the drop anyway, and they probably did with Tacoma. They won't see us coming. Let's –"

"Prez is right. *Easy.*" Roman slapped me on the shoulder and squeezed so hard it hurt. "We can't just ride in there with our dicks hanging out. You're letting your emotion do too much talking, brother. It's gonna make you a dead man."

Behind him, Brass and Rabid nodded. *Motherfuckers.*

All of them. I'd seen them working with the same manic energy boiling my blood when their girls were on the line. Yeah, the fucks were trying to do me a favor now, making sure cooler heads prevailed, but it sure as shit didn't feel like it.

"Asphalt, don't waste your energy taking swings at your brothers." The Prez stepped up, sensing the tension, looking like a wizard when the wind blew his long gray hair. "Let's huddle, son. Ten minutes. Just one of our boys getting shot because we could've used our brains is one man too many, I say. And as long as I'm sporting a patch that says President, you'd better believe what I say in this club is law."

Much as I didn't want to admit it, he was right. I tried to pay attention to everything coming outta the Prez's mouth for the next ten minutes, just like he'd promised.

Too fucking bad my mind was anywhere but here.

I couldn't stop thinking about Elle Jo. Almost as much as I couldn't wait to throttle every last sonofabitch who'd dragged her into their damned mess.

Blackjack rattled off some elaborate strategy like the sorcerer he was. I looked at the brothers one-by-one, sharing the same wicked energy brewing in their eyes.

Once he was finished, the Prez gave the order and we got on our bikes. The two Tacoma prospects rode by my side, all the better to keep them in line if nerves got to 'em. No man ever forgets his first battle, and these poor fucks didn't have as much on the line as I did.

My thoughts rambled like a goddamned freight train as we tore down the highway, weaving around cars, heading for the docks where the warehouse sat.

Hang on, Elle baby, I'm coming. I'm never letting go again, no matter how many times you stab me through the heart.

We're doing things different, babe, mark my word. I'm gonna save you, fuck you, and love you 'til disobeying me again is the last thing you've ever got on your mind.

And if you don't like it, I don't care. I don't fucking care.

You belong to me, and you always will, even when I'm telling you don't like a goddamned fool.

We're coming. You're coming home. Then I'm gonna make you come so hard on my dick I break every defiant little shred in your body.

We knew the Tacoma boys had run into deep shit when we perched on the hill overlooking the warehouse district. Roman looked through his binoculars and grunted, muttered something about rows of abandoned bikes.

He also said he saw a truck parked by the wall with blood all over the driver's seat. The lazy fucks hadn't bothered to clean up whatever the hell happened there.

I helped the big guy pull the fat tube off his bike and start setting it up. I've never handled a fucking cannon before.

Mortar, to be precise, the sorta portable shit guerrillas used when they wanted to put some explosive teeth into their hit and run attacks. This one wasn't gonna be blasting anything fatal, though.

Once we had it together, the Prez pulled his smoke outta his mouth and stubbed it out on the ground.

Blackjack looked at Brass, Rabid, and the two prospects who'd rode up from Redding. "Go."

They rode down the hill like demons, doing several passes around the warehouse, careful to shoot at anything moving inside if it looked remotely Chinese.

All hell broke loose when our group rounded the back. Orange fire exploded just ahead of my brothers' bikes, sending thick black smoke up into the sky above it. Roman's walkie-talkie hummed static, screams, and a raging curse that let us know our boys were still alive, even if they were busted up pretty bad.

Fuck, fuck, fuck...

I was already getting on my bike, the Tacoma boys at my side, before the Prez gave the order.

We roared down the same slope as the others, but this time we made a fucking beeline for the center gate.

The flash grenades Roman slung outta the mortar blew up a little bit ahead of us, just on the other side.

Perfect fucking timing.

About five Chinese assholes in suits came running out, guns drawn, just in time to get blinded. I didn't even duck as all three of us crashed through the gate, flattening it underneath our bikes.

Shots were already going off behind the warehouse, off to the side where our boys had driven into the big blast.

Fucking shit. The prospects at my side didn't have my aim. Most of their shots went all over the fucking place, but they managed to pin the mafia assholes down. A strange calm came over me, allowed me to put all five of 'em down like dogs with neat shots to their rotten heads.

I didn't kill my bike and step off it 'til I saw them stop moving. Then I charged, yelling after those fucks behind me to follow, hoping that shit Roman had on the hill wouldn't lob another flash bomb and blind us.

No way of knowing how many assholes we'd taken out. The shooting off to the side was dying down.

I hit the service door and found it locked. I swore, gave it my best kick, and cursed bloody murder when it didn't budge an inch, hellfire running up my leg.

"Get the fuck over here and pry this thing open, assholes!" I screamed at the prospects. "Gotta see what the hell's going on around the corner. Gotta –"

Another blast cut me off in mid-speech. We weren't the only ones who'd brought a few bombs to the fight.

The latest blast was just a distraction. No sooner than I looked at the latest orange plume rising high into the air, a van came tearing out the opposite direction. Fucking thing grazed Carbon's bike and nearly took out mine before it swerved.

It wasn't slowing down, not when the driver knew there was hell behind 'em.

It went tearing through the gate we'd knocked down, trying to catch it, but the motherfucker was just too fast.

I prayed to whatever gods had saved this club's ass in the past that Roman would take out their tires and cut them down before they got away. I prayed even harder that Elle wasn't inside, that we weren't too late to save her.

We couldn't be wasting our time here, killing assholes who were nothing but a distraction, while the real bastards escaped.

Too much shit was happening at once. The prospects busted open the door to the warehouse just as two more bikes rolled up, a very dazed and cut Veep with Rabid at his side.

Relief rolled through me to see them safe. Thank fuck for small favors.

They jumped off their rides and followed behind us as we pushed our way inside, guns drawn.

I almost puked when we walked through the dirty old cafeteria. It smelled like a fucking slaughterhouse. We saw why about a second later.

Men with bloody Grizzlies MC cuts were stacked up in a pile, dismembered and rotting.

"Holy fucking shit!" Brass swore, smacking himself across the forehead in disbelief. "That's gotta be half the Tacoma charter!"

The prospects lost it. They both dropped to the knees and barfed their guts out, Carbon and the other guy alternating holding each other.

I couldn't even roll my eyes. I'd expected some nasty shit before, but I'd never seen a fucking abomination like this.

Forced myself to keep moving. Had to. Not 'til I had Elle home and safe.

As the only asshole who wasn't paralyzed, I walked up and started combing through the dead bodies, holding my breath while I shoved severed limbs aside. All the guys had their throats cut, and it looked like the chop shop came later.

I held my breath, desperate to see whether or not there was a woman in there too.

Had to know if Elle was with them – even if it was gonna kill me as dead as all these poor sorry bastards.

"Christ, bro, what the fuck are you –" Rabid grabbed me by the shoulder and flung me around just as I finished.

"She's not here," I said, trying not to shake. Then the brief flash of giddy joy I hit the fucking wall. "Oh, fuck. The van..."

"Yeah, shit, we'd better check with Roman. It's all up to him now." Brass took one look at the gory mess I'd just combed through and shook his head. "Fuck. We're gonna hang this Zee asshole from his goddamned balls when we catch him. I can't believe this shit. All these guys with a Washington patch might be fuckers, but they're *our* fuckers."

"We'd better get our vengeance going fast," Rabid snapped. "We've got about five minutes to light this place up before every cop in the whole fucking Seattle area sees the smoke and descends on this place. I'd be surprised if some asshole hasn't phoned it in yet."

Shit. He was absolutely right.

Grizzlies always made a policy to cover up our battles, and we didn't have much time at all to burn this place to the ground. At least it would buy the club some time to bribe the investigators who'd find what was left, and save everybody in Washington from Fed snooping – if there still was a Tacoma charter worth saving.

"We have to find Elle. We gotta comb this place before it burns the fuck down! I'm not waiting up."

"Asphalt!" Brass swore behind me as I took off, heading outta the cafeteria through the old swinging door. "Goddammit!"

I couldn't get the van outta my skull. If they'd carted her away for more torture, more brutality, then I'd make theirs a thousand times worse. I tore through the warehouse, ignoring the pungent smoke beginning to drift through the empty spaces, all the signs this place was primed to go up like an exploding fucking blimp.

"Elle! *Ell-e Joooo!*" I screamed my lungs out, hands around my mouth to project it.

I stopped, held my breath, listening harder than I ever had in my fucking life.

Somebody tried to scream. Except they couldn't, their voice stopped like they'd been gagged. I kicked aside a few old crates stacked against a storage container – mercifully empty – and found three Tacoma boys hogtied with dirty socks stuffed in their mouths.

Fuck. Reaching for the One-Eyed Jack first, I tore off his gag and yanked him to his feet, pulling my switchblade to his bound hands to get the rope off.

It was their Veep, that battle hardened, scruffy motherfucker with one eye named Line.

"Where's Elle Jo?!" I screamed in his face.

"Elle? What the fuck? We've got to go after the van, brother, the Chinese took off with our fucking Prez and —"

I punched him clean across the face. Fucker was too dazed to fight back. I didn't give a shit about what they'd done to these poor bastards, or even the fact that asshole Gil was missing.

If the next few words outta his mouth didn't have to do with my girl, I'd knock him out cold.

Elle Jo took up a hundred percent of the space in my fucking mind, and she wouldn't quit 'til I had her in my arms.

"Is she with them? Did those fucks cart her away too?"

Line shook his head. "Storage. We need to get the fuck outta here."

He pointed with his free hand, beginning to work on cutting his brothers loose with the other. He'd ripped the blade right outta my hands, and I didn't even give a shit. I ran up the small ramp to the metal box and began pounding with both fists.

"Elle? Elle!" I shut my ass up for two seconds and heard a tiny muffled whimper. "Fuck, baby, is that you?"

I wasn't waiting to find out. The fucking door was

locked when I jerked it, a cheap ass padlock holding it shut. Guys behind me started to cough as thick gray smoke blanketed us.

The fire under my ass to get her the fuck outta there burned a hundred times hotter.

Grabbing an empty rusted barrel next to the storage tank, I went apeshit, bashing it against the lock 'til the impact practically shattered my bones. Had to hit it about ten times before the shitty plastic finally cracked, and I could reach inside, jerking on the guts. Tore them right out.

The newly freed Tacoma boys helped me pull. Fucking thing finally snapped, and I jerked open the huge double doors, rushing into the blackness.

What I saw inside should've stopped any sane man in his tracks.

Lucky me, whatever sanity I had left went flying out the fucking window about ten minutes ago.

My baby girl was slumped in the corner, her hands bound, a gag in her mouth, just like the others. I didn't understand why the fuck her jeans were down around her ankles 'til I saw the piece of shit next to her.

Elle looked up from her stupor, saw me, and started screaming through the gag. She motioned with her whole body, down at the man on the ground, rolling around on the rusty floor with his hand between his legs.

Didn't take a genius to figure out she'd kicked this fuckhead in the balls so hard she'd probably ruined him for sex forever. And if she didn't, well fuck, I was gonna finish the job.

I stepped on his gun as I approached, then kicked it across the floor where he couldn't reach. Mafia asshole must've lost it and been too preoccupied with blinding pain to pick it up, and now he never would.

I didn't even bother claiming the gun for myself. I had everything I needed right behind me. I rushed out between the bewildered looking guys, and pushed them aside a second later, a heavy metal barrel in my arms.

Elle Jo started screaming again through her gag when she saw the storm coming. She went silent, and so did the whole damned world, when I stood over the groaning mafia asshole and slammed it into his head.

His rotten skull caved with one crack. Not good enough.

Not even fucking close!

I knocked his goddamned teeth out and probably his eyeballs too on the second blow, and it only got worse from there. By the time the Tacoma Grizzlies shook off their stupor enough to grab me, and I heard Brass' pissed off voice behind me, I was a gibbering mess, my whole body burning on pure rage as I turned mafia asshole's brains into cherry mush.

Too fucking bad a man only gets one death. If I could've killed him a hundred more times, I would've.

When they finally slammed me against the wall so hard the whole storage shed echoed, what little I'd left attached to his neck couldn't be called a head in any proper sense.

"Let me up, you fucks! I have to set her free!"

"Calm down, brother. Rabid's working on it." Brass covered his mouth with his sleeve and coughed. "Shit. Fuck. We've gotta grab the girl and get the fuck outta here."

He turned to Line. "Was anybody else here tied up with you assholes?"

The Tacoma VP shook his head. I looked at my Veep and told him the same, said these boys were the only ones I'd found.

We knew exactly what happened to the others. The nasty pile of carved up brothers we'd found in the cafeteria told the entire story.

The fuckers let me down just in time for Rabid to finish cutting my girl loose. I knocked one of the Tacoma assholes flat in my rush to get to her.

"Fuck, baby, you're safe now." Rabid jumped outta my way as I pulled her into my embrace, sweeping low, reaching for her jeans.

I pulled them back up where they belonged with a growl. No man ever undressed her except me – and if I hadn't already brutally killed the motherfucker who'd tried, I'd have done it all over again.

"God. I thought I'd never see you again," she moaned, burying her face in my chest. When she lifted it a second later, we both started coughing.

Fuck, the smoke. It wasn't getting any thinner.

"Come on!" Brass' voice rang out through the haze. "Let's move our asses out right fucking now, before we all suffocate. This place'll be crawling with cops any minute too."

Elle Jo heard the man. She tried to follow me when I jerked on her hand, guiding her over the mess of the dead mobster on the ground, but she tripped on the fuckhead's dead body.

I spun, caught her, and swept her into my arms. I wasn't taking any chances.

I wouldn't let go, despite her protests. Just threw her arms around my neck and carried her all the way out, crushing her face into my chest when we went through the thickest smoke, holding my breath 'til my eyes bulged.

A couple of beat up Tacoma guys staggered through it and almost collapsed. Rabid helped them up, and we headed toward the service door, hoping none of the fires had fucked up our bikes.

Fresh air never tasted so sweet. I threw my girl on the back of my bike while the others got themselves set for the ride out. Sirens screamed in the distance. Big, loud fire engines judging by the sounds of it.

The Veep wasn't kidding, cops would be close behind the firetrucks, if they weren't already.

Shit! Blackjack and Roman gestured wildly by the gates. The look on their face said it all.

Move. Your. Asses.

We had to get the fuck out. There was no dealing with any of this shit the proper way, covering it all up. The club was gonna have to pull every damned string in the book to get outta this, especially when the officers found human bones inside.

"You hang on tight, woman," I told her, tucking her arms around me. "We're gonna be home soon, Elle Jo."

"Where's my dad?" she said, pressing her face into my shoulder as I started my bike. "You didn't find him, did you? Oh, God, he's not...dead, is he?"

I shook my head. "Dunno, babe. There wasn't any sign of him in there. You and three Tacoma boys were the only ones we found alive. We'll sort all that out later. Promise."

My words weren't much comfort. She cried for the first solid mile after me and my brothers crashed over the flattened gate.

About a mile later, we needed a whole different kinda comforting for the world shattering blast that billowed up behind us. Thought a stick of fucking dynamite blew out my eardrums. Rabid almost wrecked his bike, regaining control a second before he smashed into a concrete divider.

The lone civilian bread truck in front of us came to a total stop, and we all weaved around it in the nick of time. Elle fought to keep one arm around my waist, covering her damaged ear with the other. Her eyes in my mirrors were just as bewildered as mine, wondering if the fucking world just ended.

It hadn't, but the warehouse was toast. Whatever the fuck caught fire in there was big enough to leave a steaming crater and a small mushroom cloud that lingered in the sky for half a minute. Then the hot, orange death faded to nothing.

At the next light, I caught Blackjack's reflection. The Prez looked like he didn't know whether to smile or grimace.

That explosion had probably blown the fuck outta everything there that would've raised too many uncomfortable questions, but the Tacoma boys still had the club's name on this property. We'd be answering questions about hazardous substances and weapons of mass destruction, rather than the chopped up dead men and the mafia asshole whose head I've obliterated.

Fuck.

By the time we got to the Tacoma clubhouse, none of that shit mattered. The prospects who'd ridden out with my boys got off their bikes and hugged their full patch brothers. Their club had taken a lot of casualties, and with their Prez MIA, they'd lost their head too.

All the Redding brothers began to huddle, an improvised debriefing that would have to wait for me. I had bigger business right behind me.

I helped Elle off the bike and pulled her helmet away.

Then I hugged her so fucking hard it would've hurt, if both of us weren't running on raw, rip-your-guts-out passion.

"Fuck, I love you, babe. Forget everything I said in that goddamned park. You're still my old lady. You're my bride, now and fuckin' forever. You're my woman, always mine, and that's the way it always will be."

Her eyes were so dark. Haunted in a way that made me wonder if the Chinese had stolen part of her forever. But those blues lit up when I ran my hand over her face, amazed how her skin stayed so soft despite going through sheer hell.

"I'm sorry, Asphalt. Jesus, God, I'm so fucking sorry..."

She cracked. All my brothers stopped mid-sentence and watched as she poured her grief out all over me. I just held her, kissed her on the forehead, ready to keep her in my arms 'til she believed everything I told her next.

"Forget the past, babe. Whatever the fuck happened between us before, that was club politics. Club business that shouldn't ever involve an old lady and her man. Shouldn't ever land her in a pack of fucking jackals neither. Listen good, because I'm about to tell you how it's gonna be from here on out."

I waited 'til those bright blue eyes looked into mine. "You're home when you're with me. You're safe when you're with me. You're my whole goddamned world, and that's never gonna change. I don't let my world burn or bleed out on the ground." I paused, brushing away more tears rolling down her cheeks. "Tell me you understand. Everything's different now, the way it should've been from the start. That's a fucking promise."

"Asphalt..."

She just nodded, too fucked for words. I looked at my boys. They just nodded as I escorted her inside, walking into the clubhouse the Tacoma boys had just unlocked.

I'd find a place to lay her down, get her some decent grub, make sure she got some sleep. Then me and the boys would figure out how we'd track down the Chinese and nail their dicks to the closest fucking wall.

If her old man was still alive, he deserved the same treatment. That stupid, shit-for-brains motherfucker deserved a bullet in the brain for getting half his club killed.

As far as I was concerned, the asshole deserved worse for putting my girl in danger with his bullshit.

Elle Jo wouldn't ever work for the club and put her ass on the line again. Not for any charter.

She lived for me now, and as long as she did, I'd make damned sure she never had to suffer, bleed, or shake for this patch.

It took forever to calm her down. I made her drink water like a damned fish, and she heaved it up right away. I helped her sip more gently on the second go.

I talked to her the same way I did all those years ago when I saw her with that flattened bike tire by the road, about to go to tears from being so damned frustrated. Except this time, I put my lips on hers, stopping her before she could spill more tears with my kiss.

She didn't resist. I found her a cot and pulled her into it, throwing my arms around her. I held her and rocked her the way I'd wanted to since I put my brand on her skin.

"This is all my fault," she whispered. "Everything."

"Babe, kindly shut the fuck up. You know that isn't true," I growled, doubling down on silencing her with another kiss. "This is your old man's fault. He tried to do dirty deals with the Chinese behind mother charter's back, got half his guys killed, and almost got you fucked over on top of it. If we manage to track his ass down, he's gonna pay."

"Asphalt, no!" she snapped, shaking in my arms. "You don't understand. It wasn't like that. Yes, he did wrong. He never meant to do a real deal with them from everything I've gathered. He tried to draw them into a trap, he was going to take care of them before they became a problem for everyone, but they saw it coming. Yeah, daddy misstepped, trying to kill them first and underestimating them. But you didn't see the things they did, the way they slashed men's throats in front of us..."

She closed her eyes. I could sense the painful memories boiling her from the inside out.

That shit never went away. It would fade over the years, but a man never forgets blood and death. Couldn't be any different for a woman.

Fuck. If I could've drawn all that poison into me, wiping it from her precious brain, I would've done it in a heartbeat. Too bad life wasn't ever so magical, or so easy.

"Quiet, babe. You need rest. There's no point thinking about that shit now."

Yeah, right. The expression her face told me how stupid I was for telling her to shut down, as if it was the easiest thing in the world.

"We'll bring your old man home, one way or another," I said. "That's up to me and the club. Not your worry."

"He's suffered enough. Please, don't kill him or hurt him anymore if you do find him. I swear, he doesn't deserve what they've done to him."

I wasn't gonna debate.

Honestly, imagining Gil being tortured a hundred different ways didn't bother me. The motherfucker deserved it for the mistakes he'd made. He'd flushed a solid twenty years leading his charter down the damned drain by getting so many of his boys killed with this half-cocked ambush plot.

But having Elle there too, subjecting her to the same savage shit the Dragons cooked up? *Fuck.*

Maybe this Zee asshole deserved to die a little more than her old man. Also, rogues or not, the Tacoma charter still wore our patch. They were Redding's cousins in the Grizzlies MC.

No assholes came into our territory and hacked brothers to pieces like some Medieval shit without paying heavy. Every last Dragon was gonna die terrible when we had our reckoning.

I stuffed my desire to say more bad shit about her old man down my throat. She kept crying, and I kissed away the tears, whispering how she'd always be okay in these arms.

Just when she started to drift off, I rolled her over gently, and pulled down her shirt. Took a good, long look at the PROPERTY OF ASPHALT brand I'd put on her not so long ago, when she'd fought me all the way.

That ink meant everything. As long as she wore it, I'd make damned sure I lived by my word, and she never had good reason to bawl her eyes out again.

I closed the door gently behind me and found the brothers waiting by the bar. When Blackjack saw me, he stood up, and walked straight into Tacoma's meeting room.

We all understood, and everybody followed. Even the Tacoma boys didn't protest. That Line asshole hadn't made a peep about us taking over. He must've realized how bad his MIA Prez had fucked his club over.

Blackjack stood 'til everybody else was in their seats. Finally, the Prez sank down in Gil's beat up leather chair at the head of the table, folded his arms, and looked right at me.

"What did she tell you?"

"Nothing we didn't already know from the papers I found at her old house. Tacoma wanted to go rogue and wipe the Dragons out before the rest of the club got wise to it. The Chinese were a lot wiser to their Prez being a two-timing fucking idiot."

"That's my Prez you're talking about." Line's fist hit the table. "For fuck's sake, we don't even know if he's breathing or not, and you're all shittin' on his grave."

So much for the hour or two of brotherly love we'd had between charters.

The Tacoma boys sat next to their Veep on one side of the table, sizing us up, looking like they were ready to spit nails. Every Redding brother in the room bristled, except for Blackjack.

He wore the same iron calm on his face we'd seen a thousand times, awesome and scary-as-shit simultaneously. The Prez stood up, shook off the pain in his bad leg, and walked over to Line and his crew.

Roman's arms flexed next to me. His fists were more than ready to crack heads if they were stupid enough to try anything on our boss, the same man everybody in this club owed top allegiance.

"Asphalt's right," Blackjack said coldly. "Gil didn't have to go charging into hell's mouth after he got his little note from the Russians, did he? Redding, Klamath, and Portland would've been behind you. We could've dealt with them on our terms in massive numbers. We would've wiped them out without losing a single man."

Line snorted, trying to act tough, but he couldn't even look at our Prez. Gutless motherfucker.

"You don't know that, Blackjack. And shit, it's still no excuse for me and my guys to sit here and listen to your boys mouth off about our Prez trying to do good with the least damage possible. He was working for the whole club, dammit – honest! He deserves a little respect."

"The club? What about Elle Jo?" I jumped outta my seat and almost hit the ceiling. "That fucking dumbshit almost got my girl killed. You were there when we found her! Would've gotten that mafia asshole's dick between her legs if she hadn't kicked his balls off, and you've got the nerve to stand here and bitch about respecting Gil? Fuck!"

"That's enough, son," the Prez snapped.

Then I felt Roman's huge hand on my arm. I looked at the giant and he shook his head, urging me to sit the hell down.

"Thing is," Blackjack began, pulling out a smoke and stuffing it in his lips. "You boys have a point too. This club's all about respect – and that's got nothing to do with Gil. We all respect these colors."

He stopped, took his cig outta his mouth, and nodded at the huge Grizzlies MC banner draped across the wall. Most clubhouses had one, the same roaring bear on our patch in the middle, deadly as a modern pirate flag.

"The minute we stop respecting the bear is when we go to pieces. Every charter winds up at each other's throat if there's no brotherhood, no strength in numbers, no common cause. That won't happen on my watch."

Everybody in the room watched as he lifted his cig to his mouth and took a long pull. He made a show of turning his head away and letting smoke roll out his mouth when his lungs were full, intentionally not blowing it in One-Eye's face.

"We'll find Gil because we need to find the Black Dragons. Nobody fucks with this club," he growled. "If we let them dismember the Tacoma charter and hold a President hostage, however much he deserves it, we'll have every other group breathing down our necks in a few months. Japanese, Irish, Russians, Mexican cartel – hell, even the little shitstain MCs down in Dixie like the Deadhands and the Pistols will come gunning for their piece of the bear. It'll be open season on everybody sitting in these chairs. Killing your boys and taking Gil away in that van was a kick in the balls, no bones about it. We're not gonna fucking take it."

Line's fists were clenched so tight on the table his knuckles went white. He restrained himself, just listening. Smart man.

Before the Prez was done, I saw a hot tear spill a jagged path down Line's cheek, falling from his good eye.

"I want everybody in this room to stand up and shake hands." Nobody moved. The Prez narrowed his eyes and looked at us. "You heard me."

Blackjack waved us up with one hand. "If any one of you gets the urge to knife another man wearing your patch, you're helping the Dragons. You'll be treated like the traitorous fucking rat you are. Until we've got Gil back here and we're dealing with him *our* way, until we've killed every last one of the men who piled up severed bodies wearing Tacoma cuts like trash, no man in this room has any reason to hurt his brother. *None.*"

Fucking shit. The man talked too much sense for his own good. Sometimes it cut through our guts like a dagger.

Brass nodded and stood up first. We all watched as he walked over to Carbon, the Tacoma prospect. The lean kid stood up and shook when our Veep gave him the most aggressive, lung-crushing hug I'd ever seen.

Roman, Rabid, they all did the same. Even Blackjack embraced one of the full patch Tacoma guys we'd rescued.

I was the last one standing, looking at Line across the room. He started walking toward me, and I pinched fists so hard I thought my fingers would rupture like overcooked sausages.

The Tacoma VP came to a stop in front of me and flashed me a viper's smile. I threw my arms around him and we wrestled right there, trying to see who could crush out the other man's breath the fastest.

In the end, I let him think he won.

This brother was a damned fool for following Gil off the cliff and nearly losing his life over it. But he wasn't Elle's old man, the real SOB who'd stolen her away from me.

Gil did that with his fucked up failure of a plot. So did the Chinese when they'd held her, tortured her, left her with some pitch black poison memories I'd have to spend weeks fucking outta her sweet head.

Line and his crew didn't deserve to have the life choked outta them for obeying orders and putting my woman in peril. I knew exactly who did.

And once I found those motherfuckers, they were all as good as dead.

IX: Sweet Mercy (Elle Jo)

The devil in my dream screamed over the sound of gunfire, plus an explosion that sounded like it just ate half the world.

All Mandarin. All wicked words I wish I didn't understand.

You're going to come with me, little girl. Just as soon as you're finished coming on my cock.

It's a quickie. You and me.

You know how many hours I've been dreaming about tasting this pussy? Finding out how loud you scream? I never had American pussy before, and I'm going to ruin it.

He stared at me in the dark metal box, his eyes flaming animal lust. Zee's followers were just as insane as their leader.

Maybe it was the adrenaline pounding through my veins, or the fact that the demons hadn't even brought me breakfast. I barely knew what was happening when instinct grabbed me by the throat and slammed me down.

I couldn't let this happen without a fight. I had to stop

it, even it meant the end of me.

I waited until he started pulling down my jeans before I kicked. Hard.

My foot flew harder than I'd ever moved in my life. Hard as I wanted to live, to see Asphalt and daddy again, to avoid being used and abused in this stinking shipping container while everything went to hell around us.

The mafia man's eyes rolled back in agony as my shoe destroyed his balls. He hit the ground, groaning, clutching his gun until his fingers gave up and dropped it at his side.

Familiar voices started screaming. Someone pounded at the door, and I watched it pull aside on its rusty hinges. The love of my life stepped inside, obliterating the doubt and the mean words we'd exchanged at the park.

I knew I'd be saved. Asphalt won my heart, my body, and a piece of my soul.

Then I woke up.

I should've relished being safe and sound, alive with my man. Part of me did, certainly, but it wasn't over.

God Almighty. *It wasn't fucking over.*

I had to crawl out of my cot and find out what happened to my father before I'd ever have a peaceful night's sleep again.

A shower sounded like a good start. I walked into the tiny, grimy bathroom attached to the club room and stripped. Compared to the small, dirty space where I'd spent the last few days, it seemed like a five star hotel's bathroom. Even in the run down shower stall, it was a relief to have the filth stripped off my body by cold water.

At one point halfway through, I slapped the cracked wall tile with both hands and held myself there, crying out at everything.

If it hadn't been for Asphalt, I would've been a goner. Beaten. Raped. Dead.

I couldn't forget the insane explosion that ripped through the old warehouse while we raced away. Easily big enough to incinerate me and my would-be rapist, assuming he didn't fight through the blinding pain I'd inflicted on his balls and kill me first.

I turned off the water and stepped out. My reflection drew my eyes, and I hated it. I couldn't stop staring at the screwed up girl in the mirror, one who'd finally been bit by the life she'd tried to escape after all these years.

Sure, I desperately wanted to see my father alive again, but only so I could slap him across the face.

I didn't deserve this. Nobody did. He'd put me in mortal danger, gotten his men killed, and almost got the love of my life murdered on top of it.

Something changed when I was locked in that dirty, claustrophobic box. I reached up and touched the faded scratch on my cheek, one left by Zee that first evening, when he'd gotten up in my face, rough and menacing.

What the hell have I become?

There wasn't time to ponder. A loud knock on the little door nearly caused me to jump out of my skin.

"What?!"

"Babe? You awake?" Asphalt's voice had that concerned edge in it that turned my heart to butter.

Pausing to wrap a towel around myself, I flung it open, and his arms were instantly around me.

Warm. Loving. Reassuring in all the right ways.

"Fuck. I'm sorry I had to be gone so long. We were talking, me and the boys, figuring out how we're gonna hash out this shit with the Chinese."

"Kill them," I said. "Every last one. I don't care how, as long as you come home alive, and bring daddy back too."

"I'll bring him home, Ell-Bell. Me and the boys are real interested in dealing with his sorry ass for what he's done. We'll –"

I couldn't take the animosity. Not right now. I stood on the tips of my toes and shut him up, pushing my lips against his, hot and eager.

Asphalt growled into my mouth. His hands stiffened, caressing their way down my body. He grabbed the towel and pushed it down to the floor, then shifted his hands to my bare ass.

One fierce squeeze of those hands made me forget everything.

Sex wouldn't be the answer forever, but today, I really needed to be fucked.

He could take me away from everything – the killers I'd just escaped, all the ways I imagined they were torturing my father, the near certainty that the Redding charter would end up destroying him if the Chinese didn't do it first.

"God, I missed you," I hissed, dragging my fingers along his back. I scratched at his cut, straight across the bear patch and his bottom rocker, the symbol I'd come to love and hate in my sick, twisted life.

"Babe, you don't know the half of it. Get back in the cot, and I'll hold you 'til you sleep."

"No!" I put one hand on the back of his huge neck and held it, forcing him to look at me. "Don't leave me this time. Not tonight. I *need* you, and I need it so fucking bad."

His dark green eyes flickered. They moved in the whites of his eyes like jade pendulums, drinking me in, battling his vow to me against his oath to the club.

"Fuck." One word and a hand on my wrist told me who'd won.

He practically carried me to the flimsy cot and threw me down. He pushed me onto it, holding me down with his weight, tearing off his clothes.

His lips, tongue, and teeth teased down my shoulder, my back, stopping near the spot where I'd had his name inked on me forever. Asphalt pulled me up, and I moaned when I felt his naked torso on my back, the hardness he had between his legs, raging when he rubbed it against my ass cheeks.

"You're ready to give me your full attention, Elle Jo? Tonight, it's just you and me. Nothing else. You need it? I need to know I'm the only fucking thing on your mind. Nothing else deserves a shred of your attention except my dick. Nobody else is gonna give you *this*."

He rubbed up and down my ass, then angled his cock close to my pussy, teasing me. I shook as he pulled me up on all fours, making the position to take me deep.

I wanted to shake and die in this pleasure. I wanted to be with him. But those thoughts, those nightmares I'd just woke from, they wouldn't stop coming.

Closing my eyes tight, I tried to lie.

"I'm here for you, baby. Only you. Give me everything. Please."

Snarling, he fisted my hair. He tugged it, jerking my head around until his lips were against my ear. "No. Not 'til I can believe there's nothing on your mind except the dick that's about to fuck you senseless. I love you so fucking much, babe, and I'm a greedy SOB...you're mine. *Only* mine."

I heard him, but I didn't know what he meant – didn't *really* know – until his fingers pushed between my thighs. He shoved two fingers deep and held them in me, covering my clit with his thumb.

"Oh – Jesus!" I gasped, arching my back. "Fuck, Asphalt! Yeah..."

"Yeah," he repeated, quickening the loops his thumb

circled, digging into my clit in a hard, steady burn. "You whimper like that a couple more times, maybe we'll be getting somewhere."

His fingers moved inside me. My hips bounced back, caressing the full magnificent length of his cock. The guttural thunder leaving his throat vibrated in my bones, and I smiled.

There was something beautiful about being able to turn him on, even in this fucked up state.

"I knew you'd come for me. Never doubted it. Those words we had before were tough, and I screwed you over by listening to daddy like his stupid little girl. But I knew it wouldn't ruin this, Asphalt, this strange and wonderful thing we've built."

"Austin."

What?

"What?" I moaned, fighting for words through another full pussy stroke of his fingers, wondering if I'd heard him right.

"In this bed, you call me by my rightful name. The one that always loved you, babe. The one that watched you growing up and came hard as fucking diamond to you instead of any lesser slut. Shit, I don't give a fuck what you say, just as long as you know who owns this now, who's gonna own it 'til you take your last breath."

"Austin..."

It sounded so soft and alien after everything that happened. I'd used his name before as a curse, trying to get under his skin. Now, I whimpered it like a lover, especially when he rewarded me with more fingers, another kiss, and a quicker, dizzying lap around my clit.

"Come for me," he growled, crushing his lips down on mine.

And I did.

I came with my entire body into his hand. Sobbing, grunting, spilling out my pain, my love, my heartache.

He wrapped his free hand around my waist and kept his lips on mine. Asphalt swallowed everything, twining my twitching tongue with his, loosening his pressure when I started coming back to earth.

Tears were still rolling down my cheeks when he finally pulled his fingers out, and he turned his mouth to the nape of my neck, gliding down in soft, gentle kisses.

"No. I don't deserve this," I whispered. "Not after how I treated you."

He stopped, his muscles tensed around me. Grabbing my chin, he jerked my face until we locked eyes.

"Babe, what you deserve tonight is exactly what I'm giving you." His green eyes blazed, turning tender lover into manic killer.

I knew how badly I was fucked when that actually turned me on – turned everything below my waist to instant jelly.

"I wasn't fucking around when I told you earlier, I need *all* of you tonight. You're mine, woman, and I'm yours too. It's you and me here. The rest of the universe be fucked. And babe, I'm gonna fuck the ever-living shit outta you. Nothing barred."

"Oh!"

It shouldn't feel this delicious. Not after what I just went through.

Oh, but it did.

He pushed inside me without a second warning. Pleasure overwhelmed me, unexpected and molten hot. I arched my back and gripped the thin sheets underneath me for support.

Oh. My. God.

"All the shit that happened before?" he growled, nipping at my ear as his cock pulled back, slamming into me deeper than before. "Gone."

His hand moved up, pausing to maul my breasts, before moving up to my throat. He held me in a gentle, but not-so-gentle grip, the kind that said he'd love me and destroy me all at once.

The same grip I needed just then.

"All that shit we spat out our mouths, going at each other like mortal fucking enemies?" His cock thrust deeper, harder, faster, driving me out of my mind. "Gone."

Our breath came in long, ragged puffs. My fingers scratched, tore, ripped at the sheets until I couldn't even feel them anymore.

"Austin – don't stop!"

"No. Not 'til every last ounce of painful shit in your

life's a goddamned memory, babe. Told you, I'm fucking out everything. Killing it by making you come so hard you're blind to all the darkness." His thrusts quickened, rocking the cot between us.

It might give out, and I didn't care. Hell, I couldn't focus on anything except the lighting building around his cock, my pussy coiling around him, just a few more thrusts from sweet release.

I love this life when we're in bed.
I love this dick.
I love you, Asphalt.

A long, uninterrupted growl poured out his mouth. Long, punishing strokes filled me over and over again, so hard, so loving, he shook my entire body. My breasts swung beneath me, and he reached between my legs, found my clit, and added that miracle thumb to the maelstrom of his cock.

"I'm telling you now, and I'm telling you a thousand times, Elle Jo," he said, his voice starting to crackle like static from the pleasure ripping through him. "*You. Are. Mine.* Every last atom of shit that ever makes you doubt it? Gone. Now and fucking forever. And you'll know it when you pass the fuck out from coming on my cock."

I lost it then. *We* lost it together.

My pussy clenched his cock so hard I screamed. I came, feeling him stiffen, sputter, and add his heat to mine. Asphalt's seed pumped deep and hot, filled me until I overflowed.

We'd fused our love and hate. Maybe we fucked it away too, a healing fuck, just like he'd said. When he pulled out, he was still hard. He flopped on the cot and pulled me on top of him.

For the first time, I rode him with everything as his wife, his old lady, rather than the bitch keeping secrets.

"Fuck, babe, fuck! Just like that. Don't you stop for all the diamonds in the world, all the blood in the ocean. Love you from the tips of your toes to your ears, and everything in between. Really fucking love this pussy, too, and I'm gonna find out how much come she can take."

The second time I came, impaled on his cock, I couldn't even scream his name. I was too busy smiling, breathless and happy, numb to everything except this beautiful moment with my outlaw husband.

There'd always be more out there, waiting to hurt me. It could wait. We were too busy reconnecting, or maybe connecting for the first time.

He fucked me like the big, powerful, unstoppable badass he was, but I'd gotten a little of his spark. Nothing was keeping me from his flesh tonight. He'd ripped me wide open with soft, honest words and furious kisses.

I might bleed out and die a little before dawn, but I'd never die alone, without love.

Not tonight. Not tomorrow. Not ever again.

A couple days passed. Asphalt practically kept me under lock and key, bringing me food and fresh clothes, telling me to sleep. I spent so many hours in the cot I didn't know how I'd ever sleep again.

I left my room and walked into the empty bar, looking for something sweet and powerful to drown my worries for the next few hours. Looking at the selection made me wrinkle my nose.

These boys rarely drank anything except straight whiskey and thick, dark beers. Not exactly my style. The clubhouse hadn't been restocked in some time, which told me just how obsessed daddy and his guys had really been about going after the Chinese.

I passed on alcohol and chose a tall glass of water instead. It wouldn't make me feel better, but at least it would keep me healthy.

"Elle Jo?" A voice said behind me. "Package."

I turned around to see the prospect, Carbon, holding out a small cardboard box. I took it, feeling the confusion twist my face. Holding the lightweight box, I gave it a little shake.

"Who's it from?" I asked, turning it over. There wasn't any return address.

Carbon had gone behind the bar to dig around, coming up with a grin when he found half a bottle of Jack. "Huh? Oh, don't have a fucking clue. Found it stuffed outside in the club's big locked box for deliveries this morning. Nobody gets in there without a key except the mailman, so it's gotta be somebody who knows you."

"Hm." I reached over to the bar counter, where I'd seen a pair of scissors, and began slicing off the tape.

A strange odor hit me in the face as soon as I pulled back the flaps. The top was stuffed with a scrappy piece of paper smeared with red ink.

It took me a minute to realize what I was seeing.

"Jesus Christ!" Before Carbon could even stop sucking on his whiskey, I realized it wasn't red ink.

Blood formed blocky, messy letters meant for Blackjack, and for me.

GO FUCK YOURSELVES. NO TIME TO TALK. ONE CUT AT A TIME MAKES A DEAD MAN.

ZEE

I never should've let my hand wander into the box, searching underneath the paper. When I found what was making that stink I'd smelled before, the whole world started spinning.

My fingers gripped something cold, soft, and pliant. Fingers slipped through mine, stiff as plastic. I pulled it up and screamed, all I could do before I slid off the bar stool and hit the floor.

"Babe? Fuck, baby, wake up!" Asphalt kneeled on the floor, shaking me.

I opened my eyes and saw half the club standing around me, a mixture of bewilderment and rage on their faces.

"They're killing him!" I screamed, jerking up into my man's strong grip. "That was his...his..."

"Quiet. Don't fucking think about it. We're taking care of it. No more packages are getting to you without going through me first, woman. That's a goddamned promise."

"It was daddy's fucking hand, Asphalt! I can't just forget."

"No, babe, you can't." He pulled me in tighter, hiding my face in my chest, running his strong fingers through my hair. "But I'm gonna make you try. And you can be damned sure all those motherfuckers will pay for what they've done."

"Shit's downright fucked," the big one named Roman thundered above us. "Nobody starts carving up a Grizzlies Prez and sends us the pieces."

I sobbed all over again, smashing my face into Asphalt's chest. I still couldn't believe what I'd pulled out of the mystery package, what I'd held, feeling it ooze dead blood onto my wrist!

"I shouldn't have approached them." Blackjack walked up and laid a cool hand on my shoulder. "I'm sorry about this, girl. I thought we could lure them into a meeting, a ruse for peace, then hit them the same way we've dealt with our enemies before."

Asphalt looked at his leader, fury shining in his green eyes. "It would've happened anyway. Everything she's told me says these fucking jackals are sadistic as the day is long. We gotta change tactics. They know what we did to the cartel several months back, and they're doing the same fucking thing to us."

I staggered up with Asphalt helping me. Line stood in front of me, fists flexed at his sides, his face turning red around the eye patch.

"I'm so fucking sorry, Elle Jo." He grabbed me, pulled me away from Asphalt, and squeezed.

"I just want him home safe, Uncle Line. You *have* to help."

"Already on it." My adopted uncle gave me one more reassuring squeeze before he released me, looking at the Redding men.

"We've got to hit them hard, as soon as we can. We wait another day, another week, there won't be nothing left of my Prez and her father. What's the intel say?"

The boys started talking about war among themselves. I faded out, too numb to comprehend what they were saying.

Blackjack nodded at Asphalt, and my husband led me away, back toward the room that was starting to feel like a cell. Halfway there, I slapped his chest and backed myself against the wall.

"No. I need to get some fresh air."

For a second, I worried he'd try to drag me back into the room. Instead, a thin smile curled his lips, and he took my hand.

"I know just the place."

We headed for his bike and left the clubhouse. The wind helped dry the tears sliding down my cheeks. Locking my hands tight around my protector's waist warmed the glacier building inside me.

I barely paid attention to where we were going. Didn't look around until I heard him kill the engine.

Of course. I should've recognized it sooner.

He'd brought us to the same park where we'd clashed our first night here, when he'd dragged me down in the dirt, kissed me in the rain and lured me into bed.

"Let's go for a walk, Ell-Bell." He helped me off my bike and we headed down the trail, both of us turning briefly to the spot where we'd first wrestled with our love and hate on the ground.

"Look, I know you hate him," I said. "You think he's a demon who put me at risk. You probably want to strangle him for bringing me to the Chinese and almost getting me killed, I understand that. I just *know* it wasn't supposed to go down that way, though. Daddy got a little reckless, and he should be balled out for that, or whatever you guys do when somebody goes against orders in your club."

Asphalt's face showed nothing while I made my plea. I looked at him, moistening my lips, praying he'd truly listen to what came next.

"He doesn't deserve to die like this. You have to help him, help me, Asphalt. If he's going to be butchered like an animal by those fucking monsters, it'll kill me."

My voice cracked. I stopped in mid-step next to a tall tree with him. For a long time, he didn't say anything, just held my little hands in his, running his free hand up and down my cheek, wiping away every tear.

"God damn it, I love you," I sputtered. "And I'm sorry too. I'm sorry I didn't listen sooner. I could've talked him out of this, maybe. I could've –"

"Babe, don't. You couldn't have done shit."

I opened my eyes, blinking back fresh tears. He pulled me into his embrace and just held me against the breeze, protecting me from every kind of cold I'd been hit with lately.

Here, I was really, truly safe. Shielded from everyone who'd ever try to hurt me, every tinder of pain and terror ignited by this world and the wolves who were constantly circling each other for dominance.

The MC had caused a lot of pain and terror, no doubt about it. But it could also be a fortress when it needed to be, a place for men and the women they claimed to find what they needed to survive.

Right now, I had everything I truly needed in my arms.

"I told you before, and for some fucked up reason, you keep doubting it. I'm gonna bring your old man back here alive. Then I'm gonna bust his fucking jaw myself for his mistakes. The Chinese *won't* get another piece of him."

I swallowed the bitter lump in my throat,

remembering how cold, disgusting, and alien his dismembered hand had seemed in mine.

"How can you make that promise? He might already be dead, Austin."

"He's not, Elle. I've known fucks like the Black Dragons before. It's not all business to them. They're bastards, like big cats. They like to torture their prey nice and slow before making the kill, and they'll probably try to do it when somebody's watching." Asphalt looked at me, his green eyes going dark as the Pacific tide. "Your old man's alive, and he's in hell."

My face cracked again, but not before he reached up, cupped my chin, and pulled my face close until we were just inches apart.

"We'll bring him home. One week. I'll ride everybody in this fucking club 'til they do it, or fuck, I'll take off and deal with them myself. This is the last day you're ever gonna cry, Elle Jo, and I'm the man who's gonna make you stop."

How could I argue with that confidence?

I couldn't. Not when he jerked me close to his chest, tipped my face, and kissed me so hard I thought I'd faint all over again.

The boys were away all evening after we got back. I heard rumblings from the big meeting room next door, and the occasional shout, Blackjack slamming something hard against the table, calling men to order.

Finally, the door popped open and hit the wall, and men came filing out into the bar, rumbling among themselves.

Asphalt opened my door, came in, and sank down into the worn loveseat next to me.

"Well?" I said, trying not to let too much hope creep into my voice.

"I shouldn't be talking club biz with you, babe, but I'm gonna make a single exception to say this." He paused, and looked at me with a stare so intense it turned my blood cold. "We're sure the Dragons are holed up in an old plant just outside Portland. Intel says your old man's alive, just like we thought, though I'm not sure being handcuffed to a fucking radiator with one hand can be called living."

I didn't care. Hearing confirmation that daddy's heart was still beating was enough for me. I jumped up, threw my arms around him, and kissed the stubble on his cheek.

Only problem with kissing this man – I *always* wanted another taste. No matter how dark or strained or dire things might get, he drew me like fire.

Familiar needles stabbed at my nerves. I ran my fingers down his back, remembering how amazing it felt to have his naked skin on mine the night before.

"Not so fast," he said, pushing me away with a dark look on his face.

"What? What's wrong?"

"Busting in and decapitating the motherfuckers isn't as simple as it sounds. The Portland boys tell us this place they've got is built like a brick shithouse. Club's got their lawyers doing their damnedest to deflect the shit from the Feds after that warehouse went up like a small fucking nuke. Thank fuck everything around it was abandoned, or we'd really be up shit creek. We can't have another firefight go down like that. Our network with dirty cops in Portland doesn't run as deep, and we'll all end up behind bars if the Chinese trap this place like they did the last one, start blowing shit up when we tango..."

I wracked my brain. I wasn't even close to cut out for advising on strategy, but there had to be *something* they could do, some way to take down the bastards torturing my father without drawing too much attention.

"Does anybody in your Portland crew know Chinese?" I smiled as he looked at me like I'd lost my mind, already knowing the answer. "Thought so. Daddy was going to use me to make sure no tricks were going down when they talked among themselves, back when I thought they had a deal on paper. Maybe there's still some way I can help, figure out what they're really planning."

"Elle, no. *Fuck no.*"

Asphalt grabbed me by the shoulders and gave me a hard shake. "You're not getting within a hundred fucking miles of that city, or between our guns. Besides, even if I lost my mind and let you show up there with us, they'd know something was up, bringing you back. I'm not gonna do it. That idea's completely fucked."

"But –"

"No. We don't need to figure out what the assholes are saying to each other anyway. We just need to kill 'em dead without making too much racket."

Honestly, it wasn't like I had a master plan for dealing with the Dragons. But I wanted to help, damn it.

I wanted him to listen, give me a chance, help me help them save daddy.

"We need to get ready to leave. I've said all I'm gonna say about this shit, and we'll part ways at this clubhouse tomorrow, assuming the Prez finalizes a viable plan for cleaning up this damned mess."

"Leave? Where are we going?"

"You deserve better than this shitty cot for a good night's rest. I booked a place in town for us tonight. Let's roll."

The motel wasn't super fancy, but my aching shoulders didn't care. The bed was a *huge* improvement over the beat up cot we'd spent several nights on, and even that felt like heaven after the two unforgettable nights I'd had nightmares in the dark, rusty storage unit.

We grabbed burgers and headed to our room without saying much. I wasn't going to keep fighting him on my offer for assistance. Not today, anyway.

The tension rolling off him was so thick I could feel it curdling the air.

Asphalt's entire god-like body rippled in a constant state of tension, just how men always felt when they were about to go off to war.

Neither of us knew when the trumpet would sound and he'd have to ride off to Portland, or God only knew where. As much as I wanted daddy home and the Dragons buried so all of this could end, I feared for him.

He had to feel it in my touch. I caressed him a little more gently, and hugged him tighter than before, throwing my arms around his strong neck and pulling him to my lips.

We'd be fucking soon, both of our bodies begging for it as we twisted playfully in bed, the TV chattering away on low volume behind us. Deep down, I prayed it wouldn't be the last time, but if it was, then I had to make this the best night he'd ever have in his life.

"Fuck, babe, you've got a kiss men will kill for," he growled, pulling his lips away from mine after he'd already heated my mouth to about a thousand degrees.

"Yeah? How many men?" I teased, running my fingers down the middle of his chest, trying not to bite my lip while my touch reminded me how hard, how strong, how ferocious he really was.

"Don't bullshit me," he snarled, folding his arms around my waist and flipping me over, until I lay underneath him, my legs spread wide. "You already know I'm the only one who'll ever own this pussy. You're wearing my brand, Elle Jo, and I'm gonna live to see lightning inked all over you."

"Mmm," I said, running my ankles up over his thick calves. "Guess that means you'll have to come home to me safe, after all this is over."

"I will fucking *die* for you, baby girl." His green eyes and the thunder in his voice turned deadly serious, making my breath catch in my throat. "But not this time. I'm not leaving this earth 'til I've fucked you a thousand times and watched you get fat from all the kids I'm putting in you. *I'm not fucking leaving.*"

"Pig! You're really set on this baby thing, aren't you?"

The crass promise made me laugh. I pushed at his chest, making sure to dig my fingernails in past his shirt, just deep enough for him to feel how bad I wanted it.

"Yeah, baby, I fucking am. I've already got your ring, your brand, your heart. I want the rest, Elle Jo, and you'd better believe I'm aching every damned night to knock you the fuck up. If you hadn't already been so sloppy with that birth control shit, I'd have flushed your pills down the fucking toilet, I want it so bad."

Okay, I officially had a madman on top of me.

But instead of flipping out or cowering in horror, my pussy melted in my jeans. His insanity turned me on like nothing else, the same raw, masculine possession that made me his before I'd accepted it, when I was just a naive little girl.

"You're talking crazy, baby," I whispered softly, running one hand across his cheek. "Daddy's going to need my help when you bring him home. I need to find a good job. He sent me to college for a reason, and I'm not exactly a stay-at-home kinda gal. You know that."

"Babe, you know I do. And I don't give a single fuck," he growled, silencing me with his tongue in my mouth before I could say anything back. "You're giving me a kid, and it's gonna happen soon. I'll take care of the rest. The club'll help your old man, once we see how fucked up he is, and I'll make sure you get a good job."

I smiled, shaking my head, already knowing what he was about to suggest.

"You already learned that Mandarin shit. The club's gaining more international business all the time. No reason you can't learn Russian or German or Japanese, too. Shit, you can learn whatever the fuck they speak in the north pole for all I care, just as long as you're happy."

Laughing, I punched him playfully. Asphalt smiled, and wrestled me harder into the covers.

He'd given me too much to think about today, especially when the danger wasn't close to over. But the nightmare from this morning already seemed like ancient history.

I swore this man's sex appeal and the good heart he had underneath the roaring bear tattoo did something to bend time, rolled it back. Or maybe he just made me forget, and his body was the best amnesia a girl could ever have.

His hands pulled at my clothes. He had them off in no time, and then he kicked off his own, exposing each layer of his perfection a little at a time.

Asphalt's big chest rose and fell when he was naked, his excitement building. I pulled him into me with another kiss, feeling his cock rubbing against me.

"So fucking tight," he grunted, pushing into my wet pussy.

He stretched me, filled me, and held his cock deep. I gasped, electrified with pleasure. My legs locked around his.

The hunger was too great tonight. This wasn't a time to take it slow and explore. I needed to be fucked – hard.

I arched my body, pushing my lips eagerly against his. He growled into my mouth and began moving his hips, fucking his way into me, making my whole pussy ripple with his power.

My clit burned. Each thrust came harder, and I wanted even more.

I needed him to fling me around the bed tonight, take me, own me the way he'd promised. It had to be hard, rough, and merciless so I'd have something to hold onto, something I'd never forget.

Bad things had already happened. In this life, the worst was always around the corner. If it came, I didn't want regrets.

I had to get fucked so hard I'd remember this night

forever. Remember the raw love and energy in every bed slapping thrust.

I took him eagerly, moaning when he sucked my bottom lip into his mouth, digging his teeth in. Asphalt thrust harder, holding his pubic bone against me, grinding his dick inside me like a bull in rut.

"There, there!" I whimpered, breaking the latest kiss. "Harder."

Our eyes were electrified. I saw unbridled lust in his jade, and they reflected the same lightning in my own soft blue eyes, suddenly alive with the need to fuck like mad for just one night.

"Fuck, baby girl, sometimes you make me wanna do nasty, terrible shit." He slowed for a second, twisting my blonde locks around his fingers.

"So do it," I said, throwing my hips into his. "Do them all."

I wasn't sure what kind of challenge I'd just given him, but he accepted. Next thing I knew, he pulled out, and flipped me over, slamming me down on the bed with one hand in the small of my back.

"You'll hurt for me a little first," he growled, rubbing his stubble against my ear. "Then you'll feel so damned good you'll never know how you lived without being fucked with no limits, Elle Jo."

That was the only warning I got before he shut up and brought his open palm down on my ass. I jerked with surprise, feeling the hot, red needles shooting through my buttocks.

I'd left myself wide open. His cock pushed against my pussy, sinking into me from behind, picking up where he'd left off.

"You fuck me with everything you've got, little girl, or I'll hit you harder. Show me you fucking love me, babe. Show me you can become a total goddamned slut when you're not teasing me with those soft kisses and the fire on your lips."

Yes, sir!

I threw my hips back into his so hard the bed began to shake. I fucked him for all I was worth, feeling him slap my ass again whenever I slowed down, desperate to meet his frenzied thrusts.

It didn't take long. The molten fire building up inside me broke through my nerves, the sharp, delicious agony he'd left on my ass cheeks blending like never before.

I'd never thought I was into this kind of stuff. Tonight, I stood corrected, and I think I became the biggest pain slut who'd ever lived.

Being spanked by the wild animal fucking me from behind sent me into a universe of blinding pleasure I'd never imagined. When I came, my pussy tightened so hard on him he had to use all his strength to keep going through it, fucking me into an orgasmic frenzy, robbing all of my senses except one.

My mouth opened in a perfect circle and I tried to scream. But nothing would come out. My lungs burned to keep oxygen flowing into my convulsing muscles.

And I twitched *hard* on his cock, flopping like mad, especially when he growled. Asphalt pinned me down so I couldn't move, leaving me a prisoner to his thrusts.

I couldn't tell where the first blinding release stopped and the next began. I couldn't talk, couldn't breathe, couldn't even scream as he owned me in the deepest sense.

He played me like his personal instrument, pulled every one of my strings tight, until they snapped off in the relentless fist tangled in my hair, the savage thrusts fucking me into carnal seas that tried to drown me.

Can't breathe. Can't breathe – and I fucking love it!

Pleasure overwhelmed me. I thought the storm was breaking when I felt his fingers on my ass again, spreading me open, just above his pistoning cock.

Two stiff fingers sank into my virgin hole. He held them there, stroking me, while his cock slammed deep in my wet pussy.

I came again, panting bloody murder, somewhere between a scream and a moan.

His name was the only thing on my speechless lips. I mouthed it like a mantra as both my holes tightened on him, and he erupted deep against my womb with a vicious roar.

"God. Fucking. Damn it!"

The pleasure ripped through us. So hot, so intense, so wild I swore we'd fused into one shaking, grunting being for the next few breathless minutes.

Austin, my love.

Asphalt, my life.

The one, the only, the love I'd always have written in blood, sweat, and tears.

When it was finally over, I felt his hot seed trickling down my leg, just as he drew his cock out of me.

"Jesus, Austin," I said, focusing all my energy so I could roll into his waiting arms. "What the hell was that? Who knew sex could be so...so..."

"Explosive? Yeah, babe, it's a fucking grenade when you're with me. You think you've got it all figured out, that you know everything I can do, but you haven't seen shit." Grinning, he rested his forehead on mine, calming my lips with his before he spoke again. "You don't have a fucking clue how I'm gonna make your body shake in all the years to come. Can't wait to show you, Elle Jo. Cannot fucking stand it."

The boys were heading down to Portland soon. I overheard the whispers at the bar, sensing the tension coursing through the clubhouse like a dying autumn wind.

The Redding men who'd taken old ladies made their calls. I heard Brass, Rabid, Roman in their private moments, telling their women they were going to come home safe, the last rites an outlaw has before he puts his life on the line.

My heartstrings strummed each time. And every night Asphalt kept me at the hotel, holding me tight against his chest when we weren't fucking hot and hard.

"You're staying under lock and key, babe," he told me. "We'll keep a couple prospects playing rear guard to make sure you're safe while we make our big run. Don't fuck with them. They're trying to do their job."

I tried to keep what he said in mind. I'd grown up with daddy's prospects and brothers hanging around constantly, so having my own little security detail wasn't anything new.

Too bad familiarity breeds complacency.

The men were locked away all day in their meeting room, probably drawing up their final plans before they hit the Chinese hard. I had to get away from it, go somewhere to clear my head.

Carbon drove me out to the park where Asphalt and I formed our special connection. I was looking forward to a nice, long walk, trying not to fume that they'd completely ignored my offer to help them translate.

Okay, so maybe there wasn't a place for my services, and putting me back in the danger zone was too much. But I could've went with them, damn it, could've followed them down to Portland for moral support or more, if they needed to know what the Chinese were really saying when they spoke man to man.

Carbon wisely kept his distance. I walked the long trail up through the hills, looking back over my shoulder.

Fresh smoke curled from the prospect's mouth into the cool Pacific air. I couldn't tell if the look of boredom on his face trumped the disappointment that he was being left behind to look after me while the others rode away to war.

Dark thoughts crept up on me for the past twenty-four hours, until I couldn't hold them in anymore. Losing daddy and Asphalt both was a real possibility, and it gripped my heart like a boa constrictor, threatening to squeeze the life out of me one anxious second at a time.

No. I couldn't think like that. I had to stay strong, for both the men in my life.

They deserved better than defeatism, and so did I.

The sun picked a perfect time to break through the dull gray sky. For just a second, I stood underneath the lone beam, warming myself. Tried to absorb some sign from the universe that everything was going to be all right.

If nothing else, it gave me the strength to get moving again. I told myself I'd hit the books later, maybe figure out what other languages I could learn for the club as a backup plan.

Yes, I was actually considering Asphalt's crazy career offer.

I rounded my way off the trail and looked for Carbon. Where the hell was he?

He wasn't by the tree anymore. I shrugged, thinking he'd gone off to the public bathrooms or something.

Maybe he'd snuck inside the small service building for a nip of something from a canteen – all these biker boys had to fall back on when they got bored and couldn't get into any new mischief.

I headed for the building. Pushing open the men's room door, I poked my head in, taking a quick, cautious look inside before I called his name.

Of course it had to be one of those old bathrooms that curved around a tiled bend, the kind that didn't let you see anything without walking straight inside.

Somebody's footstep scraped the floor and a man cleared his throat.

"Carbon?" I yelled softly, staying just behind the corner. "Is that you? I'm ready to get out of here whenever you're –"

The man burst out from around the corner and tackled me to the ground. Before I could even scream, I hit my head on the concrete floor so hard my ears rang. He dragged me by the legs, and in the blinding pain, I couldn't even think to fight him.

My legs wouldn't kick. My hands wouldn't claw at the ground. He swung me around the corner, kneed me in the spine, and began tying my hands behind my back.

I caught a flash of several other devilish looking bastards in neat black work shoes, their cruel faces smiling. Each one wore the same small golden dragon head on their lapels.

I managed to scream for a solid second before the

Chinese mobster clapped his hand across my mouth. Cold, deadly steel pushed against the length of my back, making me shudder.

"Scream again and we'll cut you open like your friend." He turned my head harshly, pointing it toward the dirty stall with its door swung half open.

Oh, God.

I recognized Carbon's thick riding boots unnaturally touching the ground. Blood pooled out beneath his body where they'd laid it on the toilet, a thick, red stream that could only be coming from his stomach.

He wasn't moving. He had to be –

Shit. I sobbed against the asshole's hand, and the blade of the knife dug deeper into my back, one more ounce of pressure away from doing everything he promised.

"Just try my patience again, bitch. You got my brother killed. You're coming with us to talk to Zee, and you'll tell us everything you know before we rip your whore throat out."

Behind him, the other two laughed. They whispered several words in thick, angry Chinese, the last thing I heard before the pounding in my head caused me to black out.

Save your energy, brother Zhao. She'll have a heart attack when she sees what we've done to her idiot father.

X: Crusade (Asphalt)

"Gone? What the fuck you talking about?" I sat up in my chair, looking across the desk at Blackjack.

Roman's hands instantly fell on my shoulders, trying to keep me from getting outta line.

I shot him a nasty look. Fuck him, and fuck anyone who got in my way!

If somebody had really taken Elle Jo, like the Prez just told me, then I'd punch a hole through the entire fucking earth to get her back.

"A small strike team, no doubt, probably sent up here just for her." The Prez folded his hands neatly and looked at me, his dark eyes shining. "You deserved to know since she's your old lady, son, and we're going to bring her back. That's why I brought you here."

"You're damned right we will!" I growled, shrugging off Roman before he could get a death grip on me. "We oughta be loading up and hitting the road to Portland right now, for fuck's sake. No delay. What difference is a few hours early gonna make?"

"Not so simple," Blackjack snapped. "There's heavy storms rolling through just south of us now. The Tacoma men need time to mourn their prospect, at least a few hours to shake off the shock."

They'd found Carbon completely gutted at the same park where I'd truly owned my girl for the first time. He seemed like a good man, but I couldn't care about that shit right now.

I couldn't be fucked to think about anything except where my woman was, and what the bastards who had her were doing. That fucking animal I'd beaten to a bloody pulp in the storage container had been about to force himself on her, tarnish what was mine and only mine.

My blood seethed like a volcano. I was about half a second from going thermonuclear, blowing the fuck up, and coating the Prez and the Enforcer with my own bloody gore.

"Let me do whatever it'll take to get us there faster," I said, feeling like a hero for offering them a diplomatic way out.

Just let me get my girl, assholes, I thought. *Then we'll all walk away satisfied.*

"Can't let you do that, son." Blackjack shifted in his seat, slicking back his long gray hair while he tugged out a smoke from his pocket. He offered me one, and I shook my head.

The man didn't speak 'til he took his first long pull and blew it high into the air. "Roman."

When I saw the giant walk to the door, cover it with

his body, and stand there with his arms folded like the Berlin fucking Wall, I knew the next shit rolling outta the Prez's mouth was bound to be bad.

"This club's at war, about to go off to fight the most serious battle it's faced since the Mexicans. If we play our cards right, it'll be the last fight we face for a good, long while. We'll bring Elle Jo home safe, and whatever's left of Gil. We'll murder every single Black Dragon in our sights."

My fist hit his scratched up desk. "Yeah? Where's the fucking punchline?"

"We can't do any of that if we've got a loose cannon in our ranks. Son, for the good of this club, this mission, and your woman, I'm asking you to stay behind and help the prospects hold down SeaTac. We need someone here to protect our assets and make sure the Chinese don't hit us behind the lines while we go for the throat."

No way. No cocksucking, motherfucking way.

By some miracle, I just sat there like a stone, holding in the rocket fuel billowing up inside me, making me feel like I was about to shoot through the goddamned roof.

Blackjack's words washed over me. I saw Roman outta the corner of my eye, studying me, ready to knock me flat if my anger caused me to do something really stupid.

They had to keep order. So did I.

"You understand, don't you, Asphalt? This move's the

last one I want to make when I know how hungry you are to tear a piece out of those sonsofbitches, but my first priority is keeping anyone from getting killed. Your odds are a lot higher than the rest of us when you're so pissed off, you're reckless. The Dragons won't claim one more brother, or any of the women who are family in this club. Do your duty here, and we'll bring her home. Got it?"

Blackjack looked me dead in the eye and extended his hand. I took it without hesitation and gave him a shake, resisting the urge to tear his damned arm off.

When I pulled my hand away, the Prez and Roman shared a bewildered look for just a split second.

Too easy – what the fuck just happened?

If I made them believe it, all the better.

"I'm gonna get the hell outta here and work on the bikes. Need them tuned up in case we've got any surprises to deal with in our territory here." I stood, slowly shaking my head. "Can't wait for this shit to be over, Prez, so we can go home to Redding without these fucking worries.."

"You and all the brothers, son. You've got my thanks for understanding."

I held my rage as Roman stepped aside and cleared the door for me. Didn't show any emotion 'til I was out, and then I headed for the garage, just like I said.

I watched my brothers come out with guns, ammo, and a few first aid kits for their saddlebags a couple minutes later. Blackjack and Brass rode out ahead of everybody, leading the big war party out through the gates when everything was ready. Rabid looked at me and gave me a stern nod on his way out.

The respect in his eyes almost made me feel bad about the game I was playing. Almost.

No, fuck that. With Elle on the line, nothing – and I mean *nothing* – meant more than keeping her safe.

The boys would ride slow, probably take the long route through to avoid the lingering storms rolling through the Pacific Northwest. I could cut around them, beat them to Portland, and kill half the fuckstains who had my girl before they even rolled into town.

I waited 'til it was just me and a couple prospects who'd come up from Redding. Fished out every fucking drink I could find at the bar to keep them distracted and seal their yaps. A quick call had the hottest pussy in town on the way to the clubhouse, three escorts with virgin looks and fake tits that would keep those fucks hammered all night.

Then, when they were laughing like drunken fools with their dicks straining in their pants, waiting for the girls to show up, I stepped out into the garage one more time. The whores grinned at me when they pulled up and made their way in. I waved 'em through without a second look, not even bothering to glance at their asses bobbing in those heels.

I had better waiting for me when I got my girl home. Nobody saw the shit I took outta the vault – the only new toy the crew left behind because nobody knew how to work it. The Devils dropped it off in trade last week coming from Montana, a peace offering from Blaze to Blackjack since he'd managed to calm shit down with the rogues in Tacoma.

They said they'd send instructions later about how to use the high powered sniper rifle. I turned it over in my hands, marveling how it was just like the one I'd used at the range last month.

It was supposed to be Roman's job to figure this shit out and keep it for dirty jobs in the club's arsenal. She was supposed to be in that vault, sleeping like an angel of death, ready whenever we called her to service.

Too fucking bad I had to interrupt her sleep early.

I packed her carefully on my bike in the long case, covering it with an extra tarp in case I passed any nosy cops on the road.

I'd put that big, killer bitch to work for me at dawn tomorrow, and she'd help me get my baby girl home alive.

I rode without stopping for anything but gas on my way down. Took more than four long hours after leaving at midnight, and I approached the Portland outskirts in the same slow, brutal rain that slowed time itself to a trickle.

Stopping at the last fill up station before all hell broke lose, I did a quick call to Blackjack. The boys were at least a solid hour behind. Told him everything was fine back in Tacoma, and asked for an update.

They'd gotten slowed down by the storms more than me, despite leaving sooner, and one of the Tacoma guys had to stop for engine trouble on the way down.

Fucking great.

Great for me and the killer angel riding with me, the best chance Elle Jo had at being saved before the Dragons did worse.

Blackjack was damned right about one thing – the hunger.

I couldn't shake it, the firestorm raging through my system. My finger burned every time I thought about squeezing the trigger with those motherfuckers in my sights.

Blood for blood. Vengeance. Salvation.

They had to die so we could live. The way of the universe, kill or be killed, all I'd ever known. Except now I had something more important than that shit on the line.

I had Elle Jo, and I'd sworn an oath on everything I had to protect her. I wasn't gonna disappoint her again, if by some miracle the assholes hadn't already fucked her over.

If they'd stuck their greasy cocks anywhere near her, I swore to fucking God...a lot of men were going to die the worst deaths possible.

The old plant they'd picked as a base looked like a

goddamned castle on the horizon. I had to pull my bike into an abandoned weigh station to get a good look.

The bastards were definitely there. Saw them through my binoculars, a couple sharp dressed Dragons out on patrol, lazily walking around the edges of the high gate topped with rusted barbed wire.

Had to find my perch. Had to pray they weren't smart enough to have their own sniper, but I'd never seen anybody up against our club yet who had the cutting edge shit made for murder on my bike.

The whole area had seen better times. The abandoned power plant was flanked by several old warehouses and factories with busted out windows. Leaving my bike parked at the rear, I headed for the one I'd seen with the most smashed windows, giving me several good places to set up shop and figure out who's head I'd blow apart first.

I climbed about a dozen flights of stairs to reach some high ground. The place was a fucking disaster zone with broken floors and exposed beams. I kicked aside several ratty sleeping bags on my way in, trash left by bums or urban explorers who'd come through over the years.

Taking a careful look around on the top floor, I made sure it was just me and ghosts here. Then I stayed low, making sure nobody saw my shadow filling the few remaining windows. The rifle went up fast, and I warmed it with my greedy hands, priming myself for action as I looked through the scope.

Shit had one hell of a magnifier. I could see the Dragons better than I could through my binoculars. The early morning light coming over the horizon helped too.

Fucking waiting game. I had to be patient, wait for just the right moment to start dropping the fuckers.

All the time I'd spent on the range learning exotic weapons was about to pay dividends. I held my breath, struggling to keep my white hot rage from making me pull the trigger as I watched those fucks shuffle through my scope, oblivious to the fact that they were all about to be snuffed out like goddamned flies.

I wanted to see that fucker, Zee, poke his head out. Elle described him to a tee, so I knew exactly what to look for, an older man with graying hair and crazy fucking eyes.

If I could pop his head, it'd sew confusion in the ranks. They'd be falling to pieces by the time the boys pulled up, ripe for slaughter, and then –

"Fuck," I muttered, stunned to see the same white van that drove outta the warehouse we'd blown to kingdom come in Tacoma.

It rounded the corner and parked next to the old loading dock. The driver got out and opened the doors, waiting while several of his boys marched outside, towing a prisoner behind them.

Gil looked like absolute shit. The motherfuckers had carved up his face, lacing it with thick, deep cuts, shit that wouldn't just scar and fade if he managed to live through today. The stump where his hand had been hung limply at his side, and he walked like they'd fucked up one knee, dragging his right leg behind him.

What came out behind him was even worse. I saw Elle being dragged in chains, manhandled by two sick motherfuckers.

My vision through the scope went blood red. My finger trembled on the fucking trigger. I narrowed my field of vision to the assholes holding her, looking for a reason to shoot their heads off, plus anything that would prevent my girl from getting shot or stabbed the moment I did.

That was the damned catch.

Fuck, fuck, fuck.

They were taking them away. Relocating. Running like the vermin they were.

I couldn't let them drive the fuck off! Steam hissed out my mouth in a cold puff as I sighed, sucking in a big breath to hold.

Watching, waiting, hoping for a miracle.

The Chinese piled them both into the back of the van and slammed the doors shut. My rifle followed the van as it drove to the front gate, keeping my target fixed on the bored as shit fucknut driving it.

He'd die first. I had to kill him, and the other shithead in the passenger seat before they rolled through that gate onto the open road. Then maybe I could pick off any other assholes dumb enough to approach the vehicle, before they –

"Fuck!" I swore louder this time, banging my fist on the ground.

My boys picked the worst time in the world to roll up, just as the van stopped at the gate, waiting for it to open.

The biggest pile of shit in the universe hit the fan and got flung to the furthest corners of creation.

I locked onto the asshole driver, just as the Chinese heard the motorcycles and started to panic. The rifle barked, jerked in my hands, and the windshield exploded into broken fragments, stained red with his gore.

His fuckhead passenger in the next seat over managed to reach for the handle to pop his door before I took him out. One shot collapsed his skull, took his face clean off. His headless body rolled out the open door and flopped on the ground.

Blackjack looked almost as confused as the Dragon motherfuckers storming outta the building like angry hornets, their guns drawn.

Didn't stop him from riding behind Roman's truck. It took down the gate like a fucking battery ram, and I watched the firefight start through my scope like a civil war general, men on both sides screaming, running, shooting at each other.

The Chinese had some tricks up their sleeves, but we had more. Several fuckheads popped up on the rooftops, looking for the sniper, without having any clue I'd gone lone wolf.

I took them out in seconds. Tried like hell not to focus too hard on the van, praying Elle and Gil would be all right.

Yeah, that's right, I even hoped her asshole old man would survive, because anything that happened to him in the back of that shitty white van was bound to hurt my girl too. Plus keeping his evil ass alive would save her heart from getting torn into a million pieces.

My rifle shifted across the battlefield. I killed a few more Chinese hiding behind crates, shooting at Rabid and Brass as they smashed their way in, heading toward the door with the Tacoma brothers close behind.

Roman circled for the van, and I breathed my first sigh of relief since this shit started.

The wind blew fierce, and I saw Blackjack turn around and follow it, his eyes scanning the walls of the broken old place where I'd holed up.

I'd given them a huge advantage – the boys would just have to pick off the ones inside now. Time to get the fuck down there and fight with them, man-on-man.

I ran down the same flights of dirty stairs and climbed on my bike, holding the sniper rifle on my side.

When I rode across the street and crossed over the broken down gate, the Prez shook his head, shooting me a death glare while he tried not to grin.

I'd done him a big fucking favor. I'd saved lives. But I'd still disobeyed a direct order, and I'd pay for it later, like the defiant motherfucker I was.

Parked my bike by the loading dock as I listened to gunshots firing inside. I dropped the sniper rifle off where Roman could see it, and drew my nine millimeter, heading inside to find the fuck responsible for this shit before anybody else did.

I had to kill him. Had to put that Zee piece of shit down like the rabid dog he was.

My brothers were just coming out from behind their crates when I busted in.

Brass' eyes went big as fucking saucers when he saw me. "Holy fuck. You must've been the asshole playing sniper? What're you doing –"

I fired before the mobster asshole popped up behind him, and put a bullet through his brain. I hit the fuck in the thigh and his shot went into the ceiling as he collapsed, screaming shit in Chinese I couldn't understand.

The second miracle of the day arrived.

Zee rolled on the ground like a fucking coward when I found him. He'd been reaching for the gun he'd lost when he hit the floor and started clenching his leg. I picked it up, walked over, and stomped his hand so fucking hard his fingers snapped like twigs.

The other guys were behind me in seconds. One-eyed Line made a grunt of approval, and both the Veeps reached for the asshole, ready to hoist him up.

Wouldn't fucking let 'em. I pushed my boot down even tighter, hearing his pain echo like a song through the huge place as I ground the bones I'd broken into dust.

"Asphalt, what the fuck, man?" Rabid looked at me, reaching for Zee's leg.

"No. Put him the fuck down. Where's the Prez? This asshole needs to die right here. His scalp is mine, and it's Elle Jo's too."

They looked at me like I'd lost my mind. I'd been around for ages in this club, long enough to know the drill.

When Lady Luck sent us a head honcho like Dragon Fucker here, their ass belonged to the Grizzlies. We grilled them before we executed them, or else used them for ransom. But what the fuck could Zee tell us that mattered, seeing how we'd just slaughtered his entire crew?

It took several minutes for the rest of the boys to join us. Roman scanned the warehouse, making sure we'd annihilated every last one of the mobsters. A couple gunshots rang out in the distance, telling us he'd put one or two more outta their misery.

Blackjack walked up to me, his arms outstretched. My jaw nearly hit the floor when he threw them around me in a big brotherly hug.

"That's for saving our lives with the sniper stunt," he growled into my ear.

Stunned, I ignored Zee's groans and started to put my arms around his back. Then the meanest blow I'd felt in awhile cut across my chin like a fucking hurricane. He hit damned hard.

I reeled back, fell against several crates, and doubled over, rubbing the blinding pain shooting through my face.

"And that's for defying a direct order and lying to me, son. Next time, you'll catch a bullet in your kneecap." The Prez pointed, his finger stern and cold as a dagger. "Never again."

"Understood. Sorry, Prez," I mumbled, spitting out the blood pooling in my mouth, hoping I'd be able to talk so I could get the very last thing I needed.

"Get this sack of shit loaded for the ride to Redding," Blackjack said to Brass and Rabid. "We'll bring him home and find out everything he knows."

"Prez, wait..." I touched him gently on the shoulder, and squeezed. "I don't give a shit if you wanna torture this fuck any way you please for intel. But the kill needs to be mine. I gotta give Elle something to make up for all this. I need to –"

My words stopped in my throat as Roman stepped up, a switchblade in his hand. Elle Jo stepped out behind him, her hands cut free from the cord binding them. Her attention was totally on Gil, hanging onto her shoulder, and she didn't see me 'til I spat more blood.

"Asphalt, baby, oh my God!"

Fuck. I took one more long look at Zee, his head twisting unnaturally as the boys carried him toward the truck. He'd have a long, hellish ride to California. The tourniquet they'd put on his leg would keep him from bleeding out, but he'd suffer just the same, knowing he was completely at our mercy.

And we had none.

Shit, I had absolute zero. Negative fucking mercy, if such a thing were possible. I wanted to kill him, slice through his nasty face, lift the fucking scalp off his head and hand it to my baby girl as payment for what she'd suffered.

She needed a bloody guarantee that my word was solid, and this shit would never, ever happen again.

But she needed my arms around her more right now.

I stepped away from the cursing, wriggling mafia don and hugged my woman. For just a second, I could savor having her in my arms, something that seemed downright impossible a couple hours ago.

"Never should've let you leave the clubhouse," I said, reaching for her hand. I pulled it to my lips and gave it a kiss.

Fuck if it didn't make my dick throb. That woman could've touched me with nothing but her eyelashes, and I'd still have a raging hard-on worse than I got when most girls straddled me, feeling their pussies leaking all over my cock.

"It's not your fault. None of this is." She kissed one cheek, and then the next, before centering her lips.

I took what was mine. We kissed long and hard and deep.

Didn't give a fuck about the dead assholes laying all around us. Didn't care about Zee screaming one last time as I heard them throw him into the back of Roman's truck like a sack of trash. Didn't even give a shit about Gil and Blackjack both eyeballing me, looking like they wanted to rip my head off for very different reasons.

Then Gil looked at his daughter, and the fucker's face tensed up. He started bawling like a baby. Whatever the fuck happened out here, it was bad, awful enough to break him.

"It's over now. You're coming home with me, babe, and it'll be awhile before you ever see the Pacific fucking Northwest again."

Her old man bit his tongue when he heard me say that shit. He cried harder, his whole body quaking, dying from the shame of going completely broke. *Good.*

I motioned his way. "Come on. Let's help get him in the truck with his crew so he can get some proper attention."

Gil didn't say shit as I grabbed his other arm and we helped him walk outside. He'd taken quite a fucking beating thanks to the Chinese. His sobs slowed as we led him out.

Fucker was red as a tomato, embarrassed, probably the reason he wasn't giving me any shit or whispering threats about the glorious hold I had on his daughter. He'd never give our love his stamp of approval, and I didn't fucking care.

Right now, he was too fucked up and traumatized to say a damned thing about it.

Line stood near the open door to the truck, just waiting. I finally got a good look at him as we hoisted him inside, me stepping back so Elle could fasten his seat belt.

The man was completely, irreparably fucked. If Karma was an absolute bitch, like everybody said, then she'd decided to rip everything away from him except his daughter.

She'd taken his hand, his face, and whatever manhood he had left. Tacoma's soon-to-be-ex Prez would never ride again with that stump on his arm, and if he found a woman who'd let him bed her with that sliced up face, he'd be paying for her company.

Much as I hated him for putting my girl in danger, shit was fucking sad.

Christ, I needed a smoke. I fought the urge and took Elle's hand instead, leading her toward my bike.

"It isn't really over," I growled, jerking her into my embrace and whispering in her ear. "I lied back there."

Her sweet blue eyes turned up, a little darker than usual, fear streaking through them. "Huh? What do you mean?"

"I'm gonna kill Zee myself for what he did to you and your old man. He needs to fucking die for this, and I wanna be the one to plunge the knife in his throat, maybe do worse."

She looked around, making sure nobody else could hear. I could've rolled my eyes. The girl should've known by now how crafty I could be.

"Won't that get you in trouble?"

"We'll see." I shrugged. "Honestly, babe, I don't give a single fuck anymore. Even the Prez acknowledges the fact that I saved his ass and everybody else's today. The Chinese might've taken you and your dad in that van if I hadn't started shooting. They definitely would've given my brothers some casualties."

"It isn't worth it," she said, refusing to look at me. "I just want this to be over. For real, Austin. We've suffered enough. I don't need more blood to make this right. I'm safe, I'm with you, daddy's alive...that's all that matters. That's enough."

Her eyes told a different story. I saw the way she looked away from me, turning toward the truck where they'd loaded up Zee. Poor girl had a flood of pain building up inside her, ready to burst.

"No fucking way," I said coldly.

I grabbed her chin and jerked her face straight, locking down her eyes with mine. "I told you what's gonna happen once we get home. You'll never sleep another peaceful night if that animal's still wasting air breathing on this earth. And if we don't kill him, we'll regret somebody else doing it. Told you, babe, I'm gonna carve a piece off his carcass and bring it to you with my bare hands. That's a promise."

She gasped. I let her go and walked away before she could try to talk me outta it.

"Stay here and drink some water. There's a canteen in my saddlebag. Gotta help clean up so we can get our asses home."

I left Elle waiting next to my bike while I headed back inside the old plant. I had to help the boys clean this shithole up, dispose of all the assholes we'd killed.

The club couldn't handle another massacre in the media. A couple politicians were already screaming for action 'til we paid 'em off, and they'd start squawking for more if they saw another opportunity to fill up their campaign coffers.

It took about a solid hour with the full crew carrying bodies into a big, empty pit we'd dug out back before we finished. Their skin sizzled like a witch's brew when Roman tipped the acid barrels over their carcasses, dissolving them like they'd never existed, before we shoved the dirt over their bones.

If anyone ever came out here and found this shit in fifty, maybe a hundred years, they'd never piece together who the fuck the remnants belonged to, or what had happened here today.

That secret died with us. It was about to die a whole lot faster with Zee too. My fingers itched to feel his blood all over them when I smashed my fists through his rotten, fucked up face.

Nobody hurt my girl and lived to whine about how

sorry they were. *Fucking nobody.*

I flexed my fists, nodding to the big Enforcer as I helped him pile the empty barrels back by the loading dock for the prospects to carry. Glassy walked up and winked at me before he picked one up and hauled it over his shoulder.

"This bullshit gets old, don't you think?" Roman said, squinting into the rising morning sun. "I wanna go the fuck home and stay there this time around. I'd rather be with my wife and kid any damned day over throwing more dead bastards into the ground."

"We're getting there, brother." I threw my arm around his shoulder. "Give it a year and I'll be right there with you. So will Rabid and Brass when they knock their girls up. The Prez can be a real fucker sometimes, but he's right."

The giant cocked his head, wondering what the fuck I was talking about.

"He's helped us clear out practically every asshole who could ever threaten us. We're earning our peace by blood, and it's so damned close I can taste it. No more rogues in our ranks once the other charters hear about what happened to Tacoma and Gil fucking up. No more mafia goons or vicious cartels breathing down our throats when they find out we took out a whole crew of Dragons. Look up there, man."

I pointed to the sky, and we both stared at the big, fiery ball 'til our eyes burned. "It's a bright new day for this club and every man in it. All we gotta do is keep the peace, and make our women the happiest, most spoiled bitches on the face of the earth."

He laughed. It was still weird to hear the big guy bust a gut, though he'd been doing it more lately, ever since settling shit with Sally and his son.

A couple minutes later, Brass and Rabid joined us. We bullshitted like we hadn't since the last big hog roast a couple months ago, and when the prospects told us everything was finished, we headed out to our bikes wearing shit-eating smiles.

"Oh, God. What now?" Elle asked sadly, running her hands over my neck after we got on my bike.

"Nothing, babe. Why do you look so worried?"

She hesitated. "You're happy. Who did you kill to get a smile like that?"

I turned around, fisted her sweet blonde hair, and smiled wider. "I'm grinning like a Cheshire fucking cat because everything's gonna be different now. We'll finally be living like a man and his wife should. There's more blood in the future, yeah, there always fucking is. But I'm gonna make you the happiest woman who ever wore a man's brand, and you're gonna love every single second. I'm smiling, thinking about all the ways you'll grin in the years to come, smile at me 'til your pretty white teeth fall out."

She laughed. It echoed like the best damned music I'd ever heard as we pulled out behind my brothers, tightening our formation on the road for the long trip home.

Peace was waiting for all the brothers in Redding. No sooner than we rode through the gates, I saw all the old ladies file out, the prospects and a couple brothers at their sides. Stryker saluted the Prez, the only full patch brother who'd stayed behind, except for old Southpaw.

The old ladies practically ran 'em all down in the rush to greet us.

Christa for Rabid.

Sally for Roman, cradling their son in her arms. The kid was getting bigger all the time.

Missy blew a kiss for Brass. Even her kid sister, Jackie, was standing by her side. The teenager would have a rocking body in a few more years, and the Veep would probably have to fight off prospects from sniffing around her if she kept coming by the clubhouse.

Lucky for me, I already had everything I needed on the back of my bike. I helped Elle off it like a queen and took her helmet while brothers went running to their girls. Tugging her close, I gave her a nuclear hot kiss that rivaled all of 'em, clutching her body like I couldn't believe it was real.

Fuck, her ass was made for my hands. I held it tight, pulled her hips into mine, made her feel every inch of what she did to me.

She'd never stop being the air in my lungs, and right

now, I had to drink her deep.

We kissed for what seemed like a million years, and it still wasn't enough. Didn't take my lips off hers 'til Roman barked at the prospects, telling them to get their asses in gear unloading our arms, and putting them to bed.

Elle looked like she was about to fall over. I had something else to put to bed, and I led her into the clubhouse, trying to keep my eyes off the limp Chinese asshole a couple guys carried in ahead of us.

We took the shitty bed in my old room, one of the last nights we'd camp here before I found us a real place to live.

We were both too tired to fuck, but damn if my dick didn't hound me anyway. I held her close, feeling her curves as she mumbled nonsense, drifting off to sleep. She seemed trouble, tossing and turning in my arms. I stroked her brow, then ran my fingers softly through her hair.

This was living. Before, I'd only been alive when I had some whore on my cock with Jack coursing through my veins, or else when some sick piece of shit who deserved to die was gurgling his death rattle.

None of that shit even came close to what I had in this bed. Elle Jo slept like an angel.

A battered, damaged angel who'd been fucked over one too many times by her dad's mistakes, and mine too.

"Never again," I whispered into her ear, not even

caring she couldn't hear me.

Never, never!

"All you're gonna be doing for me is making money, making kids, and setting our bed on fire when I climb into it. You've suffered, Ell-Bell, hurt more than some brothers. That's a fucking crime, and it stops now. I'm telling you right through your dreams, babe, because I fucking own 'em. I'll make 'em happen. And I'll make sure you know how much I love you every single day when you're awake."

Pausing, I buried my nose in her hair, breathing her scent. Goddamn, she smelled good, even when she was fresh from being held by the mafia, without so much as a shower.

I wanted to rip her clothes off and fuck her senseless, fuck her 'til our bodies totally gave out. But she needed her beauty sleep, and I wasn't a total animal, even though I sometimes doubted it.

"Sleep tight, Elle Jo. You can give me all the shit you want about how I saved your life. Truth is, you saved mine. I'd have wound up dead sooner or later with my temper, if I didn't have something to keep it in check." I kissed her cheek, listening to her moan softly, nuzzling her face into me. "Only gonna let it loose one more time. Then it's done and gone forever, baby girl. I'm killing it for you."

I closed my eyes and slept like a dead man for several hours. When I woke up to the pounding on my door, I shifted outta bed carefully, leaving Elle deep in her dreams.

"Yeah?" I cracked the door, and saw Brass' dark face looking at me.

"Church, brother. Five minutes."

I nodded, closed the door, and pulled my cut off its hanger. I lingered a minute longer as I rolled it onto my shoulders, staring at the woman sleeping in my bed, the one who'd just handed me the rest of my life.

It was gonna be absolutely fucking glorious.

"Bring him in." Blackjack clenched the bear paw so tight his fingers turned white.

The tension was back in the room. Everybody in the Redding crew stared across to Tacoma. Not that the assholes would try anything, no matter how heated it got, because we outnumbered them in droves.

Our prospects waited outside. Stryker and Southpaw held the door from our side, only stepping outta the way when Gil staggered in, taking the seat reserved next to our Prez.

The motherfucker shuffled like a damned zombie. Plopping down into the empty seat, he gave the Prez that thousand yard stare I'd seen on guys before, when they'd been through too much shit. Usually, those guys snapped.

I eyeballed Roman, and he looked at me. The Enforcer understood. He was more than ready for anything fucking crazy. The prospects had patted Gil down before he entered, but who the hell knew what a man might do when he had nothing left to lose.

"You fucked up something awful, brother," Blackjack growled, giving the Tacoma Prez a look straight from hell. "You put my whole club in peril. You're not a stupid man, though I've got to wonder with everything that's happened. You, Gil, know exactly what the rules say about mother charter and her right to reign in chapters going rogue. We can do this the easy way, or the hard way, brother. It's all your —"

"Shut up."

Two words, and I knew Elle's old man had lost his fucking mind forever. Nobody cut Blackjack off, and you sure as shit didn't tell him to shut up.

All the Redding brothers bristled, including me.

Across the table, Line looked nervous, torn between his loyalty to a man who'd flipped his shit, and the full Grizzlies MC assembly here.

Slowly, Gil stood. Half the room was ready to pounce and knock him the fuck down if he so much as reached into his pockets. I didn't trust the pat check he'd received before coming in here one bit – a twenty year veteran in this club had plenty of ways to hide weapons if he wanted to kill a man bad enough.

Gil reached for his own chest with his single good hand. We watched him grab the PRESIDENT patch by several loose stitches in the corner. He pulled hard, 'til we heard the tear ripping through the dead silence.

It popped right off his leather cut without so much as a thread hanging. Shaking, Gil turned to Line, and opened his torn up lips.

"Hand out," he whispered.

The Tacoma Veep did as he asked, and everybody calmed when we saw the patch passed to him. "This crown's yours now, brother. Remember my fucking mistakes."

Gil turned back to Blackjack. Our Prez nodded coldly.

Deep down, he was probably just as relieved as the rest of us, but his face didn't show it. The bastard had given up his power without a fight, and that was all that mattered.

Blackjack looked merciless as the defeated asshole turned away, heading for the door. A lesser man would've felt sorry for the poor sonofabitch, but I had nothing except pure relief pumping through my blood.

Maybe he'd actually paid the price for losing his post and a fully functional body, too. Maybe I wouldn't try to fuck him up, as soon as I dealt with Zee.

"Let him through," Blackjack ordered.

The whole room watched while our boys stepped aside. Gil limped out, heading straight for the bar, ready to drown his agony in the only shit with a prayer of saving his miserable soul.

It was Line's turn to look at Blackjack.

"Tacoma's in your hands now," the Prez said, studying

the bear claw gavel in his hand. "Treat it right, and you won't wind up in his place."

"You've vetted me. Don't have to tell any of you what I can do. You can all count on me to set things right. I'll rebuild the Tacoma charter the way it should've been the first time, without any antsy fuckers ready to walk off a cliff. I won't do anything that'll bring down hell on the whole club."

"I believe you, brother," Blackjack said sternly. "It isn't just the Grizzlies MC as a whole that's counting on you to act on your word. It's every man in this room who's ready for some peace and quiet. That means me, too. We want to make money, build real assets, and fire a few less bullets next year. We're tired. We've had our feast on blood, and we want to trade with our friends and run our empire in peace. Help make it a reality."

Fucking shit. The place was starting to sound like a hippie commune with everybody talking about putting down their guns and living the quiet life. *Peace.*

Damn if it didn't sound good right now. I'd be ready for some of that, just as soon as I finished cleaning up the last mess dirtying this clubhouse.

Church lasted for about an hour. The Prez debriefed us and told us he'd be working Zee over later – not that he expected to get much from the beaten mafia fuck.

They had him tied up in the storage room, the same place we'd dealt with our enemies for years. Sometimes it was our own brothers who'd gone rotten, and other times it was the cartel, before we'd beaten their asses just the same.

Underneath the table, I fingered the switchblade in my belt, imaging all the ways I'd gut the motherfucker waiting for my steel.

I waited 'til church finished. The Prez disappeared for the night, and the rest of the boys gathered in the bar with their women, their kids. Family time was the real debriefing they all needed, far more meaningful than any club business we could hatch in the meeting room.

I nursed a single beer by myself, hiding in a corner while the brothers enjoyed themselves. They all started to taper off a little later. First Brass and Roman with their old ladies and the young ones. Then Rabid and Christa, leaving nobody but the prospects and the club whores.

They'd be retiring behind closed doors to put their kids to bed, or suck and fuck themselves to sleep soon enough.

Another half hour, and I made my move. I headed down the hallway, stepping over Stryker, who lay smack in the middle of the floor, locking tongues with some dark haired bitch in his lap. Glassy was passed out in the corner, his fake eye open, staring lifelessly across the clubhouse.

The lone Tacoma prospect standing in front of the storage room looked at me like he'd seen a ghost, and smiled. "You taking the next shift? Fuck, man, I've been listening to the party all night. I could really use a smoke."

"Go." I slapped him on the back. "Fill your lungs out back and have some fun. I'll take over from here."

He didn't even give me a second glance. Just handed me the key and took off.

Sometimes, the universe just hands you a kill on a silver-fucking-platter.

The storage room was permanently lit with several loud, fluorescent bulbs. The pieces of shit we kept in here didn't deserve a good night's sleep, but damn if their bodies didn't try.

Zee slumped in a chair, his head hanging down like a bird's. He didn't look up 'til he heard the door snap shut behind me.

"Asshole," he said. "You're the one who shot me. Come to finish things, yes?"

I looked him dead in the eye without saying shit. He didn't deserve any idle chit-chat. I was about to give him the last thing he needed, all he deserved before his worthless carcass wound up buried in an unmarked grave.

"You got anything else to tell the club, or should I try to beat it the fuck outta you?"

One question. The only one I'd ask before I did his ass in.

"No. All the treasure you'd ever want to plunder is

safe in Shanghai, where your pissy little club will never reach."

Fuck, did I hate the bastard's smug ass smile. Even worse that he was right.

The savage punch I slammed into his gut killed the grin instantly. He tensed up, spat blood, and tried to breathe.

"Say it again, fucknut. Men like you always think you're hot shit when you're in control, chopping hands and threatening innocent girls. You always go coward in the end, shitting your pants and begging for your life. Same fucking thing I've seen dozens of times before I send men like you to hell."

Motherfucker smiled. Again.

The asshole was tougher than most, or maybe just crazy, I'd give him that. The cartel boss we'd had back here last time cried like a bitch when the knife went through his ear, and he was one of the rare birds who'd gotten out alive because we used him as an olive branch.

"She...didn't tell...you?" Asshole spoke slow, struggling over every word when he'd had all the wind knocked outta him. "You...you were too late...asshole. You think you saved her? You fucked up. I left her with things she'll never forget...never. Your little bitch will remember choking on my dick for the rest of her life. She'll remember her daddy watched, but I wish it had been you."

What the fuck?!

I couldn't tell if the asshole was taunting me, trying to make me finish him faster so he wouldn't suffer, or if he'd really stained my girl.

No bullshit, he'd shaken me. Fucking rattled my bones real bad.

I had poison tears ready to burn trails down my face when I heard the door close behind me, spun around, and saw Blackjack standing with Elle Jo.

The Prez had murder written on his face. My woman cried, covered her face, torture and hot shame overwhelming her.

Zee just smiled. That same arrogant, wicked, demonic fucking smile that I could only kill once, when I wanted to do it a thousand fucking times, and it still wouldn't be enough.

I dropped the fucking switchblade burning in my hand. The Dragon boss laughed through the blood streaming out between his teeth.

"You prick. Stupid fuck. Thought you'd just kill me and get a neat, happy ending, didn't you?"

I'd fucking failed her. I could stand up and gut this asshole, rip his fucking throat out with my bare hands, but it wouldn't do shit. I couldn't change the nightmare that had already happened.

The asshole grinning in his hell seat would die just the same. But I'd fucking die right there on the dirty floor with him.

XI: Undefeated (Elle Jo)

Fifteen Minutes Earlier

I woke up and ran straight to the bathroom. Asphalt wasn't laying with me anymore, and I'd known it for at least an hour, suffering through a fitful half-sleep while I tried to fight the vomit churning in my guts.

I'd lied to him so well, hid what happened. I'd lied to myself, and I would've lied to daddy too, if he hadn't been forced to see it all.

My stomach couldn't empty itself enough. Mind and body tried to expel the poison in my system, the hellish memory of what happened in that run down power plant, but this wouldn't do it. *Never.*

The room spun, colliding over and over again in my head, and I retched pure stomach acid. I'd never get the taste of Zee's disgusting cock out of my mouth.

I staggered up to the sink, jerked on the faucets, and drank so many handfuls of cold water I thought I'd freeze.

They came up again a second later, barely warm. I spat dirty water in the sink and slumped to the floor, hugging the sink for support, before sliding onto the tile. I rolled into a ball on the ground.

It wasn't okay. It would never be okay. My man was going to do something stupid sooner or later, and maybe he'd find out what happened in that dirty factory too, when the mob boss forced himself on me with my father screaming through his gag, all his sick men watching in a circle.

Worthless fuckhole. That's what he'd called my mouth. And he treated it like one too, ramming himself down my throat, choking me for several minutes while I blacked out, the only defense I had against the horror.

I woke to his come drooling out my mouth. The mobster looked at me darkly and spat, zipping up his pants.

Stupid fucking cunt. Not even a little tongue. Don't get too excited, boys, there's no spark here. I'll let you all have a turn when we take the whore to the docks. It's going to be a LONG cruise home.

Come on, get her up. Out of my sight.

I was on the ground, straining for breath, spitting out his come when he yanked me to my feet and motioned to his men. They marched me out to the van with daddy at my side. He wouldn't even look at me, staring at the ground like he'd lost his mind.

We barely got in the back and felt the vehicle jerk forward before all hell broke lose.

Asphalt saved our lives. But he couldn't take back

what happened, what I vowed I'd try to keep from him – what I knew I couldn't.

I had to find him. Tell him everything, before he went and killed the devil waiting down the hall.

If he had to find out, then it was better he heard it from me, rather than the monster.

I cleaned up quickly and headed outside. Rock music throbbed through the clubhouse, a steady, low booming bass. Several guys groaned in their rooms, interspersed with the love cries of their girls. A lone figure sat at the bar, having a drink by himself.

Blackjack saw me, looked up, and stood, shoving his shot glass away from him. "Elle Jo. How're you feeling?"

His eyes narrowed as I approached. "Where's Asphalt?"

"I...don't know," I said, my heart leaping into my chest. "I was kinda coming out here to find out the same thing."

"Shit." One word, and he took off down the hallway, grabbing my hand. "Come with me. I've got a feeling I know where we'll find him."

I followed him to the heavy metal door to the room I'd seen them bring Zee into. The club President pulled a keychain from his pocket and tapped his way through about a dozen separate keys before he found the right one, shoving it into the lock.

The door opened, and we stepped inside, only to hear

the words that nearly killed me.

"...too late...asshole. I left her with things she'll never forget...never. Your little bitch will remember choking on my dick for the rest of her life. She'll remember her daddy watched, but I wish it had been you."

The world dropped out underneath me. I had to catch myself by the knees as I doubled over, and sprang back up, watching as Blackjack's face soured with rage.

The door clicked shut. Asphalt spun around, saw us.

His expression ruined me. We locked eyes, just for a second. I wanted to run to him, hold him, apologize for everything and tell him that the only thing that mattered what was lay ahead, not behind us.

It shouldn't have mattered that the wretched animal tied to the chair used me. But, God help us, it did, and my heart splintered in two when I remembered his foul taste, the way daddy flopped against the pillar, covering his eyes with his severed wrist so he wouldn't have to watch.

I'm sorry, baby, I said with my eyes. *Jesus Christ, I'm SO fucking sorry.*

I couldn't apologize fast enough. I couldn't even move my lips.

Asphalt turned away from me, dropped his knife. The clatter it made on the floor sounded like an asteroid hitting the earth.

Zee looked past him, smiling the same dirty smirk I'd seen before he unbuckled his pants. "You prick. Stupid fuck. Thought you'd just kill me and get a neat, happy ending, didn't you?"

Those were his last words. Everything happened so fast, but it felt like a thousand years as I watched Blackjack step up, grab the knife off the floor, and pull Asphalt up with it.

"Do it, son," he growled, pushing the switchblade's handle into my man's palm. "Drain every fucking drop of blood from this dog's veins."

A new stone cold calm came over Asphalt like I'd never seen before. I huddled against the wall and watched as he moved behind the laughing mobster, grabbing his face by the chin and holding it up.

Zee's laughter stopped as soon as the blade sank below his ear. He screamed bloody murder, and after the first twenty seconds, I had to cover my ears.

Blackjack turned, nodded at me, and retreated to the other corner. It seemed like the murder went on forever, an act of savagery that froze my veins.

The bastard deserved it. Every rip, every wound, every spritz of blood pouring out the fissures Asphalt tore into his flesh.

Every last bit of blinding pain.

My heart swelled with pride when I finally dared glance at them. The evil mobster's face was half-peeled away from his skull, and he was still alive, twitching in an agony that wouldn't let him do anything else.

When I uncovered my ear, he wasn't screaming any

more. Soft, terrified words in Mandarin hissed through his blood and curdled the air. I took my hands off my ears and listened.

No. No. No!
Don't do this. Don't, don't, don't –
For the love of fucking God!

I was the only one in the room who could truly understand what he was saying, but the other men got the message. They didn't need an education to understand stark raving terror.

Asphalt's face turned into a mask of grim satisfaction as he stripped the remaining meat from his bones and finished peeling his face off.

Zee rasped, then let out another vicious scream. I looked at him and we locked eyes.

"Die, you piece of shit," I whispered. "We won't even think about you after this. There's no reason to. You have no power over me, none over us."

Snarling, Asphalt stopped, turned, and looked at me. "Get up here, babe. This shit belongs to both of us."

My heart beat wild as I slowly approached, shifting my eyes away from the demon to the love of my life. Before I knew what was happening, he pushed the blade's handle into my palm, and tightened his fingers over mine as we formed a double fist.

"We kill this motherfucker together. Put his ass down forever after all he's done to us, everything he did to your old man..."

Totally insane. But I nodded, without a shred of hesitation.

We'd been wed once at the altar. Once more in bed, giving him my body, mixing flesh and passion in sweet vows we'd renew for the rest of our days. This was our third wedding, a marriage in blood, one that would wipe away all the curses we'd suffered for good.

I stared into the wild emotion tightening Asphalt's handsome face. "We'll do it on my mark, on three," he whispered.

"One," he began counting, and I moved my lips with him.

For a second, I understood the killer instinct in every outlaw biker's heart.

"Two," we whispered together.

Zee babbled like a madman, gurgling for a mercy we'd never never give him.

"Three!"

He pulled the blade in our hands back like a spear, and then slammed it into Zee's throat. The devil's body kicked like a mule one more time, and he died.

We dropped the knife, and I stumbled backward, amazed at what I'd just done. Even more incredible that there wasn't a shred of guilt.

I'd felt glee when we slayed the monster. Asphalt hovered over him, watching the steady trail of blood spilling out his neck.

I only got a tiny pang of disgust when Asphalt reached

up, grabbed him by his bloody hair, and snapped his head back until it tilted unnaturally, nearly detached from the neck.

"Babe." He turned to face me, and our eyes met, the pain fading in his bright green eyes.

I ran to him again. We crashed together, kissing so hard I couldn't believe we were right next to a dead man still dripping blood onto the floor. Asphalt's hands were covered in blood, and they caressed me, but I didn't care.

Blackjack watched from the corner, an approving look on his face. He knew better than we did what kind of therapy we needed. Nothing except ripping the demon who'd hurt us to pieces would do.

This was an exorcism. Freedom in the making.

Asphalt took my mouth with the same hunger as before, maybe more. He kissed me like we'd been apart for years, jamming his tongue down on mine and sweeping his heat through my mouth. My nipples hardened, and all the trauma I'd feared would linger from the last twenty-four hours faded.

It wouldn't disappear overnight. Oh, no.

There'd be nightmares, bad memories, and bleak doubts aplenty. But with the dead man in the chair gone forever, and his men long since buried, we'd never have to be afraid again.

They couldn't haunt us, couldn't ruin the bright future we'd have from this day forward.

"It's done, Elle Jo. I don't give a fuck what happened

before. He's dead – the only shithead responsible for your suffering. Soon as his bones are in the ground, we won't think about his evil ass ever again."

We kissed again, twined lips and tongues until I sensed Blackjack coming up behind us.

"You're doing the right thing, kids. I'll make sure he's hauled away and put away deep. You two make sure the darkness goes with him." The older man slapped us both on the shoulders and squeezed with a grip so strong it surprised me.

Then, without another word, he turned and left, closing the door behind him. Asphalt took my hand, and we turned to take one last look at the very last dragon I hoped he'd ever slay for me.

"He'll rot in hell longer than that pile of shit rots in the ground," he growled.

I turned, pushing myself into him, running my hands down my man's hard chest. "Baby, don't worry about it. We've got bigger things to worry about now."

His face tensed. "Yeah? Like what?"

"Finding somewhere to live in this town, for one." I smiled, pushing my hands harder on his chest, admiring the sharp, strong cuts between each muscle clinging to his bones. "Then I'm going to remind you the man you killed will never, ever leave a billionth of the impression you've made on me. Shit, Asphalt, you *own* me. It's been a long road getting here, but I love it. I'm proud of it. And I'm going to wear your name all over me in the years to come."

"Fuck!" He grinned and pulled me tight, dipping me in his arms for another lightning hot kiss.

I meant every word. I'd been his bride from the start of this insanity, when it was the last thing I'd wanted.

Now, I couldn't imagine anything else. He'd saved my life several times over, put down the ones who hurt me, and rescued my only flesh and blood, too.

This man deserved the moon. I'd give it to him time and time again.

"Damn," I swore, breaking the kiss as I remembered something.

"What?"

"We need to find daddy. He'll need someone to drive him back to Tacoma...I guess he's staying with the club, except as an emeritus now. It's hard enough for him. He won't want to spend a second longer than he really needs to in Tacoma."

"Yeah, I've been meaning to talk to your old man myself. Let's go."

Smiling, with his hand in mind, we walked out the door. Blackjack waited at the end of the hall with a couple prospects and the brother named Stryker.

As soon as he saw us leaving, slamming the door behind us without one more glance at the dead mafia man, the Prez nodded to his men.

"Take this sonofabitch out to the deepest part of the swamp. He doesn't deserve an eternity with dry ground and fresh dirt after the shit he pulled."

I closed my eyes for a second as we headed for the bar, savoring the grim finality.

The animal who'd tortured me and done so much damage to my father was gone forever. It was up to us to fill the void he'd left behind with so much kickass happiness, we'd be able to hear the Black Dragons screaming their envy in hell.

"You need a refill. Here." I sat down at the bar next to daddy as Asphalt walked behind it, pulled out a fresh bottle of Jack, and sloshed fresh whiskey into my father's empty glass.

He turned his head like a turtle to face my man, the slowest look in the world.

"What's the fucking point?" he growled, pushing the glass further away.

Okay, that really hurt. I tried not to think about all the emotional and physical agony ripping through him right now. But the pain rolled off him in vast, psychic waves, so black and brutal I could barely handle sitting on the stool next to my father without bursting into tears.

"Daddy, please...he's trying to help. We both are."

He gave me a sharp look as I wrapped my arms around him. At first, he moved like he wanted to brush me off, but then he relaxed when he saw his missing hand.

He still hadn't internalized it. They'd only ripped it off

him a week ago, but it might as well have been an entire lifetime, suffering with his new disability.

Undaunted, Asphalt grabbed the glass, walked out to join us on a bar stool, and set it down in front of my father on the counter.

"You're alive and breathing, Gil. You've got a future. That's more than this club can say for a lot of guys." He paused, narrowing his eyes, taking a pull off his own beer. "I can't imagine the shit you're going through. Everything those fuckers stole, the things they did...they fucked all hard. But Elle and I are moving on. We're forgetting the past, only focusing on what's ahead. You can do the same. No matter what the fuck happened, you've got a daughter who wants you in her life, even after the shit you pulled. Tell me that counts for something."

I held my breath. Daddy would either accept his little pep talk, or he'd smash his good hand across my lover's handsome face.

"You're an absolute bastard," he snarled at Asphalt, finally lifting his drink to his lips and pouring it all back in one gulp. The glass clinked on the counter when he'd finished. "Too bad my little girl loves you. I don't give a shit what the Dragons did to me. I had it coming for my fuckin' sins, my mistakes. It's what they did to Elle, right in front of me, that's gonna hound me 'til the end of my fucked up life."

"It doesn't need to," Asphalt said. "Zee's dead. I killed

the motherfucker with my own bare hands, less than an hour ago. They're dragging his carcass away right now. I'm gonna let what he did die with him. It's the only shit that makes sense, the only thing that'll keep us sane, and happy."

He left out the part about my participation in the murder. Daddy couldn't know I'd been corrupted in blood, too.

"Ass-fuck, I don't need your advice."

Ouch. I cringed when I heard the cruel name he'd used before, the one I'd been hearing for years on the rare occasions when he even mentioned his name in our house.

"I need you to keep her company. Keep protecting her, loving her like I can't." Daddy looked up, and the two men locked eyes. "You saved my girl several times. I know you love her, too. That's good enough for me."

His words took me by total surprise. Suddenly, I couldn't hold in my smile. The tears I'd been holding inside spilled down my cheeks as I threw my arms around him, thanking him with kisses on both cheeks.

His face was so rough beneath my lips. He'd have lingering reminders of the sad hell we'd experienced all over his body for years to come. But the jagged cuts were healing, little by little. They'd get a little better each day, just like the hole in my heart.

"Okay, okay." Daddy pushed me away softly, a familiar kindness shining in his eyes. "We're never gonna be one big, happy family. But, you know, I can live with the two of you being hitched for real. If you ever come up to Tacoma once you start popping out babies, you'll always have a place to stay."

Asphalt smiled. We both knew my father had just given him the closet thing he'd ever get to a stamp of approval.

"Deal, Gil. And you're welcome here in Redding anytime." He held out his hand.

Daddy took Asphalt's hand and they shook for all of two seconds, a peace for the history books. Or at least the biggest truce I'd ever seen in my screwed up world.

"You gotta be fuckin' kidding. Once I'm in the truck home, riding with Line and the boys, there's no goddamned way I'm ever coming back to this god forsaken clubhouse. I'm no Prez anymore – I don't deserve it. Shit, I'm no good for ridin', shootin', and fuck knows what else with a damned stump."

"You're still good for admitting your mistakes, knowing right from wrong," I whispered, putting another arm over his shoulder. I twisted, pushing his stool until it spun him around, ready for a proper hug. "You'll always be my dad. I don't care what happens with the club."

This time, daddy didn't resist. He held me tight as he could with both arms, and I held him. Before he let go, I leaned close, and whispered.

"That arm's still good for giving the warmest hugs I've known since I was just a kid. Mom always said the same thing, and she was right. God damn it, daddy, you're going to be okay. You're going to be happy. Everybody sitting next to each other at this bar is going to live the rest of their lives with smiles on their faces. That's how we beat the Dragons for real."

When he finally turned to the bar for another drink, he had tears in his eyes, with a smile behind them in the darkness.

Asphalt stood up, took me by the wrist, and jerked me to my feet. "Let's get outta here, babe. We've got some shopping to do."

One Week Later

"Ass up. Hands behind your back, babe." Asphalt grunted, pulling my wrists together behind me when I complied. "Fucking shit. I'm never gonna get tired of seeing my brand all over you."

I smiled, enjoying the next few seconds of naked anticipation, before he mounted me from behind with a growl.

One apartment, one move, one new tattoo later, and we were about to reap some serious rewards.

I'd gotten his name imprinted on my left ass cheek in a second brand.

PROPERTY OF ASPHALT, two lightning streaks beside it, a target for his eyes as well as his hands when he decided I deserved to be spanked.

This evening, though, his cock just slammed me raw. I pushed my fingers through his and held on, bound by his hands, his personal fuck toy for tonight, and every night after.

If servicing his body as his old lady, his wife, and his woman was my duty, then I must've been the most eager, obedient girl on the planet. We hadn't stopped fucking since the move several days ago, sharing a real bed for the first time together.

Holy shit, what a workout we gave it.

Asphalt growled a little more with every stroke, his hips crashing into mine. Sweet, familiar tension roiled me near my center. I pushed back at him a little harder each time, bucking against his cock, always desperate to draw him deeper.

We fucked like the animals we were. My vision went white after a few more bone shaking strokes, and the fist holding my wrists closed tighter. He pulled me up against him, using my arms for extra leverage, fucking me even harder.

"Sweet Jesus!" I rasped. "Fuck!"

Yeah, *fuck.*

I'd come to know that word like hello and goodbye. It was the only sound I could make before he tossed me over the edge, into the churning, white hot pleasure tearing through me.

I said it, panted it, screamed it. And I always lost everything except that word when I came, feeling my pussy clenching on his cock, hungry to wring every drop of come he had inside me.

"Fucking hell, you're hot tonight. So fucking tight. All fucking *mine.*" His tempo rose, and his cock plunged deeper, pushing me into total, blissful submission.

God, I loved this badass. I'd really fallen for his cock, too, a total junkie for the only man I'd ever have inside me, the only one who'd fuck me, please me, and knock me up when the time came.

Maybe today.

We'd both discussed it. All the drama and danger of the past few weeks meant I'd gotten dangerously sloppy with my birth control. I'd decided to go off it with his blessing, and now there was nothing between my womb and his seed, the deepest branding an outlaw biker could give his old lady.

Beyond ink, words, and love itself. He took me like a wild beast, trying to get me pregnant, and I wanted it at some deep, dark, primal level I couldn't understand.

"Oh, fuck," Asphalt rumbled, making me smile.

I loved it when he went into a frenzy. He worked for every single spark of his pleasure, fucking me harder. I had to make him explode, pull him deep inside me, grind his cock inside me.

"Fuck *me,*" I growled back at him.

He met my challenge with more savage thrusts. His free hand wrapped around my waist, pinning me down, and he picked his entire body up and slammed it into me, crashing down again and again.

His pure, masculine strength drove us both to heaven. When I reached it again, my toes curling and my fingernails twisting in the sheets, I shrieked myself breathless.

This time, he came with me. Roaring, cursing, fucking my whole body with his, wedging me against the mattress as he turned me into a vessel for his seed.

"Shit, baby girl. No fucking clue what you do to me. All I know is I'll never, ever stop." He paused just long enough to pull badly needed air into his lungs. "Come the fuck with me!"

His hand twisted in my hair. He yanked it hard while my back arched with pleasure, his cock pushed deep, and he held it there, making me feel the imminent flood as he swelled.

Damn!

My eyes rolled as he roared, holding himself inside me, hurling hot seed straight from his balls. His cock jerked, pulsed, shot his load into my depths. And every single drop burned me so good I couldn't hold back.

I came all over again, my eyes rolling into my head. Burying my face into the cool sheets was the only relief from the fireball incinerating my entire body, blinding me, lashing me from head-to-toe with the frenzied pleasure he'd addicted me to.

We came so fucking hard my breath stopped. Suspended in that timeless space of twitching flesh and sweaty skin, I wished we could stay there forever, even if the intensity would've killed us both.

His cock kept pumping, and he rubbed it deeper into my sucking pussy. My teeth bit into a rough fold in the sheets to make sure my heart didn't stop.

Pure pleasure overwhelmed me, and retreated like a hurricane, slow as sin.

I turned my face and let out a loud gasp before breathing again. Asphalt groaned, relaxing his muscles with me, holding his dying hardness inside me as long as he could.

Jesus, he wanted that kid, and I wanted to give him one.

We were way beyond sex. Every time we fucked, we healed. The new bed gave us a springboard for the only therapy we needed, a shortcut to fucking out the last of our grief, our pain, and a road straight to our future.

I moaned as I felt him slide out of me, always hating the empty shock. When two souls became one like ours did every time he came inside me, it hurt to have it stolen away, if only for a couple seconds.

He eased off. My body ached deliciously as I twisted toward him. He laid down on his back, pulling me close to his chest. My lips were instantly on his, as starved for him as the first night we kissed on daddy's doorstep half a lifetime ago.

I couldn't have imagined my disaster of a prom night would ever lead to this. Hell, I couldn't imagine *him,* his arms folded around me, running one hand down to the fresh ink forever branded into my ass.

"Wish you had a clue how much I love this, Ell-Bell." He kissed me again, smiling as he pulled away. "Shit, I'm gonna have to buy you some knee pads next. I want to see my name glistening on your skin every single time we're fucking."

"Oh? I thought we put the new furniture across from us for a reason..."

Grinning, I pointed, and we both turned to our reflection in the big mirror as he straightened up to get a better look. He'd left the furniture crap mostly to me. I'd chosen well.

His eyes lit up when he found my latest surprise. I hadn't forgotten our night in the hotel.

How could I ever? This man had bent me over and fucked me in front of our reflection, stretching my eyes wide open to see the delirious love and lust in my own eyes when he came inside me.

Now, I straddled him, spread my legs wide and pulled him into my slick pussy.

"You can see my back in the mirror, right?"

"Yeah," he growled, licking his lips, grabbing for my ass.

I moaned as his cock sprang to life, pushed up inside me, using our juices from the last fuck as extra lube. We glided to a slow, fiery release like messed up angels.

He fucked me so hard I thought I'd fly through the

ceiling, if only his hands didn't grip my ass so tight. He pinched my cheeks *hard*, made them hurt, the kind of sexy pain my brain absolutely loved.

My lips parted in the first moan of many.

"Fuck me," I whispered softly, unable to hide the rough desperation creeping into my voice.

He doubled his speed, slamming into me so hard his balls swung, clapping my flesh.

We fucked. We rocked. We kissed each time I leaned down, devouring each other.

My pussy already ached for more of his come. I wanted every last drop out of his balls buried deep inside me. My hips jerked into his, swallowing his huge length.

Deeper. Faster. Harder.

So. Fucking. Good.

As soon as he felt me tensing, racing toward another climax, he pushed one hand between my legs. His fingers found my clit and I was gone.

I threw myself backward, fucking him deeper still, catching myself with my hands behind me. Asphalt fucked me wild for the next thirty seconds, all I needed to come so hard I thought I'd found paradise several times over.

Halfway through it, he came. Growling, twisting his hips into mine, pulling me close.

He gripped me like an owner. He clenched his fingers into my flesh for dear life, like he needed me to live, and I smiled through my world breaking orgasm because I knew he did.

Shit, I needed him.

I needed *this*. Just as much as I needed my pussy to keep squeezing his cock, stealing his come, draining all the heat from the tip of his cock.

"Holy, holy fuck. Almost made me blind, woman," he growled, smashing me against his chest when we could finally speak again. "What the hell's gotten into you today?"

"We have an extra room, and I don't want it to be empty for long. I'm working overtime to give you a family, baby."

The words still sounded strange leaving my mouth. I'd never plunged into a beautiful, life changing thing like this. But after all the hurt and heartache getting here, I did it without a second more of hesitation.

I did it for him. My love, my life, my Austin.

"Guess I should've known," he said with a grin. "Fuck, babe, you know I'm ready. Only wish I had five more goddamned balls to keep you full twenty-four-seven."

I laughed. So ridiculous and weirdly sweet. Running my fingers across his face, I moved the tips over his head, feeling the stubble coming up, softer than the stuff lining his jaw.

"What's this? Don't tell me you've decided to drop the cue ball look?"

"Shit changes, babe," he said mysteriously. "Life's not

all about breaking heads and boozing. Fuck, there's only a couple brothers left riding free and wild. I'm ready as hell for a family too, and I'll be damned if I'm gonna have my son thinking he's fucked into growing up bald."

"Yeah?" I giggled, straining to wonder what he'd look like with a nice, thick head of hair. He'd be just as handsome, I knew that much. "But what if you get a girl for your first born?"

"Then she knows she'll get your good looks," he said, stamping his lips against my neck. "And I'm sure as hell not raining all over 'em by making her think she won't get this beautiful hair because her old man's got nothing on top."

I purred when he fisted my locks and pulled them one more time. "Whatever, *dad.* I see you've thought of everything."

"Babe, you don't know the fucking half of it."

XII: Drive On (Asphalt)

Six Months Later

Our turn.

Brass, Rabid, and Roman stood next to the altar, their old ladies on their arms, little Caleb squirming in Sally's. Everybody here was getting officially hitched or renewing their vows today, and now it was our turn.

I grabbed Elle's little hand and stepped up, staring the Prez and our brother-turned-priest, Angus, right in the eyes.

"You've been a fine example to everyone, son," Blackjack said. The old man took my shoulder and gave it a fatherly squeeze. He looked at Elle. "Both of you. It's only right you're joining the party today, doing this the way it should've gone down the first time."

Ell-Bell and I shared a look. Christ help her, she blushed, a little remnant of the sweet virgin girl I'd married lingering in the badass bride carrying my kid.

"Don't be shy, babe," I whispered. The church had gone so damned quiet I felt like I was talking in a library.

"I took this hand when I didn't have a choice, and I

still wanted it then. Needed to own you so bad I almost fucking died," I said loudly, so the rowdy gathering of brothers surrounding us could hear. I wanted her to hear it more than anybody else, but I didn't give a shit if the whole damned world found out the lunatic love I had for this girl.

"Today, I know I've earned it. I've killed for your heart, babe, almost died for it several times over. And I'd do it all over again without a shred of hesitation. You've given me things no woman ever will, and there's so much more on the way, sometimes it makes my fucking head spin."

She smiled and suppressed a laugh, blushing again as my eyes fell down. The girl wasn't stupid – she knew exactly what I was looking at.

The little bump on her belly got bigger everyday. I reached out, laid my free hand on it, and squeezed her hand tighter.

"Things are changing in this club all the time. Two brothers turned newlyweds today, two more renewing their vows. Who the hell knows what's next." I paused, trying not to notice how dangerously fuckable she looked wearing my brand on her new jacket. Thing had PROPERTY OF ASPHALT stitched on the backside, lightning bolts by the side.

Mine, mine, all fucking *mine.*

I was damned glad it wasn't staring me in the face just then, or I'd have lost my mind.

"Peace and plenty," Blackjack said, finishing for me with a wink. "Every man standing here with his girl has fought, worked, and bled for what we have today. There's no going back for this club. I could stand here and rehash all the battles and sorrows we've all faced. There's no need. Tell her, son. Give her your promise."

Shit. These grand speeches had never been my thing, but suddenly I had a fire in my heart.

I snatched Elle's hands in both of mine, held them up to my lips, and kissed her cool skin. Her blood burned. So did the beautiful spark rising in her clear blue eyes.

"Peace and plenty's for the club, and we're all happy to have it. But you and me, Elle Jo, we've got love. I know you feel it every night when you're pressed up against me. It's there, whether we're staring at the ceiling or the stars or just each other. Hell, I feel it every time you're on my bike, holding me so tight I think we're gonna become one right there on the open road."

I paused and turned, watching her blot away a happy tear, staring at the brothers gathered around us.

My boys all held their women close. All the girls were crying, overwhelmed by the raw fucking emotion of the day. We were the closing act.

Out in the pews, Missy's little sis, Jackie, wept like the schoolgirl she was. I grinned, briefly wondering what kinda crazy shit lay ahead for her in the years to come, if she kept close to this MC.

"Babe, that shit they say about a man getting

acclimated, getting bored with his woman – it's not true. Not even fucking close. Every day I wake up with you weighing heavier on my mind. You're sunrise and sunset. I think about you when I'm on my runs and sitting in church with the boys, even when you're laying next to me. No bullshit. Just truth, all of it."

The Prez shot me the evil eye for a second when I said the part about being distracted in church. Then, he shook his head and smiled. Club business took a backseat to all this crazy fucking love today.

"Half the guys here are gonna laugh. Everybody else standing up here knows exactly what I'm talking about." I looked at my brothers, and they all wore the same *fuck yes* expression. "Fuck if that matters. The only thing that's ever meant a damned thing to me is right in front of me."

I grabbed her, pulled her close, loving the little bulge in her belly against my abs. "Love you every damned day of my life, Ell-Bell. I'd relive our wedding every morning if I could, and I'm gonna feel the same way 'til my heart stops pounding in my chest. You're mine, baby, glued to my life like cement. You're still gonna be my girl when I'm too damned old to even tear across the country anymore."

My hand went to the back of her head. She didn't need any encouragement to smash her mouth down against mine.

I devoured that woman. Kissed her with the same

crazy intensity we'd shared for months, the flame I couldn't believe I'd ever lived without.

"I love you!" she hissed into my ear, digging her fingernails into my back, and then again, louder, when I finally broke the kiss. "Love you forever, Asphalt."

Didn't think anybody heard her except for me over the loud shouts of the crowd. Didn't matter either. This woman and me, we went to our own private universe lit with love and lust, even when we were surrounded by about a hundred people.

"Kiss her one more time and hit the road, son," Blackjack said. "This club has earned some happiness in every single mile we've won."

I nodded at the Prez. He didn't have a woman at his side – shit, I'd never so much as seen him pull one of the club sluts into his office – but he was celebrating too.

We'd gone six months without a fucking shootout. Six months with nobody in the clubhouse taking more serious damage than a bad hangover.

Goddamned record breaker. Times were changing for sure, and the bear finally meant something more than blood and violence.

We'd kept our freedom. And now we'd added all the other glorious shit to our list.

Love. Family. Brotherhood.

"Let's burn some fucking rubber!" Roman roared. "We got a long haul to Oregon and we oughta be there by sunset."

Everyone laughed. The giant had gotten unhinged today, his stoic shit wearing down. He threw a huge arm over his girl and they walked over with Brass and Missy, passing their toddler to Jackie, who'd be watching the kid while they got some alone time.

"See that shit, Elle Jo? That's gonna be us in a few more months." She smiled at me and I leaned closer, putting my lips against her throat.

"Guess you'd better fuck me a few more times to make up for what we'll miss when the baby comes," she teased.

I looked at her like she'd lost her fucking mind. The wicked smirk in her sweet lips only made my cock hammer harder in my jeans.

"You better be fucking kidding, woman," I growled sweeping her into my arms. "We'll be up fucking all night once we get to the campsite. And we're not gonna stop, not even when we're spending our nights on two hours of sleep, running after the kids. You think you're ever getting a break from this, you've got another thing coming."

I kissed her harder this time, my tongue probing deep into her mouth. Found her sweet little tongue, flicked it, and ruled it. I fucked her lips with my tongue the same way I'd glide between her legs later tonight.

Fuck, fuck. Blood pounded through my dick, anticipation streaking through me like a drug.

How the hell did she taste so perfect every single

second?

"I hope so. Last thing I'd ever want is my old man going soft," she purred, tipping her face away from mine before I could steal more. "This is like our wedding night, right? The one we should've had?"

I grinned. "Damned straight."

Everybody wearing a Grizzlies MC patch rode out in formation, probably the last time I'd ride with all my boys and their girls before Elle Jo got too big for my bike.

Fuck if I didn't love her anyway. Shit, truth be told, I loved her more with that bump in her belly, a constant reminder that we'd become man and wife the deepest way we could.

We'd said our vows at the altar. I'd renew them with her every damned year if it'd make her happy, but no vows could ever compare to the ones we'd written in flesh and blood.

We wouldn't be alone. Our club would look like a goddamned nursery in the next couple years now that the rest of the brothers had gotten hitched.

Brass and Missy. Rabid and Christa. Sally and Roman.

Even Stryker and the other prospects would probably shack up before long, putting the dwindling numbers of sluts who came to our club parties outta work for good. There's always be bastards who fucked around on their girls too, and I'd never get their stupid asses.

The girl riding pressed up behind me had felt like my bride forever. But we'd just got through with the closest thing we'd had to a real wedding, seeing how the first one was a clusterfuck of outside obligations.

Never again. There'd always be duties to my patch and my brothers, sure, but everything involving this woman from here on out was for us.

Us. That fucking phrase made me burn.

Us. That single word caused my blood to heat and my pulse to pound straight into my cock.

Us. I couldn't wait 'til we had a family in front of us, even if it meant getting older and grayer.

Shit, *especially* if it meant that. Just as long as it was with her, having our kids at the table every night or bouncing on my knee while I told them crazy tales about awesome warriors and vile bastards who deserved to die.

We rode on outta Redding, straight to our big club honeymoon getaway in the lush cedar wilds across the state line. The whole Grizzlies brotherhood was riding into a new chapter that would take years to write.

I couldn't wait to make a few more words tonight with Elle, next to the big fire we'd build, only heading back to our tent when we were good and ready to fuck, to merge, to live and love.

The guys and their girls all sprawled out around the fire. Jackie put down Caleb a couple hours ago, and we gathered around the fire, the wide starry sky twinkling above us.

"Why so heavy tonight, Prez?" Brass said, pausing to plant another kiss on Missy's cheek. "I mean, shit, you've earned it more than anybody. Don't know how the fuck you survived all those years when this club was going downhill, rudderless as all hell."

"There's always good times in the muck, son. There's always purpose. Direction. A man's life ought to have light, darkness, and enough fire to burn down the universe." Blackjack looked up, his long gray hair blowing as a wind cut through our camp. He stared right at me and Elle.

"You two, over there. Seeds grown straight from pitch black soil." His eyes moved over us, stopping on the brothers and their girls, one by one.

I held Elle tighter, giving the Prez a silent nod. None of this would've been possible without the chieftan sitting in front of us, deep in his thoughts and words. Sometimes he waxed fucking poetic, a philosopher king if there ever was one.

"Nobody sitting by the fire tonight hasn't been gutted at some point," Blackjack said. "Whether they've lost their mothers, their fathers, or just a piece of themselves some long dark night, they survived. They lived to burn higher and brighter. Damn it, boys and girls, we've all beat the odds. There were plenty of times on the road when our guns came out that I thought I'd lose good men. I thought I'd have to break news about being widows to the girls here, or else drown our brothers in booze and bitches after some sorry bastards killed their girls dead."

He stood up, slowly, shaking off the pain in his leg. Shit wasn't getting any better. And yet the crazy SOB kept leading us straight into peace and war. Nothing could keep him down – same as every man here by the fire tonight.

"We beat the fucking odds, boys, and don't you *ever* forget it." He pointed to all of us, taking a long sip off his beer bottle. "You're married. You've got families coming. You're living the good life, like every man and woman should, and it's not going to be taken for granted."

"Fuck, no," Roman belted out, pulling Sally a little closer on his lap.

"Doesn't matter how much we bled or how many assholes we've killed in the past. Doesn't matter how much more of that's ahead," the Prez continued. "If any jackals are crazy enough to sink their teeth into our happy peace, they'll die, plain and simple. As long as this big ass family's alive, breathing, and still able to love each other like brothers and sisters should, we own the world."

"Never gonna let go of it neither, Prez. The whole damned world's ours," Rabid growled, staring into Christa's smiling, scarred face. "We've got that motherfucker by the throat, tonight and forever."

They kissed. Somewhere in a nearby tent, Caleb cried, and we heard Jackie's soft, young voice trying to soothe him through the silence.

"Kids. Hope you're both ready," Sally said, shooting Elle a wink before turning to Roman. "Come on, baby. We'd better see what he wants."

The giant stood up, nodded a goodnight to us all, and disappeared with his girl. The rest of the couples all sat quiet, while Blackjack stared into the fire, knocking down his beer with new vigor.

"This fire belongs to lovers," the Prez said, throwing his bottle into the waste bin and picking up a new one from the case. "Enjoy the stars, sons. You don't know how fucking special they can be. Here for an instant, bright as a candle, and snuffed out just as easy."

Rabid, Brass, and me all shared a look.

"What's gotten into him?" I growled, just as baffled as anyone, once the crunch of Blackjack's boots on the dirt had totally faded.

Rabid shrugged, running one hand through his hair. "He's branching off from camp tomorrow, like he said. Going out to Missoula for a day or two by himself to meet with the Devils, or some shit. The Prez is always all business, all the fucking time, when he's not doing fancy ass speeches for us."

"The man's a walking mystery. He's earned it," I said, watching the Prez's silhouette disappear through the trees. "We'd all be missing our heads from a cartel blade or worse if it wasn't for him. Hope he finds whatever the fuck he's looking for, out there all alone."

"It's probably just the long trip up here," Elle said with a yawn. "God, I'm tired."

Goddamned adorable. *Really.*

Did she seriously think I'd let her sleep without fucking her completely senseless?

I pulled her onto my lap and gave her another long, fiery kiss. Didn't take long before all the brothers were trying to one-up each other with the girls on their laps.

We kissed. We made our women moan. We fought to stay by the cozy fire 'til the first man lost his nerve and headed for his tent.

"Brass!" Missy moaned, taking the Veep by the cheeks and staring into his eyes. "Let's get out of here already!"

He grinned, losing his battle. Once, he'd been a junkie, and now it was plain as fucking day my brother had a new addiction. Brass stood and mumbled a goodnight, pulling Missy with him, taking half a bottle of whiskey to help keep them warm.

I kissed Elle harder. My hands went to her ass, jerked her softly against my hips, making damned sure she felt the rock hard need I had underneath my jeans.

The fresh air out here in the wilderness had nothing on this woman. I needed her like fucking oxygen. Her legs quivered as she hooked them tighter around mine, her lips moving in a circle.

When my hard-on hit her clit through her own ivory white jeans, she nearly scratched blood down my neck. We hurt so damned good together, and we'd be doing a lot of that tonight.

"Rabid..." Christa was the next domino to fall.

I looked over my woman's shoulder and saw her hands moving up underneath his shirt, gliding along his smooth back muscles. My brother scratched his stubble, looked at me, and accepted defeat.

He stood up, holding his old lady in his arms. "See you in the morning, brother. We've gotta turn in for the night."

Some night bird caterwauled in the distance. I listened to their footsteps disappear, then the lone disruption of the zipper going up on their tent.

Alone at last. I stared into Elle's eyes, feeling her legs unhook from mine, her little hand tugging on mine.

"Come on, baby. I think I want you more than any woman here wants her man, and I'm going to prove it." She licked her lips.

Fuck me stupid. My cock ached from tip to sack.

The girl was too damned good at being enticing. So fucking enticing I almost lost my shit, flipped her around, and spanked her in front of the fire we'd have to put out before we went inside.

"No." I took her wrist in my hand and jerked her back, before she got any bright ideas about leading me to the tent. "Get back on my lap where you belong."

"Huh?"

I wasn't waiting around. I pulled her back into place, and once she was on my knee, put my hand down her jeans. Hungry fingers disappeared down her waistband, through her panties. I found the wetness waiting for me and put my lips on her throat to stifle my growl.

"Oh...Oh, God!" Elle's big blue eyes rolled toward the fire, and she moaned again.

Now, she understood. Out here in nature, with nothing but this fire watching, we could fuck like the animals we were.

I went for her zipper, tugging on her pants, desperate to free her to the night and my own manic fucking lust.

"Austin, really?" She panted, her eyes opening in disbelief. "Out here? What if somebody sees us?"

My head snapped back and I laughed. "Get real, babe. They're all in their tents, balls deep in their own lust by now, same as we're about to be."

Just to reassure her, I reached for the log next to me and threw it on the fire. Sparks shot into the night as the fire consumed the new wood, crackling and popping like gunfire.

"Come closer," I ordered, jerking her head to my chest. "You'll hear something louder going off in my blood than that shit burning up in front of us. I *need* you, Ell-Bell. Out here. Right now."

Simple, even if it wasn't rational. The crazy ass longing for this girl didn't think and it sure as fuck wasn't patient.

I ripped her pants down with a snarl, and then jerked her panties to her knees. Lifting her up, I took my own pants down, bringing her down onto my lap.

Whatever doubts she had, I wrecked them when I thrust up into her. Filled her hot, sweet little cunt with every inch of my hungry cock, stretching her open, feeling her tense and dig her nails into my back.

"You better ride me good if you want us in that tent tonight," I growled into her ear. "Give me the love and hate, babe...everything you've got. All we're ever gonna share. I want you jerking on my cock like a shot to the fucking heart."

"Bastard!" she cursed as I dragged her deeper onto my cock, filling her completely, grinding her clit with my pubic bone.

She tried to call out again, but the squeal sticking in her throat choked her off.

Loved this shit. I loved fucking her so hard she couldn't breathe.

I kissed her, moving my hips harder, faster, then pulled back to let her suck more air down her throat. This dick could've pounded her 'til she passed the fuck out, but I couldn't have our kid getting oxygen deprived in her womb.

"Breathe, baby," I growled, clenching my fingers on her ass, jerking her against me with more force each time. "You're gonna come for me, so hard and good you can't see straight."

"Please!" she whimpered, begging me to fuck her harder still.

With a snarl, I pushed her off my lap, then bent her over, grounding her hands on the rock. I took her from behind and let my balls swing, slapping her clit each time I drove deep.

She tensed up, gushed, and tried to scream within seconds. I clapped my hand over her mouth, cursing when she bit into my finger, pushing the pleasure back into her lips.

Wasn't letting anything escape into the night. Her pleasure, her moans, her screams belonged to me.

I let the fire behind us warm my ass while I fucked her like a freight train, straight through her first orgasm of many. Her pussy juiced all over my dick, growing hotter and wetter and tighter all the time.

"You're gonna kill me one of these days, baby girl," I growled, the fire in my balls growing as strong as the one toasting my backside. "I'll fuck you so hard my damned head pops from everything you've given me."

"No!" she moaned through my fingers, kissing over the bite mark the little minx had left on my hand.

"Yeah. Fuck yeah."

Had to say it twice. I wouldn't fucking settle for anything less.

She had to believe me.

I fucked this girl honest, groaning my pleasure a

minute later, my balls hitting overload, crazy to spit more come into her.

I railed her with all my might. Her tits swung like pendulums while I shook every inch of her, fucking her with everything I had, everything that said it like words couldn't.

My. Fucking. Property.

Elle Jo's perfect pussy squeezed my cock. She came again, and I fucking lost it. My head snapped back so far I could see the stars rolling in the blackness while my load hurled out my dick.

I shot the thickest ropes of my life into her since the night I knocked her up. Pushed my cock deep and unloaded with every muscle twitching, a full body release like she just took half my soul.

All these months, and the drug-like effect of coming inside this woman still hadn't faded. There was a difference between fucking the sluts of the distant past and the love of my life, the mother of my kids, the woman I'd claimed from here 'til kingdom come.

And I'd never forget it. How the hell could I?

The fire rampaging through my veins told me every time I pushed deep like this. My balls pulsed a reminder so fucking hard it made my ears ring. Elle Jo took every inch of me to the absolute limits like she did every night, pulling out my come, taking a piece of me to heaven.

I came my fucking brains out. I gave her my soul. And she gave me something I'd be dreaming about when we were finally spent – her moaning, clenching, biting release. Everything I gave to her like no man ever would.

"Fuck, fuck, fuck," I whispered, pulling outta her an eternity later.

Couldn't force my brain to think anything else after coming together like that.

She rolled, closing her legs like a good girl to hold my seed in, staring me in the eyes. I doused out the fire with a bucket of water nearby, then rolled up my pants. I frowned when she did the same, only consoling myself with the fact that I'd be ripping all that shit off in a couple more minutes, back in the tent.

"You know, I wracked my brain to tell you how much I love you back there at the church, before we left Redding," she said softly, holding my hand, looking into the dying embers in the fire pit. "I couldn't find words. Nothing comes close when it's all about you, Austin. You saved my life. Not just with the Chinese, I mean...*this*."

She brought a hand to her belly. "I never thought I could be so happy. So fulfilled. You've given me a future, a way to be inside the club without losing my mind. Thank you, love. I'll never forget it."

The girl leaned on her tip-toes and gave me a kiss so hot it was like we hadn't even fucked. My dick sprang to life, begging to be inside her again.

I turned her around, ran my fingers through her soft blonde hair, then put my lips where they belonged on hers before I said anything.

"Babe, you don't have to thank me for shit, or sing my ass sonnets. When you're screaming your lungs out underneath me and exploding on my cock, that's how I know you love me. When I see my face getting older and wiser in those blue eyes, I know. You're fucking crazy if you think you've gotta prove anything – or if you think I'd ever doubt it."

"You'd better kiss me and come closer to get a better look," she said, smiling, taking a long look at the stars before meeting my eyes. "It's such a beautiful night."

"Yeah, Ell-Bell, but it's barely different than any other. We're gonna be having nights like this for a long fucking time. Count on it, as sure as you'll be rocking our kid to sleep by winter."

"Oh, I will, you wonderful bastard."

I smiled into our next kiss. These getaways were great. The club needed ceremony sometimes, and so did we as a couple, but fuck.

Honestly, I'd be renewing our vows every single day. I did it every time I took these lips, listened to her voice, pinned her down and felt her shaking under me.

About a minute later, we managed to pull away just long enough to crawl into our tent underneath the starry sky.

We renewed our vows all damned night, and probably forged a few new ones in dirt and grit and lust.

I loved this woman so much I couldn't believe I'd

wasted so much time on other shit. I remembered the first time those bright blue eyes gave me the world when we were dumb kids, staring at me through the spokes of her screwed up bike tire as I kneeled down to give her a hand.

Half an eternity ago, and it was still as fucking beautiful as yesterday. I passed the hell out next to my woman with a smile on my face.

OUTLAW'S VOW

Blackjack's Secret:
Grizzlies MC Romance

Nicole Snow

I: No Less Bitter (Blackjack)

I watched my boys get married one by one.

First Roman and Sally, complete with a kid in tow. I'd bet my bottom dollar my Enforcer would have another kid in her by next year, giving Caleb a little brother or sister.

Rabid and Christa. The joy he'd brought to her scarred face and torn up life tugged something wicked on these old heartstrings. He'd paid her debt in blood, saved her life, and given her the world.

Brass and Missy. Once a junkie, my Veep was only addicted to his girl now. He'd pulled her out of the gutter and adopted her little sis like his own daughter. Their marriage reminded me every damned day I'd made a solid choice for my right hand man when I took this club over.

Finally, Asphalt and Elle Jo. She poured ice on the hothead, and he gave her fire. They were born in the club. They'd die someday with the patch hanging over them too, but not before their hearts were scorched to a crisp with the flame they had for each other.

Shit, their love hit me the hardest. They'd really

suffered for their love.

All too brutally familiar, stabbing me right between the eyes, reminding me of everything I'd squandered, lost, and still had on the line.

Their pain, I got on a very fucking visceral level. It hung low in my bones, worse than the ache radiating up hip since I'd taken a bullet to the leg. The old wound nipped at me now as I rode away from our happy camp in Oregon, on toward Missoula.

As far as my boys knew, I was going up there to have some serious talks with the Devils about business. That much was true, but Missoula would be at the tail end of a more personal pit stop.

I was going home. It was time to pay homage to the past and stare my future in the face, back in Spokane, the place I'd lived and loved half a lifetime ago.

I rode hard all day and night. Mountains, forests, and streams passed by in a blur, cold as time and faceless as the wind ripping through my long graying hair.

Nothing but truckers and young kids on the road at night. When they saw me coming, they moved the fuck over. Probably wondered if they'd seen a ghost when I got up alongside them.

Didn't ever smile unless somebody had a kid in the car. Especially not on this trip.

Coming so close to my girl was always a bitch because she kept me so far. Impossibly distant. She still hadn't forgiven me, after all these years, and I knew she never would.

I never told my boys about the hell behind me, the agonizing loss, and I sure as shit never said anything to the bastards who served in the Grizzlies with me under Fang. This shit was too private, even for brothers.

Spokane had the only thing in the world that could make me lose my shit. I'd rather take a dagger to the chest a hundred times than let any man sharing the patch see me break.

Outlaw Presidents don't get the luxury of tears.

Not even when they're hot, toxic, and totally justified.

My heart thumped like a big bass drum by the time I saw the little outline of Spokane coming into view. My bike roared through the mountains, and the memories hit me harder than the Washington wind.

A soft, dark morning dawned on the last stretch. Perfectly somber atmosphere for what I had to do. I turned off the main road, bypassing the town center, and headed for the sticks.

My girl hadn't ever been cut out for the city life, so no surprise I'd shuffled her off to somewhere more peaceful, the last place she'd ever live.

"Hey, babe."

So fucking pathetic, but it was all I could muster. The angel was huge, and I'd gotten her face custom made to look just like my girl. I'd used this spot for confessions the few times I'd come here over the years, telling this crude stand-in for the real deal everything I ever wanted to say to flesh and blood.

I put my hand on her, trying not to wince when I felt how frigid she was, how she wouldn't even look at me.

So cold. So quiet. So absolutely pissed – and she'd got every reason in the world to be.

This wasn't an angel of mercy. Didn't deserve one neither.

I took my hand away, folded my arms over my cut, trying to muster the same manic energy I used to wheel and deal as Prez every day.

Didn't fucking work here. It was flat, worthless, dead.

"My whole crew's just about married now. Only got Stryker and a couple kids left to get their boozing and whoring out before they settle down just the same. It's funny, watching these boys turn into proper men after being bastards for thirty years. Old Southpaw's never gonna stop fucking his whores, but you know how that shit goes. He's a lot like your old man."

I looked up with a smile, straight into the big stone angel's dark, vacant eyes. Nothing.

Fuck me, it hurt.

It split me in two from the skull on down. I'd gazed into the eyes of hell a thousand times since I'd put on this patch, stared down cartel captains and dirty rogues and kids who'd done terrible things because they were just 'following orders.'

None of that shit had anything on staring into my old

lady's face cut in stone. I had to look away, turn my back, and settle onto the dirty ground, clutching at the grass.

I leaned into her robe, feeling how stiff, immovable, and timeless she'd become. I could've moved the whole damned world without her saying boo.

"Had our anniversary last week, Lizzie," I said softly, staring at the big brass ring on my hand. "I'd have gotten up here sooner if I wasn't so distracted. Yeah, club biz, you know it, woman. Sorry I fucked up, babe. Again."

How many times had I apologized? How many times had I wanted it to do some good, to see her magically look at me, throw her arms around me, tell me the past was the past?

How often had I walked away with jack shit?

"You know I'll always love you, Lizzie. It's not like the shit in my chest gives me any choice, even if it's getting older and harder every passing year. I'd ask you to forgive me for the thousandth time, but I know you won't." I reached into my pocket and pulled out a smoke, touching the tip to my lighter 'til it caught. "I don't deserve it. Never will after what I did to you."

I leaned back against her, waiting for the morning sunlight to creep across the cool ground and warm everything up. Took about another twenty minutes, crouching there in silence, burning up my cig.

Then I lit another. And another. Must've smoked three more before the sun came out through the clouds, giving us some precious light.

Gold did funny shit to an old man's eyes. Made me think. Just enough to remember the good times wedged between the sins, before the darkness swept over us when I left, and wrecked me forever.

Wrecked us. I closed my eyes, tilting my face at my knees.

"You remember those days, don't you babe? Somewhere, somehow, I know you do. Feels like it was only yesterday." I took a long pull off my smoke, filled my lungs, and held it 'til I almost choked. "Just tell me one thing – where the *fuck* does the time go?"

II: Firecracker (Blackjack)

Twenty-four years ago

Once, I wasn't gray. I had muscle, I had venom running hot in my veins, and I thought I was God's own gift to the wide open road.

Anything seemed possible before the constant nipping fire above my knee, or half a dozen other aches that came and went.

I was spry. Young. Arrogant.

An unapologetic motherfucker with long dark hair, short on fucks to give. Everybody walking on the planet answered to me, ever since I'd joined the baddest MC West of the Mississippi, and learned to love the dark snarling bear inked on my skin.

So, when I saw her working the new club bar outside town the very first time, I didn't know she was my own President's daughter. And I didn't fucking care.

She'd be mine that night for no other reason than the fact that I *always* got what I want, who I wanted, whenever I needed it.

Oki's words echoed in my head like the big old

bastard was still speaking to me, that night he saw the way I was eyeballing her, trying to stop my dick from ripping straight out my jeans. Sometimes I wonder if I hadn't been so damned arrogant, if I'd only backed away, maybe we'd both be better off.

"I know you think you're hot shit, Blackjack, but we've got ourselves an order around here. You're gonna figure it out quick, or I'll knock your head off so fucking fast it'll spin like a fucking satellite." Oki bared his teeth, lifting me halfway off my feet by my cut. "Stay the fuck away from my Lizzie. If I find out you've even so much as cat called her, I'm putting you under, and I don't give a single fuck who your old man was."

Whatever you say, Old bastard. I stumbled backward with a nod, hating the way he rubbed my family shit in his warning.

Not like it was new. When your papa was a founding member in the club, everybody kissed your ass, resented you like you'd put a bullet in their favorite dog.

I'd had to work five times as hard as every other man wearing this patch to prove myself. I took shit from no one except the fucks who were entitled to serve it up.

Unfortunately, right now, that included Oki, a towering World War II vet who'd lost his soul on some God forsaken island in the Pacific forty years ago. How he made a chick like Lizzie, I'd never understand.

He'd barely turned back to his whiskey, grabbing the bottle and storming off to his office, before my eyes were all over her again.

Fuck. I couldn't look away.

Eighties rock blasted out the jukebox, and I thought it was Christ himself blowing his horn when I saw her, felt that pulse in my balls hitting my throat.

Green eyes. Long red hair. Shape like a fucking hourglass, perfectly crafted to activate that cave beast deep inside every man, the thing that wouldn't let me stop 'til I had her naked, screaming, digging her nails into my back while I owned her from the inside out.

Then she looked up. Our eyes locked, and I knew one of us would be a goner before the night was done.

No bones about it. I'd either fuck this girl 'til I owned her soul, or her old man would snap my dick off and toss it down the sewer.

"Whiskey, beautiful," I said, walking up to the bar and slamming my empty glass down in front of her.

She looked down, her lips twisted all sour, but playful. Couldn't decide whether I wanted to bite them more than her sweet round ass.

"Haven't you had enough? Daddy doesn't like it when his guys get real drunk. You know we're out here, kinda one the edge. He says you need to be ready for anything."

"Yeah, yeah, I know the drill. Just fill it the fuck up." I punched my shot glass down on the wood again, wondering where the hell she got off.

Pretty bold to tell me I'd had too much.

Maybe there was more to the sweet little daddy's girl after all.

"You're awful brave for a bar girl," I said, throwing my long hair back across my leather clad shoulders. "What the hell are you – seventeen, eighteen?"

Please be fucking legal, I thought, feeling my cock straining more.

"I'm nineteen, Blackjack." She smiled shyly, grabbing a bottle of Jim and tipping it to my glass. We both watched the honey brown liquid pool, catching the light like dull gold. "Just trying to do you a favor, keep you sober and responsible. You're not the Enforcer yet, but everybody says you want to be someday."

"Yeah?" I grabbed my drink and smiled. "You've been asking around about me? Shit, girl, why the hell haven't we sat down together sooner?"

"I like to keep tabs on guys my daddy hates." I caught a flash of her soft little tongue razzing me through her lips before she turned around, grabbed her towel, and went back to polishing the counters.

"Say that again. I'll come over the counter, pull down those jeans, and spank your sweet cheeks blood red."

Her head whipped around so fast her jaw was hanging. Inside, I was grinning all the way, happy to finally see some shock lighting up her face.

"Look, I never said *I* hated you. That's what daddy thinks."

"Hm. I'm more interested in *your* thoughts, baby girl.

Believe me, I know damned well how Oki feels about both of us."

"He can be a little overbearing, right? Daddy's always been like that. Mister Upright Citizen, at least when he isn't in a fight or screwing somebody behind ma's back."

"That's rough, babe. I feel you." Without a smile, I stood up, placing my hands on the counter. "But you didn't really answer my question. It's obvious you know my name. You've been looking at me, probably more than I've been watching you...what's that say, Lizzie?"

"Well, I don't..."

She stopped in mid-blush. Took the moment while her face was turned, bright red beauty blossoming on her cheeks. Threw my legs over the bar and stormed across it.

My hands went around her waist, pinned her against the edge of the counter before she realized what was happening.

"Blackjack! This is crazy...he could come back any minute, you know." Her eyes were wide and scared, totally fucking beautiful in their shimmering greens. I wanted to make them burn like forests on fire. "He's in the back...probably with that floozie, Butterbaby, his favorite..."

"You worry too much. Your old man's getting his dick wet the same way I oughta be with a woman like you. Let me guess..." My hands clamped down on her ass and jerked her closer. "You've been sheltered with the way he treats you, yeah? Always watching the brothers grab their girls and go off to fuck, while you can only stand aside and wonder."

She whimpered. I knew when I was on the right track, and right now I read her fucking mind.

"How many men, babe? One, two? Don't tell me you're a kiss-less virgin."

"What?!" She flattened her hands against my chest. The girl feigned pushing me away, but she wasn't really trying. "Do you ask every girl that the first time you have a conversation?"

I snorted. "Come on. You've been around this club long enough to know the way it's done."

Her hand shot up and slapped me across the cheek. The burn sank through my skin and hit my brain, quick as booze, and I smiled.

"Hit me again, Firecracker. Only makes me want to rip your pants off and take you on this counter here even more."

She gasped. I pulled her close. Before she could curse my name, my lips crashed down on hers.

We kissed volcanic, hot and needy as flowing lava.

I swallowed her heat, and she swallowed mine. Beautiful exchange. Gorgeous woman.

With her lips on mine, I was alive, truly hungry to devour her and stay in the moment. That was something special when I'd gotten used to draining my balls in sluts who's names I never remembered.

Fucking them was no different than blowing my damned nose.

This girl...*fuck,* what lips. Grabbing the back of her head, I tugged her face to mine, kept my nuclear hot lips on hers while my tongue conquered.

"Let's go," I growled, breaking away, taking her hand and leading her into the bar. "Bet your papa never let you ride on another man's bike, did he?"

The smile on her face overwhelmed the questioning look she'd had a second ago. "No."

Without another word, I led her to my bike. I'd give her a chance to own the road and let the wind speak before we did more talking on a motel bed, the side of the road, in the clubhouse, behind daddy's back.

Everywhere. Anywhere.

Christ, what the hell was happening?

I'd just met the first girl in my life I *had* to fuck to keep breathing.

"Just look at all that fire up there and tell me it doesn't make you want to blow this town forever." I pointed at the wide starry sky spreading over Spokane.

We'd stopped for the night on a hill, nothing between us but a blanket. Maybe she hadn't figured out this was where she'd spend the night yet, but I was gonna fucking show her.

"I can't," she said, smiling and shaking her head. "Daddy would kill me."

"Come on, Firecracker. There's a beautiful fuckin' world out there. Already been abroad, and I'll be doing more of it soon. I'll be riding all over hell – Oregon, Idaho, California. That's assuming the club doesn't send us East to make Montana our bitch. We're owning that state someday, and nobody gives a damn what Vodoo and the Prairie Pussies in the Dakotas have to say about it."

"Prairie Devils." She rolled her eyes. "You guys all hate them, don't you?"

"Only because they're in our way, love." I reached for her hand, pulled her onto my lap, overpowering her when she tried to playfully resist. Lizzie settled down real quick when she felt my heat all over her.

"I'm surprised you haven't gotten it straight yet. This club takes what it wants, and never fails to get it. We'll fuck them all – Devils, Scorps, the gangs in LA. I don't give a shit. The Wild West has always belonged to the outlaws, babe. We're the only men who can hold it, tame it, own it."

"Whatever you say." She razzed me again.

My cue to slide one hand to the small of her back. My other went behind her head and pulled her into my waiting lips.

She kissed hotter than she had at the clubhouse now that she was free. Out here among the stars, it was just her and I, man and woman.

I kissed her like the bastard I was. Found her tongue,

swirled it around with mine 'til her breathing told me she'd gone dizzy. My hand hugged closer around her waist, slipped below her jeans, feeling the wet spot on her panties.

Sweet fuck. She had the hots for me coming out her ears, assuming she didn't lose it all pooling out her pussy first.

Her whole body jerked when my fingers traveled lower, slipped below her waistband, going for her clit. That little nub made her sing sweeter than any girl I'd ever fucked before.

I'd never forget that first moan, or the thousands that came after it. Just a soft, feral little whimper, begging for my trust as much as she craved every inch I had pressed up against her thigh.

"Blackjack..." she moaned again, when I finally broke the kiss, let her come up for air.

"You've really never done this before, babe? Never had a man like me inside you, making your body tingle like it's balanced on a thousand needles?" I pulled her hair, touched my lips to her ear, and let my hot breath melt her a little more.

She squirmed when she felt my stubble, sensing the red hot words flowing through her ear. Fuck, if she wiggled a little more, I'd have to fight the urge to blow my load in my pants like a fucking virgin.

Growling, I grabbed her, flipped her over, put her where she belonged. Lizzie spread her legs instinctively, only showing a shred of fight left in her when she pushed against my chest with both hands.

"Wait, wait...this is happening so fast. It's too much, Blackjack."

"Come on, babe. Don't bullshit me, telling me you don't want this." I smiled. "Play your cards right, and you're looking at the one and only man who's ever going to be fucking you."

My hand reached around her head, fisting her perfect red locks. Pulled her face right up to my lips. She stopped resisting awful fast and her legs went slack, open for me to conquer.

I wrapped the blanket around us as I kissed her throat, working on her jeans' clasp. They came down hard, then her panties, jerked to her knees in a tangled bundle. I lowered my lips across her body, one hand massaging her breast, shoving aside her bra.

She moaned louder the deeper my lips went. My tongue grazed the sweet, trim landing strip going down to her slit, just as brilliant red as the ponytail in my fist.

My cock throbbed harder when I buried my face between her legs. My mouth completely dominated her, licking and sucking at her inner thighs, before moving straight to the goods.

And what perfect fucking goods she had!

Her pussy called to me, pink and succulent as a little rose. I can still remember her taste, stamped onto my brain 'til the day I die, the sweetest wet heat I ever tasted.

My tongue couldn't resist fucking her. I probed her virgin pussy with it, smothered her lips, plunged it against her walls 'til her thighs began to shake. Held them down like an avalanche covering an earthquake, and her hips arched a second later.

She rode me like a madwoman just as I found her clit. She came hard, scratching my scalp raw, pulling on my hair like her whole damned life depended on it.

Inwardly, I smiled, all I could manage with animal lust clawing at my veins. It'd take a fucking bullet to pry me off her right now. My mouth strummed her something beautiful as she gushed, buckled, and came her little brains out, riding my face to kingdom come.

Didn't stop 'til she pulled on my hair a third time. She practically ripped my long black locks off my scalp, and I fucking loved it. Made sure my dark stubble rubbed her thighs as I came up, slowly licking my lips, then bringing them back to hers so she could taste what I'd done to her.

"Oh, God," she moaned, still trembling a little when I broke away.

One look, and I smiled. Knew I'd be shaking her a whole lot harder before the night was through.

"You just had your first hit of this mouth on your flesh, baby girl. Pretty fucking sweet, isn't it?" She nodded, trying to hide her bashful smile as I pulled her into me. I struggled to ignore the fire humming in my balls while I held her, stroked her silky red hair, awed by how beautiful it looked even when it was getting messed up by our sex.

"Gonna ask you a favor before you take my cock for the first time, babe." She looked at me, her green eyes wide and curious. I tipped her chin up with one hand, digging my fingers into her sweet face with a master's touch. "Promise you'll come away with me. Take a leap of faith."

Her face crinkled up and she laughed. "You're crazy! It's my first time, yeah, and I want it to be with you. But this is just sex...isn't it?"

"No." I grabbed both her wrists and threw them over her head, pinning her beneath me. "You've gotta be the only girl associated with the club here who hasn't been corrupted. You don't fuck for money or prestige or just to get your rocks off with a man wearing this ink. Oki did a damned good job shaping you, hardass that he is, but it's time for you to fly. Spread those sexy wings. Let me take you the rest of the way home."

"Blackjack, I really can't. We barely know each other. It's too crazy, too –"

I shut her up with a hand across her mouth. "And I'm telling you, I don't give a fucking shit. We're about to know each other the most carnal way a man and woman can. Shit, I want more than just your pussy, too. For a bastard like me, that's a first. I know I'll want those green eyes shining into mine every damned night once I've had a taste. I'll need you under me, against me, warming my bed. One more week, and I'll know if I want to put my brand on you. Don't make me fuck with my oath to the club, babe. Because if you stay here, I know I'll be heading back to Spokane when I really shouldn't, anything to feel your pussy clench on my cock."

She gasped. Soft, seductive, and totally shocked.

"Be mine. No second guesses. Wear my brand, ride my bike, take my fire."

She shook her head in disbelief. I'd just said the most serious words a man in this club can say to a woman, and she knew it.

I pulled my hands off her, letting her move. Wordlessly, she threw her arms around my neck, inching her hands lower, over my shoulders. She pulled at my cut, desperate to have me just as unwrapped as her.

I reared up and started taking my clothes off. Fucking relief to shed the leather cut and then my shirt. I lifted my legs to tear off my jeans, my boxers, and then folded her against me, both of us fully naked.

We were hot, overwhelmed, totally desperate to be joined. My dick roared every waking second to be inside her, but I ignored it, not 'til I had an answer.

Rolled her on the ground and folded her against me. My hand reached around her thigh, pushed between her legs, and started to rub where my mouth left off.

She moaned, arched her ass into my cock, gasping when she found it.

"You'll get fucked good and hard soon. But only after

you tell me 'yes' to everything I said. Come with me, baby, tell me you're climbing on my bike when we get dressed again and hit the open road. It's the only way we'll really get to know if this black magic shit between us is half as good as I think it is. Plus it's the only thing that'll keep your old man from killing us both when he finds out..."

"Blackjack – oh!" She whimpered, temporarily losing her mind when I started stroking her clit, pushing my dick a little closer to her slit.

My tip grazed her entrance, just below her raised leg, ready to sink in, own her, claim her as mine.

"Say it," I growled. Gave her one more brush stroke across the clit with my thumb, and then I stopped, refusing to dole out any more 'til she gave it all up.

"Yes!" It hissed out her honey lips like the softest breeze.

"Couldn't hear you, babe. This dick can't go in 'til I get it loud, clear, proud. No more confusion." My cock's head ached like a motherfucker as I rubbed it over her sopping wet entrance. Somehow, I kept myself from ramming it balls deep, taking her cherry before I had the rest of her life.

"I'll do it, Blackjack. It's crazy, but I'll do it. Now, please...put it in."

"Fuck," I whispered, smoothing her throat with a kiss. "Thought you'd never ask."

My free hand slid to her thigh, pulled her leg up, and

kept it open for me. One push with my hips and there wasn't any stopping it.

I sank into her with a groan. My balls blazed like coals when her soft, slippery heat surrounded me. I pushed in steady, taking what was mine, secretly vowing I'd be the only man who ever got this pussy wrapped around my dick.

Lizzie took it like a good girl. I kissed her, steadied my strokes, pulling back and thrusting into her good and hard and slow. She only winced once, and I could tell by the sounds coming out of her that I'd already punched through her virgin pain, replacing it with sheer pleasure instead.

We fucked underneath the blanket, side to side, my hips crashing into hers. Drilled her so fucking deep I swore I could feel her soul. Her pulse quickened, and she thrashed a little more in my hands. The fist I had around her sweet red hair pulled tighter, holding her like reigns, and her thigh muscles stiffened as I pushed her to release.

"You're always gonna belong to me," I told her, just before she came. "Don't give a damn how psycho it sounds, or how many times I'll shake your delicious ass before you figure out I'm serious."

My cock deepened its strokes as I growled my next words.

Harder. Faster. Meaner.

"Lizzie, baby, fuck. You know exactly what you are,

right?" I snarled, plucking her ear with my teeth. She whimpered before I said the words. "My. Fucking. Property."

Soon as the girl heard *property*, she went off like dynamite. I fucked her harder as she tightened around me, hot and wet and wild. Her leg spasmed in my hand and she buried her face in her shoulder, trying not to scream, pulsing out her climax in savage little grunts.

We fucked harder still. I wasn't done with her, not by half, and I'd make her come two more times before I finally let go of the molten load building in my balls. I rolled on top of her, ripped off her shirt and bra, fucking her twice as fast the second time.

She moaned louder as I rolled her over, got between her legs, pushing her down. I slammed her into the ground, throwing the blanket off us. We were naked for the stars and the moon to watch the filthy show going on beneath them, and I wanted them to take a good long look at how I fucked this woman, deeper and better than I'd ever taken any slut.

I'd never believed in natural chemistry 'til I blew it all inside her. That moment, when I tensed up, my whole body burned like some bastard crept into my bones and lit them all on fire.

"Fuck, baby, fuck!" I growled, feeling her bare ankles jabbing into my ass, spurring me to shoot it deep. "That's it, that's it. Milk every damned drop."

"Yes, fuck!" If she regretted spitting that vulgar word,

I couldn't tell with the rosy red sheen across her face.

My orgasm exploded inside her, good and raw. I fucked it all out, embracing the wild, manic energy, wondering if I'd feel any different when it was finally over.

She screamed and came on my cock for the umpteenth time that night. Her pussy got a hundred times wetter as my seed filled it, and still I didn't stop, fucking straight through it without even going soft.

I wasn't gonna stop. Couldn't stop fucking her.

That told me more than anything else that this crazy spell wasn't getting broken just because I'd lost my nut.

That black magic shit wasn't going anywhere. Not 'til I owned her so damned deep neither of us were coming up from it. Ever.

The last time I came, she was right on the edge, her hands and legs both shaking. I'd spread her out under me, mounted her from the behind, driving into her so rough her breasts swung beautiful.

The pleasure of her perfect cunt sinking down on my dick over and over again short-circuited my brain. Then hers, too.

We came together, screaming and craning our backs, staring up at the pinprick stars in the sky while our bodies thrashed. Couldn't stop feeling that gentle light washing through us, like something otherworldly binding me to this woman, this chick I still wanted to fuck when I was totally spent.

We rolled together and I held her in my arms, stroking her hair 'til she fell asleep. We slept out in the open, naked before the universe, and I thought about whether or not I was serious about leaving with her tomorrow.

Yeah, fuck yeah, I was. We'd be riding out at dawn, straight down to NorCal, where we'd build a new life together.

It was crazy claiming a girl like this, but what the hell ever really made sense in this fucked up world? If I wanted to play it safe and sane, I'd have never donned the patch. I'd have sat in some office or joined a construction crew, jacking myself off and living paycheck to paycheck, never experiencing more than a moment's excitement with weak beer in a sports bar.

This was the life, the same one Lizze and me got ourselves pulled into by being born in it. We'd embrace it, squeeze it by the throat, choked the shit out of that bitch 'til she gave us everything we deserved.

And I meant *everything*.

No bullshit. For the first time in my thirty two years on this earth, I fell asleep content, ready to start a new chapter with more to it than killing, boozing, and fucking my way to respect.

III: Bitter, Bitter Fruit (Blackjack)

Five beautiful years passed like a rolling storm.

The whole damned world changed, along with the club, and so did our lives.

We settled just outside Sacramento. I'd transferred to a charter with men who rewarded me on merit, rather than my family name.

So much had happened, the kind of glorious, torturous excitement that told me I was balls deep in my prime.

Lizzie got her brand, and I started calling her my old lady. Oki rode down shortly after he heard about it, got to me at a club party one night, pulling me aside and knocking several teeth out.

I laughed at him through the blood pouring out my lips, knowing he couldn't do shit about it. I owned his daughter now, and I'd keep her forever.

My girl was addicted to me. I was addicted to her. I told him as much, and said if he didn't fucking like it, then he could skip the wedding in a few months.

Oki swore at me, threw a fucking bottle at my head, sank to his knees and cradled his bruised knuckles after I dodged the glass and heard it smash into a million pieces behind me. I laughed at him and stuck out a hand, offering him an olive branch.

"Get up, old man. You don't have to fight me."

"Fuck you!" Oki spat, slapping at my hand like a girl. "Where's my fucking daughter? She's coming home with me. I won't let her marry a prick like you. I'll fucking kill you with my own bare hands! She's not marrying you, Blackjack – Lizzie's better than some fucking pig who shot a guy twenty-one times!"

I braced myself for him to jump up and charge, but he didn't. He was waiting, just holding it all in for me to lay it on thick.

My closest brother, Wheeler, laughed behind me, his eyes glowing with respect. He had a wife and a baby son, a kid named Travis, who'd probably grow up to be just as big and bad as the rest of us. He knew exactly what was on the line.

"Don't think you want to turn this club's founding clubhouse upside down. I sure as shit don't. You know what Fang does to guys who shit on his home turf?"

The national Prez was ruthless. Sometimes so much he made my skin crawl.

"Yeah, I do, asshole," Oki snarled, his gray mustache twitching like a brush. "And I'll let myself get drawn and quartered if it means keeping my Lizzie out of this fucking bullshit!"

"You're not keeping my girl from her future husband. If you're looking for a heap of bullshit, maybe you ought to look in the mirror, old man. The second I put my brand on her I swore I'd never fuck anyone again, and I'm living by my promise."

"It's true," Wheeler pipped up behind me, nodding at my former Prez. "Blackjack's one of the most honest guys here. Hasn't so much as had a fucking lap dance since the day he came down here with the redhead."

Oki stood up, his face glowing red, fists shaking at his sides. "This shit better be true. You stole her from me, and that's a goddamned crime. But if you really love her, swear on your colors you're gonna treat her right..."

We locked eyes. I pulled off my cut, flung it around, grabbed it by the patch on the back. I gave the bear in permanent roar above my bottom rocker a kiss, right across his gnarled teeth.

"I swear on this patch, on this life and next, old man. Your girl's in good hands. I'll protect her and give you a few grandkids you can be proud to call family."

"Fuck you," he grunted, extending a hand with a skull and a date stamped on the back, 1945, the year that sent him home too screwed up to be anything except an outlaw. "Just because I'm deciding not to crack your skull open doesn't mean I'll quit saying it."

"I can live with that."

Behind us, Wheeler laughed again, and I heard him chugging beer. The good times were about to roll.

No, it wasn't perfect, but what the hell ever was?

We were into the early nineties. The club had some

dirty shit going down with the other guys, drugs flowing through our routes and rumors of war with other MCs. The Devils, the Scorps, the cartels south of the border – any last one of those motherfuckers might challenge us and put our lives on the line soon.

All the more reason to make peace, get this fucker to approve of me owning his daughter. I loved her with my entire heart. That was all I needed, love and allegiance to the club.

Men like Oki were part of an older generation, and their time was ending in this MC. The future belonged to guys like Wheeler and me.

Whenever my hair turned as gray as Oki's, I swore I'd have all the pieces in place. I'd figure out the shit the older guys couldn't while they did filthy deals and fucked around on their women. I'd make this club great, just as soon as I made Lizzie the happiest girl on this rock whirling around the stars.

At the three year mark, she gave me a son. I remembered the week we made him, right down the day, breaking in a new bed in a cozy new house just outside the city.

We fucked our brains out like we'd only been married for a week instead of an entire year.

She ballooned before my eyes, growing with my seed, turning more beautiful than any girl should as she crossed into her early twenties, pregnant and happy.

Each night, I held her a little closer, kissed her brow, reminded her how real this thing between us would always be.

My guts ache when I think about the day I met my kid with Lizzie holding him in the little hospital bed. She looked up at me, her jade green eyes brighter and hotter than ever, amazed at the miracle we'd made.

"He's got your cheekbones," she said, giving me a smile as big as the Milky Way.

"Babe, this kid's gonna be handsome as the devil himself. Straight up killer."

Her face went dark when I said the K-word. She stiffened up in bed, clutching him tighter, reaching for my hand. We'd both been raised in the MC, and Finn faced the same future.

"Look, Blackjack, we've both grown up in the club life because that's where we belong. But we also know how dangerous it can be. Promise me you'll never let him put on the Grizzlies patch and get hurt." She squeezed her fingers in mine, so soft and pleading, asking me to do what should've been the impossible. "I need this. He deserves better, Sam, and I have to know he'll get it."

Hearing my real name hit me like a rod through the fucking chest. Brought her sweet hand to my lips and kissed it, grazing my stubble over her skin.

"Deal." Her lips trembled a little, probably overwhelmed with surprise. "Don't look at me like that, baby girl. If you think I want our kid getting himself killed, you've got another thing coming. He'll have bigger and better things waiting for him than this MC. I've given it half my life, the one I can't share with you, and whatever chick he ends up marrying won't suffer the same."

"Sam!" She reared up like a lioness, despite being tired as a dog from the delivery just a few hours before. Her fingers clung to my neck, and we kissed forever. Only broke away so she could wipe the tears rolling down her cheeks.

"Mark my words, babe, nothing dirty's *ever* happening to you or Finn. That's a fucking promise. I don't give a shit if I have to die to make it happen. Whatever happens with me and the club, it's not going to hurt my family. You're safe, Lizzie, and so is our son. Forever."

When I looked into the soft, tired eyes of the kid staring up at me, I meant it more than I'd ever meant anything in my life.

Two more years. Promises were getting harder to keep, stretching me thin as a damned ghost.

The club had fallen on hard times with the Scorps sabotaging our supply runs east. Fang and the national boys fought to drum up more business in Canada and overseas for our shit, but the Feds had gotten better at intercepting cargo, too.

I sent every red cent the club gave me to my family.

Worked my balls off taking odd jobs in the meantime to earn a little more scratch – and they didn't pay well when a man had a couple felonies keeping him from anything kosher.

I'd done my time in jail, earning my bottom rocker when most kids were focused on degrees. When the club profits were good, we all lived well, but now we were living in lean times.

The men who were brothers in name only laid down the law in mother charter. Didn't trust them worth a damn, but didn't have the clout to challenge their rule.

I'd never forget the church session when Fang brought in his little brother, this utter fuckwad named Frig, suddenly our Enforcer since old Jammer's knees were too fucked up to ride anymore.

"This is a big goddamned democracy, so let's have a little squawk and vote," the Prez growled, flashing us a jagged smile that said it was anything but. "My blood brother's a good man and a real hardass. He's exactly what we need to bash the Scorps' fucking skulls in and put them under."

The Prez's eyes stopped on me. He stiffened up, giving me a darker, more menacing look, that crooked tooth in his mouth sticking out and biting his lip. "You disagree, Blackjack?"

"I've got my doubts." Half the guys in the room almost shit their pants.

Wheeler had a nervous glint in his eye, knowing if

anything went real sour with me, it might drag him down too. Fang had already fucked over a few of the older guys, forcing them into early retirements, and a couple accidents claiming other brothers seemed awfully fucking suspicious.

"What the fuck, Black-Jackass?" Frig shot up, a lean little hothead with a face like a rat. "You got a problem with me, you say it to my fucking face instead of acting like a smug little shit."

Fang put a brotherly hand on his shoulder, forced him back into his seat. "We'll figure this shit out like men. Blackjack, what's your beef?"

"Your little brother only got his bottom rocker six months ago. Not much time to take on an Enforcer's duties for the top charter in this club."

Fang snorted. "Give me a fucking break. You think Jammer was living up his full fucking responsibilities with his knees as fucked up as they were – huh?"

Wheeler coughed. We both knew damned well Jammer had arthritis, but it wasn't half as bad as Fang made it out to be. Now, we both understood he'd been shuffled off early so the Prez could ram his cronyism down our throats.

"Of course not," I lied. "Just not convinced we need to go the opposite way – appointing some inexperienced kid to head up our whole arsenal and the ground war with the Scorps."

Frig was a trigger away from shooting up and

marching over to punch me in the face. Only Fang's dirty look suppressed him. There had to be years between those two, a fifteen or twenty year age gap. Too bad their personalities were both rotten to the fucking core.

"You're mistaken, Blackjack, and I think half the men here will agree." Fang scanned the room, until he saw the brothers who were dirty or scared shitless nod.

"You're outnumbered. I've got the votes, end of fucking debate."

The look I gave him was like death. He just laughed, full on busted a gut, slapping the table with his palms.

"Look, Mr. Stick-Up-The-Ass, if it makes you feel better, you can tag along for Frig's first big run out to Elko. We've got a big haul that's gonna make us a lot of money in Nevada, plenty of coke and shit for our partners to pick up and peddle across to Utah. Lotta shitheads up there who are even more uptight than you are, and we'll help 'em get smashed."

"That's practically Scorps territory," Wheeler said, taking his turn with Fang's nasty smile.

"Bullshit. They haven't run out the clubs who come down to Reno and Vegas to party, and they're not gonna fuck us up neither. They don't got the numbers. Nevada's always been neutral territory, and it's gonna be ours next, just as soon as we kick those assholes square in the nuts."

"Tell you what, Blackjack," Fang said, leaning back in his chair. "You tag along and report back. I know I'll end up hearing how my awesome little bro saved your life, but it'll be that much sweeter to have it from the horse's mouth. Let's fucking vote already. All in favor of making Frig our new Seargent-at-Arms for Sacramento, and all of California?"

The hands shot up, one-by-one. Even Wheeler raised his, making me the lone Nay.

Fuck. That shitshow perfectly illustrated the problem Wheeler and me had when we got too drunk, talked about getting rid of Fang, and cleaning up this club.

It wasn't time yet. The only thing we'd get by going off premature would be bloody, painful deaths.

It'd take years for the day to come, when the asshole was no longer feared and respected, and we'd be waiting. Sad as shit he was bound to do a lot of damage in the meantime.

If only I'd known then just how much the fucknut would really do.

I'd have stood up, pulled out my nine, and shot him through the face. Yeah, I'd have caught a hail of bullets for it, but I'd have saved the Grizzlies MC at least a decade of pure hell.

Shit, I'd have saved Lizzie, and the next twenty years of my life.

"Las Vegas? *Really?*" Lizzie looked at me, sweet excitement building, happy as the day I'd claimed her. "Oh, Sam. It's almost our anniversary too."

It was high summer, almost four years to the day since we'd gotten married. I picked her up 'til she dropped the spoon she'd been feeding Finn with. She squealed, and our little son laughed, clapping his hands while I bounced his ma high overhead.

If only we were really just having a family get away. The real reason Wheeler and I decided to pack our families along for the ride was because we didn't trust leaving them here worth shit.

I had to protect her and Finn. That meant keeping them as close as possible, leaving them in the sanctuary city of lights while I rode with the rest of the crew up to Elko to get this bullshit over with.

We didn't seriously think Fang would fuck with our families, but the Scorps might. Fuckers were getting bolder in their jabs – they'd hit us just outside San Diego last week, on our own turf.

The Prez was out an out of control motherfucker, and he'd left the club vulnerable to anything. They couldn't stay here in case the Scorps decided to attack our clubhouse and the families in Sacramento while half the brothers were out of town.

"Go on. Get the kid's stuff packed up and go over to Wheeler's place for the night. You can share the car with Julie and Travis so we can consolidate."

I wanted to bite my tongue off on the last word. Having to scrimp and save for fuel was embarrassing as fuck, and I also had a sick inkling it made everybody a little more vulnerable in one car.

Stop the fucking crazy talk. She'll be fine. We'll dump that crap off for the Mormon dealers and haul our asses back to Vegas, flush with cash.

I looked at my son, giggling as Lizzie winked and got back to feeding him. The kid deserved a couple more toys. These two in front of me were the reason I did this shit, the only damned reason I risked my life, hoping that maybe some of Fang's big hauls would finally pay off.

They would, so long as the greedy motherfucker didn't hog it all to himself and his bastard brother...

"When do we leave?" Lizzie said, her red hair glowing when it caught the evening light through the window.

"Just a little before ten sharp, babe." The iron fists tensed at my sides relaxed when I saw her smile.

"Ohh, that should put us in around seven! Nice planning, big roller." She stuck out that tongue I'd wrapped around mine hundreds of times before, and never got tired of.

"I'm not there to fuck with craps or lucky sevens, Firecracker. Only thing I'm making bets on is how long it takes to get your sweet ass under me."

"Hm...probably a couple days."

"Bullshit." I stepped up, pulled her into my arms, and buried her lips in mine. My hand went down her pants while Finn dozed, feeling how hot and wet she'd be for me tonight.

I knew I'd keep that smoldering good through our whole damned trip. This girl's skin learned to sing for me over the last five years, and I wasn't done hearing that music.

Never would be. I'd fuck her at home, fuck her in Vegas, fuck her on the goddamned Moon if I had to, anywhere and everywhere she needed a reminder about who owned her soft little cunt forever.

Her eyes smiled when I broke the kiss, and so did mine. We stared at each other, our excitement growing to go to bed. Familiar anticipation, but always so new each time we ripped off each other's clothes.

Maybe, just fucking maybe, everything would turn out okay. We'd come back a little richer and happier to boot. If the universe really had any miracles in store, maybe the rest of us could keep Frig from any major fuck ups, but the last thing I'd do was hold my breath.

It was an ugly scene at the clubhouse. I stared at the brothers swarming around two huge trucks, big transportation rigs that looked like they'd served a tour or two in Vietnam before the club re-purposed them for hauling filth instead of troops.

I walked past the back, just before a few guys covered in piercings closed it up. I'd never seen so many fucking pallets in my life.

There were eight figures worth of powder and other junk loaded in there, maybe more. For once, I managed to shake off the guilt I always had tugging at my balls, thinking about the payday coming once we pulled this off.

Shit, we'd be set for years. I'd get Lizzie that perfect gourmet kitchen she always wanted, a new bed for Finn, and a closet full of clothes to grow into, maybe buy myself shiny new bike.

"Dreaming already?" A voice growled behind me.

I turned to see Frig standing there, a clipboard in his hands, taking one last inventory of the shit in our club code before we took off,.

"Thinking about logistics. We're splitting the prospects evenly, right?"

"Yeah, yeah," he rolled his eyes. "You worry too fucking much, Blacky. Don't worry. I'll make sure your widdle family has a full set of Swiss guards protecting 'em all the time."

He slapped me on the back. Hard as fuck resisting the urge to bust his cocky, fucked up jaw.

"Aw, don't be like that, man. I'm just jacking you off." Frig winked and licked his lips like a total psycho. "You can hang back and watch the train of prospects around their car if you don't believe me. They're safe, or else you're calling me a damned liar, and then we'll have to throw fists."

Fuck if I wasn't ready. Every finger ached to feel this weasel's bones snap under them, but I held back, walked away without a second word to the fucker.

I'd make sure he kept good on his promise. I'd been assigned to ride tail gunner with Wheeler and several other guys anyway, and we'd make damned sure nobody crept up on our column, making its way down SoCal.

We were just starting to cross the edge of the Mojave when I saw the Scorps. The fuckers were coming up on us fast, a huge train of them, more trucks than bikes. Their group split apart and covered both sides of the road.

"They're coming! We'd better line the fuck up and protect the goods. Keep on going, don't stop for anything, I need at least ten guys to hang back with me and –"

Static cut me off my screaming into the radio. I heard Frig's voice, enraged and barking orders.

"You heard the asshole! Brothers, half you fuckers hang back, and the rest of you go on and get the truck with the rest of our guys. You know the plan."

The Scorps were gaining on us fast. I drew my nine and expected the fuckers to be right on top of me, but their trucks roared right past, going on ahead, ignoring me. They went straight for the soft targets – the car with our families and the two big trucks.

"They're going for the head!" I yelled into the radio.

Fuck, fuck, fuck. I howled bloody murder, getting off a few shots that grazed their wheels, without doing much good.

Nobody was responding anymore, too busy circling, clogging up the lonely highway, lost in a panic. The Scorps' biker train crashed into us and cut our group in two, a solid distraction to keep our crew from rushing to defend the cargo.

Barely had time through all the shooting to look on ahead, but I saw Julie's car split off as the drug trucks pulled ahead. The caravan of our prospects protecting Julie, Lizzie, and the kids broke away to surround the trucks as the first Scorps closed, leaving the families defenseless.

"Fuck!" I swore, and shot a Scorp riding up on me through his chest. Several more rival fuckers got their asses blasted right off their bikes.

Our crew slowed, took aim, and thinned their numbers one by one. Their club went through men like nothing else, and few of these assholes were battle hardened. We screeched to a full stop and made our stand while everybody else blew on ahead of us.

"Shit!" I slammed my handlebars, face to face with too many killer assholes to do shit about my girl now.

Frig stopped responding, or else the bastard ignored everything I'd said.

I took over. Started roaring orders to the men who'd joined me, a mix of full patch brothers and prospects, including Wheeler.

The boys held their fire 'til my mark when the second Scorps wave approached. Then we opened up, just when they were drawing, slowing their bikes, getting ready to jump off and start shooting. Their last truck kept coming, tried to go right through us, roll a couple guys over.

Flinching was for pussies. I dug my heels into the turf, blasting away at the approaching horde, crouching behind my poor shot up bike for cover. Several guys caught lead in their chests and crumpled over, gurgling raw blood.

"He's not gonna fucking stop!" Wheeler roared, pushing another clip into his gun and firing furiously at the truck.

We'd blown out the windshield, but the fucking thing was still screaming toward us, ready to run half the brothers over, including me.

Didn't have time for this shit. Not when my old lady and my kid were fending for themselves. My gun came up with an eerie calm and I narrowed my eyes, thinking about how bad Frig had fucked up.

Rage made a miracle that day. I hit the driver in the shoulder and the truck swerved, heading off into the desert.

"Go, go, go!" I screamed, waving the prospects toward it. They didn't need to be told a second time – just hopped on their bikes and went screaming toward the big rock where the Scorps had come to a stop.

Incredibly, we hadn't taken shit for casualties, minus a couple guys who'd gotten grazed in their arms or legs. The crew we'd chewed up must've been three times our size, and now they were all dead on the open, a few last bikes whipping around and tearing back the way they came.

"Let the fuckers go," I snarled, grabbing at a brother named Ligo when he turned toward his bike. "We've got bigger business up ahead. Gotta make sure our families are safe."

"What about the haul?! That's what we're here to protect," Ligo grunted. "The junk's the priority, Frig's orders..."

I shot him a look straight from hell, and Wheeler joined me. Our lean, shaggy haired brother came to a dead stop from reaching into his pocket for some snuff to chew. Must've realized he'd said too fucking much.

I grabbed him by the collar and whipped him around, had him on the pavement in a matter of seconds, my knee slamming him in the spine.

"What the fuck, Blackjack?!"

"That's my fucking question, asshole. What did you say? What about Frig's orders?"

Wheeler hovered over us, ready to break up the fight, but I wasn't having it 'til this fuck squealed. Worst of all, he was wasting precious time. My switchblade came out while Ligo tried to fight us off, and I held it to his throat.

"Are you fucking crazy?" he screamed.

"Family shit, boy. You wouldn't understand how pissed off that makes guys like Wheeler and me. You've got about ten seconds to tell me exactly what the fuck is going on here, before I stab this shit into your throat and let your blood mingle with the Scorps' dirty muck on the road."

"All right, all right – put down the fuckin' knife!" I let his neck breathe about an inch without cold steel pressing in. "Frig pulled a few of us aside the night before last, told us to do whatever it takes to keep the drugs clear. Nothing spared. Even if it means pulling guys off the soft targets to protect the run. He said the car's expendable, just as long as we've got the trucks covered. Wasn't my idea, motherfucker, and I'm sorry. Now let me the hell –"

Up? The sonofabitch had serious nerve. I booted him square in the ass once I took my weight off, hurling him down on the pavement again.

Wheeler was already ahead of me, climbing on his bike. *Shit, shit. Fuck.*

If even half of what Ligo spilled was true, Julie's ride was in serious fucking danger right now, and so was my whole family. Wheeler and I both jumped on our bikes.

We tore down the highway so fast my balls pulled into my guts. Took us forever to see the smoke rising from a dusty old truck stop in the desert.

Had to make a split second decision whether to check it out or keep going. Some evil voodoo instinct thumping in my chest told me to take a right, and Wheeler followed behind me, racing toward the mess of metal causing the fire. We jumped off our bikes several feet away, taking in the sight.

If there were Scorps around, they'd taken off, probably after realizing they'd been chasing bait instead of the real goods.

When I saw the twisted front of the car smashed clean through the abandoned rest stop, my heart almost gave out. Wheeler and I practically broke our knees running, desperate to catch up to it, all while we tried to brace ourselves for the biggest nightmare of our fucked up lives.

The doors hung open. Nobody had died in the crash, thank Christ, but that meant we didn't have a fucking clue where our girls and the kids had gone.

If the Scorps had taken them for ransom...

My thoughts derailed when I heard somebody cough, soft and strained. We both whipped around.

Wheeler ran like a maniac when he saw Julie. His old lady was huddled against a rock, Travis and Finn both bouncing on her lap.

"Wheeler? Blackjack?" she mumbled, her eyes half open, staring at us like she'd gone blind.

The kids weren't moving. *Fuck.*

I ran so fast I put a fucking cheetah to shame, pushing my fingers on their little necks for a pulse. First Finn, then Travis. No shit, my own heartbeat stopped 'til I felt theirs humming through their veins.

I let out the biggest fucking sigh in the world when both boys groaned and rolled in Julie's arms, Travis mumbling something about too much sleepy-time.

"Oh, fuck. Fuck!" Wheeler threw his arms around the trio, pushing me out of the way. "We gotta get you up, baby. Get you and the kids a real doctor to make sure –"

Normally, I would've felt like a bastard for cutting in on such a precious moment, but there was still one very serious fucking problem.

"Where's my old lady?" I growled, tapping my hand lightly against Julie's cheek, doing best not to slap her awake. "Where's Lizzie? Can't fucking find her!"

"She took off running, Blackjack. Somewhere in the rocks, straight behind this place. Said she'd give us a distraction, anything to keep the three Scorps away from the kids..."

That was all I needed to bolt the hell up and go running. I stumbled over the rocky ass trail leading behind the old pit, past a rusty propane tank, noticing the snake trails cut by the bikes through the soil.

Three guys, she'd said. There were at least five or six trails cutting through here, which meant the motherfuckers had probably come and gone.

"Lizzie!" Cupped my hands over my mouth and belted my lungs out.

I studied the trails closer, hoping I'd see her footprints, but the bikes had obliterated everything. *Fucking shit.*

I walked on, deeper among the higher rocks, big boulders rolled together around the hills, forming miniature canyons that would make a perfect fucking hiding place.

Or else a perfect grave. Shit, I couldn't think like that.

Didn't know why the fuck she wasn't answering. Had to keep going, face the vicious music, knowing they could've done anything to my girl in her stupid, brave move to get the bastards away from the young ones.

If it wasn't for the high afternoon sun hitting the perfect angle, I'd have never seen her shoe. It stuck out a small crop of boulders, and I knew she'd climbed in to hide, if she hadn't been dumped in there like fucking garbage.

"Fuck," I growled, swallowing the lump in my throat, trying to keep my own crazed heartbeat from knocking me out.

I ran. I found her. I fucking screamed.

The pretty white t-shirt she'd left wearing this morning was stained crimson red. I jerked her into my arms, and we both toppled over, just enough for me to see the jacket she'd tied around her bleeding shoulder.

PROPERTY OF BLACKJACK, the brand she'd had sewn on the back, stuck out in dirty red. Those letters used to be lily white with the way she'd taken care of it. Now, the stitches were dirty with her blood.

I sat her down next to me and embraced her one more time, shaking from the hellstorm building in my lungs, nasty as vinegar.

I fucking screamed so loud the devil himself must've heard my grief. My fists hit the dirty desert rocks 'til my fists were scratched, bloody, raw.

"Babe, babe, babe, I'm so fucking sorry. Fuck. *Fuuuck!*" Hot tears stung my cheeks, and still I kept a few in. They had the energy I'd need to avenge her, to kill the motherfucker who'd done this.

Boots crunched gravel behind me. I should've at least put my hand on my gun, in case it was a Scorp instead of Wheeler, but I couldn't do shit.

Sirens starting blasting in the background, howling to high hell. I heard Wheeler curse before his brotherly hand slapped my shoulder, then moved on bone, trying to shake away my stupor.

"Brother, we've got to go. Let me help you move her."

"Fuck you!" I spat, jealously protecting her fragile body like my own son, the one who'd grow up completely fucked because I hadn't been there to save her.

Wheeler nodded and stepped back, muttering something about having an ambulance on the way. There'd be badges for sure once the paramedics saw the mess of dead Scorps and wreckage on the highway several miles back.

Fuck if I cared. Fuck if I'd ever give a shit about anything ever again.

I pulled her into my arms and pressed my nose into her hair, trying to burn her scent into my brain. I was still trying when the skinny chucklefuck tapped me on the shoulder, yelling some incoherent shit in my ear.

Never thought I'd want to bust a medic's jaw, but I absolutely did just then. Lucky the kid was quicker with words than my fists. He finally got a few through to me before I could swing.

"Sir, you have to let me get in there! She's barely breathing."

IV: Hello, Purgatory (Blackjack)

I sat next to Wheeler at the hospital, Finn on my lap. My son dozed like a champ, blissfully ignorant about the goddamned abomination that had just happened around him.

"We have to go once we get the call," I whispered, careful not to wake the kid.

Wheeler looked at me like I'd flipped my shit for good. "What? You're not even sticking around for the girls?"

"Jules is fine. So are the kids. My old lady's being patched up and it's gonna take her a few days to recover." I held Finn a little tighter and leaned over to my brother, my low growl becoming thunder. "Every fucking second he's still breathing, she isn't safe. Neither is my son."

"Frig? Jesus, Blackjack, you can't just think you're gonna waltz in and off the Prez's asshole brother. You'll get us killed and everybody sharing our family name, even if you pull it off, once the rest of the club finds out..."

"Bullshit. You're acting like I'm not already sitting on

a plan that'll rip his fucking guts out with nobody being any wiser."

"Shit. I'll listen because it's you, brother, but I'm fucking warning you." Wheeler sat up tall, reached over Finn's head, and jabbed his finger into my chest. "I'm out the second it looks like you're about to swing in front of the club. You saw how easy the motherfucker used our girls as bait, let the fucking Scorps come after our kids. Call me a coward, I don't give a damn, I'm not putting my family on the line a second time."

He closed his eyes, trying to stop himself from going off in the quiet waiting room like a grenade. Who could fucking blame him?

I was asking for the impossible when we were both damned lucky we hadn't lost anybody in that crunched up car. Still, my brother didn't fucking get it.

Our wives, our kids, everything we'd ever care about was still at risk as long as reckless, selfish fuckstains like Frig were wasting air above ground.

I stared through the glass window leading to the ER, where Lizzie laid, a crew of nurses, doctors, and machines nursing her back to life.

I couldn't let her go through this shit again. Couldn't let it touch my son, and no promises I'd made about keeping him away from the club held any water as long as this club was infested with vermin I didn't control.

Every part of me wanted to be the good husband, to sit pretty here for several days, holding her hand 'til she finally came out of her coma and stared at me with those sweet green eyes.

Things were never that easy in this life. As long as we had a maniac running the show in Nevada, and another one back in Sacramento, there'd never be peace.

They had to fucking die so I'd never have to see her or little Finn torn and bleeding again.

We rolled up in front of a beat up motel in Vegas. A couple prospects led us into the dingy courtroom out back. Frig had the whole place reserved as our temporary HQ, while the guys got ready to finish the run up to Elko.

The Enforcer spun around and exploded when he saw Wheeler and me. "Fucking shit-for-brains morons! Assholes!"

For a wiry little shit, his bony hands clutched my cut hard, tried to lift me off my feet. Good thing I weighed too much for his skinny ass.

A mess of obscenities blasted in my face. Took everything I had not to crash my skull on his so fucking hard I knocked him out. Bastard had the balls to act like I'd been the one who'd almost toasted his family, and that turned my blood to lightning.

"Where were you? Both you assholes? We're a whole fucking day behind schedule, all because you made us wait!"

"Our girls almost got killed," Wheeler said, straining

to hold the savagery in his voice.

"The girls, the girls! You know what, fuck your old ladies, and your kids, assholes. Saving their sorry whore asses doesn't do shit for making this club money. You're putting your personal shit above the club. That's against the rules. Mark my words, I will tell Fang about it, and we'll all have a nice family meeting once we get home."

Frig smiled like he was chewing on broken glass. Right then, I wanted to shove a whole pile down his rotten throat 'til it worked its way out of his degenerate skin.

"You shitheads brought 'em to a public hospital, didn't you? Better hope nobody's too fucked in the head and starts talking to the Feds. They're gonna be up our asses after finding all the dead Scorps on the highway."

"Didn't have a choice," I said. "My girl, Lizzie, she needed serious treatment. The kids, too."

Why the fuck am I trying to reason with this braindead prick? He reminded me about a second later.

"Whatever, Blacky. You can clean up your private horseshit when you're done shoveling it for the club. 'Til then, your ass is mine, and yours too, Wheeler. Saddle up. We've got a long road to Elko to finish our run."

Keep on talking, asswipe. I stomped off with Wheeler behind me, preventing either of us from knocking his fucking teeth out in front of too many boys who'd squawk to Fang.

My brother gave me the look. *Let's fucking do this.*

Wheeler had finally gotten the message. Frig had to die to save our families, and we'd make it happen.

We rode out just before dawn.

The journey was long and hot. I rode just a couple bikes behind the big truck, now splashed with some shoddy patch to cover up the bullet holes.

It took about seven hours to get into the county, and then another half hour to get out into the boonies, where the Utah buyers waited for their pickup.

A couple dozen of us stood underneath the evening sun. We all sweated bullets watching the prospects load our haul into the dealer's trucks, placing them into compartments along the side covered in sheet metal for secrecy.

When they finished, a couple grungy looking guys in leather jackets shoved several duffel bags toward the Prez, and then headed back to their rusted pickups parked next to several sleek black sedans. Whatever mob we were doing business with, I didn't fucking care, because I had more important shit on my mind.

Frig whistled. Wheeler and I stepped up and got on our knees, unzipping the bags. Tightly bundled cash popped out flush in our hands. We sifted through it, taking a quick estimate. There had to be about a million and a half stuffed in here. The other four bags I checked were identical.

Holy shit.

"We're set," I told Frig, disguising the hatred in my voice.

He went off like a fucking idiot. Pulled his nine out and aimed it at the sky, shooting it like the drunken cowboy he'd become.

"I'm rich, rich, crazy fucking rich! Jesus, I wish those motherfuckers in cell block G could see me now! Can't wait 'til Fang hears all about this. Fucking shit, this club's never gonna need an honest day of work again."

The younger guys behind us laughed. Guilt shot through my chest like a heavy stone as I stared at the money. Before we'd taken this trip, I was ready to risk anything for cash, whatever it took to give my family a more comfortable life.

This dirty fucking money had almost gotten them killed instead.

No, correction, the asshole shouting his lungs out and taking withering glances from the mobsters still climbing into their cars had almost put our women and kids in the ground.

I smiled so big I had to make sure I wasn't about to bite my fucking tongue off. Frig jumped when my hand slapped his shoulder. Squeezed 'til I felt bone – it didn't take much.

"You're a happy man today. What do you say we get ourselves a drink and bury the hatchet? We'll need brothers on good terms to guard all this loot."

"Ha, yeah, if you're talking about my money, Blacky."

Frig shot me the evil eye, but he didn't turn away. "Aw, fuck, why not. I'll round up all the brothers and find us a bar."

"No!" Wheeler stepped up, his big tattooed arms folded across his chest. "This oughta be between full patch brothers who need to smooth shit over. Right now, that's you, me, and Blackjack. We've got booze we picked up in Vegas. The desert's a much cooler place to crash than some dirty bar where the Scorps could sneak up and kick us in the balls. No damned good for a celebration."

"When the fuck did you grow a brain?" Frig turned to me and winked. "You could learn a thing or two from Wheeler. Think he's gonna make a fine treasurer someday when we get our asses home."

The only boy here who's about to do any learning is you.

I just smiled and nodded, watching as Frig stepped up in front of the crew, cupping his hands over his mouth. "You heard the man, boys, so listen up! I want all that shit locked up and going home to Vegas. We'll do a layover for one night, and only one night. That's all I can spare when we're hauling these many stacks. Fang's gonna want this shit in California pronto."

The small gaggle of prospects and brothers nodded. Frig thumped his chest, letting his power go to his fucked up skull.

"You boys ride on ahead. We'll catch up to you in a

couple hours. If the Scorps show up for a rematch, hit me on the radio. Doubt they'll have the balls with these fucking Feds combing around, trying to track 'em down after finding their guys smeared all over the goddamned pavement."

My hand grazed the switchblade near my belt. Perfect, just fucking perfect.

Wheeler and I shared a look. If we pulled this off, we'd definitely have holy heaven on our side.

And I'd do whatever it took to make sure my woman didn't have to wear angel wings.

I'd sinned enough, and I was bound to the club. Lizzie wasn't suffering a single fucking second after today for my mistakes.

"What's the fucking hold up?" I saw Frig coming over the horizon, stubbing out the smoke he'd just had, shooting the shit with Wheeler.

I'd gotten the hell away from his bike just in time. One second after I'd modified the brakes.

"Nothing at all, brother," I said with a smile. "Just thinking about the perfect spot for boozing. There's some great fucking views off in those hills, just a short ride through the rocks."

Frig took a long look at the jagged path where I was pointing. He snorted, then shook his head.

"You trying to kill me? How the fuck you think we're gonna handle that shit if we're riding back before we're sober?"

"Aw, shit, you're right." My voice kept an eerie calm, even though every muscle in my body turned to lead. "Let's find something else. Wouldn't want you taking a spill and fucking anything up."

His smartass stare turned into a death glare. "Wait a fucking minute, Blackjackass, are you saying I don't know how to ride?"

"You're fucking crazy, brother. That's not what I'm saying at all."

No, you really are a psycho, asshole, I thought, throwing my hands in front of my chest.

"Nah, asshole, I think it is. You're saying I can't ride and hold my fuckin' booze."

"Brothers, come the fuck on." Wheeler stepped between us, a big grin on his face. "If we're gonna hash some shit out with fists, why do it sober? I've got three solid bottles of Jack in my saddlebag, and those hills are calling for Grizzlies blood."

Frig stopped, and I kept one eye glued to his fist, ready to finish him here if it came to it.

He broke down in a wild laughing fit a second later. "You're both fucking numbnuts. Come on."

Wheeler looked at me and shrugged. We all got on our bikes, started them, and waited 'til Frig take the lead.

His ride wouldn't last long enough to waste another sip of good whiskey.

The terrain got fucking crazy, even by my standards. I

struggled to keep my bike from sputtering as it sank into the sand, tore through thick gravel, following the faintest outline of what used to be a road.

We were descending a slope, and just about to take an even higher hill, when Frig's shit gave out.

He must've been doing forty or more down the hill. He couldn't do a damned thing to stop his bike from picking up more speed when his brakes fucked up, and we watched the asshole soar halfway up the next hill, before sliding backward, screaming his sick head off.

His bike went off the road and slammed into a patch of boulders, just on the edge of a ditch. We waited 'til we heard him screaming to ride up and follow him, taking the path a lot more carefully.

"Pinned down. Just like a fucking rat," I growled to Wheeler, pointing at the hot mess in front of us.

Frig's leg was caught between the rocks and the smashed remains of his bike. Had to be broken, smashed to bits after the blow he'd taken.

He'd probably fucked up his spine too, judging by how he squirmed. I smiled. It was just enough to make his pain a special kind of hell, rather than numbing his agony.

That smile got wider as I stepped up. Fucker was still conscious enough to see us, and the light blub switched on in his head about a second later.

"Fuck! You motherfucking, cock sucking, two-timing pieces of shit!" Asshole reached for his gun, but a bullet flew through his hand before he got it.

Wheeler had some awesome aim. Almost better than mine, sometimes, though I'd never tell him to his face.

The jackass lifted his shot up hand and sucked blood from it, still screaming out his pain and rage. Then we caught up to him, and the real party started.

Wheeler got him in a choke hold while I opened my knife. There was no need for fancy explanations or even taunting.

I carved him up. Had to concentrate to make shit look right, especially when I ripped open his shirt.

Whoever had given him his Grizzlies MC tattoo had done a shitty job. Wasn't easy following the edges as I flayed him to bits, but I managed.

Frig only started screaming when Wheeler took the whiskey we'd brought, poured us a couple shots, and dumped the rest all over his fresh cuts. The asshole must've went blind from the pain, and we both knocked back a nip before we got back to work.

The sun was setting by the time he finally bled out. Thought he'd died right there, all slashed to pieces, but his head snapped up when he heard our boots crackling through the sand.

"Ass...holes...you fucking leaving me here? Your own goddamned brother...dying with the birds...fuck. Fang's gonna rip your throats out a thousand times worse, stuff your balls down the gash. You...your bitches...both your fucking kids. They're dead. I'll see every brat your balls ever make in fucking hell, assholes. I'll –"

I spun around, pulled my nine, and shot him right through the throat. Something about that shot didn't do him in instantly, or maybe the asshole was a little stronger than we thought.

We heard him choking halfway to our bikes, where we polished off the rest of the whiskey.

I reached into my saddlebag and pulled out the bloody Scorps cut I'd taken off a prospect's bike last night in Vegas.

"Think it'll work just to cover him?" Wheeler asked.

"Yeah. It'll take weeks to send a crew out here to find him. By then, Fang'll be too pissed to think sideways. He'll take it for what it's worth and rain down hell on the Scorps."

"Fuck, brother, if I hadn't seen myself naked, I'd think you've got the biggest goddamned balls in the world." Wheeler slapped my back, pouring the last of our bottle down his throat.

"Don't thank me 'til we're safe and sound. It's going to take years, a work in progress, and this is just day one." I held the Scorps cut close, heading back to where we'd left Frig's carcass, ready to toss it over him. "I don't give a shit how long it takes. I'm the man who's going to clear out this club. They'll all die, Wheeler, all the dirty ones. Some day, I'll see Fang killed too, and every other rat bastard who smears his shit on this patch. That's the only way I'll ever feel good bringing Lizzie home."

Wheeler didn't speak 'til we'd wrapped up, thrown our charade over Frig's dead face. "Wait, Blackjack, what about your woman? Are you telling me you're not planning to grab her and bring her home? What the hell you planning, brother?"

I never answered. I'd been doing too much thinking, and I had to act, even when it killed me.

The easy part was finished. Now, I'd pay a heavier price for my sins, and watch my soul turn pitch black one day at a time.

V: Twenty Year Winter (Blackjack)

Back at the hospital in Vegas, Oki's fist cracked across my jaw. I rocked backwards and hit the floor, feeling several teeth loosening. I stumbled, caught myself against the wall, and spat blood on the tile under my boots.

"This is your fucking fault. You ever come one step closer to my little girl and my grandson again, there'll be a bullet through your head. I'll put it there myself, here in broad daylight, mark my fuckin' words."

What the fuck could I say? The bastard was absolutely right.

I'd failed her. Gotten too greedy, too blind to how screwed up the club had gotten. Yeah, I'd eighty-sixed the man who'd tried to kill her, but the danger hadn't gone anywhere.

Not as long as dozens of dirty dogs shared my patch. Fuck, not while Fang held the national gavel. He'd be shaken up over his brother, no doubt about it, but he'd find a way to cling to power for God only knew how long.

We had a mad man at the helm, and that meant he'd

wreck our shit, including every innocent life we loved.

"Look at you," Oki snarled, eyeballing me as I stood against the wall. "Shit, I met Jap soldiers who had more to say with a gun at their backs. A man talks, admits his fuckin' mistakes. You're just gonna stand there?"

"I know I fucked up," I growled. "And I'm sorry, Oki. So fucking sorry, you're getting your biggest wish."

His eyes went wide, and he shook his head. "What the fuck are you saying, boy?"

I slicked back my long black hair, feeling a few stray pebbles from the dustup in the desert slip out. "Finn and Lizzie aren't coming home with me 'til I can promise they're safe. I'm not having their lives hanging over my head, always on the line, ready to get their throats cut because I fucked somebody over who deserved it, or because this club got itself too damned deep in the cesspool."

I walked up, well within range of the old man's fists if he wanted to hit me again. Wasn't going to stop him.

I deserved every fucking blow.

"Don't be a goddamned martyr," Oki said. "You're not gonna single-handedly take out the trash and leave this MC squeaky clean. We've got real dark times ahead – all of us – and it's going to last a lot longer than anybody thinks."

"Then that's the way it has to be," I said, staring out the window in the deserted waiting room. Pale Nevada light gave everything a sickly glow.

"I almost got her killed, old man, and I know it. Lizzie deserves better than that, and so does my son. I'm done putting them through the fucking grinder."

"Damned straight," Oki said. "Don't know how many years I've got left, but I'll take care of her. Finn too. You keep your filthy ass out of Spokane, and I'll do everything I can to keep the riffraff away."

Fuck. My heart sank like a stone into my guts. Grim finality set in.

This shit was really happening.

The best way to protect my family was to make sure they never saw me. Had to get them far, far away from me and the club.

I fought the urge to puke right there, so I walked away from Oki instead, heading for Lizzie's room.

"Hey! Where the fuck you think you're going?"

I stopped, turned around, and looked him dead in the eye. "She's awake, isn't she?"

He nodded. "Yeah, finally."

"She deserves an explanation."

I couldn't bring myself to tell him the truth, that was I going to say what promised to be a very fucking long goodbye.

"Don't upset her, asshole. She's barely coming around after losing half her blood. If I find out you're the reason she's back in a coma, Blackjack, I swear I'll –"

"Yeah, yeah." I put my fingers against my head, cocked my thumb like a trigger, and growled. "Trust me, old man, I'll get on my knees and suck your dick while you blow my brains out if I make her pass out. Promise."

Before he could say anything else, I marched down the hall and headed for her room. Oh, I'd be doing some damage, all right. But I'd be doing less than I would by hanging around, making promises I couldn't keep, turning my wife and son into easy targets when I finally got on Fang's bad side.

I had to do this. No excuses, no delays, no looking back.

"Babe..." I took her hand and brought it to my lips, feeling the strange coolness on her skin left by losing so much blood.

Even there in bed, with her long red hair messed up and wearing a baby blue gown, she looked like an angel. Lizzie smiled when I kissed her, bathing me in those green eyes I was about to have ripped away.

"Sam...I thought you'd never come."

"I'm here now, Lizzie. You're alive and breathing. That's all that matters, isn't it?"

Yeah, everything except the fact that I'm about to rip both our poor fucking hearts out and throw them on the floor, I thought, trying my best to enjoy the moment.

I held her quietly, leaning in so she could kiss me. Those sweet, sweet lips...fuck.

Didn't have a clue how long it'd be before I tasted them again. A couple years if I got really lucky, about what I expected to torch the cancer beginning to gnaw away at the Grizzlies MC from the inside out.

"How the fuck do you kiss like that after you just escaped the reaper?"

She smiled, winked at me. "You're a little more handsome than the angel of death. I decided to stay."

"I love you, Firecracker." I held her, kissed her forehead, and tried to savor the moment as long as I could.

Too fucking long. Time to get on with it.

"Listen, I've got some shit to say, but before I do, never forget how much I love you." Her smile softened, worry clouding her beautiful eyes. "Love you, babe. I always will, 'til I draw my last breath, even if you want to throw me straight down to hell and scratch my fucking eyes out."

"What's going on?" She sat up, wincing when her weight shifted a little to the bad shoulder. "Oh, Jesus, it's not Finn, is it?"

I shook my head, grabbed both her hands, and pulled them to my chest. "Hell no. If anything happened to our son, that's the first thing you'd know about, babe."

"I don't understand," she whispered. "You look terrible. I don't like it. What's got you staring at me like...like you're about to hurt me."

Shit. Having a dagger tearing through my ribs wouldn't have been half as painful as this stone cold agony. The longer I looked at the tension creeping up around her eyes, the more I wanted to gouge out mine, blind myself so I wouldn't have to see the sadness on her sweet face ever again.

No more bullshit. Pain time. I had to do what I'd come to do, take a bullet for her and Finn that would take them years to comprehend.

"Fuck it, I'd might as well spit it out. There's no easy way to say this, babe." I paused, looked her dead in the eye, and let the hammer fall. "I'm going away for awhile. A long time."

"Away?"

"Truth be told, you and Finn are the ones leaving California. I already talked to Oki, and he's taking you home to Spokane 'til I can sort out some nasty club business down here."

"What? You walk in here acting like everything's okay, only to drop this bomb?" Tears filled her eyes, and I saw a lump slide down her throat. "How long? Are we in danger?"

"Fuck, no. I already saw to that by killing the motherfucker who let you and Julie get run off the road." I stepped back and pushed my hand through the air, smooth as silk. "It's this club as a whole that won't be safe for a long time. Don't know how much longer I can pretend I don't see it, and when I can't pretend anymore, Fang's coming for me. The Prez'll fucking destroy anything in his path if it means smashing my guts like a fucking gnat. I'm not keeping you and Finn at his mercy, let alone any of the other venom he'll invite in, long as he's leading us."

"Goddamn it, Blackjack." She turned away from me, pushing a desperate palm over her head, through her sexy red hair.

My hand fell on her shoulder and squeezed. She wouldn't look at me 'til I rubbed that spot on her neck she loved, the one with all her heat, the target and I'd teased, kissed, and sucked a thousand times.

"It doesn't have to go this way. Leave the club," she said, pouring those bright green eyes straight through me. "It's not too late to get out, especially if daddy helps you. We can leave the country. I'll go anywhere, put up with anything, just as long as we're together!"

Wish I'd brought earplugs, as big an asshole as that would make me. I had to turn away, if only to hide the sickness in my eyes, the soul killing poison ripping through my system right about now.

"Sam – please!"

I had to face her again, folding my arms across my chest. "Not an option, babe. I told you before, I have to keep you safe. I swore an oath to this club, too. Can't just leave it, hang up these colors, and run like a fucking coward. I'm not going to leave Wheeler and the other good brothers to fight on their own. They deserve better, and so does everybody under this patch."

"So that's it, then? You're putting your oath to the club over our wedding vows?"

More questions. Accusations that sparked an inferno in my blood. I held my lava in, letting it melt my veins and blacken my heart.

"You know that's bullshit," I growled. "I'm not going to shake you 'til you believe it, seeing what you've been through."

"You're leaving Finn. Hell, leaving me to do it all alone, struggling to bring up our son when he needs a father."

I finally understood what it was like to get eviscerated. My knees burned, and I could practically feel my guts swinging, sliding to the floor, my whole fucking life slipping away from the sword she'd just pressed in deep.

I could've said a million things. Could've told her I'd be back as soon as I could, sworn it. I could've told her Finn had Oki, a good man who'd bring him up right, but it didn't change the fact that gramps wasn't his father.

I could've stood there like a fucking tool, telling her I'd send love and money, every fucking dime I earned. All my grand plans about murdering Fang and purifying the Grizzlies MC died like leaves stuffed down my throat when I thought about speaking them aloud.

The girl was right, smart as the day I'd claimed her. I was full of shit, nothing but excuses.

Too bad seeing right through them wasn't stopping me from walking out. I'd wracked my brain, burned through a hundred backup plans and a thousand alternatives, and the only one that ended with me doing right by my blood and my patch started with me walking the fuck out.

I turned my back, feeling hot tears stabbing at my eyes.

"I hate you!" she screamed. I heard something scrape off the little nightstand at her side.

I started moving, heading for the door. Totally ignored the skinny glass flower vase sailing over my head just a second later. It shattered like a bomb, spitting tiny shards everywhere.

She wasn't done yet. Fuck no. If I could've traded the sharp glass crunching under my boot for the next words out of her mouth, I'd have taken that bargain over and over.

"Fuck you, Sam! Fuck you. Get out! Don't come to me again, no matter what happens with you and the stupid, screwed up club. I'm never going to forgive you for this – *never.*"

I walked, headed down the hall to her wailing, without turning back.

Never. Never. Never. I heard that last hellish word over and over again in my brain.

You don't need to forgive me, babe. I need you and Finn alive, even if you hate my twisted ass forever.

I'm sorry, Finn. I'm sorry, Lizzie.

I'm so fucking sorry.

I lived in hell for twenty damned years.

If only all those preachers had told me hell meant silence, isolation, death.

Fang got his claws in deep. His power grew, corrupting the club, putting dirty assholes in all the right places, men without morals or club honor who'd support him 'til the bitter end.

Asshole never figured out what really happened to his brother, but it took me nearly two fucking decades to hatch a plan to kill him.

Just a couple years later, and I wore the Enforcer patch, taking the spot of his dead brother. I buried myself in work, doing every nasty deed I had to for the club, watching as good men fell.

We made money – a lot of fucking money. I sent it home to Spokane every month, emptying my account, always leaving Lizzie the same instructions about how to launder it so she wouldn't get fucked.

She never answered, holding to her promise. The only shit I ever got came from Okie, older and a little more senile, telling me to fuck off while he sent me pics of my kid.

I took a good, long look at Finn. He turned taller, older, handsomer, and stronger with each passing year. He grew up in still, faded images I burned every time after taking a good, long look.

Couldn't let anybody in this club know what he looked like, or even that he was still alive.

Assholes came and went like a revolving door. Fang

forgot all about my family, thank Christ, and Wheeler hit the bottle.

I joined him, drinking out my woes, ignoring the boozing and whoring he started to do, fucking around on Julie. He was sorry by the end, of course, shortly before our final reckoning with the Scorps MC.

Another bad deal of Fang's killed my best friend. I started watching over Julie and Travis the same way I did my own kin. She got older, aged like a widow does. The kid grew up, eventually took the patch, called himself Roman. I remembered that name, knew I'd probably have him by my side someday, when I made good on my promise to purify this MC.

I spent at least a thousand nights listening to brothers drinking, drugging, fucking themselves stupid with faceless whores. My dick got to know my fucking hand so well I could barely tell them apart.

I rode out into the wilderness and screamed 'til my throat was raw, promising myself I wouldn't betray her, even if I never got pussy again.

Another blink of my eyes, and the Scorps were just a memory. So was peace.

We fought clubs in Sturgis, several kinds of mafias, any little shit who had the balls to step onto our territory. The Prairie Devils, the Raging Skulls, the Slingers, the Deads, all of them wanted a piece of us, so we chewed them up and shat them right back out whenever they came too far West for their own good.

Threats changed. Fang got cockier, greedier, uglier. He smiled at men with that crooked fucking tooth while he held his dagger behind him, taking out anybody who got in his way. He did more dirty deals. More men died, good and evil, 'til it was hard as hell to tell them apart.

Finn hit his teens and wrote his old man, told me he'd gotten his address off his ma, the only time she'd said my name. He told me Oki died, and that he had a few more years of high school before he joined the Navy, fulfilling his promise to gramps that he'd become a Navy SEAL.

I smiled when I burned his letters, knowing my son wouldn't come anywhere near the club.

Found out where Oki got buried. I spoke to a few guys in Spokane I was still on good terms with, and had them put up an extra marker next to Oki's grave, special insurance to make damned sure my family stayed safe, no matter what happened.

I bought them fancy new names.

The cartel wars kicked up, and we had far more to worry about than the shit inside the club. Threw everything I had at the Mexicans and then some, stacking up my sins higher than I piled up bodies.

Finn wrote me a lot, especially when he joined Uncle Sam. Basic training turned into hell for him in Afghanistan, and then I heard all about BUD/S. We talked several Christmases over the phone, always cut short when I asked about Lizzie.

He told me how much his ma still hated me.

Fuck.

I made a couple trips to Spokane and stopped just short of barging in on her, talking to the angel over her fake grave instead, standing over Oki's bones.

Roman went away to jail. New boys joined the crew. Sacramento fell to the cartel, and mother charter moved to Redding. We put our war with the Devils on hold after they beat us stupid, drove us away from Montana.

Brass, Rabid, Asphalt, Stryker. They helped me rig this MC with dynamite, blow it the fuck up, and put it back together again in my image.

I saw my opening, seized it by the balls, killing the asshole who'd caused all this grief with a few good men. Fang died, and I dreamed of him roasting in hell.

I traded my Enforcer patch for PRESIDENT. The Devils become brothers instead of rivals.

Roman got out of jail and found out he had a bride and kid waiting. Brass and Rabid got their girls. Asphalt fell to cupid's blow, swerving through the same club politics I'd suffered.

His happy ending came a whole lot sooner, thank fuck.

More cleanup. More romance. More blood spilled for the club, and this time it meant something. More weddings, more brands, more babies being born.

My hair turned from charcoal to ash, and old age pounced, beat me with a fucking stick. Everything took real effort now, especially since I'd taken that bullet near the hip – riding, wheeling, dealing, sometimes just holding the gavel.

I knew I wouldn't have too many years left as Prez, but I'd done it. I'd finally fucking done it.

I watched each and every one of my boys up at the altar, renewing their vows or making new ones, before we all took off for our big club outing. They knew I'd be breaking away for business with the Devils out east, but that was only cover.

I'd come to Spokane for a final answer from the woman who'd given me nothing but silence for two wicked decades. Whatever her choice, I had to know, before I took a hit I couldn't survive and they lowered me into the ground.

I'd already died for this club, and my family. Sure as shit didn't deserve any second chances, but hope springs eternal. And right now Hope rode my ass like a jockey out of hell.

Present Day

Still had my hand on the cold stone angel when I heard his voice behind me. "There you are, old man."

I spun around. The kid looked at me. Half a foot taller than me, and even more built than I'd been at my peak. He wore his hair cut real close, just like the SEALs demanded, a jet black match for his loud green eyes.

He came up to me and we sized each other up. Last

time I'd seen him, Oki was holding him there in the hospital, just a toddler on his grandfather's lap. I'd kissed him on the forehead then, something that wouldn't do for a man this big.

I threw my arms around him before he could say another word. Finn stood there, strong and tall as a tree, shaking when my hands ran down his back, hard as I hugged my brothers.

"Finn! Welcome home, *son.*"

Yeah, I fucking choked when I said the same word I used all the time for my boys. Maybe because it meant something more here, or maybe because I couldn't believe he'd become real, more than just a ghost I'd abandoned years ago.

"I oughta be saying the same thing to you, dad. I'm only here because of you, plus it lined up with them giving me some fucking R and R for once."

I laughed, slapped him on the back, and watched as the big, rough SEAL pressed his fingers into his eyes. The boy hid whatever tears he had pretty damned well.

He had every reason in the world to hate my worthless ass. Amazingly, he didn't.

Finn looked at me like family, something I'd forgotten for twenty fucking years, only coming close when I was with my crew.

"Your gramps would be proud, son. Hope you know that. He was a good man, whatever our disagreements." He stood at my side, and we both stared at Oki's tombstone.

"Yeah." He looked at me, his eyes catching the sun just right to show me his love. "I'm changing my name back to Reno this year. So is ma. We've run from this family long enough, and it's about time we fixed that shit since you gave us the all clear."

Had anybody ever had a heart attack from pure joy? I had to wonder as I hugged him again, chewing on the last part about his ma.

"I'll pay more money to have the dates chiseled off." I nodded at the big angel standing over Oki's grave, where Finn and Lizzie's ashes had supposedly been added about a decade ago.

"Nobody ever signed off on the death certificates," Finn said.

When I whipped my head around, he was grinning. "What?"

"Ma always said you were way too paranoid. She used some of the money you sent to brush off the guy who came up here to change our whole identities. Dude was pretty fucking happy to get paid double for doing nothing except these fake grave markers."

"Goddamn it," I growled, shaking my head. "She always was a Firecracker. Figures she'd fuck me over like that."

If only I'd been able to talk to her then, remind them what kind of danger they were in. Whoever or whatever had watched over them, knowing they hadn't switched names, deserved my thanks.

"Don't tell me," my son said, slapping a big hand on my shoulder, turning me around. "Say it to her."

My knees almost dropped the fuck out when I saw the trim, beautiful forty-something woman heading toward us.

Rosy red hair. Bright green eyes. Curves just the way I remembered, calling my old hard-on to attention like a soldier shaking off a hangover.

Finn leaned in and whispered in my ear. "I'll be in my car, old man. Looks like you've got a lot of catching up to do."

The kid was smart – shit, of course he was, I'd made him – but he didn't know the half of it.

VI: To Eternity (Lizzie)

I'd fucked him. Worn his brand.
Married him. Loved him.
Lost him. Hated him.
Today, I forgave him. I came out to the cemetery where Finn said he'd be, wearing the leather jacket I hadn't worn since the day I was shot. PROPERTY OF BLACKJACK was sewn on the back, the blood long since bleached out.

For the first time in years, I meant it, too.

Sam aged so well. The long black hair I used to run my fingers through had gone gray, and he walked with the faintest hint of a limp, but I recognized the man I'd married the instant I saw him.

Beautiful gray stubble. Eyes so dark and sharp they reminded me of all the nights we'd spent together. Those flush lips beneath the scar on his cheek were the same ones that kissed me, commanded me, told me he loved me, and killed me the day he walked out.

He took big, eager strides toward me. I think I ran faster, feeling my heart do a dozen loops at once.

It was all coming down before we embraced, years of

bitterness and silence just crashing apart. I'd planned to get the first words in, but the sobs ripping at my throat wouldn't let me once his arms were around me.

They'd lost none of their strength with time. He held me, pressed me to his chest, reminding me how amazing, how right, how delicious it felt to be here, snug against his muscular wall.

"Never stopped loving you, babe," he said, stopping to smother my neck with kisses. "Not once. I'm too damned old to quit now, so I'm gonna keep on doing it. Don't care if you like it. Don't care if you want it. It's all I'll give you, all I've got 'til the day I die."

Smooth talker. *Too* smooth.

I never imagined how much hard it would really hit me to hear his voice, the dark, savage cadence rumbling in his chest. Nuzzling deeper against him, I didn't resist when he reached for my chin, tilted my face up to his.

Did he brace himself for our first kiss in twenty hellish years? Did I?

I'd never be able to tell. Because once our lips locked together, everything went fiery and white, tearing the rest of the sadness and pain from my heart.

"God! I love you too, Sam. I forgive you." I wept when the words finally came out. "Life's too short for this. I want you in my life again, even if you can't let go of the club. You said it's safe. You invited me in. So, here I am."

"Fuck yeah, you are. And you're never leaving me

again, Lizzie. I'm not going anywhere this time. You're all I thought about the last twenty years, and you're gonna be the last thing on my whacked out brain in twenty more."

"Blackjack...Sam..." My tongue fell all over itself, hungry for his taste, twisted into knots by raw emotion.

In the distance, somewhere behind us, I could feel our son watching and smiling. We were just feet from daddy's grave, a family reunion I'd dreamed about forever. But it wasn't supposed to turn me into a mess, so full and warm I could barely talk.

"God damn it, why did we waste so much time apart?" I said, shaking my head.

Blackjack took me by the temples, held my face steady, and planted his lips on mine. We kissed harder than before, and I sank into him, happier than I'd been since the morning before I took a bullet so long ago.

"We were young and foolish, babe. Let's be old fools together." His calloused palm swept over my face, touching my cheek so gingerly I wanted to break down all over again. "Let's see where you've been living and book a dinner with our son. We've got a lot of catching up to do. No more tears. We'll be out here all damned day if I've got to catch each one with kisses."

I stopped crying. His lips swept across mine again, igniting a fire I'd forgotten for ages.

He'd see everything tonight. The happy home I'd built with Finn before he left for the service, the cats, my dad's old cut framed on the wall, along with the wedding photographs I'd grudgingly hung up last year, when I couldn't stand it anymore.

Later, I'd show him the bedroom. I couldn't wait for that.

I'd lost so much growing up in the MC, but without it, I wouldn't have him or Finn at all. I held my arms around him, digging my fingers into his neck, drowning myself in his scent of oil, leather, and raw masculinity.

A real man always comes back, no matter how many times you shove him away. He'd been my dirty secret all these years, and I'd been his, but now we were out in the open.

Today, there'd be no more secrets, not even when he got gruff and said the usual crap about 'club business' like all biker badasses do to their women.

As long as these lips were within kissing distance, I'd be happy.

I'd be honest.

And I'd never, ever let my old man go.

Thanks!

Want more Nicole Snow? Sign up for my newsletter to hear about new releases, subscriber only goodies, and other fun stuff!

JOIN THE NICOLE SNOW NEWSLETTER! – http://eepurl.com/HwFW1

Thank you so much for buying this book. I hope my romances will brighten your mornings and darken your evenings with total pleasure. Sensuality makes everything more vivid, doesn't it?

If you liked this book, please consider leaving a review and checking out my other erotic romance tales.

Got a comment on my work? Email me at nicolesnowerotica@gmail.com. I love hearing from my fans!

Kisses,
Nicole Snow

More Intense Romance by Nicole Snow

FIGHT FOR HER HEART

BIG BAD DARE: TATTOOS AND SUBMISSION

MERCILESS LOVE: A DARK ROMANCE

LOVE SCARS: BAD BOY'S BRIDE

RECKLESSLY HIS: A BAD BOY MAFIA ROMANCE

STEPBROTHER CHARMING: A BILLIONAIRE BAD BOY ROMANCE

STEPBROTHER UNSEALED: A BAD BOY MILITARY ROMANCE

Outlaw Love/Prairie Devils MC Books

OUTLAW KIND OF LOVE

NOMAD KIND OF LOVE

OUTLAW'S VOW

SAVAGE KIND OF LOVE

WICKED KIND OF LOVE

BITTER KIND OF LOVE

Outlaw Love/Grizzlies MC Books

OUTLAW'S KISS

OUTLAW'S OBSESSION

OUTLAW'S BRIDE

Outlaw Love/Deadly Pistols MC Books

NEVER LOVE AN OUTLAW

SEXY SAMPLES: <u>OUTLAW'S BRIDE</u>

I: A Piece of Him (Sally)

I remembered him like it was only yesterday.

The heat of his kiss, the raw power in his arms as he pushed me down in the back seat, fisting my hair and making me scream when he sucked along my throat. He was going to be my first. I never dreamed in a thousand years he'd be my last.

He conquered me, and I fucking let him. I loved it. I didn't love him – at least not *yet* – but I lived giving him my innocence.

Sex came natural to him. He forced me to recognize his awesome talent in everything he did, from the way he shoved himself inside me for the first time, to the cadence of his voice, growling in my ear, twisting my head perfectly to bring my ear to his rough lips.

"Follow my lead, Sally. You're too damned hot to tell me fucking doesn't come natural." He paused, flicking his tongue over my earlobe until I squirmed. "Just watch and feel and learn. Every time I push my dick deep, you grind back. Meet my hips. Fuck me like you mean it, babe. Fuck me like you want it. Keep going 'til it feels like you're gonna blow, and I'll give you the final push. I'll teach you how to use that hot cunt between your legs to suck every drop of come outta a man's balls. Especially *mine*."

God.

And just like that, he fucked me. My best fuck, my *only* fuck. Roman shook the whole truck with his thrusts as he plowed into me, sending me screaming toward the sultry release.

I didn't know him, and it didn't matter. I was too deep in the pleasure zone after about five seconds to even care.

The way he handled me...sweet baby Jesus.

I hadn't meant to lose it this easy. Sure, I wanted to, but I didn't know this would be the day until he started pulling off my clothes.

I went down easy. One kiss was all it took to seal my fate forever.

Maybe it was his strength, or just the rogue good looks in his massive, tattooed body and chiseled face. His dark eyes told me he knew *exactly* what to do with a woman like me in every glance.

And I listened. I melted. I surrendered.

I'd never been a small girl. Growing up on my Uncle's ranch left me strong and well rounded beneath my curves. Stronger than the skinny twigs with palm sized boobs most of the biker boys in this town brought to bed, anyway.

I was pretty voluptuous, actually, which made it all the more amazing when Roman followed through on his promises.

It started with him walking me into the back, showing

off the work he'd done on my Uncle's truck. He'd done the job quickly and efficiently, just like a good mechanic could, and I was gawking at him like a schoolgirl with a bad crush every time I twisted in the machine, pointing out some gear or strut.

My thoughts went everywhere. Mostly, just wondering what those big, thick hands could do besides tuning up vehicles in record time.

If only I'd just wondered, fantasized, and left it at that.

I shouldn't have let him pull me inside for a closer look. All alone too – nobody else was in the garage. It must've been a light day for the Grizzlies Motorcycle Club, or maybe his brothers had other business.

I should've put up a fight, especially when his hands grabbed mine, bringing my trembling fingers to his lips. It couldn't possibly mean anything good except some incredible sex.

I was young, but I wasn't stupid. I knew the average badass wearing the Grizzlies MC patch offered nothing except a heart stopping romp between the sheets – or maybe somewhere wilder.

These boys didn't do relationships and dinner dates. They flirted, they fucked, and they moved onto the next hot ass within grabbing distance.

I knew better, and I didn't listen to common sense. The second we locked lips, lust did all the talking.

Maybe I shouldn't look back and be so hard on myself.

After all, it's hard to say no when you're twenty-one years old and still a virgin, and suddenly the biggest badass in all of Redding has his hands reaching for your bra clasp. And it's even harder when a tattooed giant like Roman shoves his fingers on your thigh and squeezes until it hurts because you want it so bad.

Lust never lies. We melded, a perfect fit, even before he maneuvered his huge frame between my legs, pressing the swollen cock behind his jeans to my panties. The honest *need* in his body fed hunger in mine.

Nature took over. Before I knew what was happening, my shirt was off, and the seat flopped back, leaving ample space for me to open my legs.

The things he did with his mouth set my pussy on fire. When he shoved his hands between my thighs and brushed my wetness, asking me if I'd ever been with a man like him before, I couldn't hide it. I told him I'd never been with any man.

The look he gave me was like a wild animal locking onto its prey. He told me not to worry. He'd take care of everything. He'd teach me all about pleasure, the flesh, *fucking.*

Lesson number one didn't truly sink in until he stripped me naked, shoved his broad face between my thighs, and ripped down my panties with one rough hand. I creamed the instant he started sucking my clit.

Sure, I'd read about the wonderful things a man's tongue can do in dirty romance books and even seen it in some porn. But it was *nothing* compared to having him there, shaking his huge head from side to side, pulling my clit between his teeth and crashing his tongue against it until my entire body exploded.

I came so fucking hard I almost went blind.

Five minutes later, I'd barely come down from the high, and he'd flipped me over in my stupor. One hand pulled me open, baring my virgin slit for his cock. His pants were off, and I caught a quick glimpse of his rock hard, throbbing, insanely huge dick.

I didn't know how he'd ever fit. He didn't care.

There wasn't time for any questions before he pushed himself inside me, all the way, stretching everything wide open for his cock. He sank deep, held it for a moment, shaping my pussy to fit his length.

It didn't hurt much. After several seconds, it started feeling pretty damned good actually, and then *fucking amazing* when his thrusts picked up speed. A dozen strokes in with my legs splayed wide, taking his massive cock, and I couldn't think straight.

I couldn't bother with right or wrong, or what time Uncle Ralph wanted me back with his workhorse on wheels, or even the fact that I couldn't check if the outlaw between my legs rolled on a condom first. Roman taught me a lot that day, especially about losing my mind.

Good sex was worse than good whiskey.

A woman couldn't think about *anything* when her

nerves were on fire, blowing all her circuits. I stopped trying when he rocked my body harder, shaking the truck along with it, quaking my whole fucking world apart.

The things that came out of my mouth probably made mama spin in her grave. Especially when he slowed his thrusts, just enough to let me form words, urging me on.

"You like that, woman? Fucking tell me you do. I wanna hear you beg for this dick. Start talking. You'd better practice talking dirty awful fast if you don't want me to pull out right now and shoot my load on your tits." Then his hand came down, slapping my butt for emphasis.

"Oh, don't stop! Please don't pull out. Please *keep fucking me.*" If only I would've known those words sealed my fate.

"Fuck you like what, babe? I don't give a shit if you're a virgin. I don't do gentle. I don't do slow. I only know how to fuck sluts."

"Then fuck me like one." His hand reached around and cupped my breast. Pushing into his palm, I moaned, praying he'd understand my body's needs.

"Bullshit. You're a good girl, Sally. I've never seen you so much as hanging around a hog roast out here before. You're not a biker bitch. You're not a club whore. I can't fuck you like one unless you make me believe it." Growling, he pulled out, resting his cock between my ass and rubbing it up and down.

"Anything. Do you want this?" My cheeks burned

bright red as I shoved my ass cheeks against him. Yes, he had me so drunk on his body I offered him everything that moment, and I would've given it to him too – anything to bring him back to the fire he'd kindled inside my pussy.

Silence. Until I heard the thunder building in his throat. With a snarl, he tilted my head to the side, jerking my hair in one fist, pushing his lips close to my ear again.

"You're lucky the thought of fucking a virgin cunt no man's ever been in makes my dick pulse lava, blondie. Turn the fuck over. I'll take all your holes another night." Another slap on the ass, and I obeyed.

I was so vulnerable, so exposed beneath him. His dark hazel eyes flashed. He took a good long look, bathing me in his hungry gaze.

"Lock those legs around my waist, and don't you fucking let up when I make you come. Consider this a test. We'll see if you're worth more than one fuck. I hardly ever do girls twice, and never when they've got hooks on 'em, trying to pull me into some shit. I'm a *free* man. You hear me, babe? You down with that? I'm looking for a fuck. Not a girlfriend."

My eyes narrowed. I can't say he didn't give me many chances to run. He told me straight up he was the world's biggest asshole with a gladiator's body and a tiger's stripes going up his arms. The roaring bear inked in the middle of his rock hard chest should've been warning enough.

I ignored it all. I wanted him that bad. I'd play along to keep this going, to feel him shaking me again. I'd already gone too deep, and now I wanted my virgin innocence obliterated.

For one night, I just wanted to feel his cock inside me as many times as I could. I'd deal with the guilt in the morning.

Reaching up, I ran my fingers down his chest, stopping just above his throbbing cock. Steam shot out my pores when I really *felt* how hard he was. *Holy shit.*

"You talk a lot about wild and free, don't you, Roman? Why don't you shut up and show me what that means?" God, I sounded nervous, but I managed.

I hooked my legs around his waist and gave him a squeeze. I teased him, and I loved it.

His cock jerked, letting out a steady trickle of pre-come. For several seconds, I watched the thick, pearly liquid dribble down to my soft belly. Then, I reached down and swirled my finger through it, instinctively raising it to my lips.

One drop was all I needed to be addicted to his taste. And apparently, one stunt like that was all it took to tease the animal inside him, the beast that took hold of his body while he pushed his magnificent cock deep into my virgin wetness again.

"Fucking shit." He shook his head, sliding in to the balls. "Don't you know you're playing with fire, baby girl?"

"Mm. I guess I'll just have to be your pyro for the night."

His whole body shifted forward. Taking my wrists in both hands, he slammed them onto the leather seat beneath me, holding them over my head. Then his hips moved, and he resumed thrusting. He pistoned in and out a little easier this time because I was twice as wet.

He melted me alive, or at least turned everything below my waist into napalm.

I came apart. Panting. Pleading. Impossibly wet and hot and wanting, ready to blow up the entire biker clubhouse attached to this garage if he refused to finish fucking my brains out.

Thankfully, he did.

Roman throttled my whole body. His deep, hard strokes shook my breasts and vibrated through my bones. My lips popped open, forming an O, a release valve for the fireball exploding around my clit. I barely had time to reach up and wrap my hands around his neck before it went through me, scorching everything, promising an earthquake.

"Roman!"

"Come on, babe. Keep it the fuck going." As if it was so damned easy. "I wanna feel you clenching this dick 'til I blow."

Hugging his powerful ass, I lost it. I thought I knew what an orgasm felt like from using my vibrator, but having my pussy wrapped around his dick drilled it into my brain, introduced me to a new sensation a thousand light years from earth.

It's different. It's incredible. Shit, I think I'm addicted.

I could've said the same about him – not just the sex. Something about being fucked by an outlaw giant three times my size fueled the hormones blazing in my veins.

I couldn't hold back. I didn't try. I came as hard as he commanded, throwing my head back and screaming my lungs out, so loud I wondered if any of the other rough bastards inside the clubhouse would come storming out to find out what all the commotion was.

Nothing would've stopped them from seeing us tangled together through the half-fogged windows, locked in ecstasy.

Roman's hips didn't stop either. If anything, they fucked harder, deeper, so fast and relentless I started to worry something would break in our bodies. But then his hips jerked to a stop, and he pressed me deep into the leather with all his weight.

"Goddamn, you're *fucking tight.*" One more ragged breath and Roman couldn't speak. "This pussy's mine. *Mine.*"

His cock pulsed, buried deep against my womb, making me feel him swell and twitch. He came with the same raging intensity. The deluge instantly fed my own orgasm like kerosene, and my legs squeezed his waist so hard they hurt.

His come flooded me in molten jets. Pulse after pulse hit my womb, so hot and powerful I swore I could feel it. I came so fucking hard, so long, I didn't know if I'd ever be able to walk straight again. I wondered if he'd left me paralyzed.

A small eternity slipped by in the heaving, rocking, sweating mess of us pinched together. My pussy refused to let go until he began to soften, and then I started my long glide down from the high, awakening to his salty lips on mine.

"You fuck pretty hot for a girl who's never done this before. You sure you're not bullshitting me about that virgin thing?" he asked, gently pulling out and wiping his dick. "Never felt a pussy ramp up to a hundred degrees and stay so damned tight."

Smiling, I caressed his legs with mine, feeling his seed trickle down from my middle. Ugh. I should've been worried, but I told myself there was plenty of time for that later. I'd been taking my birth control as steady as I could, hoping for the big day, and now I could finally put the pills to use.

I couldn't worry. The deed was done. I just wanted to enjoy the moment, the hazy afterglow we'd left in the truck, the smell and warmth of smoking sex.

"Fuck me," he growled, cupping my mound and feeling our cream pouring out into his hand. "I think I'm in love with this pussy."

"Yeah? Does that mean I get a second date?"

Roman looked at me, wiped his brow, and laughed. "You gotta be shitting me. You think fucking in an old truck's some kinda date?"

My cheeks flushed and I looked down. Of course not.

How dumb could I be? Dumb enough to entertain love-at-first-fuck, I guess. Suddenly, I wasn't so keen on being so naked before this man.

Embarrassed, I started reaching for my clothes, somewhere in a heap on the floor, when he put his hand on my cheek. "Ah, what's this? I'm just fucking around, Sally. Come on, get dressed and we'll go have some grub. Every chick deserves a sit down date when it's her first time."

The next week defied belief. The fun didn't end with a late night breakfast and another romp at his place.

I *dated* a bad boy, an outlaw, a man who'd probably strangled guys almost as big and bad as he was with his bare hands.

Roman picked me up a couple days later for a ride on his Harley, and the sweet autumn breeze blew through my hair. Having my hands wrapped around his body was sheer heaven. On his bike, holding him close, all my problems faded into a big fog of masculine spice and rippling muscle.

Roman saved me from having to think. With him, I didn't have to worry about the bad economy, my pissed off cousin, or hurtling toward permanent farm girl status.

I didn't fret skipping college, or feel my stomach twisting in knots when I remembered the only places hiring in Redding were even scarcer and lower paying than Uncle Ralph's ranch.

Him and his bike took me away from all that. He teleported me to an alternate universe of motor oil, dark inks, and pounding hearts, a paradise so awesome I never wanted to come back.

One evening became two, and then an entire week of hard riding, hard fucking, quality time together.

Roman picked me up every sunset, and we tore through the countryside on his bike, occasionally stopping in town for drinks or food. It always ended the same way – my bare ass bouncing beneath him in the bed, or sometimes in the tall, cool grass.

We fucked our way to happiness. We used sex to wipe ourselves clean. Me, with my boredom and mundane worries. Him, with his dark biker obligations, his mysteries, the scary warrior bloodlust I saw darkening his hazel eyes.

Club business, he said, warning me not to wander too deep into his world. And I didn't because when we were alone, the only business he had was me.

We fucked underneath the stars and in his little apartment. We kissed until each other's taste was inscribed on our brains forever. We fucked until neither of us knew night from day, right from wrong, heaven from hell.

One day, he woke me up early at his place. I wiped the sleep from my eyes, and realized he'd just ended a call.

"Get moving, babe. I gotta get you home." The tension in his strong face told me something was wrong, but he wouldn't say what.

I kept pressing him about it the whole ride home. My heart thudded like never before on the bike, and it had nothing to do with the road tearing by underneath us.

I was scared for him, terrified at his silence.

When we pulled up the dirt path to my family's farmhouse, he ripped off my helmet, and told me he'd call me later. I couldn't let him leave without trying one more time.

"Roman, please...what's the big secret?" I asked, frustration heating my blood. He gave me the same icy stare and looked away, mumbling something about it being nothing I needed to worry about.

I grit my teeth. "Fine then, keep it to yourself. Guess you can tell me now, or I'll just find out later when I come by the clubhouse."

Shaking his head, he got off his bike, and grabbed me by the shoulders. Then he shook me – and I mean *really* shook me – so hard I stumbled back scared.

"Don't you fucking *dare*," he growled. "Not now. I told you the rules our first night out – I come to you, Sally. Never the other way around. There's a damned good reason for that, and I need you to fucking listen."

"Listen to *what*? How can I trust you if you won't tell

me what's going on?"

"It's club business," he snapped, making me hate that two word sucker punch for the first time. "Not yours. I've gotta put my brothers first, second, and third. That's what a man does when he's in the Grizzlies MC."

Thanks, I thought, feeling the chill realization of how far down the ladder I must be.

"I swore an oath to this patch." His right hand formed a fist and slapped his chest, right where he wore the roaring bear tattoo underneath his shirt. "What's going on today's between brothers *only*. You've gotta understand that. Look, you know I like you a lot, but I can't fucking bring you into a world where you don't belong. I'm not gonna be responsible for you getting hurt."

Hurt? So, it was just as bad as I thought. Maybe worse.

Without another word, he turned his back, and began revving his engine.

Fuck it. I went after him, too upset to worry about the loud motorcycle drawing Uncle Ralph's attention from the fields. He'd look at me with horror if he knew I'd been hanging with a Grizzlies MC man for more than a week.

But it didn't matter. Him leaving did, especially when the chill current swept up my spine, telling me this could be it.

Whatever was going on threatened to pull him away

from me forever. It scared me senseless.

"Wait!" I yelled, stepping in front of the bike before he could dart away. "Will I see you alive again? Just tell me the truth. Just that. Please, Roman, don't do anything that'll get you killed. *Please.*"

Frustration stormed in his eyes. "You'll see me in one piece if you step outta the way *right fucking now.* I'm going, babe. Don't make me run you over. I've got my orders. Yours are to calm the hell down and let me go. I'll be back for you. Promise. Right now, there's shit I have to do, and nobody's standing in my way. Not even you." His cold, angry voice chilled me.

I wilted. My feet dragged on the ground as I reluctantly stepped away, watching as he sped off without so much as a wave goodbye.

I thought it was the last glimpse of him I'd ever have. Forever.

Turns out, forever was actually a little under two years.

Weeks rolled by, and there was no call. No note in the mailbox. No breaking news in the paper or on TV about a bloody battle that left men dead anywhere in NorCal.

Nothing.

I couldn't take it. I had to find out what happened.

My next visit to the clubhouse was a fucking disaster. I drove in about a month after he disappeared, circling past the gruff faced guards by the gate, hoping I'd see some sign of him.

But if I did, that would've been worse. If he'd chosen *this* way to dump me...

I bit my lip, trying to keep it together, especially around all these scary, rough strangers.

An older man with long gray hair named Blackjack answered all my questions. Thank God, because he was the most approachable of the bunch. He told me Roman was in prison, part of his service to the club for...God only knew what.

"Club business," the weathered warrior said.

I hated those two words before, and now I fucking loathed them. For any woman unfortunate enough to be in the Grizzlies MC's orbit, it was like having the door slammed in her face.

Of course, I broke down in my car. I wasn't just chasing him because I wanted to find out he was still breathing, though that was a big part of it.

I had something to tell him, a slow motion disaster building by the second.

"Why are you crying, girl? Look at me." Blackjack's eyes were surprisingly soft, far kinder than any ruthless killer's had any business being. Looking at the ENFORCER patch on his cut told me he ranked higher than Roman, which probably meant he'd been into even darker things for far longer.

"That's *my* business," I said. "Mine and Roman's. Is there an address where I can reach him? Maybe visiting hours or something?"

Blackjack shook his head. "It's too dangerous. Where he's going, rival gangs use visiting time to sneak up on a man and cut his throat. He knows to keep his head down, refuse everybody, even from the club. Sure, the guards will come in blazing, but by the time they break up the fight, he'll be bled out like a slaughtered hog if somebody gets a lucky stab."

Jesus. Telling him in person would've been hard enough.

Now, this old vulture was telling me I wouldn't get a single chance for nearly *two years?* If ever?

"Stay there a second," Blackjack said after a moment, watching new tears pulling at my eyes. "I'll get some paper and pass along a PO box where you can send him letters."

I hated sitting there and staring at the clubhouse wall. A huge mural of a ferocious grizzly bear leered out from the side, its mouth stretched wide, ready to devour everything. Right now, it was chewing my world apart, piece by bloody piece.

I barely knew the club, and I hated it. I certainly wouldn't be the first in Redding to feel that way. Uncle Ralph told me they were no good, though my cousin, Norman, always said they were the only thing stopping even bigger rotten apples from rolling into town and taking over.

My Uncle only had me take the truck to their shell

repair shop because the other guys in town screwed him over one too many times. Talk about a dismal situation when the most honest mechanics around were honest-to-God outlaws, smugglers, and possibly murderers.

It was surreal. A few weeks ago, I'd been scared to death over Roman going off for an evening, wondering if he'd come home alive. Now, after hearing about jail, I knew I'd be feeling my nerves burning out for the next twenty-two months.

He's not the only one in prison. You're going to pay for your mistake, I thought.

Karma's come to collect her debt, and it's him. He's gone. You're going to do this alone, whether you see him alive again or not.

My thoughts pulled knots in my intestines. Or maybe it was just the changes in my body, the shadow left in my flesh by too many unforgettable nights with a bad boy.

"Here you go," Blackjack said, sticking his hand through my car's open window. I felt so tiny in my own crappy rust bucket after driving Uncle Ralph's truck most days. "Write him anytime. I'm sure he'll answer you. Remember, the boys who run that place read everything before it gets to him. My number's there too. You really ought to call it if you need anything, rather than coming to the clubhouse. It's a bad time for too many outsiders."

I blinked. Blackjack put both hands on the window's frame and leaned in. "There's things going on in this club right now. That's why our boy's in jail. We're not interested in babysitting civilians, or receiving them at all unless it's absolutely necessary. You look like a smart girl, and I know he wouldn't want you fucked over by any bad business that isn't yours. Stay away from this patch for awhile, Sally. If you care about him at all, you'll listen."

I didn't say another word. Neither did he.

A crater blew open in my heart. Two years. No contact. No way to reach him at all except a note by pigeon that would be intercepted and poured over by the guards before it ever made it through.

No privacy. No help. No more loving – if I could call whatever we had that without being totally delusional.

As soon as Blackjack walked back into the garage, I turned my car around and waved to the prospects manning the gate. I couldn't wait for it to slide all the way open before I gunned it out of there, fighting the fiery tears in my eyes.

I was alone. The sooner I learned to accept it, the better.

I didn't send a single letter the entire time. I couldn't bring myself to pick up the pen, couldn't put my hands on the keyboard. It would've written the lamest note in the world, and also the one guaranteed to stop my heart when I thought about how he'd react.

Two long years passed in a painful haze. I tried to

forget, at least until he got out. *IF* he got out...

We never spoke once. Not until last week, when I finally mustered up the courage to walk into the clubhouse and try to tell him everything I'd been terrified to say by letter.

He'd only been free for a few weeks. His twenty-two months in prison were a lifetime to me.

I'd heard the rumors around town. The Grizzlies were fighting for their lives the past few years. They'd been warring with everybody across the wild west, rival MCs like the Prairie Devils up in Montana, and bigger worries closer to home. Nothing hit them harder than the Mexican cartels coming north, muscling in on the territory they'd held for decades.

Every other week, there was a new gruesome headline. Missing people on both sides of the border, bombings and gunfights in every major city, especially Sacramento and LA. Thankfully, the war zone hadn't really hit Redding yet.

Oh, except for the club's infighting. Their old President, the notorious old thug named Fang, was deposed. Blackjack took over the entire national organization, and he'd made Redding the MC's permanent headquarters.

Change was in the air, and nobody on the outside knew what it meant. Not yet.

Now shops funded by the Grizzlies MC sprang up all over, gun shops and strip clubs and biker bars. They cleaned up other dirty clubhouses as far as Klamath Falls and San Diego, and even ran a few charity events.

No one was going to roll over and call these guy heroes. Honestly, it didn't take a perfect vision to see through the PR stunts, and some of the new businesses they'd helped set up were likely fronts for money laundering.

Other things stayed the same.

Their cartel wars weren't over. New violence somewhere in the state cropped up every week, except now it sounded like the Grizzlies were beginning to gain the upper hand.

Me? I stayed out of it.

There was plenty to keep busy. I'd never grown beyond the ranch, and now I was managing a lot more of it since a stroke took Uncle Ralph's life last year. Cousin Norman and I shared the farm, managing the machines and the family's old employees, including a few younger guys who'd become hangarounds with the Grizzlies MC.

They were my source for most of the rumors. I never contacted Blackjack or anyone close to Roman, deciding to keep my distance until I was good and ready, and Roman was free.

Days passed. I heard he was back in town, and apparently the club's Enforcer now.

It took an entire summer week to gather my courage. I let Norman know I was going into town for a few things, but really, I was heading for the clubhouse.

The fresh paint on the place instantly looked brighter when I pulled up. Two prospects were guarding the gate, and I struggled to explain who I was while they gave me cold, skeptical stares.

But as soon as I said "Roman," the man who's name patch said Stryker walked over and punched the button. The gate slid open, and I walked through it, leaving my car parked on the curb.

It was early evening. Two men were arguing over drinks at the bar. I'd never been inside the place before, and it was about what I expected. Dark, smoky, dizzying.

The sharp stink of booze and testosterone clung to the air, and I stumbled forward along a narrow corridor, trying to get my wits.

"Sonofabitch!" A man growled. "Hey, lady! Look out!"

Something sharp whizzed past my face. There wasn't time to dodge, or even wonder if it was a bullet. It smacked the wall just a few inches from my head, a long metallic dart, lodged in the wood like a stray missile.

An angry looking bald man looked at me, straightening his cut. When he saw it hadn't taken out an eye, he spun around to face his partner, a strong, younger man I'd seen riding around town.

"Asshole! What the fuck is wrong with you? Are you trying to get somebody *killed?*" Baldie slapped both hands against his brother's chest.

The other man took a swing, missed, and drunkenly

hit the floor. Before I knew it, I was watching a mini-biker brawl, two men on the floor cursing and throwing fists.

Ugh. Not exactly how I wanted to re-introduce myself to Roman and his friends. I was about to say something and try to ease the scuffle when I heard footsteps.

I looked up, and there he was, coming toward me. My heart thudded like a bomb's aftershock, and it didn't let up until he'd closed the gap between us, two fucking years apart.

Roman and I locked eyes. The words I'd practiced so many times died on my tongue.

I couldn't believe it. I couldn't believe how he'd changed. Could I even believe my own eyes?

Was he always so huge – or did prison add a few inches to his bulging muscles? His face looked tougher too, accented by a few more lines in his forehead, a sharper angle to his powerful jaw. He'd probably just passed his thirtieth birthday in jail, and he had all the insanely hot finishes of a man aging into his prime.

Jesus. Before I came here, I told myself over and over I wouldn't feel the old heat. This was going to be business like, personal, but I wouldn't let my old attraction take over. Not before I saw what he was like.

Yeah, good luck with that.

As soon as his dark hazel eyes sucked me in, I lost it. The tattoos on his muscular arms rippled in my peripheral vision, forcing me to remember those hands on my body. They'd held me down so tight while he fucked me, fingered me, warming me up for that battering ram between his legs.

The men stopped fighting when they saw him coming. The young guy with the sandy hair helped himself up, holding onto the bar, nursing his ribs after they took some cringe-worthy kicks from Baldie. One look at Roman, and he started shaking, making excuses.

The bald guy retreated behind the bar, fixing himself a drink. Roman stormed right past his beaten up brother, giving him a quick shove, muttering when he tried to stand up. "Get the fuck outta my way."

I'd stolen all his interest. While we stood there staring at each other, lost in our memories, everything else in the clubhouse might as well have been happening on the dark side of the moon.

"Sally." I flattened myself against the wall the instant he said my name.

It wasn't just his body changing behind bars. Prison or age deepened his voice, given it a smoky richness to go with the deep baritone he'd had before. My mind went wild, recognizing the same wicked cadence and thunder I heard that summer when he growled into my ear, ordered me to suck his cock, to come each time he fucked me senseless.

"What the fuck are you doing here?"

Good question. My lips tasted bitter against my tongue, as if they didn't want to move, didn't want me to remember why the hell I'd come to confront him.

"I had to see you. I heard you were out of jail."

"Yeah, word spreads fast." He folded his huge arms, and his biceps bulged so thick I swore they'd bust his seams. "What the fuck is this? I'm surprised you showed up. Pretty sure you'd forgotten my ass when I didn't hear from you. It's been – what? – two goddamned years?"

Ouch. Steeling myself for this crap before I walked through the door was completely different from actually facing him. The lump in my throat didn't want to go down, and it had to before I could form words.

"I'm sorry, Roman. When I heard the news from Blackjack, I didn't know what to do. He said I couldn't see you in person, told me it wouldn't be good to visit you –"

His hand shot up, right in front of my face. "And he was right. You were wise to stay the fuck away. This world's not for you, babe. If I'm not worth writing to, then I'm sure as shit not worth your time now that I'm out."

I sucked in a sharp breath. *No, no, you don't understand.* I couldn't force the words out, and he just kept talking.

"What? Don't give me that fucking look. You always had a good head on your shoulders, woman, and it's time for you to put it to use. You know it's too late, too far gone for us. Mistakes were made, and they weren't fixed. If you've got any sense, you'll pick those long legs up, turn around, and walk out that door."

I froze. The cold energy in his eyes danced over me, sucking the life out of me. "What? *Why?*"

"Because what happened that summer two years ago was a big goddamned mistake. I'm sorry the memory's left you hanging. If you're still wrapped up in me, then I don't know who the hell you are. I don't wanna know. I should be ancient history by now, and you should be settled down with some civilian and a couple kids. This clubhouse never was a place for a real lady."

Real lady? Was he patronizing me, or just trying to let me down easy? Shit, the fact that he was letting me down at all hit me in the chest and shredded my heart.

Before I could say anything else, he turned, heading for the bar. "Wait! Roman!"

The blade he'd pushed into my chest just sank deeper when I heard myself saying those fucking words. *Wait.*

Haven't I been doing it for twenty-two fucking months? All alone, hiding my memories at the ranch, suffering in silence?

My brain flipped to a different mode. I couldn't let him get away from me again like this. I had to get his attention – *now.*

Running after him, I grabbed a bottle off the bar and threw it.

I wasn't trying to hit him, but the glass made a hell of a noise when it hit the floor, right by his boot. Roman whirled.

How could those eyes that were so sexy and full of life be so dead and glacial? I stared back at him, hoping he caught pure hell in my dark blue eyes. Maybe I'd see a spark of something that was still alive.

My temper took over. This wasn't the man I knew, even if this stranger had the same incredible body, the same face I'd imagined night after night.

"Go ahead and walk the fuck away again, you coward!" I screamed, my voice surprisingly steady. "At least this time I know it's not the prisons and the courts holding you back! You're not man enough to handle *us*."

Christ, that idea scared me too. But I still said it, I still offered it to him, even after all this time.

I expected him to strike back, shove me to the wall, get in my face. Instead, he just turned around and kept going.

He left me alone. I was about to storm out when the brother who'd taken a beating with the bald guy stepped in front of me.

A few minutes later, I sat with him at the bar. I let Rabid – what a ridiculous name, right? – pour me a shot of whiskey. We talked about bad luck and love.

He was nice enough, and I actually felt better by the time I had a couple drinks. We must've sat and talked for hours. If he wasn't so hooked on some redhead he was chasing, I might've leaned over and kissed him just to spite Roman.

Maybe to spite myself for being so stupid, thinking

this would be easy.

"Good luck, baby," Rabid said, just before I gathered up my purse to leave. "Try coming by in a few weeks. Maybe then we'll have sorted through some of our shit."

""I hope so," I told him. "Thanks, Rabid. I've got a feeling you'll sort whatever's got you by the balls just fine."

His chances were definitely better than mine, anyway. When I left the clubhouse, the only thought rattling around in my head was how much I never wanted to see that overgrown asshole, Roman, ever again.

If only it were that simple.

At home, the reason why I practically walked over broken glass to see him at the clubhouse sat in my arms, soft and sleepy.

Soon, Caleb would be growing into a real toddler. I've tried like hell to raise my son alone, to forget about Roman and walk the fuck away, never looking back.

But every time I looked into my son's dark brown eyes and saw the same powerful jawline forming on him, I knew. I understood what he deserved, what he needed.

The kid had to have his father – even if the man who shared his DNA turned my heart to ice.

No, no, I couldn't give up this easy. God help me, I was the only one who could bring Roman into his life, or else I'd keep them apart forever.

Look for Outlaw's Bride at your favorite retailer!

Printed in Great Britain
by Amazon